Kinetic

Kinetic

The First Alliance

Herro Raymond
and
Laz Matech

iUniverse, Inc.
Bloomington

Kinetic
The First Alliance

iUniverse books may be ordered through booksellers or by contacting:

iUniverse
1663 Liberty Drive
Bloomington, IN 47403
www.iuniverse.com
1-800-Authors (1-800-288-4677)

ISBN: 978-1-4759-5000-7 (sc)
ISBN: 978-1-4759-5001-4 (hc)
ISBN: 978-1-4759-5002-1 (e)

Library of Congress Control Number: 2012917095

Printed in the United States of America

iUniverse rev. date: 9/21/2012

We would like to thank; George, Nikki, and Justine, not to mention all of our friends and family for the tremendous amount of support they have given us. Without them none of this would be possible, and we dedicate this book to them for always believing in us.

CHAPTER 1

Farewell Days of My Youth

THERE'S RARELY EVER A time in a person's life that they're ready when called upon. Usually, it happens at the most inconceivable moment, but when thrown into an intergalactic war of worlds, what choice do you have, really? Right and wrong, good and evil, heart and mind—it would be so much easier just to run away from these conflicts. Alex, however, was about to learn that courage is not the absence of fear, but rather the judgment that something else is more important than fear, but even more important, is knowing real heroes are just people who fear running away from conflict more than they fear death itself. However, the irony of life is that without struggle, you'll never know what you're truly capable of; something Alex was going to find out the hard way.

Mankind may never understand how thin the line between good and evil really is. Who decides who is right and who is wrong? Usually, it's decided by the victor, but this time around, we're supposed to entrust the survival of humanity to the hands of a teenager who's only sure that he is impossibly unsure. What kind of messed up joke is that? The smart thing to do would have been for him to forget that night, and live the rest of his short life as a normal, boring adolescent. Then again, no one said being a hero would be easy, or at least, it definitely wasn't smart.

Despite his best efforts, Alex couldn't shake the pounding headache that abruptly started an hour ago. Usually, sitting on his favorite couch watching old game shows with his grandfather put him at peace, but it didn't offer any letup from the pain that night. Alex had always been cautious about taking pills of any kind, but the pain was steadily increasing. The flashing lights from the screen felt unbearably intense, and all the applauding was like a power tool drilling through his mind. He glanced at the tempting bottle of aspirin on the small TV dinner table to his left but decided against it. It was getting late anyway, so he decided to go to bed and sleep it off, hoping he would feel better in the morning.

"Grandpa, I've got a killer headache, so I'm fista' go to bed. Okay?"

"Want me to call a doctor?" As usual, his grandfather was overly cautious at the slightest sign of trouble.

"What? No, I'm fine," Alex responded.

"Of course you are." He smiled slightly. Alex's grandfather instinctively looked at the framed picture of Alex's late father above the mantle and told Alex for the hundredth time how much he resembled his father in both appearance and demeanor. Alex thought it was a bit eerie, almost as if looking at his future self in that frame. With his fair skin, blue eyes bright enough to pierce someone's very soul, yet hair so jet-black that light would never be able to escape from its void, Alex was undeniably his father's son. They even smiled the same way.

"Just like your old man, trying to tough it out," he said, but before Alex could even open his mouth to respond to the comment, his grandfather looked up with tired eyes, and smiled.

"Sir?" Alexander replied.

"Nothing, goodnight, son," he added.

Alex gave a sliver of a smile back. "Goodnight, Grandpa." Alex nervously paced to his bathroom, hoping not to fall over from being so nauseous. He leaned over his sink, wanting to wash the day away. He cupped his hands under the faucet and splashed the lukewarm water across his face; it offered only a split second of relief before his headache began thrashing around in his skull again. He took a look in the bathroom mirror and stared at his reflection. His grandfather's remark once again forced him to think of his parents, who had died when he was just an infant. Since then, he had been raised by his grandfather, a decorated and retired police sergeant with more than thirty years of experience on the force. Alex had so much anger inside of him and no one to direct it at. He was proud of his parents but angry at them for not being there. With no one to blame, he once again buried his resentment deep inside and dragged his feet down the hall toward his room.

He reached for the door handle with apprehension. *Maybe tonight will be different,* he thought to himself. He slowly turned the handle and went in his room without incident, thankful that at least one thing went his way that day. Upon entering his room, he took off his shirt, revealing his toned body—a body he'd acquired from years and years of running track in middle school and high school. Behind him was a wall dedicated to his accomplishments in the sport, everything from ribbons to two-foot-tall trophies was on display.

Alex traced the frame of his bed with his hand before lying down; he wasn't sure if he could climb in without missing the mattress from being too disoriented. He crawled into bed with his laptop in hand; it had become routine for him to plug in his headphones and fall asleep to the songs in his music library. He reached over to plug in the charger but instead watched as it sparked and shorted out upon contact with the outlet.

Son of a …, he thought to himself and prayed the battery would last long enough for him to fall sleep. He tried his best to settle in bed and scrolled through the thousands of songs he had illegally downloaded. Alex was confident the worst was over, but he hadn't even gotten past the *H* section of his playlist before two drops of blood splattered on his keyboard. Puzzled, he wiped his nose and stared at the streak of blood running from the end of his wrist to the tip of his finger.

"Seriously? It's official … I'm cursed," he said to himself. Alex gripped his head in agony. For some reason, his headache was getting much worse. Alex finally gave in and turned to his nightstand to get an aspirin. He popped the pill in his mouth, but not even a minute after swallowing, he saw the silhouette of a figure behind his adjacent window's curtain. Alex was startled out of bed. He took a couple steps back and again grabbed his head, wanting to literally rip the throbbing torment from his scalp. He squinted his eyes and looked up, but he couldn't make out who the figure was behind his slightly transparent curtain.

"Who the hell is there? Get out of my room!" demanded Alex as he frantically looked around for a weapon. He picked up his aluminum baseball bat and pointed it at the figure.

"Drop your bludgeon immediately! I am not here to harm you. I came to help you, human," the mysterious voice said.

"Screw you…I'm not dropping a thing," he nervously responded.

"*Screw me* you say?" The figure took a step forward.

"Look, I'm not afraid to use this." Alex tightened the grip around his bat's handle and inched over to the wall. He was close enough to his light switch to flick it on. The figure stepped out into the light and revealed itself. Alex couldn't believe his eyes. The thing in front of him stood up straight with perfect posture and had amber-colored skin with black tribal markings that circulated and flowed in steady motion throughout the surface of its body and face. Sleek, battle-scarred armor covered most of its body, and perfectly placed cryptic medals that signified to Alex this creature had seen many battles were attached to its sleeves.

It proudly walked over closer to Alex and sternly said, "You would dare raise a hand to me? I could leave your planet to die right now."

But the words were all a blur to him. Alex couldn't get over its appearance. It had the curvatures of a woman, but her eyes had pitch-black corneas and white pupils—the opposite of human eyes. However, the real distinction was that they were sideways cat's-eyes, which reminded him of the frogs his science teacher had forced him to dissect in middle school. He gauged her to be about six feet tall and noticed that she had thin black tendrils on her head instead of hair, which she had tied back. Her armor radiated its own dazzling light and was mostly royal blue with white accents and silver-colored plating. Her pants were white with a blue stripe that ran up her thigh and accentuated her curves.

"I … you—" Alex dropped the bat and gasped for air. He backed himself up against the wall as he prayed for the power to phase through, but the best he could do was look around for something to grab on to so he wouldn't fall down from the shock. He was either looking at the best Halloween costume he had ever seen, or there was a real-life alien in front of him.

"I have not the time nor patience for this, so listen well. I am known as Shyra, from the distant world called Kalryn." With speed faster than Alex could react to, she closed the gap between them and grabbed his forearm. "I have come here to prepare your race to fight. Now let us go." Her skin was clammy but warm, not like anything he had felt before.

"Whoa, what? You're hurting my arm; let go of me," Alex said.

"Either your race is slow to learn or unable to grasp the concept of total annihilation, but if we do not act right now, trust me when I say you will perish. Zenakuu means to kill you off, but it still may be possible to save your kind," Shyra said.

"Zen-a-what? How do you even—" Alex started, but his ability to form complex sentences escaped him at that moment.

"Do I look to be in a gaming mood?" She let go of his arm and let out a deep and frustrated sigh. Negotiations clearly were not her strong suit. "I know you are scared, human, but we have not the time. This is your life from now on, like it or not. Now we must go and prepare for training."

"I'm not going anywhere with you. Just stay back okay?" Alex couldn't find his bearings.

"What did you say to me? Did you not hear what I said?"

"Oh. No, I heard you. Now it's your turn to hear me. That is the best damn cosplay I have ever seen, but if you don't get out of my room, I'm calling the cops."

"Why you insolent little— to die for your planet in the line of duty is a great honor!"

Die? He thought to himself. He was nowhere near ready to die. "Granp—" Alex tried to scream, but the creature threw her hand over his mouth to muffle his cry before he could finish.

"I sincerely hope it is not always going to be like this with you," Shyra removed her hand from his mouth. "Allow me to show you why I am here." Shyra approached Alex like someone meeting a dog for the first time. Hesitant, her hand slowly got closer to Alex's forehead. Alex began to sweat, frozen in place from fear. He clamped his eyes shut as he prepared for his end, but he only felt her slightly coarse skin on his forehead. In an instant, a flash of light blinded his vision, but he was okay. Much to his relief, the alien was gone.

"That's it. I'm never taking aspirin again." He got up from bed to see if his grandfather was still awake. Even he would love a crazy hallucination like that, but it was too quiet. Alex slowly walked down the steps and saw the TV was blown and smoking.

"Grandpa Henry?" he cautiously said, but there was no answer. On the last step, Alex could see his grandfather's head sticking up from the couch.

Must already be asleep, he thought as he walked over to wake him. "Grandpa, you're not gonna believe the dre—" but when Alex finally stood in front of him, he was mortified by what he saw. His grandfather had been stabbed and cleaved open, and as if having been carved like a turkey wasn't enough, there was a single bullet hole centered on his forehead.

"Oh my God … Grandpa, what the hell is this?" Alex felt powerless and paralyzed. His grandfather was dead because he hadn't been there for him. Alex heard the back door to his house slam and immediately looked up. The murderer was still close.

Alex clenched his fist and went off running to the door. He saw only a darkened figure run out toward the street. Alex stayed in pursuit but couldn't make out who it was. He quickly made it to the streets, but his neighborhood looked different. Fires were scattered sporadically across the area, and row after row of two-story houses had been partially blown up, the streets laid to ruins. He ran forward not knowing if the trail of destruction was the right path but praying he would get answers at its end. His heart pounded out of his chest, faster than it ever had before. Tremors of crippling fear ran down his spine, but his legs would not stop moving.

The image of his gutted grandfather was all the drive he needed. He persisted halfway down the street when suddenly an ear-shattering whistling stopped him in his tracks. He looked up again and watched as a small black orb with a fire-lit tail descended to the ground. On impact, the orb exploded. A loud crack went off in the distance, and a mushroom cloud emanated from its location. Alex was distraught; it looked as if World War III had started without him knowing it. The light from the explosion faded the night sky, blotting out any stars from sight. The only things visible were the dozens of gigantic black mother ships, the likes of which he'd never seen. In seconds, the blast brought a shockwave and blinding light that vaporized Alex in seconds. He snapped back to reality in a cold sweat, gasping for air, unsure of what was real or fake. The process left him debilitated, as all his senses felt like they were on fire.

"What … the hell was that? Where was I? What did you do to me?" Alex stammered.

"Calm down. I showed but a glimpse of what fate will befall your planet if you do not take action now. Earth is very large yet very insignificant in the grand scheme of things, but it is the only world you have ever known. Am I correct? Your people have not gotten past your own galaxy, yes?" she inquired.

It was all just a vision; his grandfather was still alive. Alex gritted his teeth in unfiltered rage.

"I'll kill you!" Alex said in a fit of blinding rage. He raised his hand to strike, but she flicked her wrist and slammed Alex to the ground. He landed with a thud, and immediately got the wind knocked out of him.

"Enough. You are a hundred years too early to be challenging me. I am not your enemy, human. The Zenakuu did far worse to my world, and unlike yours, we actually stood a chance. Understand I am here to help you."

"If you want to help me, get out of my room and never come back. I cannot help you."

"If you want to save your family, you have no choice."

Thinking that he might still be hallucinating, Alex rubbed his eyes and reached for a nearby doorknob. "So, why me?" he asked. "Am I like *the one* or something?"

"No, I am afraid you are not that special. You just happened to be the most inclined for this type of battle."

"I see. Well, that's cool," Alex said in a sly fashion.

The creature noticed his attempt to escape and telekinetically locked the door shut. "Your planet is being threatened. I believe you have the ability to save it. Now tell me, will you?"

"Look, all this is really too much. I won't tell anyone I saw you, so please just go," Alex stammered.

"I cannot. You are a very unique young—I suppose—man? I do not know when your species reaches adulthood, but regardless, you are meant to stop the greatest evil that has come to pass in both your history and ours."

"I can't. Even if anything you say is true, I can't just leave. I start college in the spring," Alex answered.

Seeing that the conversation wasn't going anywhere she paused momentarily. "That device over there seems to run on electricity. Hand it to me."

Alex was dubious of her intentions, but he didn't feel like he was in a position to argue. She cut the computer's charging cord in half with a snap of her fingers, and Alex's eyes widened. "I had to work hard for that computer!" he shouted.

"Stop being such an infant. You are technologically a millennium behind schedule anyway." She took his hands in hers and put them over the ends of the cord. "Now make it work."

"How?" Alex asked her.

Her eyes locked on his. "My ship's scanners detected a strong reading for electrokinesis from this residence. Now fix the cord."

"This is a waste of time. I don't even know what that is. You've got the wrong person," he said.

"Do not"—her tone dropped to a threatening modulation—"waste my time, earthling."

Fear took over Alex. "What do you want me to do? Just press the wires together and see what happens? I could die."

"My patience wears thin, earthling. Make a stream of electricity to bond the two cords.

"I don't know how!" he frantically said.

Shyra placed her hand over her mouth; her body language suggested she was concerned with his lack of kinetic comprehension. "Perhaps my father was right about the potential of this planet." She moved in closer until she was face-to-face with Alex. "Visualize an electrical connection between the two cords," Shyra instructed.

Confused, Alex held the wires and tried to see some sort of electrical bond between them in his mind. Nothing at first, but then he felt some sort of warm sensation flow through his arms to his hands but kept his eyes shut, as he was focused on imagining. The computer turned on and began rebooting.

"Good, very good indeed," she remarked. "What do they call you?"

"Alexander Carter, but everyone just calls me Alex."

"Very well, Alexander, I have come as a guardian to save your planet from invasion. Now gather your things. We are leaving."

"I keep telling you, I can't just pick up and leave. I have a life here. And how do I know you aren't just trying to abduct me to perform gross experiments on me? I've heard how this kind of stuff usually goes."

"Trust me, human. If I wanted to abduct you, I would have done it by now."

"Fair enough," he responded. Alex stared in disbelief. He always hoped he was meant for something greater in this world—that he wasn't just another kid out of Houston, Texas—but never in his wildest dreams did he imagine this. "What about my grandfather?" Alex asked.

Shyra replied, "No one can know where we go. Our training must be in seclusion. I will give you one last chance to say goodbye."

"What kind of training?" Alex asked.

Shyra reminded him, "You have ten minutes; better make it quick."

"I can't just leave him. I'm all he's got," Alex said.

"Then your grandfather is already dead. Odd, though, I thought you a hero, but I was mistaken. I pray the Zenakuu at least slaughter you and your family quickly and without torture. Good day, Alexander Carter." With that, she turned and headed for the window.

"Wait," Alex called after her. She grinned upon his stopping her but wiped the smile from her face before turning around.

"Swear to me that if I go with you, he'll live," he said.

"I will guard his life myself if need be," she promised him.

Alex stared at her. Doing nothing was a risk he could not take. Putting family first was something he learned from an early age. Though petrified, he finally gave in. "I'll go with you," he finally said.

"Of course you will. Now go make your preparations so we can depart."

Alex walked out and headed toward his grandfather's bedroom. Quietly and carefully, he entered the room. "Can I talk to you, Grandpa?" Alex asked.

"Of course, Alex, come in," said Grandpa Henry with a smile.

Alex walked through the doorway and looked in awe at the wall of plaques and awards his grandfather and late father had earned through the years like he always did before finally confessing what was on his mind. "You have always told me I was destined for great things," Alex said.

"Because you are, Alex," his grandfather proudly told him.

"Well, there is something that I must do. It's the reason I was born, I think, but I promise that I will come back."

"What are you talking about, son? I'm confused."

"Please, Grandpa, you gotta trust me on this," Alex continued. "I have to go now, but I love you."

"Absolutely not," his grandfather said. "I lost your father. I'm not losing you too; you're all I have left of him."

The last thing Alex wanted to do was abandon his grandfather, but he knew his grandfather was strong and still had a lot of life left in him. He would be fine, but the thought of leaving broke his heart nonetheless.

"Granddad, I promise I'll be back, and I'll make you proud of me. Just watch."

"Alex, I'm already proud of you. Whatever you're thinking about doing, you don't have to do. I don't wanna hear another word about this now. We can discuss it more in the morning."

Alex looked straight at him. "Yes, sir. Goodnight, Grandpa." Alex walked back to his room with his decision already made. "This time, Grandpa, I do."

Alex came back to his bedroom to pack his stuff, while Shyra stood at the edge of the windowsill, drawing her fingers along the frame.

Mildly bemused by the dust, she murmured, "Dirty creatures."

"Ahem." Alex cleared his throat to make her aware of his presence.

She turned to him and asked how it had gone. Alex didn't respond to her intrusive question. Instead, he just glared at her and went to grab an empty duffle bag as he wiped any trace of tears from his cheeks.

"Very well," she said, "grab your things and let us be off."

Alex packed for a trip that he knew he may never come back from. If he was going to die, he wanted to be surrounded by the things that meant the most to him. Even though Shyra instructed him to pack light, he brought along clothes, a few medals, wall posters, his laptop, and framed photos of his grandfather and late parents. He followed Shyra out the window, and Shyra shot up in the sky with Alex on her back. If Alex had any doubts to her story, they were gone now. Shyra traveled under the blanket of night to a spot in the woods. When they landed, Alex rubbed the sleep out of his eyes.

"What are we doing here?" he asked.

Shyra replied, "I need to gauge the current level of your power so I know where to start training you. It is something that every esper goes through."

"I don't know what you're talking about. What's an esper?" Alex asked.

"An esper is someone with extrasensory perception. Now show me your power."

Once again, Alex wasn't budging any. The alien expected too much from him. She attacked Alex with a telekinetic push that flung him into a nearby tree. He slammed into its bark with an echoing thud and then crashed to the ground on his stomach. With the little breath he had remaining from the blow, he screamed, "What the hell was that for?"

"Motivation, Alexander. Do you require more of it?" Shyra jumped into a fighting position. She lunged after Alex, ready to throw another telekinetic push. Alex ran away, though, through the trees, over logs, and picked up speed. He recklessly closed his eyes and began concentrating; a spark flashed, and he vanished in the night. Alex looped around and tackled Shyra to the ground. They both rolled on the ground for several feet before stopping.

"Electrokinesis—like I thought. It would appear that it only manifests when your life is in danger, though. Interesting," Shyra said. "Get some rest. We train in the morning."

"What? Here?" Alex asked.

Shyra grinned, and with a few pushed buttons on her wrist gadget, she revealed her once-cloaked spaceship. "No, in there," she corrected.

The spaceship looked deceivingly meek at first glance, like a metallic stingray. Alex peered inside and was left speechless at its vastness. There were long hallways that lead to plenty of bedrooms for a crew of people. Shyra's ship had many features. To Alex, the technology looked like it was straight out of a Hollywood movie. The craft's most important attribute was its ability to cloak by either becoming invisible to the human eye or changing into the shape of any proportional object that Shyra could download through a connection to Earth's Internet. The ship was docked in a treeless patch she'd found in the forest closest to Alex's high school. When uncloaked, it looked like a very high-tech alien spacecraft.

The ship was round but not perfectly round, it had its own shape. The bottom of the ship was flat and around the edge shifted up and down like a ripple effect. The thrusters were all around the edge and one thruster on the bottom for lift off and landing. The tail of the ship was long and it acted as a stabilizer. Turret guns were located to the front, and the dimmed lights on it glowed and seemed to hum in the darkness.

"Hurry, Alexander. We are moving the ship to the mountains of Call-o-rah-dou," Shyra said.

"You mean Colorado? Why there?" Alex asked.

"That is where the first guide crashed."

"You mean there are actually more of you here?"

"All your questions will be answered in due time, Alexander, but now we must leave."

They entered the craft, and Shyra had Alex sit down while she prepped the ship and activated its cloaking device. They soared through the sky under the veil of the nightfall and within a half hour were nestled away in a remote location half way up Mount Elbert in Colorado. Alex was assigned a room that was completely bare and stripped of everything besides the essentials—a bed, a metal chair and dresser, and a lamp. He resided there for the rest of the night, though he got no sleep for hours. He spent the entire night staring out the window into the endless forests of Colorado. He must have questioned himself hundreds of times, wondering if it was all real or if he was going to wake up any minute and find himself back at home with his Grandfather Henry, but it never happened. Alex was going to get the chance to be the hero he dreamed of being whether he liked it or not.

The woods were the perfect training spot—plenty of ground, cover, and privacy. Hunting season was over, so there wasn't another human in sight. The brisk mountain air was much colder than Alex had anticipated, and the wild animals howled, making sounds that shook his very core. Shyra woke Alex at the crack of dawn, and while his eyes were barely open, she flung him outside and began training. He landed face first on the ground motionless, still unable to shake the headache he suffered from the night before.

"Rise, Alexander; you can sleep when you are dead."

He glared at her for the unnecessary comment. "Not cool, Shyra. I'll sleep when I'm tired."

"You will sleep when I say you can sleep," she firmly said, but Alex just rolled his eyes at her, completely uninterested in what she had to teach.

"This is dumb. I can shoot electricity from my hands. I don't need to train, why don't you just show me where to point and I'll shoot," he said.

"You insolent little…Is your entire species this abrasive or is it a pubescent thing? Listen here Alexander, you having these abilities is like tossing an X-57 plasma cannon to a new recruit and sending him into battle without any training. He is going to get a lot of people killed. By itself, having kinetic powers does not make you any more qualified to be a superhero than having a gun makes you qualified to be a soldier. Now stop wasting my time and prepare yourself." Shyra moved in closer and slowly closed her eyes. "First off, Alexander, take a deep breath and channel the power that has always been within you. Meditation is the beginning of mastering your ability. Once you grasp that, you can utilize your power, and the headaches I know you have been feeling will go away," Shyra explained.

"What's the deal with that anyway? Ever since you showed up, it's felt like bombs continuously going off in my head."

"You are not used to kinetic pressure. Beings with a high signature naturally emit a kinetically charged, pressurized aurora. What you are feeling right now is mine. With time, you will grow accustomed to them and even learn to mask your own," she explained.

"The sooner, the better. I don't know how much more of this I can take."

"Focus. Feel the energy surging through your body; visualize the spark that flickers, begging to be released."

Even though Alex was listening intently, he couldn't help but laugh. "You sound like Mr. Miyagi."

"I do not know who this person of whom you speak is, but I will advise you not to interrupt me again. Now bring your hands inches apart and concentrate that energy between them."

"Alright, whatever," he said to her.

"Depending on the person or species, there can be several different kinds of kinesis. To this day, we are still discovering different types."

"Understood," he said. Alex began sparking electric current surges from one hand to the other. It was pathetic at first, but for the next hour, he focused on holding it.

"The more you use your kinesis, the stronger and more in control you will be," Shyra explained.

Alex smiled with enthusiasm at the possibilities. "Do you always have to talk so cryptically? Look, you ripped me away from my family because of some alien war, so stop beating around the bush," he demanded.

"Listen here *human*, I 'ripped' you away from your insignificant life as you so elegantly put because the Zenakuu will be here someday, and you are nowhere near ready for them," she retorted. Clearly frustrated, Alex finally snapped.

"Okay, new plan, *you* deal with them when they get here! I'm going back home," he said as he started walking in the other direction.

"I will have no choice but to Alexander Carter, they will undoubtedly pick up on my Lygokinetic signature and track me down," Shyra explained.

"Good, problem solved. Now beam me back home or whatever it is you do," Alex said.

"Though faint, they will find yours as well. Along with anyone else who emits kinetic energy, and they will most likely hunt you down one by one, and then kill your loved ones. I am the only chance you have to prevent that," she confidently said.

"Ugh, enough of this crap. I want to know exactly what I'm up against. Who are these Zenakuu?"

"I could try to explain them to you, but I do not think you are ready for it," she responded.

"How about you let me be the judge of that? Tell me what happened."

"To appreciate the horrors of war, it is something that I must show you."

"Okay," he responded in confusion.

"I am going to telepathically link with you now. Just relax your mind and clear your thoughts."

Alex did as instructed, and Shyra's eyes began to emit a white glow. In a flash, Alex was seeing the collective memories of the citizens and soldiers of Kalryn, but what was truly shocking was the landscape. He looked around and marveled at its sheer beauty. All the trees gleamed with luster and were covered with pristine white bark and shimmering golden leaves. The lake next to them was crystal clear and shined like the glint of light on broken glass. In the distance, he saw deep blue mountains that scaled the land. Towering skyscrapers shrouded the city; the beautifully crafted architecture was on a level he'd never seen before. Everything was peaceful until he finally reached a horrifying reality. He was stuck on an alien world with no way to get back.

Chapter 2

It's Nothing Personal, It's Only Revenge

Alex's psyche was brought back through space and time, years before he ever existed to bear witness to the events that would forever shape his life. It was exceptionally quiet that day in Trifa, the capital of Kalryn. The Savant members were deciding whether or not to go on a salvage mission to the late Zenakuu Empire to confirm casualties. It had been twenty years since the last communications with Zenakuu had ended, and there were no signs of recovery. The planet essentially went black. During the meetings, city hall was always heavily guarded, which proved to be a lackluster job for the highly trained military personnel. These soldiers were equipped with kinetic-imbued swords for close-range combat and small powered plasma rifles in case of intruders, but the only action they ever really saw was keeping out kids who liked to hang around.

Jeramine was one of the soldiers patrolling the top of the building. He began dozing off when he was awoken by a rumbling. As he regained his balanced, he horned in, "Tremor!" He jumped from the top of the building and regrouped with the rest of his team.

Another soldier, Henarai, looked up. "What the hell is that?" he asked as he pointed skyward to a colossal black spaceship entering the Kalryn stratosphere. At closer look, the object was unmistakably a Zenakuu ship; confusion overwhelmed the Kalryn guards, as they had never witnessed an attack on Kalryn before.

"Impossible. Zenakuu was wiped out. What is going on here?" Jeramine wondered aloud.

Soon, the warship began its assault on the vibrant capital. Bombs started dropping like hail, and gunners began shredding the capital with Zurekium bullets eviscerating anyone unlucky enough to be caught in the crosshairs.

The tall, plate glass windows of city hall were the first to shatter. Rows of them stretching the length of the building shattered into a million pieces, leaving the once-elegant silver silk drapes that covered them tattered and unsightly.

The small group of soldiers who initially guarded the building now hid for cover behind it. "Call Rayvaar right now and counterattack immediately," Jeramine ordered. He was the acting commander of a small group of guards for good reason. He was proficient in all manners of weapons and tactics, kept a cool head, and excelled at combat training.

"Yes, sir. I will reach Rayvaar and the Captain," responded Shielza, the communications expert in the group.

A telepathic link was sent out to the head Savant Rayvaar. "This is Shielza of the Savant guards. We are under attack by a Zenakuu warship. One was reported, but there could be more, sir. Please get to the panic room with the others at once."

"Understood, Shielza. Thank you, and good luck out there. Rayvaar out." After signing off, Rayvaar turned and announced, "Councilmen, I just received word that Zenakuu has attacked. We need to move to the panic room."

"Rayvaar, what of the citizens of Kalryn?" someone asked.

"We will launch a counterattack, but at the moment, there is nothing we can do for them other than pray they can find refuge,

Hartell. If your loved ones are near, bring them quickly, but we need to survive this attack."

"Of course," the man responded.

The Savants rushed down the long corridor, which was lined with elegantly hand-woven tapestries and paintings of the founding forefathers. They scrambled for the panic room, as the building was falling down around them. While some could call their actions selfish, the Kalryn always thought strategically, and the Savants dying would no doubt be considered checkmate.

"My daughter," Rayvaar said. "Has anyone seen my daughter?"

Rayvaar's daughter Shyra was never around when she was needed.

The Savants members all made it into the panic room safely, but Rayvaar was not satisfied. "Shyra, where are you?" he called to his daughter telepathically.

"Father, I am fine," she responded. "Your guards messaged the captain on the first recon infantry and air force, and I am boarding a plane now with Jeramine to fight these savages back to the hole they came from."

"What! Shyra, I forbid it. That boy is going to get you killed. You must get to the panic room at once! That boy always has trouble following him."

"I am well aware of your displeasure for him," she answered, "but I love him, Father. He will keep me safe. You have to stop treating me like a child. I can make a difference out there; no one has my level of focus and my kinetic abilities." With that, Shyra set a mental block to her father's brainwaves. *I am sorry, Father, but I must do this,* she thought to herself.

"Shyra, close the hatch. We have to get going," Jeramine said.

"I am coming." Shyra took a deep breath and kissed the locket Jeramine had given her during their courtship for good luck. The doors on the fastest two-man flying craft available in the Kalryn airbase closed and prepped for flight. It was difficult to hold herself together, but if she was to die, she wanted to be by her love when it happened.

The Zenakuu ship bombarded the remaining parts of the once regal city hall into rubble. It was no match for the raw power of Zenakuu engineering. Luckily, they built the panic room underground and about a mile away from city hall.

"This building is not giving us significant cover, Kipshiro," Henarai said. "We have to move. We are sitting ducks here."

"Agreed, but Jeramine told us to hold our position," Kipshiro said.

"Well, Jeramine left to find Shyra. It is just you, me, and Shielza out here, and I intend on living through this."

"I hate to say it, but you are right," Kipshiro agreed. "We can head for those trees over there and stay low." The three-man team hunched over and traveled fast while rocks and debris flew past their heads.

"Air support should be here soon, along with the Calvary," Shielza said.

"The military base is thirteen miles west. If we make it there, we can gear up and fight back," Henarai said.

"Good idea, Hen, but it is a wide-open field between us and the base. We will be spotted for sure."

"Do not worry about that. I have an idea. Just be ready to go on my mark, and you better move your ass too." Kipshiro ordered.

The Kalryn people had an ace up their sleeves, however, a kinesis of their own—their signature lygokinesis, the ability to use one's mind to create pure energy into whatever object they wanted. With lygokinesis, the Kalryn race could create psionic force fields, enhanced weapons, and various kinds of devices to help them in war situations.

Kipshiro strained to send half of his lygokinetic power through his gun and the other half to shield his body. "Go now!" he yelled as he jumped out in plain sight. He lined up his sights on the massive ship as it was pounding giant rounds into civilization. With every round that went off, the ground shook, which made lining up his sights hard, but he was aiming for something big and hoped not to get killed before he could fire at least one shot.

The barrel of his weapon grew brighter and brighter with his power until finally he released the bullet satiate with lygokinetic energy. As the bullet left the barrel it left behind a trail of celestial light, but he knew pretty light shows would not win that war. Kipshiro fell to the ground, but heard jets and other aircraft whizzing over his head. He felt a sense of relief, as he knew backup had finally arrived. The bullet flew true and hit its target; the lygokinesis inside exploded and created a crater in the hull of the Zenakuu ship. Smoke poured from the vessel as the occupants abandoned ship, some in escape pods that jettisoned out from every angle and others by parachute. Kipshiro tried to get back up, but he lost sensation in his body. He struggled to turn his stiff neck away from the blinding rays of the sun.

His pupils dilated, and he couldn't handle the bright light anymore. The mental strain was too much for him, and Kipshiro entered the early stages of a brain aneurysm; nausea intensified as his vision blurred. The others turned back, but it was too late to save him. Kipshiro felt a heavy pop in the back of his neck, and blood filled his skull until he met death. He honorably sacrificed himself for the sake of his team. The skies soon filled with not only Zenakuu but other races from the shared solar system. The fighter pilots who flew by couldn't comprehend why other worlds were helping the Zenakuu, but they did not have the luxury to stop and think.

Shyra and her betrothed Jeramine caught up to the Zenakuu warship and realized that it was dropping out of the sky. The Kalryn Air Force was broadcasting a chance to surrender to the Zenakuu, but as the enemy parachuted down, they opened fire.

"The audacity. We offer to spare their lives, and they shoot at us? They are truly deranged. Open fire on the survivors!" Jeramine ordered.

The Kalryn pilots sprayed plasma rounds and effectively annihilated some of the falling troops. A few dozen soldiers made it to the ground; some were caught up in the sparkling trees, while others with bullet-riddled parachutes landed too hard to survive the impact. The small portion that did make it formed a tight group and remained tactical. The Kalryn infantry followed up at the landing site and lay to waste the remaining Zenakuu soldiers, losing a few good men in the process. Jeramine and Shyra's plane approached fast, but as they flew over the battlefield, they only saw the crashing warship

"Is it over, Jeramine?" his fiancée, Shyra, questioned. The Kalryn military infantry rushed in and secured the battlefield, making sure all assailants were taken care of. The patrolling was almost over when they heard another shattering rumble, the second one that day bestowed itself upon Kalryn.

Jeramine heard the sound and remarked, "That is the same rumble that woke me earlier. I have to let the other fighters know."

Jeramine broadcasted the telepathic distress message: "First recon air deployment, we have a possible second warship entering the atmosphere. Be ready to defend."

More warships came in through the troposphere, crashing through the skies. They were all fixed on Trifa, the capital of the Kalryn—a very bold move.

The blackness of the dreadful Zenakuu warship entered the atmosphere, eclipsing the sun and shading the battlefield. Several squads of the Kalryn Air Force fell into a V formation and flew toward the enemy to engage.

"Okay, men, give them hell!" Jeramine shouted over the open communication channel. The men used their fighter crafts to spring their counterattack on the descending ship. Jeramine and Shyra headed the pack. The warship's main weapon activated with a small glint of light. The only one who saw it fast enough was Shyra herself, and she immediately shielded the plane she was in with a lygokinetic barrier. With not enough time to react for the Kalryn Air Force, the main Zenakuu cannon fired. A purple beam of unfamiliar plasma shot down and disintegrated everything in its path except Shyra, Jeramine, and the protected plane. The mental strain of guarding the plane rendered Shyra unconscious.

"Shyra, talk to me. Are you okay? Your father will kill me if I do not bring you back safe. Dammit!" Jeramine tried to patch himself through to headquarters. "Field Officer Jeramine to base. First recon and air infantry has fallen. Requesting backup. There is another Zenakuu warship."

Jeramine started heading back when the third Zenakuu warship dropped down in front of his airspace. Jeramine bled the speed and slowed down to a slow hover.

"Mayday, Mayday, there is another Zenakuu warship descending. Requesting to bring out the Chrentex squad into battle."

"Request denied, soldier," came the response. "We cannot risk losing a single Chrentex at this stage in battle."

"But, sir, the enemy has developed a new weapon. It took out the entire air force in one attack."

"Captain, sorry to interrupt," Henarai cut in, "but I have seen this weapon, and he speaks the truth. My Communications Expert, Shielza was annihilated, from the blast. It can wipe out an entire base with ease. I cannot comprehend your decision to not deploy the Chrentex, we need to end this fast, sir."

"Well then it is a good thing comprehension is not a requisite of compliance. What is your name, soldier?"

"Sir, Lieutenant Henarai, sir."

"Solider, where are you?"

"Sir, I am behind enemy lines. We need the Chrentex; it is the only way to assure victory."

Brigadier General Kai-neth paused for a moment. The Chrentex were the planet's greatest military assets—elite super soldiers—and he didn't want to risk losing even one. But if he didn't turn the battle around, there would be nothing left to defend.

"Sir!" Henarai yelled out again.

"Very well, Lieutenant. We will deploy them immediately."

"Thank you, sir." Jeramine ended transmission. Jeramine knew full well what deploying them meant; they could easily change the tide of this war or seal its fate. He'd never seen the Chrentex in real life, but he remembered what he'd read about them in the history books.

The Chrentex carried equipped assault rifles that linked to their battle suits. The suits, being very high-tech, powerful, and dangerous, were weapons of mass destruction that no other Kalrynian could handle and were actually connected to each soldier's cerebral cortex and, subsequently, his brainwaves. Chrentex were chosen at birth and trained for combat from a very early age.

The suits covered their entire bodies from head to toe. Their helmets were very plain with small blue circles centered on their forehead that connected to the smaller blue circles on their hands, which generated and fired lygokinesis and magnified its destructive power tenfold. There were two ocular lenses that analyzed the battlefield to determine who were threats, heart rates of the surrounding area, and a complete heads-up display. The lenses also provided infrared, X-ray, ultraviolet, and night vision, depending on the soldier's selection. The Chrentex had perfected these suits and every aspect of lygokinesis, which is what made these fighters so rare and so valuable. Armory was integrated into their suits, and just by thinking of a weapon, a Chrentex could access that weapon. It would fold out and build itself around the user's hand, ready to fire.

The two warships were relentless as they decimated Kalryn's cities. The explosions painted skies black as they filled with smoke. Heaps of rubble and twisted metal fell from the buildings that until just yesterday had gently kissed the skies. The death count continued to rise, and there was no foreseeable end to the lives lost. A Kalrynian drop ship flew over, harboring the elite military advanced Lygokinetic soldiers. Zenakuu landing vehicles came to eliminate any threats on land and fighter jets to take care of any airborne threats were deployed from the warships. Now, Zenakuu ruled the sky and land. The Kalryn drop ship hovered above the Zenakuu warship just long enough for the five silent and powerhouse-like Chrentex to jump down and land on its outer hull with thunderous force before the drop ship was shot down.

These elite soldiers also had a bottomless supply of kinesis, though the power came with a high price. Chrentex exchanged their incredible power for the length of their lives, shortening their life spans each time they used the battle suits that were permanently lodged into their brains. It was a double-edged sword, so to get the most out of the warriors, they were kept in cryogenic stasis. The life of a Chrentex wasn't glamorous at all, and even though it was considered to be a great honor to serve as a Chrentex, parents often wept uncontrollably when their infants were selected for the program.

With these fighting machines on Kalryn's side, it was clear which nation possessed the greatest soldiers. The five Chrentex were now on the top of one of the warships; they blasted a hole through the roof and jumped inside. The leader, who was codenamed Unum, led the rest to a passage through the ship. They ran down a long hallway and then turned a corner and faced a room full of Zenakuu and other planetary races armed to the teeth with ballistic weapons. Unum charged his Lygokinetic energy, and the blue circle on his helmet started to spin faster and faster. As it spun, it grew bigger and emitted a two-dimensional azure energy circle in front of him. In a flash, his helmet shot a stream of lygokinesis that ricocheted through the room, killing all enemies so efficiently that he seemed to control the beam's route with his mind.

The Chrentex never spoke. In fact, nothing could be heard but the thud of bodies hitting the floor. They communicated telepathically, and the five of them were always in each other's minds. Unum guided the rest of them in a single file line—Unum, Duobus, Tribus, Quattuor, and finally Quinque. The five readied their rifles simultaneously as they marched down the passageway. Their lenses analyzed the entire craft and guided them to the control room to bring the ship down. They took out Zenakuu after Zenakuu, as well as any other species in their way. The Chrentex displayed no feelings; because there was no room for emotions in war, they were like heartless machines.

In passing, other planetary warriors on the ship who had heard tales of the godlike Chrentex dropped their weapons immediately. In the control room, however, Admiral Jassal of the Zenakuu invasion party was ready. When the Chrentex reached them, he had a squadron of soldiers with their guns aimed at the doors. Unum turned on his X-ray lens and saw the horde of trigger-happy soldiers guarding the main deck. The five each charged up all three of their lygokinetic generators for a total fifteen shots. They waited until fully charged before Quattuor and Quinque kneeled, while the first three remained standing. They pointed their hands at the control room where twenty-five Zenakuu soldiers waited and blasted the entire room out of existence, leaving only the doorway the five stood behind intact.

Jeramine flew by the falling warship and patched through to the base "Sir, another warship is going down," he reported.

"Damn, those Chrentex mean business," the captain said.

"Yes, sir, but we still have another one. Let the Chrentex take down the last ship," Jeramine said.

"Negative, solider, they are needed on the ground. I am bringing them back down. Send the air force to finish the job."

"Yes, sir. Alright everyone, you heard the captain. Now get it done." The full force of the Kalryn Air Force lifted off to attack the remaining Zenakuu warship.

Jeramine touched down his plane back at base and handed over the still unconscious Shyra to the medical bay. He kissed her on the forehead and promised to be right back. He quickly sprinted back to his fighter craft, fired up the thrusters, and took off. Several carriers and turbo jets took flight and made their way toward the Zenakuu invasion party. The ensuing dogfight was bloody and brutal. One by one, most of the Kalryn Air Force was shot down by the superior Zenakuu pilots.

"I need three planes on my six. We are going to wrap around and out flank them." Jeramine took control and planned on finishing the fight.

"I will be your wingman today," stated a mysterious voice.

"Adel, is that you?" Jeramine asked.

"Who else would be crazy enough to cover your ass in the midst of all this?"

"It is damn good to hear you, man. I was not sure if you made it out."

"Save the tears for later. We have a battle to win."

"Copy that. Everyone stay tight and watch each other's backs," Jeramine responded. As the squadron drew closer to the warship, they did all they could to not get blasted out of the sky.

"Evasive maneuvers!" Adel shouted. Heavy machine guns sprayed the sky, and missiles flew through the air, anxiously searching for targets. The remaining squadron was the academy's best and shot down a dozen enemy aircraft before a missile finally connected with Jeramine's plane.

"Damn! I am hit," Jeramine called out. "Attempting to stabilize." His plane shook violently, and black smoke visibly seeped from the engine.

"Jeramine, there is empty field beneath us. Touch down over there. I will cover you," Adel said.

"I am not going to make it. I cannot seem to gain control."

"If you have no other choice, eject, but be careful. The airspace is dangerous around here."

"Got a better plan. I have the control room in my sights. I am bringing this plane down and taking that entire ship with me," Jeramine said.

"Have you gone insane? That is suicide. Engage the autopilot."

"None of the guiding system controls are operational. I have to do this manually, Adel. With all these missiles, I can bring that thing down," Jeramine shouted.

"No, we will find another way," Adel said.

"This is the only way. Gentlemen, it has been an honor. Adel, tell Shyra that I am sorry for breaking my promise."

"Jeramine, no! Do not do it," his friend screamed.

Jeramine knew his sacrifice was noble, but in his last moments of life, he felt regret over breaking Shyra's heart with his death and never being able to feel the warmth of her love again. But the brave pilot did not decelerate; he drove his plane deep into the front of the control room. No one could confirm the damage, because the smoke acted like a screen. When the dust settled, it was clear that part of the control room was severely wrecked but still functioning.

"Damn you, Jeramine. Why did you do that?" cried Adel.

"Yes, but he did open up a shot," another pilot pointed out. "We will not let his sacrifice go in vain. All fighters open fire on that hole."

Before long, every available missile in the air force was sent into the small hole Jeramine had created. The very last warship made its descent; half of it was blown to pieces, while the other half spiraled down to the ground and crashed in the ocean.

The assault forces of the Zenakuu had entered the lower atmosphere. They had been stymied by the fighter jets launched from various hangers on the surface of Kalryn, but a large amount of the Zenakuu landing crafts with large, drop-down doors on the front had survived the defensive plasma cannons and missiles. The majority of Kalryn's armed mobile forces stood at the ready, forming up around a gate that protected the center of the Savant's sanctuary under the once crystal-clear sky that was now turned horrid by black smoke. They understood the task that lay before them. Large portions of the Kalryn infantry were armed with guns, Lygokinetic swords, and shielded weapons. The mission was clear—they were to keep the enemy from bypassing the front line. If they failed, the chances of keeping the Savants safe would be next to zero.

The commander of the infantry made a speech minutes before the bulk of the enemy ships would appear.

"My brothers in arms, hear me. This day we stand against the single greatest threat to freedom in the galaxy. You, however, are the best of the best, the greatest of the elites. Our planet has had many trials only to always come out victorious, but long years of victory do not preclude eventual defeat. Down there are our countrymen, children, friends, and family. We will not let them down this day. Failure is not an option! Today we fight for all that we hold dear. These Zenakuu bastards picked the wrong planet to mess with. Through this battle we achieve immortality. Today we seize glory! We are the chosen arm of destiny, and the enemy will not escape our righteous judgment. For Trifa and for Kalryn!"

In response, came a chorus of thunderous cheers. Kalrynian soldiers took their duty to the Savants seriously. His words ended not a second too soon, as the first of the crafts touched down.

As the landing ship approached the ground, its cannons began to glow. Shots were fired all at once and colored the skies violet. The first assault took the lives of dozens of Kalryn soldiers. As the doors began to lower, the Chrentex began their counterassault. Soldier after soldier charged forward only to be hacked down to size by the Kalrynian super elite. Both limbs and lives were lost as the Zenakuu boldly attempted to gain ground. The hostiles' numbers were heavily decreased as they continued forward. Several more troops were cut down when they charged the front line with Chrentex warriors who stood ready to defend. The first wave had been fended off rather easily. The cheers at their victory were cut off by the sounds of the orbital cannons opening up again, aiming at the ground troops.

"Men, the true battle is about to begin! It seems our final hour may yet be at hand," the commanding officer of the group stated, eliciting anxious noises from the men serving under him.

Suddenly, a small squad of heavily armored support vehicles pulled in on the right side of the trenches. They turned their heavy cannons skyward and fired at the landing ships, adding to the Zenakuu casualties.

However, when a Zenakuu cruiser dropped out of the atmosphere and began firing on the ground troops, even the most courageous warriors lost heart. They crashed down, scorching the skies and vaporizing everything in their paths. The greatest lost was Tribus, who died when a blood vessel in his brain ruptured as he attempted to put up a barrier over the entire battlefield and overexerted his parietal lobe. The act that cost him his life shielded the Kalryn troops momentarily, but the cover that the Kalrynian infantry had been using was now partially destroyed, just in time for half a dozen landing crafts to touch down and drop open. "Sir, Chrentex Tribus has gone offline," a soldier back at the base announced.

"Dammit. This is exactly what I was afraid of. We cannot afford to lose anymore. Reclaim all the Chrentex and make sure that dead suit is recovered," the commanding officer ordered.

"Yes, sir."

As the Zenakuu advanced, they fired Zurekium cannon shells and small arms at the demoralized Kalryn. A single soldier stood and watched her comrades lose their lives. She observed one man get maimed as he lost his intestine, while another was ripped open from a grenade that exploded near his torso and sent shrapnel through his body. She began to scream, a single, feminine screech of fury. All the pain, all those gruesome deaths—it was expressed in that single outburst of emotion from the female-born Kalryn. That one voice seemed to be the only noise on the battlefield for the four seconds that it lasted before she leaped out from behind her cover and led a charge down the Zenakuu's throat.

The half or so of the remaining troopers admired her passion and rallied behind her, giving battle cries of their own. At that single moment, the empire's assault soldiers finally realized who they were up against—soldiers who were not even afraid of death. Unfortunately for them, they found out just a little too late, as the grenades thrown by the charging Kalryn landed, filling the enemy ranks literally full of holes. The Zenakuu Empire that had declared war stood no chance against extremely zealous warriors fighting for one of the few things that mattered to them—their survival. As the larger Zenakuu soldiers fell to the ground from the counterattack, they spilled their sage green blood everywhere. Suddenly, the hostiles found themselves outmatched and frightened. There was no hope for them; their reinforcements were being cut off in orbit.

All because of one courageous charge and more than two dozen grenades, the newest attack force in the galaxy was being forced to retreat. Ground troops whimpered in a variety of languages. They screamed and pleaded for mercy, but there was none. Others threw down their weapons in hopes of surrender but only earned a more agonizing slaying. Heads of innocent

Kalrynian rolled that day, so forgiveness was no longer an option. Kalrynian soldiers began to reclaim their positions in the trenches, and even though they were battered and bruised, a handful of them had survived the brutal fight. Some were only kids who never knew of true battle. They'd only read of it in their history books, but on that day they were forced to grow up. They finally saw what harsh battle really was. The remaining forces feared the worst—that their friends and family who also fought or tried to hide may not have survived the fight. The battle on this sector of the planet was done. Meanwhile, it was still raging on other parts of the planet and in space.

Elsewhere, the Kalryn defenses were rushing to regain control of the upper space area of their planet and block any more approaching Zenakuu armada.

"This is Captain Kody. I am located near sector 1-40-7. I need immediate assistance. I repeat—immediate assistance," said a voice over the radio, which was heard through the main command center of the base. Kody had served proudly in the military for many years, had seen many battles on domestic and foreign worlds, and even had bionic limbs for his legs, which he'd lost when he was unfortunate enough to step on a land mine in the years of combat. "Captain Kody, this is General Yendero. What is the emergency?" General Yendero asked.

"We have detected three Zenakuu warships coming in at our position. We do not have the forces to fight them at this moment. A large Zenakuu fleet has approached from sector 1-40-1-10. My men met them in combat about ten minutes ago, and we narrowly beat them. We need assistance immediately."

General Yendero turned to his men in the command center. "You heard him. The Zenakuu are approaching on the city of Vourn, and we are the reinforcements. Let us move, men. Get four command ships over to the city now!"

Vourn was forty miles away, but for a Kalryn command ship, it would only take twenty minutes to get there. Four command ships left the base and headed for Vourn. When they were about halfway there, they got the message.

"We have pushed them back. I repeat—we have pushed them back," Captain Kody informed.

With no more need for them, the command ships flew up into the air. When they saw space open up before them, there was a battle raging to their right. They darted in to bring aid to the space units. Fighters raced out of the hanger of Kody Kadeem's ship.

"Okay, Captain Kody. We will take the ones to the left," the squad leader said.

"Uh, Kody, what are those?" a lieutenant asked. He pointed out to the left of the battle.

Captain Kody Kadeem looked out and saw three more enemy ships advancing. "Squad 11-2, go for the—" A large explosion erupted near them and sent the ship rocking. Captain Kody looked out and saw that three large fleets approached. "Dear God," he cried.

"Captain, they are all over us!" the deployed squad leader shouted. "We cannot … Ah!"

The captain looked out at the fighters. To his horror, the insurmountable Zenakuu squad had taken down the entire squadron. "They have surrounded us!" Captain Kody shouted.

The only Kalryn fighters in the air at that moment were the four command ships that came from Kazda and three command ships from Vourn. The Zenakuu fleets had pushed them in and surrounded them. They had no escape.

"Mayday!" came a voice over Captain Kody's radio. "This is the captain of the 5-11 commander ship. We are going down. I repeat—we are going down!"

Captain Kody looked out and saw the command ship in flames, plummeting to Kalryn as a fiery heap of metal. Then, Kody looked over at his crew. "Contact home base. Tell them if we do not get back-up soon, do not bother. We will be dead by the time they reach us."

"Captain! Two Zenakuu warships are on our left," a crew member warned.

From their left came the two ships bellowing through space. From small crevasses in the ship came little orb devices. At least a thousand of them shot to Kody's ship. When they hit the command ship, they stuck like ticks to a hairy beast. Sparks began to fly as they started to eat their way into the ship.

"Sir, our ship is falling apart fast. We cannot—" The crew member's attention was turned to a red blinking screen. "Sir! Our engines are off-line."

"Everyone, prepare to abandon ship," Captain Kody ordered.

"Sir, we will not make it to the escape pods. Those things have made holes all over our ship. We will be sucked into space before we get to our pods."

"Those smart, little—" the Captain started. He felt like sitting there and cursing the Zenakuu until he ran out of breath, but he knew that wouldn't do any good. Instead, he took a deep breath and then continued, "Okay, if we are going down, we are taking them with us. Compress the drag fins. We are going to run right into those godforsaken creatures," he ordered.

"Sir, here comes the Kalryn forces. We are saved."

Kody looked out and saw a large fleet of Kalryn. No doubt they would be able to push these guys out.

"This is the Global Kalryn Forces. We are coming in. Hold your position; we are sending a rescue team," they announced over the radio.

It wasn't long before a rescue team got the others out of there. They took them back to base. Then the general of the third command ship took part in the fight. As he stood at the bridge of his command ship, he got a message. "General, we have spotted enemy forces coming in quickly," a control operator said.

"Get all the squads in your command and send them after the ships that have already arrived. Destroying those things is our top priority," the general responded.

"Yes, sir. We will have them down in no time," he replied.

At that moment, four squads moved into attack formation. They flew near the first fleet.

"Okay, this is it!" the squad leader said. "S-57, you go in at the right. Everyone else, stay behind me."

As they flew in, the Zenakuu quickly engaged them.

"Here they come!" a squad member said.

The two Zenakuu reached the Kalryn fighters first, but they were quickly shot out of the air by two missiles. Then the real Zenakuu squad flew in. The Kalryn were quickly split up and thrown into a dogfight, scrambling for dear life in the cold vacuum of space.

"Good job! First one down," the leader shouted. "Do not give them time to breathe. Go for the next one."

"We are on it, General."

The General now stood looking out at the battle. He was thinking of victory. It seemed like they would win easily. Then he got the message.

"General, uh … there is another fleet headed our way. They have surrounded us."

"What!" the general shouted.

"Sir, if we do not make a move, we are done for," a crew member said.

"Okay, here is what we will do. We will split our fleet up. Half go for one side; half go for the other, pushing their fleet away. Okay, we need some more fighters to take out those ships. Those are our main priority." The orders were given, and they were ready.

As the battle above Kalryn got hotter, it seemed like every time they took down a Zenakuu command ship, another showed up. And after about three hours of fighting, the general got another call.

"Sir, our fighters are down. I repeat—our fighters are down. Another Zenakuu ship has approached at sector 7-40. Sir, we are not going to hold much longer."

The general stood in thought and then finally said, "We need to retreat. We will not last up here. Call the base near Kazda; tell them to get all the turrets ready. We are not going down without a fight."

"General, this is Captain Matokay. We will hold off as much as we can. You and your men retreat. If we all run at the same time, most of the fleet will be destroyed."

Captain Kody responded, "You are a good man, Captain Matokay."

"I have about six fighters jets in the hanger. They will help."

"Okay, everyone," the general said as he contacted every personnel on board. "Everyone, this is your captain speaking. I am issuing a full-scale retreat. All hands on deck; prepare for departure. We are pulling out of here. Good luck, Captain."

The Kalryn ship pulled away. As they neared the planet's surface, they noticed that the Zenakuu were not following. Captain Matokay's ship flew down in the atmosphere, so they stood in the way of the Zenakuu. As the Captain waited for the Zenakuu to show, he told all the fighters to get in defensive positions and prepare to attack the Zenakuu on sight.

"Here they come!" the squad leader warned. "But they did not bring the whole fleet, not even half. They must expect an ambush."

"This just makes our job a little easier. Kill them all!" the captain said.

His staff sergeant turned to him and asked, "We are not making it out of this, sir, are we?"

With a somber face, Captain Matokay turned to his fellow soldier and told him what he was taught in boot camp during his early years. "Son, go into battle determined to die, and you will survive. Go into battle praying to live, and surely you shall not."

The staff sergeant thought about his words for a moment and responded with a passionate, "Yes, sir!" He looked around at the crew, which now had all eyes on him. "The rest of you men, you heard him—prepare yourselves. Hell's hounds draw near, but this is where we leave our mark in the pages of history. My life for Kalryn!"

The Kalryn fighters approached and began to pick off the invaders. Then four Zenakuu Command ships came into view.

"Here comes trouble," one of the Kalryn pilots said to himself.

The Zenakuu warships let out two more squads of fighters. The Kalryn fighters were quickly taken care of, and the four warships attacked the only ship standing between them and the Kalryn planet.

Back on the ground, the general asked for contact to the captain who stayed behind.

"Sir, we have lost contact. They must have been destroyed," a crew member informed.

"So they have. Okay, the Zenakuu will be here any minute. Everyone get—" The general paused as he looked up in the sky and saw three Zenakuu command ships darting to Kalryn and covered in flames. One was even broken in two pieces.

"He took three ships with him. That crew's sacrifice will not go to waste. Finish them off, men! When these monsters arrive at the gates of the underworld, they will tell the gate guards that Kalryn gives their regards!"

The battle raged on for what seemed like an eternity. So many Kalrynian lives were needlessly lost that day. Parts of the planets lay in ruins, and the slaughtered remains of people piled in the streets as far as the eye could see. Truly, this was a day that would forever lie in infamy. An entire planet too prideful and arrogant to believe that they would ever fall victim to an attack from a world that they believed to be dead was nearly destroyed that day.

The entire time Kalryn believed that Zenakuu were done for, they were actually recuperating from the Myriad attack. The Zenakuu bided their time and spent many years repopulating their planet and building advanced weaponry to seek their revenge. They used that initial attack to gauge the strength of Kalryn.

Word got out to the Savants that the battle neared its end. Kalryn was battered but victorious, and they began to surface from the panic room. The Savants were made up of seven nominated and usually elder Kalrynians and included Unarec, Kagoli, Nabire, Iyendo, Rayvaar, Tejourne, and Hartell. Even though Rayvaar was the youngest, he quickly climbed the ranks to be revered as the wisest and most tactical of them all, so naturally, all eyes averted to him.

"What are we to do? City hall is ruined, and the capital of this entire planet and neighboring cities are in shambles. I even heard that there were not only Zenakuu on those ships, but other races as well," Tejourne said.

"The Zenakuu have always looked upon us with distain and a jaundiced eye, but who could have helped them attack us?" asked Kagoli, one of the few female Savants.

"I need not guess. Surely it was the planet Purix; they are the next closest," Hartell attested.

"This is not a time to lose composure. We need to hold a meeting to assess the damage done," Rayvaar replied.

"And where are we to have this meeting? At the town library down the street? We have no city hall, nowhere to reside," Unarec said.

"We will just have it here in the panic room. There is room for all of us plus communications equipment. Now let us get to work." Rayvaar replied.

The seven Savants got together for another meeting, but not for the salvation of Zenakuu. This time, it was regarding the apprehension or possibly annihilation of the once amicable race.

"Let us get to it then. Now does anyone have any ideas on how to proceed?" Rayvaar opened up by letting his fellow councilmen bounce ideas back and forth.

"What other fate can we afford them? We should send the full force of the Kalryn military right down their throats and finish what the Myriad started!" blurted Hartell, who had always been a loose cannon.

"Do not be brash, Hartell. We have no clue how powerful they are and how many planets they have turned against us."

"A wise observation, Kagoli, but something must be done."

"What if they did not turn against us?"

"How do you mean, Rayvaar?" Nabire asked.

"What I mean is what if they had not a choice. What if they were forced by Zenakuu. The planet Purix is strong but not foolish and never favored confrontation. If they were forced into fighting, then we need to help others from falling into that same fate. Otherwise, we may not be able to fend them off the next time they attack with more military force from even more enslaved planets."

On cue, a transmission came through. "Calling out to Kalryn. We are in need of immediate assistance. The once silent planet Zenakuu has come to the planet of Belum and demanded help in destroying your world. When we declined, a giant warship blackened the sky and took us by surprise, forcing us to fight in their army. I had to send this distress call on pirate frequencies so that they couldn't track it. I pray it reaches you before they deploy for your planet." The feed ended and then looped until it was shut off by Iyendo.

"I cannot believe you were right, Rayvaar."

"I did not wish to believe it either, but it was the only explanation," proclaimed the young Savant.

"Agreed, but what to do about this? It is too late to help them or most planets in our solar system that lay vulnerable to invasion," Tejourne panicked. "Is no one safe from their wrath?"

"Do not despair, Tejourne. It looks like we have to warn the neighboring solar systems in hopes that Zenakuu has not reached them yet. Perhaps we can station small armies on each planet to defend. What say you?" Rayvaar's idea was well thought out but would require leaving Kalryn.

"I must protest! After we send small armies to all these planets, who will defend our world?"

"I see what you mean, but do you have a better idea, Nabire?"

"My decision is thus: we send a single emissary, perhaps a kinesis trainer, to train these planets to defend themselves. That way, we can keep our army here, and there is chance for salvation for other planets."

"Brilliant idea, Nabire. While here, we can begin to organize a strike on Zenakuu and start the beginning of the end of this already heinous war."

"The people of Kalryn can and will rally. From this depth, we are destined to rise," swore Iyendo.

The Savants found themselves in agreement and set off to let the rest of the world know. They organized a summit where the Savants' decision would be broadcast.

Rayvaar went to find his rebellious daughter and punish her severely for once again not listening to him. As he walked, he mumbled to himself, "I will not tolerate that girl disobeying my orders any longer. She is lucky to be alive, no thanks to that infernal pilot Jeramine." But as he entered her chambers, he found her crying over the death of her love as she gazed upon Jeramine's holographic image, which her locket projected. The seemingly stern father didn't have the heart to reprimand his bereaved daughter and left her to mourn in peace.

Chapter 3

Heart Full of Pride, and a Head Full of Anger

ALEX CAME OUT OF the flashback overwhelmed. He fell to his knees and wrapped his arms around his body. He had witnessed firsthand the carnage Zenakuu bestowed to people of Kalryn. Because of his clear moral definition of what was wrong or right, anger and rage flooded his heart. The hair on his head stood up as electrokinetic power swelled inside of him.

"Calm yourself, Alexander," Shyra said. "There will be a time to avenge lost lives. This is not it."

"I'm sorry, Shyra. I've just never seen anything like that before. What was that?"

"That was a Kalrynian memory bank. We Kalrynians are able to share our memories and store them in a records container that is guarded and preserved by the Savants. What you just witnessed were the collective thoughts and memories of my people during the invasion attempt," Shyra explained.

"I see. I'm sorry about what happened to Jeramine." Alex said.

"I apologize, Alexander, you were not meant to see that memory," Shyra held her shirt tight where her locket rested underneath; "Jeramine was my entire world, and the reason I still fight. He had the uncanny ability to metaphorically see right through me. All the farces I used on other people never worked on him. He would keep me in check but let me get away with so much at the same time. He figured me out as if he had me down to a science." Shyra gave a reminiscent smile. "I remember how he thought he knew it all, but even when he was wrong, I would smile and let him ramble on just so I could hear his voice. He could make my sides hurt from laughing and my throat hoarse from yelling all in a few minutes. Looking back now, I know he made me a better person. There was really no one else like him. I loved him, and he is gone now thanks to the Zenakuu." Shyra turned her head away so Alex couldn't see and made a motion that looked like she was wiping her eyes.

"I'm sorry, Shyra."

"It is fine. Do not give it second thought, Alexander."

"This power of mine—how did I get it?" Alex asked, changing the subject.

"Alexander, there are a handful of humans like you on this planet. I have sensed a few when I landed, and after our training, you will be able to sense them too. After we track down the others, I will explain the origins of your powers to all of you."

Alex complied with her and listened closely to all she had to say. Shyra told Alex everything about Zenakuu and their Karyokinesis, the apparent ability to manipulate your body on a cellular level. Alex soaked in all the information he could from Shyra like an impetuous sponge, dedicated and willful. In the beginning his performance was pathetic at best; he was not accustomed to the high altitude of the mountain. The elevation and lack of oxygen caused him to run out of gas in mere minutes. He kept training though; determined to be the best and hopeful that he'd make his new teacher proud.

Weeks went by, and Alex's training continued as he learned how to manipulate electricity and use it in new and creative ways. At first, the sensation felt strange to him; the electricity was surprisingly hot. As if he were slow cooking his hands, the pungent smell of singeing skin was thick in the air, and filled his nostrils —yet he endured on until his hands callused over, and his body became used to the sensation. Alex excelled before Shyra's eyes, justifying her anticipation in traveling and training earthlings. Shyra's studies were right; the power that Alex was showing actually surpassed her expectations. Excited with her findings, Shyra walked to the control room of her ship, not knowing Alex was right behind her. He eavesdropped as she opened a communication line to her father on Kalryn.

"Greetings, Father, how is everything on Kalryn?" asked Shyra.

"We have been very busy sending guides to the *important* planets in the universe," replied Rayvaar.

"Stop it, Father. I want to show you my findings on Earth," said Shyra.

"Whatever findings, as remarkable as you think they are, I assure you are insufficient to hold my attention. We have a war to win, and thanks to that damned invasion, we're down and missing one Chrentex suit."

"But, Father—"

Rayvaar then yelled, "You went to that waste of a planet against my will on a hunch that they had some kind of hidden power, and because of their primitive nature, you did not even know if those apes were capable of intelligent speech! Do not prattle on to me about your so-called findings." He sighed in frustration before continuing. "There is a forged bond between us, daughter, but do not waste my time with such frivolous matters. Just come home safely when your mission is complete."

The computer screen read "Communication End."

Shyra had faith the human race could level the playing field and give the Zenakuu a taste of their own medicine, but she was obviously upset after the talk with her father, and Alex noticed.

"What happened, Shyra?" Alex questioned.

"It is nothing, Alexander. Let us start the next lesson—flight."

Alex replied, "Did you say … flight?"

"Now, do not be afraid, Alexander. Almost all electrokinetics can fly."

"Fly, huh?" Alex grinned. "I've always wanted to fly."

"Now, Alexander, it is sort of tricky when it comes to flying. There are two ways to fly. One way is to use your powers to propel yourself through the air like a rocket. The other way is more passive. You have to concentrate very deep at first. Calm yourself and quiet your mind. Then, in your case, it is a matter of picking yourself off the ground through electromagnetism. Imagine yourself floating and then soaring through the air."

Alex didn't quite get flying down. After falling flat on his face all day and night, he finally got his fill of eating dirt. The thought of not being good enough to fly struck Alex hard, and he retreated to his quarters for the evening to be alone.

The next day Alex tried flying again but was stopped by Shyra when she decided to expand on the group from two to hopefully more. Shyra told Alex about how there should be a few more espers like him. While Alex was training, Shyra was searching the country for others and has found at least four more espers with high kinetic readings.

"Alexander, your shortcomings are going to have to wait. I require your assistance to help recruit the rest of the team. I have marked this map and will teleport you to the cities that they are in. One by one, recruit them and bring them back."

"What if they don't want to join?" Alex asked.

"Then you will just have to be persuasive, Alexander."

"I'll try, but do me a favor, Shyra. Cut everyone else some slack. If you wanna take your frustration out on me, fine, but you'll never get anyone to follow you if you keep acting like this."

She gave him a puzzled look. "I see. I will try to be nicer, Alexander."

Nervous yet excited to meet others like him, Alex set off. He knew they would be mankind's only real defense against the invasion sure to come.

His first stop was New York, and after he geared up, Shyra teleported Alex behind a local pizza parlor in Manhattan. The jump hit him at millions of miles per hour, and in an instant, he was plastered in place like an astronaut strapped in during takeoff. The heat made it feel as if his eyes were going to melt from their sockets, and he couldn't walk straight for a few minutes after his arrival. With legs made of JELL-O, Alex fumbled across the busy street. He had never been up north before, so he didn't know what to expect. It was almost sunset, but the streets were still very crowded. While wading through the hordes of natives, Alex basked in the smell of vendor almonds being roasted until he felt an unusual pressure on his frontal lobe that began to pulsate. Being more sensitive after receiving some quick training from Shyra, Alex knew it was a power similar to his emanating from the group of people in front of him.

Without warning, an earthquake struck New York. As the tectonic plates shifted, streets cracked, sending sewage covers shooting through the air like a soda cap bursting off its bottle after being shaken. Alex saw some of the unsuspecting civilians abandon their cars and run for their lives, while others crawled underneath trucks for shelter from the falling debris. He was scared but wanted to save everyone somehow. The thing that stood out like a sore thumb was a teen that was standing in place straining his arms out as if to control the earthquake with his will alone. Sure enough, the cracks closed, and the quake subsided, but Alex's eyes were fixated on the boy who did not even try to run. After the earthquake stopped the teen attempted to vanish in the crowd of spectators, but Alex was on pursuit. He dodged and weaved between people, trying to always keep one eye on the person running away.

His chase led him to a back alleyway, but he lost sight of his target and faced a literal dead end. Alex turned around and was sucker punched square on the jaw. The hit knocked him back flat on his ass. Somewhat disoriented, he stumbled to pick himself off the ground, and dusted off his pants.

Alex thought he had just been struck with brass knuckles, but much to his dismay, his attacker was unarmed. The young man standing before Alex was African American and seemed to be six feet tall with a muscular build, dark brown eyes, and perfectly symmetrical, short, wavy hair. The few hairs on his chin made him look older than he really was, but the expression on his face was filled with murderous intent. Alex had always heard that people from New York were dangerous, but he never thought he'd be mugged in just a few short hours. The assailant wore a plain black hoodie and baggy blue jeans; on his feet, he sported work boots. He demanded to know why Alex was following him. The tension between the two was thick enough to cut with a knife. Alex didn't know why he felt so uneasy with this kid, but he really didn't want him on the team. When he looked into the mysterious teen's eyes, Alex couldn't help but think about the bullies who terrorized him and his friends throughout high school. He could already tell the conversation was not going to go as planned.

"Who the hell are you?" the boy once again demanded to know.

"My name is Alex, and I'm not here to pick a fight with you. I just came to talk," Alex replied.

"Are you the one who caused my power to go out of control?" he asked.

"What are you talking about?" Alex curiously questioned.

"Out of nowhere I got one of those headaches I get from time to time, but it felt different than before—more refined, more concentrated. Next thing I know, my powers reacted to the strain, and I lost control," the teen explained.

"Wait. Are you saying you did this? You caused the quake?" Alex asked. "Listen, we have to talk."

"You and I have nothing to talk about. Just what kind of freak are you anyway?" questioned the teen.

Alex snapped back, "You're one to talk, buddy. You think I didn't notice you during that earthquake? What did you do to that crack anyway?"

"Not a damn thing," he said in a condescending voice.

"Don't bullshit me. I honestly don't have the time for it. There's something important I have to talk to you about," Alex explained.

"What's your name?" Alex asked him.

"Friends call me D."

"Okay, D. There's—"

The other teen cut him off immediately, "You can call me Dimitri, though."

Alex was more than annoyed at this point. "As you wish … *Dimitri*. Let me paint a rosy picture for you." Alex went on to tell Dimitri the entire story, and yet, Dimitri just didn't care.

He explained that he didn't turn down going to a technical institute for nothing; he had a family to look after and a sister who had been gunned down in a drive-by shooting to avenge. He wouldn't leave them—not after what had happened to her. He was determined to provide a better life for them.

"Look, I know how it feels. You think you're the only one who is being taken away from his family because he has to save the world?" Alex shouted back. "I get it. It's a lot to take in, but this is our calling—this is what we're meant to do." Alex calmed down and said with sincerity.

Dimitri's demeanor changed, and with a serious tone he asked, "Do you have any brothers or sisters?"

Alex responded with an inquisitive, "No."

"Then you have no idea what it feels like to have someone ripped away from you, someone who you've known your entire life!" he snapped back.

"Yes, I do actually. I didn't raise myself. I had to leave my grandfather—the only family I have—to fend for himself while I'm gone," Alex said defensively.

"You left your grandfather all alone? I guess I just love my family a little more than you love yours then," Dimitri said snidely.

Alex's hands began to glow in anger over the comment thrown at his face. He would have love nothing more than to fry this guy to ashes, but he couldn't forget the greater good.

"I didn't leave my grandfather. Ever since my birth he knew I was different. He more or less accepted that I had to go."

"Not for nothin' man, but I really don't care. I've had a hard enough life—a deadbeat dad, a sister killed in a drive-by, and now a family to look after. I've got enough on my plate without having to worry about killing aliens. Your sob story doesn't interest me."

With an unwavering voice, Dimitri told Alex that he had made a promise to protect his family at all costs, even if it meant his own life. Under no circumstance would he break that promise, especially not to some "superhero" wannabe who wanted to fulfill his fantasy of running around in tights. It took everything Alex had not to hook Dimitri in the face; he was determined to complete the mission Shyra had given him.

Dimitri verbally came at him again. "You wanna stand there and tell me about this alien race that *might* attack us? Get out of my face before you get hurt."

"You think I asked for this? You think I asked for this power? It's a gift—one that I can see has clearly been wasted on you," Alex shouted back. Alex wasn't sure if the static in the air was coming from him or this tense situation he found himself in.

With an almost thunderous roar, Dimitri said, "It is what it is okay? I'm not leaving my family, so kick rocks!"

To which Alex shouted, "Then your family is going to die with everyone else. Is that what you want?" Alex wasn't thinking rationally anymore and let his emotions get the best of him.

Dimitri's hands began to glow with a greenish hue, and stones and rocks started to float in midair. A superpower fight was the last thing Alex was looking for.

"Dimitri, right? I didn't come all this way to fight you, you've just met me, and I'm asking you to travel around the world to prepare for an alien invasion. You have no reason to believe me, but I swear to you that I'm speaking the truth right now, and I know deep down you know it too."

The icy stare that Alex got back from Dimitri was intense, and it seemed like the only way to make him believe his story was to show him.

"I was really hoping it didn't have to come to this, but if this is the only way, fine." With that, Alex closed his eyes and began to concentrate. Shyra was teaching him how to control his powers and not have them be just a reaction to his emotions. He visualized the spark within him growing bigger and brighter. Just with that, Dimitri saw a crackle of electrical power surge through Alex's hands. They began to glow with a brilliant light that illuminated the entire alleyway.

"Looks like you're legit. Dammit, I was really hoping you were fugazy," Dimitri said.

Alex spoke up. "I've learned a lot more, and so will you, but you have to come with me, Dimitri. Not for my sake, but for your family. Gain the power to protect them and the world."

Dimitri thought about all that was at stake and reluctantly agreed. "Fine, but don't get it twisted. I'm not doing this for you; I'm doing it for them," he said and promised he would become stronger to protect his family.

They agreed to meet back four hours later after Dimitri had a chance to say good-bye to his family. He had to go home and somehow explain to his mother and sister why he would be leaving them. During the entire train ride back to Brooklyn, it felt like he had the world on his shoulders.

They agreed to meet back four hours later after Dimitri had a chance to say good-bye to his family. He had to go home and somehow explain to his mother and sister why he would be leaving them. During the entire train ride back to Brooklyn, a whirlwind of emotions swept him away. Anger, denial, frustration, and regret plagued his thoughts without any sign of relinquishing their grip. Even the usual subway car performers stayed clear of him, scared of the intense look painted on his face. The flashing tunnel lights threw him in trance, hypnotized into a zombie-like state of consciousness. It was only the conductor's announcement that Flatbush would be the next stop that finally snapped him out of it. Things were finally starting to look up for him; finally finished with high school, a decent paying job, a loving girlfriend, and now this… No matter how hard he fought, life could never just go his way.

Dimitri dragged his feet up the subway steps, back to surface level, once again forced to come to terms with his new reality. *I can't believe mom was right about aliens existing… How am I going to explain to them that I need to leave? Maybe I can just go, and they'll think I died in the earthquake earlier,* he thought, although he knew they would never fall for that. Besides, he didn't want to put them through that kind of pain, but a lie surely had to be better than the truth. After getting off the subway, Dimitri made his way to his apartment and prepared for what would undoubtedly be the hardest talk of his life. He and his family had been through so much between their father leaving and his older sister dying. It felt like they couldn't catch a break, but he knew he had to do this. He knew that Alex kid was telling the truth. It couldn't be random that he had these powers.

Dimitri turned the key and slowly opened the door to his small apartment, but was immediately stopped in his tracks. Once again someone had locked the door chain, despite knowing he'd be coming home late. He squeezed his lips through the door and shouted.

"Ash! Open the door!"

"Whooo is it?" She mockingly asked then laughed.

"I swear to God, Ashley…" Dimitri said, growling through his teeth. His sister Ashley casually pranced toward the door, and undid the lock, smiling at her big brother with her usual cornball demeanor. In that moment, life was normal again and made sense. He tried to savor the peace and familiarity for as long as possible. Ashley darted back out of sight as soon as she granted him entrance, eager to get back to whatever she was doing. He walked past the kitchen where his mom was cooking and the living room where their couches still had their original plastic covers. Dimitri found his sister Ashley sitting on one of them watching their mom's favorite paranormal activity show on their thirty-two-inch TV, which was located directly underneath the Jesus painting.

She was always a "true believer" that aliens existed ever since she claimed she saw a UFO twenty years ago, but Dimitri just disregarded her ramblings as superstitious contradictions. How could she believe in aliens and Jesus at the same time? He wanted to know, but his mom's answer to every argument was that God created all life—including aliens. It infuriated him to no end, but learned to ignore it throughout the years. He decided to join Ashley and asked her how her day was. Then he helped set the dinner table and took out the trash for his overworked mother, at least he could do one last thing for her before in his mind he abandoned them.

Twenty minutes later he heard the doorbell ring, and wondered who it could be before remembering. *Aw damn, I forgot Rose was coming over.* His girlfriend of the past year, with everything that happened he forgot she promised she would bring over dessert. They met when he was filling the position of medical data entry at a temp job. She was breath taking, way out of the average guy's league, but her innocent yet alluring smile dug its hooks into him deep. He mustered up the courage to talk to her, and with a few suave remarks they immediately hit it off. Dimitri felt like his day couldn't possibly get worse; there was no way in hell she would go for him leaving. Still, he opened the door, and gave his girlfriend a sincere kiss as she passed him a strawberry cheesecake.

The four of them sat down together for what would be their last meal as a whole family for a long time to come. With Dimitri gone, at least there would be one less mouth to feed. But there would also be no protection from the neighborhood gangs and drug dealers who roamed the streets. Dimitri knew in his heart he would be back to clean the streets, but he had to get stronger first, and to do that, he had to leave.

His mother placed a plate of brown rice with green peas and chicken drumsticks in front of him before finally sitting down herself at the dinner table. The smell of that lemon-peppered chicken was enough to make his mouth salivate, but he couldn't wipe the sullen expression from his face.

"How was your day, baby?" Dimitri's mom asked to break the awkward silences.

"You wouldn't believe me even if I told you," Dimitri responded.

"Why is that?" she inquired. "You weren't anywhere near that earthquake today were you?"

"Yeah, but not too close. I barely felt it," he lied.

"Good, I was scared to death about you today," she said. "At least I had your sister Ashley here with me. I couldn't bear to lose anyone else." She was being her usual melodramatic self.

"Mom, I'm okay," he responded. Another awkward silence ensued. Dimitri rolled the peas on his plate around with his fork.

"Babe, you promised you'd be more careful," Rose said with heartfelt eyes. She was always worried about him, and often subdued his reckless ways. As tough as Dimitri lead on to be, he always melted in front of her. He was but a mere peasant in front a queen. She was petite, but held a very athletic build from all the times he dragged her to the gym with him. Luscious black hair woven like silk, she always kept it tied back away from her face, but it was the little things that Dimitri loved like they way she would always tuck it back behind her ear when it would fall out of place. He was in love with her flawless olive skin, the way she laughed, and the way her sweet smell lingered even after she left a room.

"Honey, is everything all right? Did something happen?" His mother asked.

Dimitri looked into the eyes of his concerned mother, then Rose. He just wanted to be honest with them but didn't know where to begin. "Mom, there's something I have to tell you, and as crazy as it's going to sound, I'm just gonna come out and say it."

"Okay. What is it, Dimitri?" she replied.

He gave another long stare, and exhaled deeply. "I'm leaving, Mom." A moment of silence filled the air.

"What?!" Rose shouted in horrified confusion. His mom furrowed her eyebrows in anger.

"The hell you are, boy. What are you talking about?"

"You don't understand. This is something I have to do. I have this… ability that I need to harness to protect you guys," Dimitri tried to explain.

His mom snapped back, "You on drugs? You're not making any sense."

Dimitri took a deep breath. It was never the way he wanted reveal his power, but he found a focus point on the table to stare at and concentrated. Rose and his mother watched as nothing happened, and gave each other an arched eyebrow. Two minutes passed, but the only visible difference was the bulging, pulsating vein on his forehead.

"You constipated D?" Ashley asked.

"Shut up, just give me a second," he fired back. It took a moment or so, but he cleared his head and thought of his murdered older sister as motivation. Sure enough, the empty table chairs started to rumble, and then the walls pivoted back and forth. The dinner table felt like it was vibrating, and soon a ketchup bottle fell over. After a full minute it felt like the whole apartment building was shaking. Ashley immediately ducked underneath the table, but Cecilia, Dimitri's mother, and Rose just gawked at him in disbelief. He didn't intend to scare them but simply illustrate his point, which, from the look on their faces, came through loud and clear. With his eyes open again, he stared at his mother, whose mouth gaped wide open. Dimitri looked at her and prayed for acceptance. "Mom?"

"For how long, Dimitri? How long have you been like this?" She responded.

"I don't know exactly, I remember it starting when Gina was killed. It doesn't hurt or anything. I'm just different."

"Baby, I don't understand," Rose said and reached her arm out on the table toward Dimitri, "How could you not tell me about this?"

"I didn't tell anyone," he said, almost ashamed for keeping it a secret.

"I can't believe they got to you too… How could you at least not tell me?" His mother asked while his sister reemerged from the tablecloth.

"I don't know. I didn't wanna freak you guys out—wait, what? Who's they?"

"Never mind that, Dimitri, I am your mother. I will love you no matter what you are, but why you? Why not someone else?" she pleaded.

"Mom, I don't know, but I need you to listen now. This ability is not a coincidence. There is an alien race on their way here to invade, and I have the chance to make a difference. I have to go."

"No!" Cecilia and Rose shouted in almost perfect unison.

"I have to," he protested.

"I said no, Dimitri Williams. I'm not burying anymore children. I don't give a damn what's happening. The world could be burning for all I care, you are not going anywhere," his mother explained.

"My God, are you even listening to yourself?" Dimitri said.

"Boy, don't use the Lord's name in vain in my house." She ordered as she pointed her finger at his face.

This is impossible, he thought to himself. There were no words in the English language he could articulate that would relinquish a mother's love for her child. Dimitri was foolish to believe the three women who loved him the most in life would let him run off to fight aliens.

Rose's facial expression suggested that she somehow felt betrayed by this new discovery. It's not like he lied to her however, he just omitted certain truths.

"I'm leaving mom, no matter what you say, I have to do this," Dimitri bravely said.

He could see the tears begin to well up in his mother's eyes; his sister just sat there in disbelief from it all. Rose pulled back her hand, and stood up, she hid her face as she cried and ran out the front door.

"Dammit," Dimitri said, and got up to go after her.

"Dimitri, you're not going anywhere, sit your narrow ass back down!" His mother barked. Dimitri hadn't even fully made it to his feet before he froze in place.

"Mom… please, you have to trust me this time. I swear on everything I love, I'll be back," he pleaded.

"We can go see a doctor, there has to be a cure for this," his mom said.

"It's not a disease Mom, this is who I am." Dimitri argued back.

"Ever since your sister died, all I wanted to do was keep you two safe, and now this," she said.

"Mom, you have kept us safe, but now it's my turn to keep you safe. Please believe in me," he begged.

"No Dimitri, I'm scared," she revealed to him.

"I'm scared too, but I'll be back. I promise I will be. I'll get stronger, and then there will be nothing to be scared of anymore."

"No, no, just no! This is too sudden," Cecilia affirmed.

"I'm sorry mom, I'm leaving one way or another."

"What about school? What about your job? What about us? Isn't anything I can say to change your mind?" she asked.

"Not this time, my mind is made up. Please understand, I'm not going anywhere just to die, I'll come back."

"Mom no! You can't let him leave." Ashley screamed right before she got up and ran to her room.

Dimitri's mom looked at her son—all grown up—wrapped her arms around him tight and demanded that he call her as soon as he got to wherever it was he was going and every chance he could, which was the only way she'd agree to any of it. Dimitri nodded in compliance before getting up from the table to get a few of his clothes ready. Once finished, he went to Ashley's room where he found her with her head buried in her pillow crying.

"Ash, listen. I need you to look after Mom while I'm gone. You gotta be a big girl for me and keep her out of trouble."

Holding back her tears, she asked him if he was ever coming back.

"There is nothing in this universe that could keep me away from you. No matter what, I will be back."

Ashley nodded her head, and Dimitri went toward the door where his mother was waiting for him with a bag. "I've packed a couple lunches for you," she said.

"Mom—"

"Dimitri, I don't wanna hear it."

He knew it was futile to dispute this with her, so he graciously took the food. "I love you, Mom," he said.

"I love you too, baby. Come back to me safely."

He nodded and walked past her. With his heart broken and his mother devastated, it took every ounce of strength not to look back at the life he was leaving behind. At the bottom of the stoop to his building he found Rose crying her eyes out. Even when miserable she was breathtaking.

She pulled herself together long enough to ask,

"Why D? Is it something I did?"

"Babygirl, you didn't do anything wrong. I love you; I'm not leaving because I wanna be without you. I'm doing this because I want to protect you. I know it sounds like a line, but you have to trust me on this one. I'll be back, real talk," he told her. Dimitri would have given anything to see that pearly white smile and her dimples one last time, but he settled for a deep kiss instead. The way he felt when their lips touched could not be duplicated. It lifted his heart off the ground, and tempted him to stay.

"I don't believe you, don't expect me to be waiting when you come back," Rose attested. She couldn't be serious... Would she really throw away all they had? *There's no way* he thought. Dimitri was sure she was saying it out anger; they loved each other too much. He would miss the funny, little way she laughed, or how the vastness of her dark brown eyes could stare right through to his soul. He wiped the tears from her cheek, and wrapped his arms around her tightly. Dimitri kissed her on the forehead, and told her goodbye.

Dimitri walked back to the subway with a heavy heart and once again boarded the Q train, except this time he saw no light at the end of his tunnel. He met up with Alex at their designated location, finally accepting his fate whatever it may be, even if it meant his untimely death.

Chapter 4

When the Dust Settles Who Will Be Left Standing

"How did it go?" Alex questioned when Dimitri arrived.

"Don't worry about it," Dimitri said. "Let's just go."

Alex then telepathically called Shyra for a teleport pickup to travel back home. In the next second, they were engulfed in a flash of light and dematerialized. Dimitri came out of the teleport gasping for air and not knowing up from down.

Alex helped him up and began coaching him. "Stand straight up to open your lungs. I learned that in track."

Dimitri looked around and didn't notice anything unusual. Shyra released the cloaking device, and all of a sudden this huge spaceship appeared out of thin air. Dimitri looked in amazement and was turned into a complete believer.

Shyra stepped out of the craft and welcomed the new esper, "Welcome, Dimitri Williams. Alex and I are so glad you have decided to train with us to defend Earth from Zenakuu."

Dimitri was in shock from the sight of an alien and said nothing at first. He was finally able to spit out, "How do you know my name?"

Shyra answered, "I can read your mind using telepathy, and from what transpired today, I see you are a geokinetic. That is an incredibly strong power to have. I will help you channel it."

Dimitri turned to Alex. "There's no going back, is there?" he asked.

"I'm afraid not," Alex replied.

Without sparing a moment, Shyra continued training the two boys. During the next week, Shyra had Alex and Dimitri travel to other parts of the country in search of more espers. Alex was sent to Orlando, Florida, while Dimitri was sent to Perth Amboy, New Jersey.

When Dimitri was sent to New Jersey the initial teleportation left him queasy and shaken. It seemed Shyra failed to mention how having your atoms rearranged may upset your stomach. He threw up behind a dumpster, composed himself, and commenced his mission. He trailed a young man using his new sensory perception powers to find the kinetic energy within people. Living in such a big city, he learned from an early age to block out static noise and focus on a single point, so finding his target came easily to him.

Dimitri followed the kid from his home and infiltrated the boy's school to get a better understanding of what he was dealing with. He noticed that the boy was antisocial and kept to himself; he didn't seem to have many friends or the desire to make any, as he kept his head buried in comic books during the lunch period where he ate alone. When the school day ended, Dimitri followed him to what appeared to be the local comic book shop where he saw the youth sit for a while and read up on the latest issues. D didn't like his look at all. The kid was five foot nine and kind of stocky. It was obvious he didn't work out much; he sported a military buzz cut hair style and wore hipster glasses. Lastly, he rocked a graphic T-shirt with fitted jeans. Honestly, he had somewhat of a goofy look to him.

"God, I wish this kid would get a life already." Dimitri's patience wore thin while he waited for the teen to leave the shop and go somewhere more secluded so they could talk. After a long wait and much boredom, the boy finally headed home. There were many kids running around in front of the apartment building; looked like they were his siblings or perhaps his cousins. The lawn was small, and the grass was brown. The yard was boxed in by a chain-link fence with toys scattered about arbitrarily. Dimitri watched him as he went in the building. Not wanting to lose sight of him, Dimitri climbed the fire escape and looked through the windows until he found his target again. He was in a small bedroom, which was more like a closet with a window. The kid lit every candle in the room. He jumped into bed and started playing a portable gaming system. Dimitri knew that moment was as good as any and tapped on the glass pane to finally confront the kid. Startled at first, he fell out of bed and shouted through the window, demanding to know why D was outside his room.

"I need you to come with me," Dimitri said.

Not satisfied with his answer, the teen manipulated the fire from the candles and shot the flames toward Dimitri. The fireball crashed through the window, sending shattered glass in all directions, and then knocked the failed diplomat off the fire escape. Dimitri hit the ground hard. Disoriented, he was barely able to get his thoughts together.

"Damn. Fire powers? That's a good one to have," Dimitri muttered.

Springing out the window the kid screamed, "You government agents aren't taking Christian Mercado alive!" Dashing down toward Dimitri with fire in hand, the misinformed teen started throwing flame-engulfed fists at his supposed captor. Dimitri dodged every punch, but some were so close that the fire singed his skin. Christian, being a heavier kid, wasn't able to get a hand on Dimitri.

The battle started to heat up immensely, and the air around them became dense and humid. To Dimitri, the self-proclaimed Christian looked like he was out for blood, and with his powers, the blood would be boiling. Using his pyrokinesis, Christian sent balls of fire toward Dimitri. He didn't think Christian would be capable of launching orbs of fire, but they exploded behind him sending char and embers flying in every direction. The fight made it very clear that Chris had a firmer grasp of his ability than D had of his own. Christian stood his ground, and for a moment didn't move a muscle. The act confused Dimitri, but not enough to engage. Hissing steam started rising from Christian's body as his sweat evaporated. He flung his arms, and the same fires that originated from his shoulder blades fled down his arms and shot out of his hands like an erupting volcano. The fireball collided with Dimitri in the chest, lighting his hoodie ablaze.

He immediately threw it off, and Christian charged at him, tackling Dimitri to the ground. He was deceivingly strong and like a mixed martial artist, Christian straddled Dimitri and started the game of "ground and pound." Dimitri could hardly defend against the flurry of punches Christian rained down on him. Surprised that such a portly kid had such a fighting prowess, Dimitri decided to turn the tables and go on the attack. Kicking Christian off of him, Dimitri sent him flying into some nearby garbage cans. Fed up with being beat down, he decided to use his own powers giving Christian a taste of his own medicine. Dimitri's left eye began swelling shut from the damage taken in the fight; he could hardly see, but the rage inside him didn't let him give up.

Now smelling rank, Christian got up from the garbage cans angrier than ever only to find Dimitri with a vengeful look on his face and ready to fight. Christian was firing on all cylinders too, and began lunging toward Dimitri with his fists ablaze. Concentrating, Dimitri dodged the right hook from Christian and hit him with a hard knee in the midsection, knocking the wind out of him. Chris stumbled back but regained his posture.

"Not hard enough?" Dimitri mocked Christian. He gathered rocks to surround his fist, forming a boxing glove solid as rock. "Maybe this will knock some sense in you."

Dimitri sprung forward swinging and throwing punches at Christian. Christian blocked most of the swings, but their sheer force brought him to his knees. The last thrusting punch that Dimitri threw connected, breaking through Chris's defense and sending him flying into a brick wall. Going in for the knockout punch with his rock-hard hands, Dimitri punched right next to the side of Christian's head to scare him. Dimitri's hand went through the brick wall with ease.

Christian wasn't one to quit that easily, though. He pushed Dimitri away and started building his strength; the fire in his eyes was almost visible. He conjured a flame in his hands and readied himself to release an onslaught of infernal attacks upon Dimitri. To block it, Dimitri used his geokinesis to lift a slab of ground from under them as a shield. A charred piece of concrete fell to the ground, and Christian came at Dimitri with a rising kick right to his chin.

Remembering he wasn't there for a fight to the death, Dimitri pleaded with the boy, "I don't want to hurt you, and I'm not from the damn government!"

Christian fell to the ground, winded. Now he was pissed; smoke began to emanate from his body. He started concentrating, and both hands ignited in a blaze.

A concerned look grew on Dimitri's face. *Shit, not again,* he thought to himself.

Christian threw out his hands, and as the air around his hands distorted, massive fireballs were sent hurdling toward Dimitri. He dodged them by bouncing off walls and diving out of the way. He was amazed no one saw the spectacle and grew tired from all the evading. After dodging and blocking fireballs for a while, Dimitri became fed up with the game of cat and mouse. Dimitri lifted two boulders out of the ground—one to block the incoming fire and the other to put Chris down. Out of thin air, a masked Shyra teleported in to break up the fight and entered Christian's mind to show him what exactly her plans were and what Earth would become if he didn't stop the pointless fight. Christian's eyelids fluttered, as he stopped breathing for the duration of the vision. Overwhelmed at the sight of cosmic war atrocities, worlds being invaded, women and children being killed for nothing, and the Zenakuu armada heading toward Earth,

Christian came out of the telepathic link gasping for air, his eyes rolled to the back of his skull, and he ultimately passed out. He woke up after a few minutes later disoriented and saw Dimitri and Shyra bent over him. Dimitri assisted him to his feet. After careful consideration, Christian decided to join. He saw it as finally getting the chance to be his own comic book superhero, but he didn't know how he was going to break the news to his parents.

Christian told Shyra and Dimitri that he must get his things prepared. Shyra welcomed him to the team and left the rest to Dimitri before returning back to the ship. As reality hit, an even grimmer look spread across Christian's face. "Aw crap, what am I gonna tell my folks? They won't even let me outside if the streetlights are on. There's no way they will let me leave to fight aliens."

"Don't worry," Dimitri said with a grin on his face. "I've got a plan."

Puzzled, Christian looked at him and said, "What are you going to do?"

"Tomorrow we're gonna give your parents the performance of a lifetime. Be at your window this time tomorrow."

Chapter 5

Maybe You'll Miss Me When I'm Gone

The next day at school felt like an eternity for Chris. All he could think about were the visions Shyra had showed him. He had always been considered weird, and people thought of him as a freak, but he knew better. He was about to save the world. In his mind, he was the ultimate galactic defender. He ignored the usual harassment he suffered at the hands of his peers with a smile on his face. Finally, the school bell rang, and Christian ran home too excited to remember he took the bus to school. It was his senior year, and he didn't have any friends, so there was no one to say good-bye to.

Hours later, he arrived at his front door winded. He came from a small, overprotective Spanish family. His mom stayed at home to look after his brothers and sisters, while his father usually got home around eight-thirty in the evening. He still wasn't sure how Dimitri was going to pull this off, but he had no choice but to trust him. He stepped through the door and greeted his mom, Gabriella, with a kiss on the cheek.

"Hey, Mom," he said.

"Hi, baby. How was school? Make any new friends today?" she asked.

"Something like that," he said to her. "I have a lot of homework to do, so I'm going to go upstairs for a while. Okay?"

"You mean you're not gonna head to the comic book store first? You feeling okay?"

"Yes, Mom, I feel fine," he responded back to her as he sprinted up the steps. Carlos and Mary, his little brother and sister, ran past him down the steps as they chased each other. Christian also had an older brother named Pietro, but they couldn't be more different from each other if they tried. Pietro had his choice of any girl at school and was one of the best defensive linemen on the varsity football team. It wasn't that Christian really cared about being the middle child, but he hated living in his older brother's shadow. It was a very simple formula to Christian—whatever Pietro did, Christian did the polar opposite.

It was a miracle Christian had his own room when he thought about it. He used to share a room with his older brother, but Pietro wanted more space so he moved into their oversized attic. That way, he could have some privacy and leave Christian to his own devices, which suited Christian just fine.

Tonight is the night my real life begins, Christian thought. He could hardly contain himself. He went straight to packing the essentials. He grabbed a few clothes, underwear, a toothbrush, and, of course, his first-edition comic books. There was no way he was going to leave those in the destructive hands of his younger siblings. After an hour, he was all set, but his father, Isaac, had not yet come home. Time never moved so slowly for Chris. What was the point of doing homework if he was leaving to go fight evil aliens? Slowly but steadily, time progressed, and his father arrived home. This was also about the time Dimitri said he would come back. Christian could feel the knots in his stomach getting tighter.

Christian ran downstairs to greet his father. His dad didn't speak perfect English, so he always spoke to him in Spanish.

"Bendiciones, Papá," he said.

"Dios te lo bendiga, Christian," his father replied. "¿Como estas?"

"Estoy bien, Papá. ¿Y tú?"

"Bien bien."

It was a very subtle greeting and exchange, asking for the day's blessing between father and son, and yet the love came across clear every time. Christian had a lot of respect for his father who had come to the United States with nothing but made something with his life and now supported his wife and four children. Christian headed back upstairs to wait for Dimitri. He passed the time by reading one of his favorite comic books, but not long after, he heard a tap on the window. Chris sprang up and unlatched the window only to receive a pebble to the forehead.

"Dammit. Ow! That freaking hurt!" he shouted.

All the way from the ground he heard a faint, "My bad."

"Whatever, just come up here." Dimitri climbed the fire escape and entered Christian's window pane dressed in a ridiculous outfit.

"And who are you supposed to be?" Christian asked.

"I'm the army recruiter here to take you away, so you can better serve your country." Dimitri must have found some costume store, because he was dressed up in Army fatigue and donned a fake mustache with a five o'clock shadow.

"You're joking, right? That's never going to work. They're already super pissed about the broken window from our fight. I'm grounded."

"Look, will you just leave it to me? I can be very charismatic," Dimitri said.

Christian felt his dream of fighting crime slowly dissipating into nothingness. "You just go along with everything I say. Okay?"

"I think you underestimate my family, but okay," Chris responded.

"Nice room, by the way," Dimitri shouted back as he leapt out of Christian's window.

"What's that supposed to mean?" he asked back but received no response. Christian's walls were lined with shelves that supported action figures, comic books, and an extensive Japanese manga collection, that he was actually quite proud of. Within the next minute, the doorbell downstairs rang. It only took a few moments before he was summoned by his mom.

"Christian, come down here, now."

He knew he was in for it when he reached the last step and saw the perturbed look on his mother's face. "Yes, Mom?"

"First Officer Williams here was just telling me how you signed up for special placement with the ROTC, which will give you a full academic scholarship when you enlist with the Army. Is that true?"

Christian began to sweat. He was never good at lying to his parents. "Heh heh, yep. What can I say, Mom? I want to be all I can be." The doubt about this working started coming at him like a flood. *Oh man, I am so dead!* He thought to himself. His mom translated what Dimitri came for to his father, and suddenly both parents were staring at him. He couldn't take the pressure anymore, and just as he was about to come clean about everything, his mom threw her arms around him.

"This is great, baby! I always knew you would mature sooner or later. The Army is a great place to grow up, and they'll help you with college. We're so proud of you."

It would have been nice if there was someone there to pick Chris's jaw up off the floor, but sadly, he had to snap back to reality himself.

"Um, thanks, Mom. Is Dad cool with this too?" Christian looked over at his father who gave him thumbs up.

"I'm gonna take that as a 'yes,'" his mom answered. "I wish you didn't have to leave so soon, but when opportunity knocks, you have to answer. Also, First Officer Williams has assured me that you would keep up with your schoolwork. Now, go upstairs and pack."

"Yes, ma'am." Christian kissed his mom on the cheek and ran upstairs where his stuff was ready to go. "That guy is pretty good," he thought out loud. Twenty minutes later, he walked back downstairs with his things. "I'm all set, Mom."

"Aw, my little boy is growing up," she sighed.

Christian's father pulled him aside and said. "Estoy orgulloso de ti, hijo."

Christian looked up at his father; it meant a lot to hear that he was proud of him. With a smile on his face, Christian responded, Gracias, Papá."

"Now you listen here, Officer Williams, you better take care of my baby. If anything happens to him, I'm coming after you first."

"You have my word, Mrs. Mercado. We'll take good care of Christian," Dimitri assured her. "Now we must be on our way. It's lights out at 2200 hours."

"I understand. Chris, come over here and say bye to your mama."

Christian walked over to hug his mom and give her loving kiss on the cheek. "Te amo, Mom."

"Te amo, también, mi hijo. Now go on."

Christian waved to the rest of his family, picked up his things, and went out the door with Dimitri.

Once they were far enough away, Christian finally asked, "How the heck did you pull that off?"

Dimitri grinned and chuckled. "Renting the costume was the easy part. It was all the phony badges and documentation that was the tricky part, but don't worry. I got friends in very high places."

Confused, Chris looked at him. "Um, okay."

"Shyra, I've got the target and await transport," Dimitri said into the open air. Christian looked left and right but saw no one.

"Who or what are you talking to?" Chris looked at his hand as it started to dematerialize. *Awesome,* he thought. And then he vanished.

Chapter 6

Cloudy with a Chance of Rain

Alex's next journey sent him to another place he had never been. This time it was Orlando, Florida. The humidity there was insane to him; he felt as if he were being roasted alive for a slow-cooked meal. He couldn't help but wonder why the state was so hot given that it was almost completely surrounded by the ocean. He wanted to know where that ocean breeze he heard so much about was. That aside, the place was beautiful. There was no denying the appeal of living there, sans the heat. The palm trees were gorgeous, and the air was so clean and fresh, it was definitely worthy of being the Sunshine State.

Alex scanned around and felt the esper not too far away. *Shyra had some pretty good aim today,* he thought. Still, it felt too far to walk, especially in that blistering heat. As Alex walked the streets in search of new means of transportation, he discovered a pay phone with a phonebook on the other side of the road. He flipped the pages to a taxi cab service with hopes to reach the new esper in some level of comfort. He was low on funds but prayed he'd have enough for the ride over.

The trip itself was short, but in the time Alex had, his mind started to wander. He couldn't help but think about all that had happened. For so long, he thought he was some kind of parentless freak, but now his life had meaning and purpose. He also wasn't alone like he once thought. There were others out there like him—people who would understand what he went through.

The cab ride was over, and the feeling that the esper in question was giving off had brought Alex to a local park where tons of people were outside enjoying the weather.

"He's close, but who?" Alex said. He tried his best to narrow in on the feeling, but he hadn't yet perfected his technique, so he couldn't single anyone out. Alex scoured the crowd for what felt like hours with no luck.

The park was majestic looking, with its richly soiled grass and crystal blue lake, but that wasn't what he was there for. The children playing with their parents did bring him down a little; he always wondered what that would feel like. Grandpa Henry tried his best but was just too old to be the active parent Alex wanted growing up. Those thoughts were distracting him from his goal, and he knew he needed to focus on the task at hand. He continued his search but wanted to take a rest, so he found a secluded lake to lie by and took in the scenery. A refreshing breeze finally cooled his baked skin, but he noticed he wasn't truly alone. There was a girl sitting by the side of the lake.

She's really cute, Alex stopped and thought to himself. The teenage girl who sat there had long, scarlet hair that she'd tucked behind her ear. The color was deep enough to make any rose contempt with jealousy. Her high cheekbones sat atop her dimples, and she had just enough freckles to make you want to connect the dots scattered across her ivory skin, which in its own respect surprised Alex. He thought all Floridians had tans.

She wore a blue-and-white horizontally striped shirt and beige capri pants topped off with black sandals—perfect beach attire, which made sense considering the weather. To Alex, she looked like a fallen angel, much more different looking than the girls he was used to. Alex had never really been a ladies' man; in fact, he was painfully clumsy at it, but he felt compelled to talk to her. She hadn't noticed him yet, so he approached with caution.

Alex knew he was on a mission, but it had been so long since he'd had a pleasant conversation with someone who would be considered "normal." He missed that human contact, and considering the life he was about to have, it might be his last chance. He mustered up the courage and continued to walk toward her. Then, he saw something that stopped him in his tracks.

"You gotta be freaking kidding me," he said under his breath.

The girl who made his heart skip a beat was manipulating water around her hand with ease. Making it look like child's play, she bent the water up and down, side to side with her mind.

It's her ... She's the one I've been looking for this whole time, Alex thought. "Okay, be cool. I gotta approach this the right way. Damn, I had this whole thing planned out in my head, and my mind's gone blank," Alex said quietly.

The girl still hadn't noticed Alex, so he slowly moved in closer. Alex was about ten feet away when she was finally alert to his presence. The water splashed down on her lap, drenching her thighs. Startled, she stumbled back. Her face had lost some color over the scare that someone had discovered her secret. She stared up at him, and as their eyes locked, it felt like time itself slowed down for a moment. Her hazel eyes left Alex stuttering as he looked for words to speak.

"Who are you?" she asked.

"I ... I ... I'm really sorry for scaring you. I didn't mean to. I just want to talk," Alex began. "My name is Alex, and I have something really important to discuss with you."

The girl furrowed her eyebrows and responded, "I've heard that before. Sorry, but I'm not interested, so please walk away. I'd like to be alone." She turned her whole body the other way so as not to face him anymore. Rejection didn't come easy, and Alex's hopes were shattered against the sharp, jagged rocks of reality.

Crap, I blew it. Why am I so bad at this? He thought to himself.

"It's not like that," he told her.

"Then what's it like?" she asked.

It was clear that he was very rusty at talking to girls, as the charm he thought he had seemed to be fading fast. It was difficult to convince Dimitri, but this was on a whole new level of epic failure. He thought how he'd rather be fighting him than awkwardly bumbling his recruitment with this girl. His palms grew increasingly sweaty.

"Look, whatever you're selling, I'm not buying, and I don't appreciate being spied on," she said.

Now on the defense, he declared, "I wasn't spying … I just saw you from a distance," Alex explained, "and trust me when I say we need to talk."

"About what? Whatever you *think* you saw, you can trust me when I say *you didn't*. Now if you don't mind, talking to you is really giving me a headache. Maybe it's your accent, where are you from?" she questioned.

"Houston," he revealed.

"Ah makes sense… well southern boy, you're a long way from home, but if you start now maybe you can make it back by 'supper,'" she sarcastically said before giggling.

But Alex wasn't giving up. "Lemme start over. My name is Alex Carter, and believe it or not, I've traveled a long way to meet you."

"Does that line work with all the girls? I don't even know you, and I find it really creepy that you claim you came so far to meet me."

"It's not a line. I don't really know how to explain it, but something big is coming—something really bad—and you are a crucial part of stopping it."

She stared at him a moment before speaking again. "What are you talking about?"

"There's something I have to show you, but don't freak out. Okay?" Alex said.

"Whoa! What kind of girl do you take me for? I'll scream right here," she retorted back. Alex looked confused, *What is she talking about?* he thought before it finally registered in his mind. "Oh … God no! That's not what I meant at all!" he said. As he thought about how this was turning out, he decided there had to be a way to turn things around. Alex held out his hands, and they immediately begin to glow with a yellowish, electric hue.

"See," he stressed. "You're not the only one."

She almost passed out as a sense of relief and fear rushed over her. "You're a freak like me?" she attested.

Alex arched an eyebrow. "I don't know if I'd call myself a freak, but I do have abilities," he said. "Can I see yours?"

She looked at him intently. She still didn't know if she could trust him, but her instincts were telling her to see where this all went.

"You did show me yours, so I guess I can show you mine." The girl was extremely nervous; she'd never opened up and completely divulged her powers to anyone before. She calmed herself and turned toward the lake. She took a look around to make sure no one else was watching before taking one final glance at Alex. "Here goes nothing," she said.

The girl closed her eyes and raised both her hands. It took a minute or so, but using her hydrokinesis, she formed a vortex in the water. It was swirling at a steady rate and growing in strength. She looked back at Alex to make sure he was still there.

Alex's jaw had dropped open completely. It was always breathtaking to see someone's ability for the first time. The fact that he was not the only one with powers still freaked him out from time to time, though. The girl lifted the water into a stream from the lake and manipulated it so it took flight.

The water bent to her will, and Alex was amazed at her control. She had never received praise for her ability before and reveled in the moment, putting on a bit of a show for him. The water became an assortment of different shapes and sizes.

"Incredible," Alex declared. "I've never seen anything like it before. It's truly beautiful."

The girl blushed. "Um, thanks. You're actually the first person I've really shown my power to."

"Something so beautiful should be shared with the world," Alex said.

She couldn't help but smile. No one ever truly accepted her and her ability before.

Who is this boy, and why am I suddenly so flustered? I've been hit on before, but this is different—he's different. He's like me … But I have to keep my cool. Keep it together, Cassie. He might just be a smooth talker, but he's also really cute. Dammit all, she thought to herself.

Cassie was torn inside. For her entire life, she'd learned to only rely on herself, but now she was finding herself being swayed by his words. She knew the first thing she had to do was wipe that ridiculous, cheesy smile off her face.

Alex spoke, interrupting her thoughts and getting back to business. "Like I said before, there is something very important I have to talk to you about. Trust me, it's not gonna be easy to believe, but I promise you every word will be the truth."

Alex started from the top—his first encounter with Shyra, the Zenakuu, the invasion plans. He told her all he knew, but what shocked him wasn't the fact that he was able to be so honest with this person he'd just met; it was that she took it so well. No dropped jaws, no bloody screams, not one demeaning laugh. Her eyes and ears just processed his every word. He knew it was a lot to take in, but so far, she'd handled the news of her planet being potentially annihilated by an evil alien race bent on total planetary supremacy like a champion.

"So … that's about the gist of it." When he was all done, Alex waited for a reaction. He knew it was coming—that snickering, snide laughter.

It never came, though. In fact, the only thing she asked was, "How much time do we have?"

"You believe me?" he asked as he staggered back.

"Basically. I can tell you're not lying. Also, I never thought my powers were an accident. I never imagined it would be for this, but if these are the cards we're dealt, I say we play them."

Alex smirked. "So what's your name?" he inquired.

"My name is Cassandra Daye, but everyone calls me Cassie."

"I can't tell you how nice it is to meet you, Cassie," he said with a smile. "I'll meet you back here tonight, and we will head out."

With a raised eyebrow, she questioned him. "Meet me back here for what?"

"Why do you think? You still need to pack your things and say good-bye to your family," he conveyed to her.

Only one word came to Cassie's mind with the deliverance of the news: "Shit."

Damn, how could I be so careless as to forget that? This guy really messes me up. I need to be careful about that, Cassie thought to herself. *He's really cute, though … Cassie, no! Stay focused. He's right. What am I gonna tell Katelyn?*

"Okay, I'll meet you back here tonight at eight o'clock," Cassie finally said aloud.

The walk home for Cassie was a long one—so much coursed through her mind. She always had to look out for herself and her little sister, because her parents were completely oblivious to them. They just focused on fighting with each other about money problems until they divorced, and then their mom obtained full custody. Cassandra couldn't stand to be home and see another one of her mom's alcoholic fits, but she endured for her sister's sake.

Of course, not all products of a broken family turn out horrible, and Cassandra was a perfect example of that. It was because she came from a broken family that she had grown up spending most of her time reading books, escaping her harsh reality and sharpening her mind in the process. She had few friends in high school, but the ones she did have could never be replaced.

Her powers didn't manifest until she was about seven. She had been at the local swimming pool with her younger sister. What all seemed like innocent fun turned almost fatal when her powers erupted and nearly drowned her younger sister. Ever since then, she has been somewhat afraid of her potentially destructive powers.

Always the A-plus student, Cassie excelled very quickly, but she had a sense of longing for something bigger that she never quite understood. The only thing she could do to keep her mind distracted from the sheer bizarreness that was her life was submerse herself in her precious puzzles, which gave her extraordinary problem-solving skills and a more technical mind than anyone she knew.

Life as Cassie knew it was about to be flipped upside down. She mulled over in her head how she was going to break the news to her sister. She could care less how her mom would react—if she reacted at all—but her sister would surely be devastated.

"God, I hope I'm doing the right thing here," Cassie said aloud as she approached their driveway. She walked inside their house, but there was no one in sight. She treaded to the kitchen, passed the table with the mountain of overdue bills piled up, and saw a note left on the refrigerator from her mom.

"Gotta head out for a minute. Be back soon. I left some money on the counter. Order pizza for you and your sister."

Typical, Cassie thought. She definitely wouldn't be sad to leave her mother, but she wondered where her sister was. Cassie crept down the hall to Katelyn's door. She pressed her ear against it but heard nothing. Anxious to know if Katie was in there, Cassie cracked open the door just enough to peek inside. Katelyn was on her bed lying on her stomach with some headphones in her ears doing what looked like homework.

Cassie didn't disturb her at first; she wanted to remember that moment for as long as she could. It was gonna be a while until she could see her again it seemed, so she made the most of it. Once she had her fill, she finally interrupted.

"Katie," she said, but no acknowledgment followed. "Katie!" she shouted.

A frightened Katie looked up. "Geez, Cassie. What is wrong with you? You scared the bejesus out of me."

"Sorry, but I have to talk to you," she expressed.

Katelyn responded back in a wavering voice, "Okay … what's up?"

With a somber expression on her face, Cassandra announced that she would be leaving for a while. "It's tough to explain, but there is something I must take care of. I don't expect you to understand, but I have to do this."

"Is this about your ability to control water?" Katie asked.

For the second time that day, Cassie's face turned ghostly white.

"H-how did you know about that?" she asked.

Katelyn confessed that she'd known for a long time. "It's not my place to out you; I always figured you would tell me when you were ready."

Cassie was suddenly filled with a sense of relief that Katelyn knew the entire time her older sister was a freak of nature but always treated her with the same level of love. She smiled and nodded to confirm her sister's suspicions.

"If you're aware of my power, trust me when I say I'm doing this to protect us all. But I don't want to leave you alone with Mom."

Katelyn smiled back at her big sister and reassured her. "Don't worry about me. I'm tougher than I look. I learned from the best."

Try as she might, Cassie could no longer hold back the tears. She pulled in her little sister and embraced her tightly to hide the fact that she'd broken down with such raw emotion.

"Katie, this isn't good-bye. I'll be back. I promise," Cassie assured her sister.

"What's up with you today? I know you will. Bring me back something cool," Katie said with a big smile.

"You got it," Cassie responded. She left to pack her things and headed out a few hours later. With the boy who inspired her, Cassie was eager to start what would undoubtedly be the greatest thing she had ever been a part of, but there was something about his words that made her heart tremble. Her only daunting question would be—could she separate the two feelings?

Chapter 7

With the Pack Completed, an Alpha Must Rise

Not too far away, Alex waited for Cassie at the park.

"Shyra, I've picked up another esper," Alex communicated. "She'll be meeting up with me soon."

A voice beckoned back to him, "Good job, Alexander. I am ready whenever you are."

Twelve minutes later, Cassie joined up with Alex.

"How did it go?" he asked her.

"Well enough. So where do we go from here?" Cassie inquired.

Alex extended his arm toward her, but she looked baffled by the gesture. "Hold on tight and take a deep breath," he instructed.

"Are you getting weird on me again?" she asked.

Alex just smirked. "Shyra, we're ready," he said.

"Who are you talking to?" Cassie asked. She had her question answered immediately as she heard a voice speak inside her head.

"I am preparing the transport," the voice said.

Startled, Cassie asked, "Um, who was that?" With her last word uttered, she and Alex were gone—transported in a bright beam of light.

Cassie and Alex were brought back to the entrance of the ship, which was now cloaked to resemble a Shaolin Temple. Shyra was waiting for them. Cassie immediately hunched over and hurled her lunch.

"I apologize about that, Cassandra, but I promise you get used to it," Shyra said.

"Not really," Alex added, leaning in close.

Cassie slowly but surely raised her head and tucked her hair behind her ear. She was embarrassed. She had never vomited in front of anyone before, and it certainly wasn't the dignified persona she liked to exude. Hunched over and on her knees she murmured, "Never again … I'd rather walk."

The atmosphere was a bit tense after that, but Alex attempted to break it. "Teleportation is still statistically the safest way to travel," he joked. Cassie just glared at him. Alex quickly continued, "Cassie, I'd like to introduce you to Shyra, the person whom I mentioned before—the person who found me and helped me to find you."

"Good day to you, Cassandra Daye. We have much to talk about," Shyra revealed.

The young girl simply answered back, "Okay, I'm all ears."

"Um, Shyra, quick question," Alex interrupted. "Why does the ship look like a monastery now?"

"I have designed the ship to provide an adequate training ground for all of you, and this structure seemed most fitting. I downloaded the layouts from your *Interweb*."

"It's actually called the Interne—ya know what? Never mind. Looks cool."

After traveling all over the country recruiting espers for the alliance, four were assembled. They introduced themselves to each other, and Chris and Alex instantly clicked. After narrowing down the next esper to Los Angeles, California, Shyra described to her team the next target. "My ship's scanners have located the next addition to our alliance, she is an esper named Tori Hannon," she explained. "She is an aerokinetic and seems very powerful. Therefore she is to be considered very dangerous."

The team looked at each other and wondered what was in store for them.

"How dangerous can she be? She only controls air?" Chris asked.

"She can remove the air around you, extinguishing your flame," Shyra replied.

Chris looked down with an appreciation of his power's weaknesses.

"You are all going to California," Shyra ordered, but she looked confused as to why the team got so excited.

"I could use a vacation," said Alex.

"This is not a vacation. We are still on a mission," Shyra added.

"C'mon, Shyra. We have been working so hard—a little rest will do us good," Alex pleaded.

Shyra looked at her group; sometimes she forgot they were really just kids. "Very well, I suppose it could not hurt—but only after we recruit the next esper," she agreed.

Everyone prepared for transport and at twilight, the alliance found themselves in Los Angeles. The air was noticeably thick, and the whole town was lit up like a Christmas tree. People roamed the streets, enjoying the crisp night scene that Los Angeles had to offer. Many couples sat nearby water fountains that filled the atmosphere with love and passion.

The team focused on the mission at hand, so they could have a little bit of rest and relaxation afterward. They rushed to the last location they'd felt Tori's power. Tori was still around; she was sitting at a chic outdoor café and noticed the alliance before they noticed her. They clearly weren't California natives from the way they dressed, and the way they suspiciously looked around made them stand out like a sore thumb. When Tori realized they were there for her, she got up, left her money for the bill, and started walking away.

Alex, who was first to realize she was the target, signaled for the others to follow. Tori cut a corner and jumped up on the roof of a building to lose them. Tori began leaping with ease, almost as if she was floating from rooftop to rooftop.

"She's on the roof. After her!" Dimitri shouted.

At first, they climbed the building's fire escape and followed her. They came to the end of a building only to see Tori had stopped running. She was squinting one eye, while her hand held her head. Other than looking like she was in throbbing pain, she was gorgeous with a perfectly fit body gained from either extensive physical fitness or cosmetic surgery. The girl was draped from head to toe in designer clothes. It was painfully obvious she paid close attention to how she looked in the mirror. Her blonde hair looked like a golden waterfall, with each strand falling perfectly into place, as if she had personal assistants who meticulously brushed it for hours. Even her bangs were perfectly linear. Her eyes looked as if they'd been cut from the highest quality green emerald, and she had the kind of slender nose and drawn out eyelashes that movie stars would kill for.

"Why are you following me?" she asked. "Is this about the blown over lifeguard tower, because I had nothing to do with that."

"No, we just want to ta—wait. What lifeguard tower?" Alex asked her.

"Don't worry about that. I know why you're here," Tori continued. "I'm obviously on a reality show. You really thought you could trick me? This kind of stuff happens all the time around here. You play some prank on me, and then hidden cameras pop out."

"What are you talking about?" Dimitri replied.

"If you guys want a show, I'll give you a show," she shouted back. With that, Tori pushed through the crippling migraine, and the wind started picking up to incredible speeds. The trees down below swayed and stirred as she began to hover, creating a small tornado around her.

"I've got her, guys," Chris said as he channeled his fire, his sleeves combusted into flames reducing them to nothing but ash. He blasted a fireball at her, only to have it sway and flicker violently before being extinguished in the raging winds. Suddenly, there was a change in air pressure and it felt as though they were being lifted up. Tori focused her wind speed at the team and almost blasted Alex, Chris, and Cassie off the building. Dimitri was the only one who stood his ground.

"Listen to me," Dimitri yelled over the wind's noise. "We need your help."

"Why would I listen to you? I can do anything I want, and I have everything I need," she laughed.

"If you help us, you'll have the chance to save the world. You can't be any more famous than the savior of mankind—they'll put a statue up of you in your honor."

The wind began to die down, and Tori slowly walked up to Dimitri out of breath and worn out. "Okay, but if you don't make good on your promise, I will literally snatch the air right from your lungs. We clear?"

Dimitri didn't take kindly to idle threats, but he swallowed his pride for the mission's sake. "Yeah, we're clear," he replied.

"Good. You know, you're kinda cute." Tori blew a kiss at Dimitri, who was still trying to catch his own breath.

Everyone else was surprised that Tori was willing to help out. Dimitri explained to the rest of the team her motives, and her bizarre obsession to be a famous reality star. Alex didn't like her reason for joining, but they weren't in a position to be turning away help. He reported in with Shyra and requested to start their vacation. After getting her consent, the group got two motel rooms for the night—one for the boys, and the other for Cassie and the newest member, Tori. Throughout the night, Alex had to continuously pull Christian away from the adjoining wall between the two rooms. Chris was obsessed with placing his ear to it, desperately trying to hear what the two girls were doing in their room. As he listened, fantasies of pillow fights and kissing practices filled his hormone driven mind. Hours flew by, and the boys and girls awkwardly did their best to bond while watching their provided free cable. But even Christian, who was the last one up on the guys' side called it a night after secretly going back to the wall a few times, and not hearing a single peep coming from the girls.

The next day, the team kicked back on the torrid sand and clear waters of Venice Beach.

Alex, living in Houston, had rarely been to the beach. Surprised that the water was so luminous and the sand so warm, he feared he would never want to leave. Alex swam toward Cassie and asked, "So how do you like it out here? Any better than Florida?"

Cassie replied, "It's not so humid here. It's nice and breezy, but I couldn't handle the earthquakes."

"Sounds like the perfect place for me," Dimitri laughed as he floated toward them on his inner tube.

Anxious and wanting to start training to save the world, Tori whined about wanting to leave; the beaches were nothing new to her. She didn't appreciate how hard the other four teens had been working during the weeks prior.

"Hey, Alex, is the water getting warmer?" Chris asked with a menacing smile on his face.

"It's you isn't it? You're like a walking water heater." Alex said then splashed him.

"Oh my God, gross! That better be your power!" Cassie yelled.

The teens were finally having fun and enjoying each other's company, but it all ended prematurely.

Shyra contacted the group telepathically. "Everyone needs to get back now."

"What's going on, Shyra?" Alex questioned.

"We have a situation at home. I will brief you when you get here."

"One of you guys is a telepath?" Tori asked. "That is so impossibly cool."

The original four gave Tori a puzzling look but decided to let it go. The alliance quickly changed from their swimsuits to regular clothes.

"Finally," Tori said to herself, although it was loud enough for the others to hear. She looked very excited to finally get in the spotlight. However, she did not know of the Zenakuu or of any alien species.

They rushed so not to keep the impatient Shyra waiting.

"Alright, Shyra, we're ready," said Alex.

"Very well. Teleporting now."

The gang of five found themselves in the quiet, secluded parts of the Colorado mountainside, high above civilization near Shyra's spaceship—what they would come to know as their training grounds. Tori appeared to be a little queasy, but completely blown away at the tall evergreen trees that swayed in the wind and surrounded the compound. She had never seen the sky so blue, and the breeze that brushed against her face was gentile and cool. The peaceful climate that Colorado had to offer was ideal for anyone looking for some tranquility.

"Nice place you got here, but I don't see where you would install the tanning beds. So yeah—what's the situation with that? Tori asked, but only received puzzled looks in response.

Hesitant at first, Tori started exploring the area. She saw the area where they would train. There were already trees knocked down, burnt grass, and turned up ground. Tori wasn't quite sure what abilities the others had yet, but she was eager to find out.

"I think a proper introduction is required," Tori declared.

Alex did an about-face. "Seems fair enough. My name is Alexander Carter. Over there is Cassandra Daye, Christian Mercado, and Dimitri Williams."

"Okay, next question," Tori continued. "Why did we have to come here in such a rush?"

At that moment, Shyra stepped out of her tremendous spaceship, which took up a large amount of the mountain. Shyra didn't look like any person Tori had ever seen. "Oh my God. What the hell is that thing!?" she blurted out.

"That *thing* is named Shyra, and she is the alien preparing us for the war," Alex corrected her.

"This whole thing is about aliens?" Tori asked.

"Easy, Tori. She's on our side," Cassie said.

"Enough of introductions," Shyra interrupted. "We have to begin training to master your abilities. The Zenakuu will undoubtedly send a scouting party to canvas Earth. I need to get you five warriors ready for the fight."

"Whoa, whoa, whoa. Who are these *Zenakuu* or whatevers, and what scouting parties? I demand to be filled in before we start anything," Tori said.

"Just us five? I thought we would have an army of espers, Shyra," Alex said.

"Sadly, I am afraid not. You five are the only ones I could detect, and now that you are all here, I will explain how you received your abilities. After the invasion, the council of Kalryn wanted to start training neighboring worlds in the ways of kinetic abilities—a power that usually lies dormant but resides in every living being in the universe. However, some of the council opposed the idea of being forced into war. They had enjoyed peace for so long and had hopes of resolving these issues. But, as planets began to fall to Zenakuu, Kalryn set their plan into action. They sent some of their most powerful lygokinesis practitioners to scattered worlds across the galaxy, praying they would have enough time to teach them defense before the Zenakuu arrived.

"My father Rayvaar, one of the most revered Savants, saw Earth as a planet of simple-minded simians at first, but I knew of your world from my intergalactic studies. While a little rough around the edges, your physiology showed immeasurable potential for kinetic power, perhaps even greater than my species. Though my father did not want to listen to me, I finally convinced him to send a trainer to Earth. He was a low-level guide named Kadir who was supposed to more or less warn Earth of the impending doom, but failed in his mission. Kadir was meant to arrive on Earth without notice and locate the more heightened earthlings still young of age and train them in solitude until Zenakuu attacked. Unfortunately, in his brilliance, Kadir did not think to activate his cloaking device. According to his last transmission, he was shot down and crashed somewhere around these mountains. I scanned the area but found no sign of wreckage. Your government must have retrieved his ship."

"Okay, but that still doesn't explain how we got the powers," Dimitri said.

"Crash landing over the continental United States and mortally wounded, Kadir must have known he was not going to make it. It is only a theory of mine, but I believe he concentrated his kinetic power and exploded into pure energy. The radiation from the resulting aerial shockwave must have expanded outward and changed the DNA of a few kinetically sensitive humans. He sacrificed himself with the hope that it would reach enough people to give your world a fighting chance. He may not have been the brightest among us, but his courage will never be under question. After reports of his death, I volunteered to be the next guide for Earth. Of course, my father highly disagreed; he did not want his only daughter to risk her life for—in his words—a worthless planet like Earth, but he could not see what I did. No longer wanting to be coddled like a newborn baby, I snuck out and set toward Earth, despite my father's wishes. He did not know what I did until it was too late. I was halfway across galaxy."

It was a lot to digest for the teens, but Cassie spoke up. "Shyra, about how long ago did that happen?"

"If my calculations are correct, I would say roughly about twenty or so Earth years ago."

"But that doesn't make sense. I wasn't even born yet," Cassie said. "That must mean it happened to my parents, but I'm pretty sure they don't have any superpowers."

"No, they would not. You see, Cassandra, unlocking your brain's kinetic ability is a lot for the mind to handle. It is mostly likely that your parents' minds were too old to adapt to the change, so their powers never manifested. With their genetic coding changed, though, they could possibly pass the recessive gene on to their offspring whose minds would be young and fresh enough to be successfully kinetically altered."

"Oh … I guess that makes sense in a weird, sci-fi novel kind of way," Cassie replied

"Yes, well by the time I arrived on Earth unnoticed, the espers were pretty far along in their lives and somewhat aware of their unique powers. It is by no means as many as I was hoping for, but we have run out of time. We have to make up for eighteen years of unexercised kinetic power in presumably less than a year."

"Sounds like fun," Tori chimed in.

"Tori, come with me. You were the last one here and still do not know why this war is being waged. The rest of you practice your meditation." Shyra brought Tori into the monastery-looking vessel; even though it was the rudimentary workings of a tangible illusion, it was still quite breathtaking. The front of the building had huge pillars that were almost as high as the trees around it. There were a dozen stairs leading up to the ten-foot entrance doors. In the open area when Tori first walked in, it looked like an endless foyer with several rooms to the right and left. When not cloaked, this foyer would appear as the control room of the spaceship.

Shyra gave Tori the complete tour of the ship, so she would feel at home. She went from room to room, showing her where everyone resided. Each room was a personification of the person who dwelled in it. Shyra showed Tori to her own room; it wasn't the luxurious accommodations she was accustomed to, but she tried to get used to it.

"We are in the middle of a war with an advanced alien race known as the Zenakuu. Once a peaceful planet, they are now hell-bent on revenge," Shyra explained to Tori.

"Revenge? Why?" Tori asked.

With a heavy heart, Shyra explained to Tori everything about the Zenakuu and their conquest. Tori was in disbelief at first. All her problems seemed petty and insignificant in comparison to what was going on out there. Knowing what she had to do, she joined the others who were outside in meditation while they waited for Shyra to give the next order.

"Okay, I know we got off on the wrong foot," Tori announced to the group, "but I want everyone to know I'm actually a really good person. Yeah, I was born to a wealthy family and was kinda given anything I wanted. I guess I took advantage of that … but I'm not like that anymore, I've changed ya know? Like I really wanna help," Tori smiled and continued "I've only been around you all a couple of days, but I feel a stronger bond to you than I have with anyone else. This is as close to a real family that I have ever had."

The group was speechless. There was a long, awkward pause as they stared at her, trying to figure out where this change of heart had come from.

"Right," Tori continued, breaking the silence, "other than that, I guess you could say that I can control the air around me—also slow or speed up winds to create vacuums and stuff." Shyra stood in the shadows as everyone expressed themselves while waiting to start the real training.

Chris continued breaking the ice with his background. "I had to leave my family for this which sucked, but the cool thing is it made my dad really proud. Let's see, what else? I read a lot of comic books, but they're nothing like this. I don't make friends easily, so I'm glad I met you all. Oh, and I really think we need to be careful, because the government is going to try to capture us and experiment on us." The other three teens shot an even more befuddled look at him than they did Tori.

Next up was Cassie: "I wish my folks were protective of me—" Cassie explained before she was cut off.

"Oh, and I can control fire! I forgot to mention that. Sorry, Cassie," Chris shouted out, causing Alex to bust out laughing.

"Yeah, well, like I was saying—my dad is a drunk, and my mom is a vengeful bitch," Cassie continued. "She is more concerned with the child support money than me or my little sister. The worst part about all this is that I had to leave my sister with her, but I know she'll be strong enough to take care of herself. I can control water, wherever it may be."

Dimitri kept it going. "I mean, there's not much to say … My dad left when I was a kid. Raised on the streets of Brooklyn, I have seen some really messed up things. My older sister was killed in a drive-by, a casualty in the gang wars that run my streets. From that day on, I vowed to protect my family, and now my girlfriend Rose. I won't let them down again. Other than that it is what it is, I have the power to control earth, rock, stone, etc., but I don't know the limit to the minerals I can control."

Hesitant at first, Alex apprehensively revealed his past. "I never knew my mom or dad. They both died when I was a baby, so I was raised by my grandfather. Ever since I can remember I've been really good at running."

"More like running away," Dimitri interjected.

"Shut up Dimitri," Alex said as he glared at Dimitri. He finished his story after the unwarranted interruption. "I can create electricity from my hands and charge my body to dangerous levels of voltage. Really, I'm just here because I want to make a difference. I want to do the right thing."

"The Boy Scout routine never gets old?" Dimitri taunted.

"Will you give it a rest man and get off my case already?" Alex snapped. "I'm tired of you always trying to start something."

"Stop it the both of you," Shyra demanded as she stepped out. "We do not know when the Zenakuu could reach Earth, and I need to get all of you in shape. Some of you are better off than others, but we need to build your endurance. These battles can last days on end. Everyone will need to learn to handle such strenuous work. Think of it as a kinetic boot camp."

The team quickly changed their attitudes.

"Boot camp? I thought we were just gonna keep using our powers," complained Chris.

"How are you supposed to beat the enemy if they are running circles around you?" Shyra replied. "Training will consist every morning of stretching, push-ups, sit-ups, running up and down the mountainside, and other endurance exercises. Alexander, being a track runner, will show everyone how it is done and what to do. I am putting Alexander in charge for now."

Surprised by the news, Alex sat up straight. He'd never led a group before. That amount of responsibility was foreign to him, and he wasn't sure if he was ready.

"What! That's bullshit. Why does he get to lead just because he's good at running away? I have fighting experience, so I should lead," Dimitri shouted.

"Your bodies are not ready for combat training yet. You need to be physically prepared. Do not question my logic, Dimitri. Things will be as I see fit."

"Whatever, man. I'll be damned if I let that suck-up order me around."

Despite objections, Alex began his workout regimen the next day.

"Alright, team, let's start off slow and work our way to the top," Alex instructed.

They all tried to keep up with Alex who had more or less become use to the high elevation and thin air, but their bodies could not cope. They were out of breath in seconds, and collapsed to the ground gasping for air. All except one. Tori was jogging steadily right behind Alex.

"How the heck are you not out of air?" Cassie wheezed as she asked Tori.

"I don't know, I just take deep breaths," she said with a grin painted on her face. She jogged back and threw Cassandra's arm over her shoulder and helped her up.

Most of the group knew that the mission was more important than all of them combined, so they did as instructed and tried not to complain. They put their trust in Shyra, hoping not to be let down. For the next two months, they trained their bodies day in and day out. Most of the team became used to Alex leading the way—everyone but Dimitri, that is. He didn't like taking orders and felt Alex wasn't quite up to the task. He knew he could do a better job and started missing a lot of days training. After one month of sporadic absences Alex was fed up, and went to look for Dimitri. Alex found him sitting outside near the rear of the ship. To add insult to injury, he was on Alex's own laptop sending an email to someone named Rose. Alex couldn't let the blatant disrespect slide and confronted Dimitri about his absences.

"Where were you today, Dimitri?" Alex questioned.

"I don't answer to you, pretty boy."

"Shyra put me in charge for a reason. If you don't like it, do something about it," challenged Alex.

"It's about time, punk. You don't know how long I've been waiting to hear you say that. I'll definitely make you eat those words." Dimitri stood up and shoved Alex's left shoulder with his right hand. In complete shock, Alex looked at his shoulder, then back at Dimitri, and chuckled.

"Fools jump up to get beat down, Dimitri, so make sure you don't regret this," Alex said back.

Dimitri clenched his fist, "Don't talk about it, be about it," he shouted, and the ground underneath Alex sunk in before fully collapsing. He fell, cutting himself on the jagged edges of rocks that were buried in the dirt. The ground began closing in around Alex as he frantically tried to escape from the tomb Dimitri had created for him. Alex blasted the ground, propelling himself upward enough to leap out of it, but Dimitri immediately sent a couple of boulders toward Alex. One by one, Alex threw both hands out and sent out a scatter shot of mini electrical bombs to take care of the multiple targets. He reached Dimitri and landed a hard-as-nails punch to his left collar bone, knocking the wind out of him. Trying to gain back his footing, Dimitri landed an aerial kick that hit Alex in the head, stunning him and almost knocking him unconscious momentarily. Dimitri grabbed him by his shirt and attempted to perform a judo flip, but Alex charged his own body with a dangerously high electric current that electrocuted Dimitri and put him down. Thinking it was over, Alex started walking away, but Dimitri refused to stay down. He lifted the ground from under Alex.

"Where do you think you're going?" Dimitri demanded to know as he lifted Alex high above him. Turning the piece of rock over, Alex fell back to the ground. Dimitri brought the platform of rock down and began chasing after him. Alex hit the ground hard with a heavy thump followed by the rock, which would have surely crushed him to death if Shyra hadn't run in and telekinetically stopped the boulder.

"What is going on here!?" Shyra demanded to know.

"I don't think Alex has what it takes to lead us!" Dimitri shouted.

"Alex was only in charge of the endurance training—that is it. Come with me, Dimitri; we need to talk, and bring that dreadful computing device with you. You all are supposed to be training. There will be no more access to the outside world."

Cassie followed in behind Shyra and tended to Alex's wounds. Things were falling apart before they ever really started for Shyra's team. If she couldn't find the source of Dimitri's rage she knew she would have to kick him off the team—forever.

CHAPTER 8

Keep Your Boots Laced if You Want to Keep Pace

IT WAS JUNE AND two months had passed since the team was fully assembled, but things were far from perfect. Shyra was learning a lot about human social culture from watching the five teens. Alex spent most of his time training, while Cassie appeared to be more of a recluse, only associating with the others when necessary. Christian spent his time cracking jokes and trying to get the attention of Tori who had horrible hygiene habits. She left her workout clothes scattered about the floor and dishes piling up in the sink as if she expected someone to clean up after her. Dimitri, who walked around like he had a chip on his shoulder, occupied his time working out. Shyra sat Dimitri down in her room and explained to him why she chose Alex over anyone else.

"I think you are a fine warrior, Dimitri Williams, and you have a lot of potential, but despite my efforts to channel your rage, so much more of it remains. Alex has a good head on his shoulders and is genuinely concerned about the team. He also has a clear understanding of right and wrong, which is what we need."

Dimitri didn't want to hear any of it. "He's weak, Shyra, and he's gonna get us killed."

"Not every battle is won with brute strength, Dimitri. Strategic thinking and brains are a lot more important to winning war. However, strength is a very useful tool in war, and our team covers all bases—everyone plays a role," Shyra replied.

Dimitri knew he couldn't fight Shyra with this decision, so he just agreed and walked away. The rest of the day proved to be tense, but Shyra had high hopes the next day would be smoother.

Shyra knew time was a luxury she couldn't afford, so she decided to train the team on how to defend themselves in a fight. She focused on teaching them a fighting style that resembled Kalrynian combat but on Earth was best described as Wushu.

"Alright, everyone, today we start working on hand-to-hand combat," Shyra announced.

"Finally, I get to show you guys my moves!" Christian jumped up in excitement. "Dimitri already knows what I can do. Remember the cut above his eye? Yup, all me."

"Shut up, Chris. Or do you want to go for round two?" Dimitri challenged.

"That's enough. Now let's hear what Shyra has to say," Alex interjected.

"Kiss ass," Tori said under her breath.

"Save it Tori, okay? Why don't you pick your crap off the floor sometime for a change? This place looks like a tornado ran through a beauty salon," He snapped back.

"Oh, I got your tornado!" Tori said,

"If you five are done acting like infants, I can get back to what I was saying," a silence swept over the room. "Now some of you know how to handle yourselves in a fight, and others do not know the first thing about defending oneself. The next two months will be dedicated to learning the advanced martial arts of Wushu. The fighting style is similar to the techniques we use on Kalryn; your version is just more basic. Now the fact that a style close to ours is in the hands of Earth is entirely coincidental, so, no, we did not visit Earth and share our knowledge." Shyra went on, "First, it is all about clearing your mind; concentrate only on breathing. With every strike, exhale and use the power within to force your hand through your opponent. Speed is the key to winning a fight. Without speed, your enemies will dodge anything you can throw at them.

Shyra stood in front of her class while she went through the motions of the martial art taught on her home world. Like a mirror, each member of the class tried to copy her every move, learning what it took to effectively defend themselves. Wushu was its own practice but consisted of kickboxing, traditional Chinese martial arts, Muay Thai, and even a Chinese wrestling style that was known as Shuai Jiao. What is called the "Eighteen Arms of Wushu" utilized weapons and integrated them in the fighting style. Each member of the group practiced to find his or her comfort zone within the art.

"We are a little behind schedule, so we need to move right on to the kinesis training," Shyra said. "I will have to do this one by one, because all of you have different abilities. In the meantime, keep exercising and keep practicing."

Roughly six months had passed since Alex's life was thrown into the chaos it is, and the team became proficient in hand-to-hand combat. The training was longer than they hoped for, but well worth it and they had a lot to show for it. Shyra moved on to what would undoubtedly be their most important lesson yet—how to master their kinetic powers. She decided to go in order of team members that she felt needed the most training. Shyra started with Cassie—she was the most strategic but lacked the knowledge and confidence in her power. Shyra was determined to get to the bottom of it and asked Cassie why she didn't like her abilities. She tried to get the truth out of her, but Cassie resisted. Shyra saw she wasn't getting anywhere and called it a day.

"We will start this again in the morning," she said. "In the meantime, join the others and think about how we can get further in your training."

It took about a week of personal counseling to open up, but Cassie revealed the time she almost killed her younger sister in their swimming pool to Shyra. That day was forever seared into her mind.

"Cassandra, that is a grave misfortune, but it is all in the past. You must not let past mistakes control your future. These gifts that you have are Earth's only hope for salvation, and you and the rest of the team must utilize them to defend this planet against any threat. I know you will come around Cassandra, but for now, we need you to understand and have full control of your powers."

"I didn't ask for any of this Shyra. I feel like these gifts are really a curse and someone is going to end up dead because of these powers, if not from our own hands but from the hands of others."

"The more we train and better control your abilities, the less likely any misfortune will occur by your hand. These powers you all have are meant to protect the ones you love, not hurt them. Ask yourself this, Cassandra: with the power you have, do your friends and family stand a better chance of survival with you doing nothing or standing up and fighting?"

The words resonated in her mind for a while; Cassie turned her head and gave a look at Alex as he was practicing his electrokinesis. She turned back to Shyra, "I understand."

"Okay, so we can start training immediately." Shyra was in haste, because she already missed a couple of days trying to get Cassie out of her shell.

"With hydrokinesis, everything flows—from your mind to your hands and feet—it is all fluid," Shyra explained. "Your kinetic energy is a current that travels throughout your entire body. First, we will practice the motions. Never rushed but never too slow, the perfect medium—water is all about perfection. There is no form it cannot take, and with enough force, there is no place it cannot venture."

Shyra showed Cassie the basic motions of a successful hydrokinetic. Her arms swayed up and down, left to right, mimicking the motions of streaming rivers and waterfalls. "You have to connect with the water," she said. "Become part of the water, and the water will bend to your will with ease. Now it does not seem like you can create it, but you can certainly manipulate water."

"Right, but what if I'm not around water, Shyra?" Cassie asked. "I'll be useless."

"Not true, Cassandra, in my studies of kinetic power, I have learned about your specific ability. Keep in mind, there is almost always water around. You are special because you may have two abilities. I will teach you the possible other half of your power—cyrokinesis, the ability to control the temperature of liquids. There is always hydrogen and oxygen in the air, and with that, you will always be able to make water. The more you train, the faster you will be able to do it, and that is what I want you to practice. From there, I will try to teach you how to freeze it at will." The training went on for the next two weeks until Cassie was able to memorize each motion of hydrokinesis.

Alex was next up for training. Even though Alex had been with Shyra the longest, that didn't mean he was the most advanced. As Alex was learning the basics of electrokinesis, she explained to him that lightning and electricity are almost impossible to predict. It took a level of focus that not many were able to achieve. She taught him that his strikes needed to be quick and precise; his ability was one of the most dangerous and without the proper control, he could harm the very ones he wished to protect. Along with the setbacks of electrokinesis were the rewards; the ones blessed with this power may not have been the fastest flyers, but they were without a doubt the fastest runners. All of Alex's track-and-field trophies stood as a testament to that. His power was not only great for offense but defense as well. Shyra went over extensively how to create continuous streams of electricity, and in a short while, Alex learned that the capabilities of his powers were endless. He spent the next two and a half weeks shooting bursts of electricity from his palms. He was getting used to the sensation, but the current of electricity always made his arm twitch and tingle. Every hair on his arm stood up at attention from shoulders to hands as the current surged through.

Chris was up next, and Shyra understood firsthand how deadly and powerful his ability was. Pyrokinesis was all about destruction.

"Christian, there is not much I can teach you, I am afraid. You seem to have a firm grip on your gift, but to perfect it and not let your emotions affect your powers is a whole other fight. Only deep concentration and dedication will allow you to have complete control. I want you to think of the fire as an extension of yourself. Think about the attributes of fire. What can it do?"

Chris looked at her, "I don't know. Burn stuff?"

Shyra knew this to be true, but it wasn't the mind-set she wanted the young hero to have. "Yes, but so much more Christian," she said. "With your power, you can create weapons and attacks, and more impressively, you will be able to fly. I will show you the motions of pyrokinesis. Use powerful and explosive movements that cater to your kinesis. Practice these moves, and your kinetic energy will be gathered and released with explosive results."

Chris was a fast learner, and Shyra only had to show him a few times before he mastered the basics. In only a few weeks he could send powerful balls of fire from his hands with almost pinpoint accuracy.

It had been seven and a half weeks since Shyra started kinesis training. She approached her most withdrawn student, knowing it would take a lot to get through to him.

"Dimitri, you are up," Shyra said. "Please step forward. Everyone else continue practicing."

Try as he might to hide, Dimitri was really curious what new techniques an alien could teach him about his powers that he'd had all his life.

"Dimitri, your ability has the potential to be the most powerful out of everyone. You can control Earth itself. When you are ready, you will be able to move the very mountains we train on." Shyra showed Dimitri the movements and let him practice picking up and throwing various kinds of heavy stones.

"Remember that the moves for a geokinetic are very solid and grounded—no pun intended. Strike hard and fast when you attack. Feel the earth move underneath your feet with every kick, and envision the rocks flying at your enemy with every punch thrown. This planet has bestowed upon you a great gift, and you need to use it wisely. Every natural mineral out there is a weapon at your disposal. Use them well."

"You are strong and tough, Dimitri, but do not forget about your allies," Shyra reminded him. "Protect them with your power. Together, the five of you can do anything." Two and a half weeks passed, but by the end of his training, Dimitri was much better at causing earthquakes and separating the ground.

Tori stepped up to be trained next. "Unlike the others, Tori, you embrace your powers and most likely have the greatest understanding of them. I expect the most from you."

"Great, and here I thought there was gonna be pressure," Tori sarcastically stated.

"I do not follow you, Tori," Shyra began, obviously confused. "The only pressure is that your species' survival rest in your hands."

"No, Shyra, I was being sarcas … never mind. What tricks do you have to teach me?"

"Aerokinesis can be the most deceptive power of them all; while it may not appear sinister, when concentrated the wind can cut through almost anything. The motions of an aerokinetic are closely derived from the phrase 'go with the flow.' That is what I want you to practice. Your goal is to remove any stiffness and rigidness. Your movements need to be swift and razor-sharp. I will also teach the power that should come natural to you—the ability of flight."

Tori's eyes lit up. "I knew it! I knew I'd be able to fly. I feel it sometimes, ya know? Like I've always been able to kind of glide and stuff, but this is awesome."

"Yes, Tori, as your people say, I suppose it is *awesome.* Now, as I was saying, you must learn to extend that feeling you get when you are gliding. Remember that gravity holds no bearing with you. Feel the current of the wind lift you off the ground and ride the wave, so to speak. Supersonic flight is only the tip of the iceberg with your powers. Aerokinetics can create hurricanes, tornados, cyclones, and so much more. With practice, you will be able to do it all."

Shyra spent the next two weeks helping Tori master her craft and then summoned the rest of the team.

"Everyone, there is something that I want you all to know. On my home world of Kalryn, the Savants that govern my planet did not want to involve your world in this battle. Their plan was to let this world fall victim to the Zenakuu, because they did not believe you could change the course of the war. I believe them to be wrong; there is something very special about your species that I believe they are overlooking. You each have unfathomable power and potential. Together, we shall prove them wrong and drive the Zenakuu back to the darkest regions of space. Now that everyone is somewhat on the same level of understanding with their kinetic powers, all we have to do is keep training and practicing. The Zenakuu scouting party will most likely be here soon. In the time we have left, I want you all to continue mastering your power," Shyra revealed.

For some of the espers, the time went by slowly. For the others who weren't looking forward to fighting an alien race, the seven months felt more like seven days.

Now in November Shyra gathered the team. It was time to reveal names and send them out into the real world to gain much-needed experience. "Gather around me, team, and listen. On my world uniforms are point of pride among my people. They represent honor, loyalty, and teamwork. You five have demonstrated all of these qualities, so I have a surprise for you all."

"Now this is more like it!" Chris shouted.

"I fashioned some uniforms and have chosen names for you all to protect your identities, so I hope you like them," Shyra continued. "Christian, here is your costume. You will be known as Irascible Flame. Your pyrokinesis will reduce the ones who stand in your way to ashes."

He held up his costume and awed at the attention to detail that Shyra had put into it. It had broad, armored shoulder pads. The chest plate had a ball of fire with an intricate design of what would appear as flames spreading throughout the lining of his body. Matching plated gloves and boots looked like something lifted from one of his comic books. The color scheme was black, red, orange, and yellow. The straps that held his body armor were golden and matched the clips on his gloves and belt buckle, which was another flame symbol. His boots were multicolored and consisted of a heat-resistant hard plastic type of armor that ran up to his knees. The pants were charcoal black and had flames that ran up the sides of each leg. Every inch of his costume was lined with flame-retardant materials so it did not burst into flames. Chris finally added a full-body, black trench coat with crimson red trim to finish the costume. The training that the team underwent transformed him into a very fit, muscular kid. The once pudgy teen now possessed the physique of a Greek god.

Next, Shyra turned her attention to Tori. "Tori, you have grown so much since you got here, and I am happy to present you with your new name and costume. You will be known as Whisking Wind. You will use your aerokinesis to take your enemies' breath away."

Tori's outfit was breathtaking to say the least. Sporting the color white with black trim, the tight-fitting costume contoured to every curve on her tone body, which was ravishing to begin with. The high leather boots were sewn into the kneepads, which made for an easy change of clothes if need be. Her gloves climbed all the way up her biceps; her left glove sported two little black padded cushions, while the right had only one. The same setup was on her legs, only reversed. She had a symbol of a small tornado on her abdomen and her belt. The cape Shyra gave her was black on the outside but white on the inside. It was a half-sized cape that came down to the small of her lower back. Tori smiled at Shyra, and secretly leaned in to whisper to Cassie.

"Kalrynians aren't much on color are they? I wish she would have talked me before designing this thing, there's like no space for accessorizing," she complained.

"Shh," Cassie hastily responded.

After the first two costumes were presented, the rest of the team waited with bated breath, anxious for their turn. All the regrets from this adventure were forgotten for a brief moment. Almost a year had gone by since Alex and the others were summoned by Shyra in this almost surreal event that had been forced upon the five exemplary teenagers. Overwhelmed with excitement, there was only one who quelled his eagerness. Dimitri was in the back of the crowd still in disagreement with Shyra on the matter of who should be leader and the thought of running around dressed as "superheroes."

And then it was his turn. "Dimitri, please come forward," Shyra said.

"I'm up? What you got for me?" he replied.

"Dimitri, you have made incredible progress since you have been here, and I am glad you can make peace with your inner demons. This is yours." With that, Shyra handed Dimitri his costume. "From now on, you will be Seismic Earth. Your geokinesis will be the cornerstone to our victory."

Dimitri's costume was tailored to his personality. It was a myrtle green leather hoodie with the sleeves cut off to show off his muscle definition. He also wore a predominantly black biker's glove on his right hand, while the other forearm was wrapped up in boxing bandages. The brawler of the group had an outfit that gave his hands and arms freedom and loose movement. Baggy black-and-green cargo pants and work boots helped him stomp out anyone crazy enough to be looking for a fight. Around his waist he sported a forest green samurai-inspired custom kusazuri, a thick cloth that shielded the hips and waist. The symbol on the left side of his hoodie was a blue Earth symbol with a crack through it, representing an earthquake. The hoodie was lined with white, while his undershirt was solid black.

Shyra walked over to Cassie, placed her hand on her shoulder, and smiled. "Cassandra, what can I say? Your strategic prowess and intellect have almost challenged my own. You are levelheaded in combat and will be the deciding factor in any skirmish. This outfit was designed especially for you. Your new moniker is Effervescent Rain." Shyra handed the costume to Cassie. "Use your hydrokinesis to wash away the sins of the universe.

Cassie was presented with a formfitting cerulean top with long sleeves and skin-tight black pants, along with a flowing custom blue hanfu. Crashing waves were depicted on her midsection, while a floral design hugged her shoulders and spread to her chest. The same floral design was repeated at the bottom of her hanfu. Her uniform was accentuated with violet trim; even the top and bottom of her knee-high boots showed off her affinity for violet and unique style. Lastly, a rain cloud adorned the left side of her chest, while on the right side of her chest was a backward E connected to an R, representing Effervescent Rain. She then tied a blue ribbon on her right leg and left arm for fashion, and on the top of her left forearm was a padded guard with a raindrop in the middle.

"Last but not least is the first person I encountered. Without you, Alexander, I would not have been able to get this far. You have been a huge help to me and are the rightful captain to this team. You can handle any situation you put your mind to. You went from not being able to control your powers to mastering them almost completely. I am very proud of you. Alexander, you will be dubbed Voltaic Cloud." Shyra handed his uniform over. "With your electrokinesis, you are the light that guides the team through the darkness."

His costume included a fitted, black Japanese-style karate gi with yellow trim as an undergarment and a vest-styled leather tabard that was connected on the outer sides by buckled straps. He had a padded arm guard covering his left forearm, while on his right he wore the powerful Raiden stone, which had been given to Shyra by her father in case she ever found herself in a tough battle. It was quite legendary on Kalryn and had the ability to amplify electric power. Around his waist he wore a broad, black belt lined with red trim and his symbol for lightning in the middle that sat atop a traditional Japanese haidate. His pants were loose and somewhat baggy. They were all black besides his trademark lightning bolt going down the sides. They were cuffed off by metallic shin guards with ninja boots. On his back he donned a cape that was yellow on the inside but black on the outside and held together by the lightning pin on his right shoulder.

They were finally feeling confident in their abilities, but Shyra had a message of warning for them that she felt they might have overlooked. "All of you have gotten a lot stronger, but never overdo it. There is a limit to the amount of power you can release. I always want the five of you to be wary of that."

Christian stepped out in front to speak. "What happens if we use too much of our powers at once?"

"Well, Christian, it depends on the extent to which you overuse it, but remember your powers are kinetic, and stem from your brain. If you push that strain on your mind too far, you will suffer what your planet calls a brain aneurysm. It differs from species to species, but you will mostly likely suffer from severe headaches, nausea, vision impairment, vomiting, and loss of consciousness. If severe enough, the aneurysm may rupture and will leak blood into the space around the brain. This is called a subarachnoid hemorrhage. Depending on the amount of blood, it can produce a hemorrhagic stroke, which you very likely will die from."

"Oh, is that all? And here I thought it would be bad," Christian bitingly replied.

The entire team looked as if they felt sick to their stomachs over the thought of bleeding out to death.

"Yes, that is all." Shyra said with a confused look on her face.

"No, I was being sarcastic," Christian said as he tried to correct her.

"Oh, this planet's sense of humor and what you call 'sarcasm' escapes me, I am afraid," Shyra noted. "Moving on, though, we have a big day ahead of us tomorrow, so you five try not to stay up too late."

Everything was really coming together for the alliance. They trained hard physically and mentally. It was time to put all they had learned into action. Smiles spread across the room. Even Dimitri could not hold back the grin over the thought of making a difference like the promise he'd made to his mom and sister. It was running smoothly for the first time, and the alliance was getting along, but this peace was not meant to last.

Chapter 9

Murphy's Law

Shyra was in her room meditating when the alarm went off. It was loud and reverberated throughout the entire ship. The team, who was relaxing in the living room watching TV, all jumped up very startled. The sound was new to them, and they didn't know what to make of it.

"What the heck is that about?" Tori asked.

"I don't know, but I'll find out," Alex answered. He got up and bolted toward Shyra's door. The team followed right behind him.

"Shyra, what's going on?" he asked.

Truthfully, not even she knew the cause of the alarm. Alex had reached her with his super speed faster than she could check the security room.

"It is nothing but a drill to gauge your reaction time, Voltaic Cloud. I am impressed how quickly you were ready to arms." She did not want to lie, but there was no need worrying the team over possibly nothing.

Alex arched his eyebrows and looked at her inquisitively. "Okay then … I guess I'll let everyone know to breathe easy."

"Thank you, Alexander. That would be most helpful. If you will excuse me, I must get back to meditating."

The door to her room closed in front of Alex's face, and he walked back to the others. Shyra could hear him though through the walls. "It's okay, guys. False alarm," he told the others.

Shyra knew she had bought some temporary silence. Once the coast was clear, she left her chambers to check the security room, but she was not prepared for what she found in the least. "Damn, I thought we had more time," she said.

It was clear as day. A Zenakuu ship had been picked up by the sensors, and its trajectory showed it was headed straight for Earth. Even the usually cool, calm, and collect Shyra found herself slipping into a stage of panic.

"They are not ready," she said out loud but low enough so no one could hear her. She tried to establish a communication link to her home planet—she desperately needed her father's advice. Surely he would know what to do in this time of emergency. She waited patiently as the screen displayed "Attempting Communication." Finally, it went through. She was patched through to one of the advisors who was second only to the official Savants of Kalryn.

"Advisor Brevitan speaking. Guide 5142-K, what is the nature of your hail?"

"Please, sir, it is imperative. I need to speak to Councilman Rayvaar," Shyra said. "It is a matter of urgency."

"Guide 5142-K, Councilman Rayvaar is very busy. We are in the middle of a war, Child, and he cannot be disturbed over trivial matters."

"Advisor Brevitan, this is no trivial matter. As we speak, the Zenakuu are on their way to my stationed planet. I must speak with him."

"I see … Very well, but know this Shyra: your patrilineage privileges wear thin. You shall be connected to him now." Brevitan's image cut out and was followed by a moment of silence before her father appeared on the screen.

"Father, I seek your council. There is a Zenakuu ship speeding toward Earth, and I fear my team is not ready for this attack. What should I do?" Shyra asked.

"Shyra, my advice is the same as before. Abandon your efforts for that insignificant planet and come back to Kalryn. Your talents could be put to better use here. The most the Zenakuu will gain from that world are resources and mining slaves. Their race holds no true potential for kinetic combat."

"You are wrong, Father. I have seen it with my own eyes. I believe this planet could change the tide of this war."

"You are stubborn and foolhardy as ever, Shyra," her father replied.

"Please, Father, I need your help."

"There is nothing I can do to help you. If they are on their way as you claim and your team is not ready, I recommend you hide them until the Zenakuu are done ravaging the planet or at least have the decency to let them make peace with their God before they are slaughtered. I must go now, Child. The Zenakuu armada is spreading over this galaxy like a plague, and we must focus our attention on winning this war," he scolded.

"But—" was the only word she got in edgewise before being cut off.

"With these pressing matters, my thoughts and prayers are with you, Shyra. Rayvaar out," her father concluded. With that, the picture cut out, and all that was left of her father was a screen that blinked "Communication End." His harsh words filled her with fear and doubt. She wanted to have faith in her team, but they were just teenagers. She couldn't alarm them of the danger, so she masked her intentions as benevolence, giving them each a "day off."

Because Shyra could only train one pupil effectively at a time, she decided to give each member of the team the chance to see their families one by one before they jeopardized their lives fighting the oncoming Zenakuu scouting party. If anything should happen to them before they got the chance to say good-bye, Shyra would never forgive herself. They would each have one day to see the people who meant the most to them.

Tori, who was giving herself a pedicure at the time was the first up. She would be teleported back to California immediately. Before departing, she turned to her friends to say good-bye. "You guys, try not to miss me too much." She waved to them, winked at Dimitri, and vanished right in front of everyone's eyes. The rest of the team shot a puzzled look at Dimitri as he stood there awkwardly.

"As if I would miss someone like her," he said in an attempt to break silence, but they only picked up on his denial even more. "What the hell are you all looking at?" he shouted and stormed away.

"Hey, Alex, do you think there's something going on between Dimitri and Tori?" Christian asked.

"Uh, I don't know. I don't think there is. Dimitri doesn't seem like he's into her," Alex answered.

"Yeah, if anyone, he's probably into Cassie," Chris added.

Defensively, Alex responded to Chris's statement. "Why would you say that? Not that I care, but did he say anything?"

"No. It's just a hunch," Alex said.

"Oh, right," Alex agreed.

"Okay, well I'll see you later. I'm gonna go make brownies for Tori's return."

"You can bake?" Alex asked.

"Well no, they're the instant kind, but you can't even taste the difference," Chris walked off to the kitchen and left Alex to his thoughts.

"There's no way Cassie would ever go for someone like Dimitri," he said to reassure himself.

Tori wasn't particularly excited to head home; her parents were never around anyway. They did a lot of globe hopping, leaving Tori at home with plenty of spending money and a less-than-capable caretaker who was only interested in spending the cash on herself. Tori didn't mind, though. It wasn't the money she cared about but the freedom. She and her guardian Nancy had an understanding—Nancy got the money, and Tori got to do whatever she wanted. This time was different, though. This time her parents would be home from their jobs. Tori's father Andrew was a renowned architect who had accumulated a large sum of money in his younger years while Tori's mom Rebecca rode his coattails. She later convinced him to give her enough money to start a clothing line that, much to everyone's surprise, took off. Tori felt nervous heading back home. It was easy enough to elude Nancy, but her parents were a different matter.

They were actually pretty sharp and business savvy. That's how they'd gotten where they were, and they expected Tori to follow suit. She, however, couldn't care less how they got their money. Tori wanted to be famous no matter what, which was always a disappointment to her parents. She arrived to a golden front gate and entered using her access code. She was first greeted by their gardener Patrick.

"Welcome back, Ms. Hannon. Nancy didn't tell me you were coming home from studying abroad."

Tori looked confused for a moment but went along with it. "Yeah, I just flew in this morning," she responded. It must have been some lie Nancy came up with to explain her sudden absence. *Fine by me*, she thought as she made her way up the driveway to the front doors.

Tori couldn't even place her key in the lock before she was greeted by Thomas the caretaker of her house, who was a slender man that stood six feet tall with silvering aged hair.

"Master Tori, welcome home."

Tori figured they must have been watching her through the security cameras. "Hi, Thomas, is Nancy around?"

"If I'm not mistaken, I believe she's upstairs," he answered back.

"Okay, thanks, Thomas." Tori took the long flight of steps passing the overly extravagant chandelier that hung from the ceiling and the freshly picked bouquet of exotic flowers that served as a centerpiece for their dining room.

No sign of my parents yet, she thought to herself. She really wanted to corroborate the story with Nancy before facing them. She found Nancy in her room doing the usual, which consisted of online shopping while she listened to game shows in the background on her flat-screen television. Tori cleared her throat to get her attention. Nancy's head snapped back and was absolutely relieved upon sight of Tori.

"Where the hell have you been!" she shouted at Tori. "The only thing I've had to go on was some two-bit note saying 'be right back' and the occasional e-mail saying you were okay, which I didn't even know was really coming from you. You're lucky I haven't told your parents. In fact, if it weren't for the jail time I thought I might've faced, I probably would've."

"Nice to see you too, Nancy, and thanks for the concern. I had no idea you cared so much," Tori responded sarcastically.

"That's not funny, okay? Seriously, where have you been?"

"I don't know, okay? I've been making a difference. You wouldn't understand, Nancy. Just know I'm not involved in anything bad or illegal, and I don't plan on staying here long. I just wanted to get our story straight. What's this I heard about me being in school?"

"It's the lie I had to tell everyone to keep from them asking questions. I even forged a couple postcards in your name," Nancy admitted.

"Classy … So what's the story?" Tori asked.

"You are finishing your junior year of high school studying abroad at a prestigious film school in Paris, France, called Château de une Actrice, and you absolutely love it there. You've made lots of friends. It's the first time you've been serious about something, so you want to see it through, but you promised to send letters, check in as much as possible, and be back for holidays," she explained.

"Okay, I got it. But is there such a place in France?"

"No, of course not. I just made it up, but it sounds real, right?"

"I guess so. Where are my parents, Nancy?" Tori asked.

"They are in the den. Seeing you will be a real surprise."

"Let's hope it's a good one," she said back snidely.

Tori didn't need to pack much—only enough for a few weeks—but the faster she got out of the house and back to her friends, the better. She crept down the hall to the den where her parents were relaxing. So many conflicting feelings came up when she thought of them. The main reason she acted up was for their attention. She didn't want the nanny, money, or nice things. What she really wanted was her mom and dad to be there for her as she was growing up. Many of her feelings toward them had turned cold and bitter. The family hardly knew each other, which, at that point, suited her just fine. She approached the room and just stood in the doorway.

"Mother, Father, I have returned from school," she announced.

"Ah, Tori, how is the acting thing going for you? Make any friends in Toulouse?" her father asked.

"Yes, Darling, you simply must tell us about it over dinner," her mom added.

Tori remembered why she couldn't stand when they came back and began to furrow her eyebrows. "The *acting thing*, as you put it, Dad, is going very well. And it's Paris, not Toulouse."

"Are you sure, Tori?" her dad asked. "I'm almost positive that it's Toulouse."

"Well, Dad, since I'm the one attending the school, I think I would know."

"If you say so, Love. Now why don't you freshen up? The cooks will have dinner ready shortly."

"Yes, Father. I can't wait," she replied sarcastically. Tori quickly stormed out of the room and darted straight for her bedroom, the only sanctuary she had in that loveless excuse for a home. Her room seemed to be a manifestation of her personality; it was decorated with old-time movie posters with some of the most recognizable actors Hollywood has ever produced. She also had a map of the world with pins on various locations of places she wanted to visit, a queen-sized bed, and a stockpile of make-up and jewelry that she rummaged through to spruce up her bland uniform. Though, it was when she sprang open her closet doors that her eyes truly lit up. Tori completely forgot what it was like to submerse herself in high fashion and caressed her cheek with her cashmere sweaters, then frivolously tried on a couple one of a kind couture dresses. What really caught her eye was a skimpy outfit that she knew Dimitri wouldn't be able to resist. She collected a few fashion magazines and some keepsakes for the teleport back to Shyra's ship. They were the only mementos that made her feel like she was home. For the next few hours, she contemplated all she had gone through in the past months and wondered what her friends were up to, especially Dimitri. Before she knew it, it was time for dinner. She was summoned by Thomas to join her parents at their very elegant dinner table; it was set up with fine china, sterling silver utensils, Roman candle holders, a silk tablecloth, and, to top it off, a breathtaking centerpiece that could make the cornucopia given to the pilgrims a run for its money.

"Tori, so nice of you to join us," her father said as she entered the dining room.

"Sorry, Father. I lost track of time," Tori said back without making eye contact.

"Indeed," Mr. Hannon muttered.

Tori's mom Rebecca jumped in. "So, honey, tell us more of this school."

"Well, Mom, I'm doing really well, and I've already made some close friends. My teacher says I show great talent."

"Wonderful, Darling, it sounds like fun. I saw a play in Milan, and the actors there were truly talented. You could learn a thing or two from them."

Tori glared at her mother, anxiously awaiting the moment she could leave.

Her father chimed in. "Well, I think the whole thing is a waste of time. When are you going to grow up, Tori, and follow in our footsteps?"

"I think you're a waste of time," Tori muttered under her breath.

"Excuse me? What was that, Tori?"

"Nothing, Father," Tori answered.

"I just don't understand it," he added. "We provide you with the best schools money can buy, and yet you still turn out like this. Where did we go wrong?"

Tori finally had enough. "You want to know where you went wrong, Dad? It was when you thought you could buy my future! I don't give a damn about your money. I wanted my father; I wanted my mother. Surprisingly enough, stacks of money don't keep you too warm at night unless you burn them. You watch, though; I'll do more for this family name than you ever did. Now if you'll excuse me, I can't stand to be here any longer. I'm going back to Paris." Tori stood up and threw her napkin on the table. She marched upstairs to gather her things.

"I can't believe them sometimes!" she mumbled on her way upstairs. "They don't know a thing about me. I'll only ever be a disappointment to them." Ten minutes later, Tori cinematically walked down the steps to the front doors. "As always, Mother and Father, it's been a pleasure."

"Aw, honey, don't be like that," her mom retorted.

Tori reached for the door handle and opened the door. "Yeah, whatever." She slammed the door shut, and the gust of wind from her swing broke every window on the downstairs level.

Outside, she pressed her back to the front door and slid down until she was sitting. Tori closed her eyes, and did her best to slow down her breathing. The twitching in her arms and legs, and quivering of her lips were all signs that she'd been rattled. Angrily she made her way to her feet.

Thomas drove her to the front gate and opened the car door for her. "You sure this is where you want me to drop you off, Miss Hannon?"

"Yes, Thomas, I'll be fine from here."

"Very well, young master. Do take care of yourself."

"Thank you, Thomas, I will. You take care too."

Thomas got back in the car and drove off as the main gates closed behind him.

Tori looked up at the sky. "Shyra, I'm ready. Get me the hell out of here." Tori began to dematerialize, and before she could blink, she was back with her team. She stood at the front doors and angrily walked in.

"Jerks!" she shouted. "Ugh, I can't believe how incredibly ignorant they can be!"

Chris walked in with the freshly made brownies that he'd kept hidden from the rest of the team until she came back. "Hi, Tori! Welcome back. I made you these bro—" Tori knocked the tray of brownies high into the air with little regard for Christian's feelings.

Alex, who saw the whole thing, was disgusted by her actions. "Tori!" he yelled.

"Not now, okay? Just leave me alone." Tori left for her bedroom and wasn't seen again for the rest of the night. Alex walked over to his friend and helped him pick up the mess.

"You okay, man?" he asked.

"Yeah, man. It's cool."

The two teens cleaned up, and Chris distraughtly walked back to his room for the evening. The next morning it was Dimitri's turn, and from the way his eyes gleamed, it was obvious he was excited to be reunited with his mother and sister. When he was done getting his affairs in order, he alerted Shyra that he was ready. She wished him luck and teleported him to New York. While Dimitri was gone, Christian decided he wasn't going to give up on Tori so easily. That morning, once the coast was clear, he walked back to where the others were relaxing with a newly hatched plan to get Tori to notice him. Cassie was resting her head on Alex's shoulder as they watched TV, but Tori was around the corner in the kitchen making a late morning snack.

"I don't know what he's talking about," Chris said abruptly in Tori's general direction. She turned to face him.

"What who is talking about?" Tori asked. Christian walked over to the kitchen counter and took a seat. "Oh nothing really, just Dmitri saying that the girls are nothing but dead weight."

"Excuse me?" Tori rhetorically snapped.

"Yeah, something about you being *a lot* of dead weight, emphasis on a lot. I don't see it though, I think you can hold your own in a fight," he replied.

"Wow! Ok well, when he gets back, *he's* gonna be dead weight, literally." She was seething mad, but calmed herself long enough to put her hand on Christian's shoulder and say, "thanks for telling me Chris." Tori walked out the front doors to train in hopes that it would relieve some stress. Alex popped around the corner and noticed that Chris had a cheesy smile plastered on his face. He snapped out of it as Alex approached him.

"Did you see that bro? She touched me, tenderly."

"Yeah I saw and heard the whole thing. Did D really say that?" Alex asked.

"Well no, but she doesn't know that," Chris said with a smirk.

"That's not the way to get her to like you," Alex replied.

"Oh yeah! Please, remind me how things are going with you and Cassie." Christian snapped back. Alex was a little taken aback by the intentional low blow.

"Ok, I don't know what your deal is, but Cassie and I are just friends and teammates," Alex said.

"You're joking right? The only way it could be more obvious is if you grabbed a loud speaker and shouted it off the top of this mountain. And, in case you haven't noticed, nice guys finish last, so say goodbye to Mr. Nice Guy. That's what my *deal* is, so please just let me do me," he said bitingly, and walked off toward his room. Chris was determined to have Tori acknowledge him even if it killed him, and when Dimitri came back, he probably would.

CHAPTER 10

Strong Dogs Seldom Bark

The thought of leaving his mom and sister behind never sat well with Dimitri, and he was anxious to see their faces again. It had been close to a year since he was able to sit down and enjoy a meal with them. He wanted one more chance to spend quality time with them in case the unspeakable happened. Upon transport to his old neighborhood, Dimitri saw that nothing had changed. All the convenience stores and pawn shops looked exactly the same, and there was a liquor store on every other corner. None of that mattered to him, though; he knew he would somehow bring peace and prosperity to his city but not today. If there was one thing Shyra was teaching him, it was patience. That night he just wanted to spend some real time with the women he loved.

Dimitri picked up some flowers on his way home to surprise to his mother. He remembered his mom's favorite kind, so he bought a dozen pink carnations for her and proceeded to walk up the stoop that led to his old building's door. Recalling how run down and depleted it looked made him appreciate the clean quarters of Shyra's ship. Dimitri hit the button for his apartment number to be buzzed in. Through the speaker he heard her voice: "Who is it?"

"It's nice to hear your voice again, Mom."

"Baby, is that you? Honey, what are you doing home? Never mind, it doesn't even matter. Come up, come up already."

Dimitri was glad that some things never changed. His apartment was on the third floor, but after all the physical training he had undergone, it might as well have been three steps in total. There she stood, waiting for him in the doorway—the woman who raised him to be a man and his only anchor in this insane world. Next to her was his reason to keep fighting—his little sister Ashley.

"Welcome home, baby. No alien race is gonna take out my son, that's for sure!" she joked. "But you need to stop taking so long to visit."

"They haven't come yet, Mom. Don't you think you would have heard about it if they had?"

"Not if you kicked their asses first."

Dimitri laughed at the thought of his mom shouting from the bleachers and rooting him on as he bashed alien faces in. "Not yet, Mom. Hey have you heard from Rose at all? I haven't gotten the chance to talk to her lately."

"Sorry baby, I see her every now and then but I haven't heard much from her. She is probably hanging out with friends. You know how it is," she reassured him.

"Yeah… I guess I do," he said. Dimitri turned to face his sister Ashley and smiled.

"Did you get taller, D?" she teased.

"No, I think you just got smaller, Short-stuff." Dimitri prodded back.

They both laughed, and the reunited family headed inside.

"I wish you would have given me more notice, but I'll whip up something for us. You sit down and talk to your sister, and then you can tell the both of us all about what you've been up to."

Dimitri cringed at the thought of having to explain to his mom that he lives with a bunch of kids from around the country—and girls too; she definitely wasn't going to like that.

"Um, sure, Mom. First let me catch up with Ashley, though." Dimitri led his younger sister to his old room and sat backward on his desk chair facing her.

"Have a seat on the bed," he said. "I wanna hear how you guys have been holding up."

"You're such a drama queen, D. You've only been gone a few months. Mom and I are doing just fine. I even got a job at the grocery store to help out."

"I'm sorry that you have to do that, Ashley."

"Don't be," she said. "I kinda like it. I've even made new friends."

Dimitri raised his eyebrow. "Is that right? Well they better be *girl* friends."

Ashley laughed at her overprotective brother. "Or what? You gonna lunge huge rocks at them, Earth Boy?"

Dimitri corrected her. "The name is Seismic Earth to you, Munchkin."

"You serious, D? Is that like your superhero name or something?"

"It's my alias. It's not like I can go around telling people my real name. That might endanger you and mom."

Ashley sat up with an immeasurable grin on her face. "That is so cool! I want one too!"

Dimitri picked a pillow up off the floor and threw it at her. "Sure. You can be the Annoying Avenger." Dimitri felt genuinely happy for the first time in months as he caught up with his sister, but not before long, their mother called them for dinner.

Dimitri didn't know why his mom was griping about having too short of notice for dinner. What she'd laid before them was a three-course meal fit for a king.

"Really, Mom?" he turned to her and said.

"It's just a little something-something I was able to throw together."

Clean living conditions were one thing, but Shyra could never touch his mom's soul food cooking—Cornish game hens, collard greens, fried catfish, mac and cheese, wild rice, cornbread, and sweet potato pie for dessert.

"Look it's not every day my superhero son comes home. The grocery store is only a block away, and I get a discount now that Ashley works there. Never mind all that, though. Sit, eat, and tell us all about it."

The three of them sat down and said grace before diving in the feast that sat in front of them. One bite, and Dimitri's palette was in ecstasy. After a few minutes of silence, his mom interrupted and looked right at him. "Well?"

"Well what, Mom?" he responded.

"Don't make me drag it out of you, boy. Tell me what you've been up to."

The long-awaited moment was finally upon him. He had no idea where to even start, but he figured the beginning would be a good a place as any. He cleared his throat and saw the anticipation in his mother's eyes.

"Well, Mom, I met up with some kid named Alex who has powers like me, only he manipulates lightning. We both got teleported to some spacecraft where I met an alien named Shyra, and she told me all about what our planet was in store for. She kinda went over how we got our powers.

"Apparently, her race came here in hopes of selecting people to help fight this war, but the first guy crashed or something, which released all his energy into the air. That affected certain people, giving them powers."

His mom's eyes were wide opened as she hung onto her son's every word. "Well don't that just take the cake?" she said. "You met an alien already, and one of them blew up, making you a superhero. My friends wouldn't believe me even if I told them."

"Well, it's really important that you don't, Mom," he said. "No one can know about any of this. I've probably told you too much as it is, but if anything happens to me, I want you to know the truth. After Shyra told me all this, I went out to recruit another teenager with powers in New Jersey. This one had fire powers, and his name is Christian. When the two of us got back,

Alex arrived with a girl named Cassie who can control water. The last girl we went to pick up is named Tori, and she controls air."

His mom interrupted again. "Girls, you say? Were any of them pretty, son?"

Frustrated, Dimitri looked at her and responded, "I don't know, Mom. I guess Tori is kinda cute, but I'm not really focused on that now."

Ashley jumped right in and added, "D has a girlfriend. D and Tori sitting in a tree, K-I-S-S-I-N-G. First comes love then—"

Before she could finish her sentence, the apartment began to shake.

"Shut it, munchkin," he demanded.

"Rocks for brains!" Ashley said and then promptly closed her mouth.

"Dimitri Williams!" his mom yelled.

The apartment immediately stopped shaking. "Sorry, Mom, but she started it."

"And I'm finishing it. Now continue on with your story."

Dimitri had forgotten how his mom's anger could scare him way more than any threat of Zenakuu invasion.

"Okay, from there we've been doing mostly just training. It's kinda like boot camp—we run, do push-ups, practice combat training, master hand-to-hand combat, and hone our specific powers. Right now I have much better control of my powers. I can cause earthquakes, geokinetically lift stones, and form dirt into whatever shape I want, which comes in handy because I can turn it into armor and stuff."

"That's great, baby," he mom said. "I bet you're the strongest one there. You're not the only one who's gotten tougher, though. Your sister Ashley got a job and helps out around the house now, and you're dear old mom got a raise." A sense of relief waved over Dimitri with the news.

"That's great, Mom. I'm proud of the both of you."

The three of them talked and ate until they felt like they were going to explode. It was good for Dimitri, laughing and smiling with his family. It reminded him why he was doing all this. An hour or so later, he received a telepathic message from Shyra. "Seismic Earth, it is time to come back," she said.

Dimitri nodded and addressed his mother and sister. "I have to head back now, guys. They're calling me."

"Aw, so soon, bro? You just got here," Ashley said.

"I'll be back soon, Ash, and next time I'll bring you back some cool alien tech."

Her eyes lit up like the Rockefeller Center Christmas Tree. "I'm gonna hold you to that, D!"

Dimitri's mother got up to make a couple plates for him to take with him. After a few moments, she handed him some plastic containers filled to the brim with food. "Here you go, son. Be sure to share some with those teammates of yours. I'm sure they could use a good meal after working so hard."

"You got it, Mom." Once again, he could tell she was trying to hold back the tears from forming.

"I'm very proud of you, Dimitri, and I love you very much."

"I love you too, Mom. I'll be back soon." He turned to his sister. "Continue to hold down the fort while I'm gone, Ash, and for the love of God, stop growing up so fast."

His sister laughed and answered, "I've got you covered on the first part, but on the second, I promise nothing." She gave him a bear-sized hug and wished him luck.

Like the strong warrior he was, Dimitri knew that real men depart without words. He turned to face the door and, with some mementos in hand, walked out, hearing the door close behind. If his family needed him to be strong, that's exactly what he was going to do for them. He headed down the steps and out of the building. Dimitri walked to the alleyway behind his apartment building and stood tall. "Shyra, I'm ready."

With a burst of light, Dimitri dematerialized and was transported back to the ship. As Dimitri passed the others who were relaxing in the living room quarters, he couldn't help but smile from the experience of spending time with his family. He went straight to his room to lie down and reflect.

A few days later, Shyra approached Cassie and told her it was her turn. Though going back home was bittersweet for Cassie, she was dying to see her sister Katie again. She dreaded running into her mom, however. The time spent away from that house really allowed her to clear her head. The minute she touched down the smell of the ocean breeze hit her nose, and once again, she knew she was truly home. Shyra transported her behind a surf and turf restaurant next to the beach. Her house was a few blocks away, but before walking over, she wanted to unwind by the scenic view of the beach at sunset. Cassie walked across the street to the beach and let the warm sand fill between her toes. She remembered fondly how peaceful it was lying underneath the piers while the waves crashed against the rocks. It was there she learned that she could manipulate the tide to bend to her will.

So much had happened already that it felt like she had been gone for years as the world passed her by, but in actuality, only months had elapsed. Unsure how much time Shyra was going to give her, Cassie took a mental picture of the beach and proceeded to walk home. If her sister wasn't in good health, she swore she was going to drown her mother in the kitchen sink. The thought of her defenseless sister left in her care sickened Cassandra, but it was a necessary evil for the sake of the human race.

So many memories came rushing through her mind while she walked back home. She passed a local ice cream parlor where she would often take Katie after school. On the next block was a pet store where Cassie bought her salt water fish for their tank. She thought to herself how being back for such little time could already fill her head with that much doubt, but nonetheless she trudged on.

Finally, she arrived at 133 Mulberry Grove Avenue—her house but never really a home. She looked at her old mailbox where she would sometimes wait for letters from the father she never really knew. Cassie was happy to see that there were no cars parked, so there was a good chance that her mom wasn't home. That also means that her sister was left alone to fend for herself. Cassie had never met such an irresponsible person in all her life.

She'd had the good sense to bring her old key, so she approached the door and let herself in. The house was eerily quiet, especially considering a preteen had the place to herself.

"Katie, you home?" Cassie called out.

A head carefully poked itself out from what used to be their shared bedroom. "Cassie, is that really you?"

"You expecting someone else?" she answered back.

"Oh my God! Cassie, it is you! I thought you forgot about me."

"You really thought I would leave you here? I'll always come back for you," Cassie said. "Now where's Mom?"

"I'm not sure," Katie said. "She said she was running late."

"Yeah, I bet," Cassie sarcastically responded back.

Katie looked at her with a very serious face. "She's been pretty down since you left."

The information didn't register with Cassie at all. "What are you talking about? Why was she so shocked? I'm eighteen, and she's absolutely horrid. The only reason I stayed as long as I did was for you."

Finally frustrated enough, Katelyn broke it down for her big sister. "I know that, and you know that, but since you didn't leave any contact info, I guess she's been worried about you."

Cassie didn't know how to feel about this new development. She didn't think her mom was capable of such things, but her thoughts were interrupted by Katie.

"So, what did you bring me back, or did you forget?" Katie asked.

"No, Katie, I remembered." Cassandra pulled from her pocket a small box with cryptic writing on it.

"And that is … what exactly?" Katie asked.

Cassie smiled at her baby sister. "It's something for your garden. I brought you alien plants from another world."

Katelyn's initial jaw drop turned into a smile that quite possibly may have stretched from ear to ear. "Are you freaking serious? Oh my God, that is so epic!" She leapt forward and threw her arms around her sister's neck.

"I love you, I love you, I love you. Thank you so much, Cassie!" Katie released the grip on her sister and leaned back. With eyes still gleaming, she took the box from Cassie's hand. "Wait, these aren't gonna like grow teeth and eat me, right?"

With a smirk on her face, she retorted back, "I guess that depends how much you water them." Both sisters got a good laugh after that.

"So, how much can you tell me about your new life?" Katie asked. "Are you Aphrodite, Queen of the Sea, yet?"

"No, and that's Poseidon." Cassie didn't want to worry her sister with the news that Earth may be destroyed in the upcoming year, so she tried to stay positive and generic.

"I'm pretty good with my control of water, but really it's just like joining the Peace Corps. I go to places where water is scarce, and I locate larger sources for them." It didn't feel right lying to her sister like that, but it was for her own good.

"Oh, that's cool of you to do. Here I thought you were in some kind of danger."

Cassie gave out an awkward laugh. "Me? Danger? No way."

Their talk was interrupted by the sound of a car pulling in the driveway. Cassie turned her head to the window and saw that her mom was indeed home from God knows where.

Shit, she thought to herself.

"Looks like Mom's home," Katie said.

"Yeah, looks that way," Cassie responded

"You sticking around, Cassie?"

Unsure what to do, Cassie looked back at Katie. She didn't feel like she'd had enough time with her sibling to justify ducking out the back door. Besides, it wasn't as if she were afraid of her mom, just disgusted.

"I'm staying for a little bit longer, but then I really gotta head back." Cassie heard her mom putting her house key in the lock.

Why is this moment taking so long, and what's this horrible feeling I have in my stomach? Thoughts ran through Cassie's head. The doorknob turned, and her mom walked through the doorframe. She walked past the dining room and tossed her keys on her usual spot of the kitchen counter where mail and bills seemed to be piling up. It wasn't until she turned around that she notice both her daughters sitting in the living room, and that's when she dropped her purse.

"Cassandra!"

Cassie stood up and acknowledged her mom. "Hello, Mother," she said.

Cassie's mom, Lillian, took a few steps forward across the green carpeted floor to confirm her eyes weren't playing tricks on her. "It's really you!" She sprinted forward and grabbed Cassie by both shoulders. "Where have you been? I've been worried sick!"

Cassie wanted say, *Stop this senseless façade*, but all that came out was, "I moved out."

Angered by what she perceived to be insolence, her mother began to show her true colors. "That's it? That's your explanation?"

"I didn't realize I owed you one, Mom. Last time I checked, I was a legal adult."

"Watch your mouth, Cassandra. I am still your mother, and this is still *my* house."

"Well, then it's a good thing I'm not staying long. I just stopped by to see Katie, and now that I have, I'll take my leave."

As Cassie started heading for the door, her mom firmly grabbed her by the arm. "Excuse me? I'm not done with you. You will show me the respect I deserve!"

"Right now I'm showing more respect than you deserve. You leave us here as much as you want so you can go out and do what? You think I'm dumb? All those pills you have in your bedroom were what? Prescription? Give me a break, okay?"

It was a heated battle now between the two women with no sign of cooling down.

"And you think you're just so high and mighty. Right, Cassie? Because why? You stick your nose in the books? You think they're going to teach you about the real world and what it takes to survive? Well, smartass, if that's the case, what are you doing back? What's the matter? Life got a little too real for you out there, and you came crawling back? Everything you are is because of me."

"Go to hell, Mom. Everything I am is in spite of you," Cassie snapped back. "I came back to see the only person in this house that I give a damn about, and as soon as I'm done with some personal affairs, I'm coming back for Katie and taking her with me."

Searing with rage, her mom lashed out. "The hell you are! I may not get to claim you on my taxes anymore, but I still get money for her."

"Are you serious? Is that all we are to you? A paycheck?" Cassie paused. "I really didn't think I could despise you anymore, but once again, you've proved me wrong."

Cassie's mom raised her hand high and slapped her daughter across the face with such ferocity that the strike echoed throughout the entire house. A stream of blood trickled down from Cassie's lip. Without wiping it away, Cassie raised her face and looked her mom straight in the eyes. "The first one is free, Mother. The next one will cost you." Cassie walked over to her sister and kneeled down. "I'm sorry you had to see that, Katie. I have to go now, but I swear I'll come back for you as soon as I can. Then it will just be you and me again."

Crushed that her sister was once again leaving, Katie was left speechless. Cassie wrapped her arms around her younger sister so she could lean in and whisper in her ear. "You're all I got in this world, so stay strong until I get back. Okay?" With that said, Cassie felt her sister nod her head against her shoulder. She stood up to face her mom once again.

"If anything happens to her, you'll be answering to me, Mother."

Cassie's mom immediately became instilled with fear, and Cassie walked toward the door. She slammed it shut and walked to the side of the house where she could not be seen. She planted her back to the siding of the house and proceeded to break down and cry. It wasn't easy for her to be tough in those situations, but she needed Katie to see that it's alright to stand up for yourself. She didn't at all feel right threatening her own mother, but enough was enough. Wiping away her tears with her sleeves, she looked up at the sky and was reminded of Alex's warmth and initial kindness. It's the only fond memory she'd had in so long. After that, she was finally ready to depart.

"Shyra, please get me out of here." Cassie dematerialized and vanished without a trace.

Upon her return to the ship, she was greeted by Tori. "How was it? Did you see your sister?"

"I don't want to talk about it." She walked down the hall and vanished from sight. A confused Tori couldn't help but wonder what had happened in Florida.

What's her problem? Tori asked herself. Cassie passed Shyra in the communication room of the ship, but she was looking for Alex. Cassie knew seeing his face would make her feel better.

"Excuse me, Shyra. Have you seen Alex?" she asked.

"Yes, Effervescent Rain. It was still early enough, so I just teleported him to Houston a moment ago. Is there anything I can help you with?"

"Oh, no … that's okay," Cassie said. "I'll wait till he gets back." She went to her room for the rest of the night, but after a few hours, she was visited by Shyra who knocked on her door. Cassie, who was in a deep state of depression, quickly wiped the tears from her face and responded, "Come in."

Shyra walked in and sat down beside her on the bed. "Is everything all right Cassandra?"

"Of course. Why wouldn't it be?" she tried to deny.

"Well, for starters, you appeared to be upset upon returning from home, but the greatest give away is that it is raining outside."

Cassie looked out her window in confusion. "So?" she rebutted.

"You really have not noticed that whenever you are depressed, it appears to rain?" Shyra asked.

"What does that prove? I know plenty of people who get depressed when it rains," Cassie stated.

"No, Cassandra, it rains *because you* are depressed."

Cassie could no longer keep up the front and let the tears roll down her cheeks. Outside, the torrential downpour could be heard.

"I do not know your mother well enough to cast judgment, but if I were your mother, I would be proud to call you daughter." Shyra embraced her pupil in her arms and reminded her of something she may have overlooked. "Earthling feelings are no different from Kalrynian feelings, and should you ever want to talk, I will always be here to listen."

Cassie hugged her back, and they sat together until she felt a little better.

Chapter 11

A Hero is Born

Alex was nervous to once again see the man who raised him. Since he was a child, his grandfather was the only family he knew. For some reason, the rest of his family never bothered to stay in contact. Alex had always asked why this was, but his grandfather would always tell him that they were ignorant, and people are afraid of what they don't understand. It never made much sense to him as a boy, but after awhile, he let it go.

It was 8:12 p.m. when Alex materialized at his house in Houston, still slightly smoking from the teleport. The air was humid—just how he remembered it. In the distance he heard the cicadas buzzing and saw fireflies sporadically glowing. Lines of various cars were parked on both sides of the roads, and streetlights were lit. It was all so nostalgic; underneath his bravado he truly missed his old neighborhood. He walked up to his porch steps, and the sensor lights immediately went on. Peering through the window curtain, he saw the faint glow from the living room TV, and there was the man he admired so much sitting in his reclining chair with his feet snug in his favorite slippers. Alex rang the doorbell, and much to his surprise, he heard a dog bark.

Well, that's new, he thought to himself. Alex's granddad, Henry, took a moment to look through the peephole, but it was too dark to make out the mysterious silhouette.

"Who's there?" he shouted out.

"It's me, Grandpa. It's Alex."

Henry unlocked the deadbolt and swung the door wide open. "Alex, is it really you, son? Step inside and let me see you."

Grandpa Henry took a step back to make some room for his grandson and began to well up with tears. Alex stood tall, but he looked different. He looked like he had been through a lot. In short, Alex looked like a man and his granddad could tell.

"I was afraid I'd never see you again, you back for good, Alex?" his grandfather asked.

"Not yet, Grandpa. I still have some things to do, but I wanted to check up on you," he said.

"Poppycock, boy. I'm the picture of good health. I don't need checking up on. Now come over here and have a seat so we can catch up."

With a grin on his face, Alex complied. He knew Henry was just trying to sound tough. "Okay, but do you have enough money? Are you going out to be social with other people?

"Alex, will you give it a rest? Your granddad can take care of his own. After you left, I went into retirement so I could work on my model airplane collection. The government sends me more money than I will ever need, and with my second paycheck, I went out and picked up ol' Constantine here. He's been keeping me company."

Constantine was a midsized Manchester terrier that had a gorgeous black sheen of fur and chestnut brown paws; he resembled a tiny Doberman pinscher with floppy ears. The pup was obviously very protective of his master, as he glared and snarled at Alex. The two made their way back to the living room where the old antenna TV was still humming in the background, and game shows filled the room with thunderous applause. Henry sat back down in his comfy red reclining chair, and Alex found his usual spot on their hunter green couch.

"Cute dog, Grandpa," Alex began.

"He's not cute; he's ferocious. Isn't that right, Constantine?" The pup barked at his master's command. "So, what really brings you back, son? Is everything all right where you are?"

Alex's grandfather always had the uncanny ability to see right through whatever wall of defense Alex put up. Alex sighed and decided to open up to his grandfather. "There's a lot I want to tell you, but I don't know how," he said to his mentor.

"Well that's simple, Alex. You just try."

Alex could never understand how, with just the simple spin of a few words, his granddad could make everything seem so easy.

"Well, okay. Let me start with why I left." Alex told him the whole story. He explained Kalryn, the Zenakuu, and the others with abilities. By the time he was done, it felt like the weight of the world had been lifted off his shoulders.

"That's about the gist of it, Grandpa. What do you think? As crazy as it sounds, I swear I'm telling the truth."

"I know you are, Alex," his grandpa said. "If you're one thing at all, it's honest. Still, though, it's a tall drink to swallow."

"Tell me about it … I keep thinking that I will wake up, and there will be no alien invasion, and I won't have to fight."

"I can see why, son. This does, however, explain a lot."

Bewildered, Alex looked at his grandfather. "What do you mean?"

Henry looked at his grandson, who was now the spitting image of his father. He took a deep breath before he spoke. "I think it's high time you knew what happened to your parents, Alex."

"Grandpa, what are you talking about? I know about them already—my mom died giving birth to me, and my father died in the line of duty while he served on the police force."

"Yes, but there's more to it, Alex. You're grown now, and I think it's time you knew the full story."

"Um, okay." Still confused, Alex settled himself in for what he believed would be a long story.

"Your parents loved each other tremendously, and you were the embodiment of their love. Everything that was good in them was copied into you. I tell ya, the months leading up to your birth were some of the happiest times for our entire family. Sadly, such happiness was not meant to last, though. It's all still fresh in my mind, even though it happened almost twenty years ago, a night like that I'll never be able to forget."

Henry received an urgent phone call from his son saying that there was an accident. When he asked for an explanation, the only sensible words he managed to mutter were that the two of them were coming back from dinner and there was a brilliant, blinding light that knocked Alex's mother on her back. Henry never saw the light, but the news reports say it lit up the skies of the entire country for a full forty seconds.

Apparently, the shockwave from that explosion induced labor prematurely, and they needed to rush her to the hospital to give birth to Alex. Henry flew out of his house like a bat out of hell and made it to the hospital as fast as he could. Thanks to Alex's father Aiden's quick thinking, which Henry was sure he inherited from him, he got Alex's mother to hospital with enough time to save him.

From the very beginning, there were issues. The machines kept shorting out, and Alex's mother, Madison, was losing a lot of blood. The doctors told Aiden and Henry that they couldn't save the both of them. If Madison went through with giving birth, she was going to die. A decision had to be made, but before Aiden could even speak, she demanded to go forward with the delivery. Before they even met, Madison loved Alex more than life itself, and that night she proved it. It brought everyone in that room to tears, especially Aiden, but if given the chance it was a decision Madison would make every time, a mother's love is unshakable.

Madison did get to hold Alex at least once. She was bleeding a lot, though. They could tell she was fading fast, but her smile was unmistakable. The sound of Alex crying was everything to her, and she was grateful just to meet him, even if only one time.

Her last wish was for Aiden to love Alex until it hurt and do everything in his power to give Alex the best life he possibly could. With tears in his eyes, Aiden agreed and watched his love pass on to the next plane of existence, undoubtedly with no regrets. Henry was in the waiting room when Aiden came out and told him everything that happened, he'd never seen his son so heartbroken in all his life. It crushed his spirit like it was an empty soda can. Nonetheless, Aiden had every intention of carrying out Madison's last wishes. The doctors never could explain the reason behind all the malfunctions, but at that time, what did it matter? Alex was all that was left of his loving mother, but he was alive.

Henry stayed with his son for a while at his house to help out, but there were so many mishaps surrounding Alex's early years—light bulbs exploding, electrical sockets catching on fire, power fuses burning out. It was all really bizarre, but no matter how many tests the pediatricians ran, they could not make heads or tails of what was going on. Besides all the freak accidents, Alex was a normal, bouncing baby boy. So they counted their blessings regarding his health and let things be.

A year passed with no serious accidents, but one fateful night, the unthinkable happened. Despite the two of them constantly fixing them, one of those electrical sockets ignited and caused an electrical fire to spread throughout the house like a brushfire. The damn thing must have surged to the other outlets, because before they knew it, the whole house was up in flames. Smoke was everywhere; they couldn't see two feet in front of them. The two of them ran to Alex's bedroom, but he was nowhere to be found. Alex must have somehow crawled out of his crib and instinctively searched for safety. Henry and Aiden tried to search every room, but flames spewed out of almost every doorway. The sound of wood splintering from the immense heat, and the floors crackling underneath their own weight was unforgettable.

Growing increasingly frantic, Aiden told Henry to leave, but he told him "To hell with that," there was no way he was leaving his side, and that was about the time Henry felt a right hook across his face and lost consciousness. Next thing he knew, he woke up outside on the front lawn with a bunch pigeon-necked spectators but no sign of Alex or his son. Henry tried to go back in, but those damn neighbors held him back. He screamed for the two of them, but could only watch from afar as his home was reduced to ash. Floating embers filled the night sky like fireflies, and several minutes passed before Aiden finally emerged with Alex safely tucked in his arms.

Aiden immediately collapsed and started wheezing for air. The fire department and ambulance arrived on the scene a few moments later, but by that time, the damage had been done. It seemed Alex was unharmed, but Aiden had severe burns and was having serious problems breathing. They gave Alex to Henry and rushed them all to the hospital. Henry sat right beside his son in that ambulance, praying to God that he was gonna be all right. They operated on him for hours, but he was badly burned.

Those were the longest hours of Henry's life. When that surgeon came out of the operating room, Henry rushed to him with Alex in hand. They told him they did all they could, but it didn't look good. The bastards actually told him to prepare for the worst, and if he wanted to say his good-byes, he should do it right then.

His heart sank to the bottom of his gut. It felt like his world was coming to an end all over again. He carried Alex over to his son's room so he could pay his final respects to his only son. Henry opened the door, and there he lay, bruised and burned and barely able to speak. He scorched the inside of his lungs, and the burns were too severe to move. Most of Aiden's face was bandaged so he couldn't even see them, but Henry would never forget the last time he spoke to his son.

And then Alex's grandfather recounted their final conversation:

"Hey, son, how are you holding up?"

"Is that you, Pop?"

"Yes it is. I have Alex with me. You saved him; you're a hero. How are you feeling?" He gave a gurgled laugh.

"You kidding me? I'm the picture of good health."

"That's good, Aiden. Now I want you to save your strength."

"Let's be serious, Dad. I'm pretty banged up. I don't know if I'm fista' make it this time. Everything hurts so much."

Alex's grandfather recounted how he was almost glad that his son's eyes were bandaged. He didn't want him to see his old man with tears pouring out. And then, at that moment, Alex began to cry, his grandfather remembered.

"Dad, listen. There's something I need to tell you about Alex."

"It can wait till you're better, son."

"No, Dad! I have to tell you now. Despite the flames, it was black in the house from all the smoke. I couldn't see anything … I called out to Alex dozens of times and tried to listen for his cries, but I couldn't find him. The only reason I finally saw him is because I saw that same kind of bright light from the night he was born shining through the cracks of the utility closet. I ran over, and when I opened it, I saw my son crying and glowing like the moon itself.

I didn't know how to make sense of it. For a moment, I thought my own son was a freak or a monster. It was in that very moment it all made sense—the inexplicable birth when the machines went haywire, and his mom died. It was all because of him. I'm ashamed to say that for a moment I resented him. I blamed him for his mother's death, but then I remembered my promise to love him unconditionally no matter what. That's when I picked him up and ran out of the house."

Henry looked intensely at his son and then at Alex. Alex was still crying but stopped for a moment and stared back. Henry thought for sure that his son was delusional.

"Son, you must have been seeing things. There's no way that can be right."

"No, Dad, it is. Alex is special. I was wrong about one thing, though—he's no monster. He's my son, and I'm sorry I ever doubted him. Forgive me, Alex."

The bandages covering Aiden's eyes finally became saturated, allowing his tears to flow down.

"You can tell him you're sorry when he's older," Henry told his son. "You're gonna be just fine. Okay?"

"Not this time, Dad ... Promise me you'll take care of him. He's all that matters now."

As Henry finished recounting the conversation, he turned back to Alex and continued, "That's when I faced reality, Alex. Your father was going to die soon, and he left his most valuable treasure to me. I grabbed his hand and told him that he had my word that I would meet death before I let any harm come to you. He smiled and thanked me. He then gripped my hand and told me he loved me. Almost instantaneously after he finished that final word, the grip around my hand loosened and he passed away on that hospital bed. You were too young to understand, but I mourned your father's death for years. I suppose that's why I was always so hard on you. I wanted to protect you. It was your parents' final wish."

Alex had a steady stream of tears rolling down his cheeks. He'd never heard the real story before, but it wasn't at all what he expected.

"Your parents were as honest as the day is long, and they loved you unconditionally."

"Both my parents gave up their lives so I could live."

"Yes, son, they did. So you have to promise me never to squander that gift. Be careful out there. You're truly all I have left of them."

"So the reason none of my relatives visit," Alex began, finally putting the pieces together.

"Those superstitious fools think you're bad luck. Frankly, I'm glad they weren't around so you weren't infected by their ignorance."

"I see," Alex said with a disheartened look on his face.

"Don't worry about them, son. You were meant for great things. I understand that now. Now go make your parents proud and carry their love with you wherever you go."

Alex cleared his face and stood up. "Thank you, Grandpa. I promise I will."

Henry slowly stood up as well. "Good. Now let me at least walk you out." Henry led Alex to the front door and opened it for him. He placed his palm on Alex's left cheek. "Now don't you worry about your granddad. I've got Constantine to look after me. You just be the hero you were meant to be."

Alex proudly nodded. "Count on it, Grandpa Henry."

Alex walked out the door and down the steps. He turned around to get one more look at the man who raised him to be a hero.

Henry smiled at his grandson. "Don't be a stranger, son. I'm always here for you." Constantine followed his farewell with an audible bark, and Alex just returned the smile right back at him.

Without a doubt, I'll make you all proud, Alex thought to himself. "Shyra, I'm ready to come back," he finally said aloud. Alex waved good-bye and dematerialized right before his grandfather's eyes.

Henry chuckled. "Crazy kid. I know he'll go far. He's got the blood of heroes."

Alex arrived back on the ship later that evening and was welcomed back by Christian. "How did it go, bro?"

The two had become like two peas in a pod, and Chris was happy to see his friend.

"I learned a lot," Alex said.

"That's cool. Cassie's been looking for you."

"Why?" Alex asked.

"I don't know, man. I still have to get my stuff together for my trip back," Chris said. "Ask her."

"Well, where is she?"

"I think I saw her out back."

Alex ventured through the ship until he finally found Cassie. She was still alone and was staring out the window in a vacant room.

"Cassie, I heard you were looking for me," Alex said.

"Alex … it's nothing really. How was your trip?" she asked.

"It was good. How was yours?"

"It went pretty much how I expected," Cassie said.

"I'm sorry to hear that. I'm glad you're back, though."

"Really?" Cassie credulously said as smiled and began to blush.

"Well, I mean … it's just that …" Alex immediately looked to the ground and desperately tried to make sense of his words, but he awkwardly stuttered instead.

Dimitri, who was passing by, added a verbal jab. "Get a room already, you two."

Alex and Cassie immediately stood up straight.

"Well, I should probably get going," Alex said.

"Yeah, I've got some training to do, so we'll talk later," Cassie responded.

"Right, sounds good." Alex finished, and they uncouthly walked away.

Smooth, Alex, real smooth, he thought to himself.

Chapter 12

Something That Burns Twice as Bright Shines Half as Long

Two days later it was finally Christian's turn to go home and see his family, and he could hardly contain himself. He really wanted to show his father how much he'd grown in the past year.

Christian approached Shyra, who was waiting for him in the teleportation room. "I'm ready, Shyra," he announced. "Send me to New Jersey."

"As you wish, Irascible Flame." Within seconds, he was gone and once again standing in his home state.

Chris was kind of nervous to go back home. He had gone over the story of his fake training in boot camp what felt like hundreds of times. To be fair, the only thing fake about the story was that the training he was receiving was not for the United States government. Nonetheless, he was a horrible liar and feared his parents would see straight through the story. He was teleported about one block away from his house. He took a moment to take a deep breath. *Dammit. Why is my stomach in knots?* He thought to himself.

Around the next corner he saw two familiar cars parked in his driveway and wondered if his parents would be able to see the difference in his new look. Christian had trained so hard and was no longer the pudgy, nerdy kid who left New Jersey. He was in shape and more confident than ever. More than anyone, he knew his father would be proud of the transformation. The grass in his front lawn was as brown as ever, but it had acquired some new dead spots.

Chris approached the doorstep and remembered that he'd brought along his old key. It was the moment of truth. The metal screen door creaked as he pulled it open and held the doorknob tight. He took one more deep breath and walked inside.

"Everyone, I'm back." It was eerily quiet in the house—way more quiet than usual. It was early afternoon, so Christian understood that his little brother and sister would be in school, but where were his mom and older brother?

"Anyone home?" Still no immediate answer. *What the hell is going on?* He thought to himself. Finally frustrated enough, he shouted out, "Mom!"

Just then, a head popped out from around from the kitchen entrance. "Christian, is that you, hijo?"

Relieved his house wasn't completely empty, Christian's spirits began to lift. "Yes, Mom, I'm back. Where is everybody?"

His mother wiped off her hands from the dinner she was preparing to give her son a hug and kiss. "My God, Christian, where have you been? We've been trying to reach you for months now."

"I've been at the boot camp, Mom. You know that."

"Yes, but we were trying to reach you, Chris. All of our letters came back to us with 'return to sender' stamped on them."

Christian grew increasingly nervous over the thought of being interrogated by his mother and looked to end the inquisition with a quick retort. "Look, Mom, you must have written down the address wrong or something. Now where is everyone else?"

His mom cracked a faint smile. “Well, hijo, your little brother and sister are at school, and Pietro picked up another job to help out around here.”

Christian looked confused. “Another job? Not that I care, but what about his football career?”

“Well, he hasn’t given up on it, but he wanted to support the family more so he’s taking a break.”

That was when it finally hit him—why would his brother have to quit football to help the family? “Mom, where’s Dad?” Christian finally asked.

The sorry excuse for a smile his mother had on her face completely diminished. “Baby, you should sit down. There’s something I need to tell you.”

A disheartened Christian took a seat on the couch. “Mom, what’s going on? Where’s Dad?”

Christian’s mom, Gabriella, took a deep breath and with a somber face, gave the doleful news. “Baby, your father passed away.”

“What! What are you talking about?”

“It happened a few months ago. He came down with a fever and started getting these stiff neck pains. We brought him to a doctor, but they couldn’t figure out what the problem was. Then his symptoms got worse. Within a week, he started throwing up a lot and couldn’t handle the sight of bright lights. We brought him to the hospital where they gave him antibiotics, but his condition only worsened. By the time the doctors figured out what was wrong with him, it was too late. His body didn’t take to the medicine, and he was pronounced dead in the hospital hours later.”

Christian’s eyes welted up with oncoming tears. “No! It’s not true, it can’t be true!” he yelled. “Dad was too strong for that. There’s no way he would die.” It was pretty clear to his mom that he was in denial.

“Sweetheart, listen, your father was a prideful man. He didn’t tell any of us he was sick until there wasn’t much we could do, because he didn’t want to be a burden.”

A waterfall of tears flowed down his face. "Why? Why didn't anyone tell me about this?"

"Sweetheart, we tried to find you, but no matter who we contacted, they had no record of you. Christian, tell me what's going on. Where were you really?"

Riddled with raw emotion, Christian couldn't keep track of the web of lies he and Dimitri had spun. "Mom, for the last time, I was in boot camp training. Okay? They selected me to be part of a special team. It's top secret, and I'm not allowed to talk about. That's not important right now. What did dad die of?"

Christian's mother looked at him. She understood this was coming as quite a blow to him and thought this was not the best time to pry information out of him. "He died of a condition called bacterial meningitis."

Christian was angry and confused over the news. "What? I've never even heard of that!"

In that moment, Gabriella witnessed her son's heart break right in front of her. The sight of it made the tiny amount of closure she had acquired in these past months vanish.

"It's an illness that took my love away from me," she said. Christian's mom buried her face deep in her hands. She lost the strength to not cry. Those past months had been so hard for her, and Christian was nowhere to be found. He felt disgusted by his own selfish actions. How could he have forsaken his own family in their greatest time of need?

"Mom, I … I'm so sorry."

"Chris, why did he have to leave me all alone like this?" At this point, she was an emotional wreck, and try as he might, the only thing Christian could do to console his grieving mother was to hold her tightly. His whole world was just flipped upside down, but he would have to figure out his feelings later.

"It's gonna be okay, Mom. I'm back now, and I'll help out." The words felt bitter coming out of his mouth, but if it came down to saving the world or saving his family, Christian would pick his family every time. His mother revealed her face again to wipe the tears from her eyes and clean her nose.

"What are you saying, hijo? I thought you were in some special training for the government."

"To hell with them," Christian snapped. "I'm needed here."

"I didn't raise you to be a quitter, and besides, you'll be court-martialed."

"I don't care, Mom. There's no way I'm leaving you guys again."

"Then you're a prideful fool just like he was!" Her sorrow was being masked by aggravation.

Chris was taken aback by her response. "Mom, what are you talking about?"

"We're not as helpless as you may think, alright? It's not your job to watch over this family. It's mine now. Your father was too stubborn to ever admit he needed help, and I won't have that same trait develop inside of you. You have to grow up."

"I'm sorry, Mom, but I've made up my mind. I'm staying," he insisted.

"Christian, do you know one of the things your father told me before he died?"

"No, what?"

"He told me how sorry he was for not being able to see all of you grow up into proud men and women. He also told me how much he loved all of us and especially how proud he was of you. For whatever reason, your father always saw the most of himself in you. Your older brother may be big and strong like he was, but you inherited his will and passion. I know how proud he was of you, because he smiled as he said your name. If there's one thing I'm certain of, it's that he would not want you to quit just because things got tough."

Christian broke down again and jumped into his mom's arms. "Mom, how am I gonna do this without him?" he asked.

"You don't have to, Chris. His greatest qualities were his inner strength and love, and he left those things to you."

For the next several minutes, Christian mourned the loss of his father by crying into his mother's shoulder while she lovingly embraced him.

"It's okay, Christian. There's nada to be sad about. This family will always be okay as long as we're together. Now clean your face off. Your little brother and sister will be coming off the school bus any minute now, and I'm sure you don't want to see them for the first time all sad.

Christian nodded his head and went to stand up. He could see that his mom had been crying too. This was all happening so fast for him. One minute he was going to be an intergalactic superhero like his favorite comic books, and the next minute he'd lost his one and only actual role model. He wiped his nose on his sleeve and headed toward the bathroom.

Before entering, he turned around and faced his mother. "Where is he buried?"

"What, baby?

"Dad. Where is he buried?" Christian asked again.

"We buried him at St. Peters," his mother answered.

"I see." He turned back around and went into the bathroom. He closed the door behind him and took one good, long look in the mirror. He wondered how in the heck all of this could be happening to him and how maybe if he was around he could have saved his father. It was a dangerous spiral of doubt and guilt. He grew to despise the image in the mirror that stood before him.

"You're weak, Christian. You've always been weak," he said to his reflection. "How can you save the world if you can't even save your own father?" He slammed his fist against the sink and for a few moments stood there wallowing in his own self-hatred. As he raised his hand to punch the mirror after not being able to stomach the sight of himself, he was interrupted by the sound of the front door opening. His younger siblings had come home, and it was time to pull himself together.

He could hear his mom through the door. "Guess who's home," she said to her youngest children.

"Who?" Carlos asked.

Christian took that as his cue and exited the bathroom to greet his little brother and sister.

"Christian!" Mary shouted out. The two kids ran over to him and jumped into his arms, simultaneously knocking him down in the process.

"When did you get back?" his sister asked.

"Just now," Christian answered. "I've been catching up with Mom while you guys were at school."

"Yeah, Dad passed away, but he left me a ton of cool stuff to remember him by."

It was funny to him how children tended to take things a lot better than adults. They knew life went on, and tomorrow was still something to look forward to.

Their mom cut in. "That reminds me, Christian. Your father left something for you too."

"Really? What was it, Mom?"

She smiled at him. "It's upstairs. I'll go and get it." She exited the room and left Christian alone with his brother and sister. "How are you guys holding up?" he questioned.

"Um, we're okay. It was hard at first, but we're being strong for Mom," Carlos said.

Christian looked back at them and responded, "That's good."

"Yeah. Besides, Pietro is home more, and he helps us with our homework now," Mary added.

As sad as Christian was over the death of his father, he was happy to be back with his family. After a short time, his mom came down the steps with a small box.

"Here, Christian. This belonged to your father, and he wanted you to have it." She handed him a small, blue velvet box, and he eagerly opened it. Inside he found his father's cross that he'd worn around his neck for as long as Christian could remember. Christian looked back up at his mom. "This is another piece of him that you can carry with you," she said.

Christian stepped forward and once again threw his arms around his mom. "Gracias, Mamá."

"De nada, hijo." For the first time during his visit, Christian smiled. His sorrow, if only for a moment, was replaced by a new sense of purpose. He would let his father's will burn brightly inside of him. Christian knew what he had to do—train harder and make his father proud as he watched from above.

"Mom, I have to go. My bus is going to leave soon, and I have one more place I need to go."

"Okay, hijo. You come back to visit whenever you want, and be sure to call or write. You understand?

"Sí, Mamá." Christian leaned down to give his little brother Carlos and sister Mary a warm embrace. "You guys be good, okay? Don't give Mom any trouble."

"We won't," Carlos, who seemed to be the spokesperson for the duo, responded.

"I love you, Mom, and I promise I'll be back the moment I can."

"We're fine, Christian, and I love you too. Now hurry before you miss your bus."

Christian walked backward a few steps to take some mental photos of his beloved family. It was a shame he couldn't see his older brother, but he knew he was working hard to keep the family together and that was enough for him. He faced the door and begrudgingly walked out. Once outside, Christian let out a huge sigh. There was still a lot of hurt dwelling inside of him, but before he could sort out his feelings, there was one thing he had to do.

Christian ducked behind a corner and contacted Shyra telepathically. "Shyra?"

"Yes, Christian, I am here," she responded.

"Before I come back, there's somewhere I need to go. I need you to send me to my father's grave. I have to say good-bye."

"Certainly, Christian," she agreed. "What is the address?"

"To be honest, I'm not sure."

"It is all right, Christian. Leave it to me. What was his name?"

"Isaac Mercado Jr."

"Understood. Doing a search for Isaac Mercado of Perth Amboy, New Jersey." After only a moment, Shyra had a listing for several Isaac Mercado and narrowed it down to one buried in St. Peter's Church Cemetery.

"Christian, I have the coordinates locked to Latitude: 40.503684, Longitude: -74.265491. Are you ready?"

"Yes, Shyra"

Christian was teleported to St. Peter's Cemetery an instant later. He was always a little superstitious as a child, and cemeteries definitely gave him the creeps. Regardless, he trudged through the hardly recognizable pathways that were nearly covered with unkempt grass. Luckily for him, it didn't take too long before he was standing before his father's tombstone. It was so surreal to him. It felt like only yesterday that he stayed up late to watch his favorite cheesy horror films with his dad, and now he was gone forever.

Christian kneeled down in front of the grave and placed his hand on the tombstone. He read out loud the words engraved on the front side of it: "Here lies Isaac Mercado Jr. Good-bye to a wonderful husband and father. He lived a long and wonderful life and was loved by all who knew him. He will be dearly missed but will live on in our hearts forevermore."

"I miss you, Dad. I don't know why, but I always thought you'd be in my corner to root me on. To be honest, I don't know if I can do this without you."

"That doesn't sound like the mind-set of a proud Mercado male to me." The voice came out of nowhere and spooked the life out of Christian.

"Dad, is that you?"

"No, you idiot. Turn around."

Christian quickly did a one-eighty, and there standing before him was his older brother Pietro. "Pietro, what are you doing here?"

"I left work for my lunch break, and after Mom told me you stopped by, it wasn't hard to figure out where you would go."

"It's just that … I can't believe he's really gone," Christian told his brother.

"Yeah, he was definitely a stubborn guy. There were times I thought he'd outlive us." The two brothers chuckled together, and it was nostalgic of better times.

"Pietro … I could come back—you know, to help out with the bills."

"Don't worry about things here. I've got things under control. Okay? It's my turn to look after this family," Pietro reassured him. "It's how Dad would want things to be."

"But what about football?"

"I'm not giving up my dreams, and neither are you. I don't know what you've gotten yourself into at that base, but whatever it is, it seems important. Follow through with it, bro."

Christian gave his older brother a nod, and there was silence as they reminisced of their late father.

"Hey, remember that time Dad brought us to Tia Rayna's house so we could play on her trampoline, and you jumped too high and fell off?" Pietro laughed over the poignant memory.

"How could I forget? I sprained my ankle and was using crutches for weeks."

"Man, Dad was so pissed at me for not watching you. He made me hold my arms out straight for like twenty minutes and threatened to beat me if I let them drop." Once again, the two took a break from reality to share some laughter.

"You were always his favorite. You know that, right Christian?" Pietro said.

"What? Are you on drugs? Clearly, you were his pride and joy—the eldest son who looked just like a younger version of him and was a star athlete. The house is covered with your constant accomplishments," Christian pointed out.

"Maybe, but he adored you. He would always tell me how you were gonna do great things in life and how I should look after you."

"He hardly ever said that kinda stuff to me."

"I'm sure he didn't want to inflate your head too much, but trust me—he saw things in you that to this day I will never understand."

"Thanks, Pietro," Christian smiled.

"Yeah, yeah, whatever," Pietro replied. "Now hurry up and finish what you have to say to Dad. I'll drop you off at the bus stop before I go back to work."

Christian turned toward his father grave and spoke his final words to his beloved father. "I'm sorry I wasn't there when you needed me, Dad. I want you to know I'm not gonna stop fighting. I'll continue to be the man you raised me to be. I'll miss you a lot, but I'll carry you with me wherever I go. I love you, Pop."

Christian stopped for a minute to pray but was interrupted by Pietro. "This is all very touching, but I'm gonna need you to take off your Sunday dress so we can get back."

"Shut up, Pietro."

Christian's older brother smiled and put Christian in a playful headlock. The ironic thing was that Christian was stronger and far more powerful than his brother but chose not to ruin the moment. They walked out of the cemetery together and got into Pietro's car. On the way to the bus stop, Christian let his head rest on the passenger side widow and gazed out toward the setting sun. He couldn't help but think there was more he could have done. His family wouldn't condone him blaming the death of his father on himself, but for God's sake, he was supposed to be a superhero. When he got back to the base, he knew he would have to do some deep meditating—anything to clear his mind and make any kind of peace with his dad's untimely demise. Perhaps that's why he didn't hear his brother shouting at him.

"Pukeface!"

"Huh? What?" Christian finally responded.

"We're here, man," Pietro repeated.

"Here where?"

"Are you serious, bro? What's up with you? We're at the bus stop. Remember?"

"Oh right, of course. I knew that."

"Whatever, man. Listen, take care of yourself, okay? I can't watch the family and you at the same time."

"You got it, Pietro. I'll be fine, and I'll come back as soon as I can," Christian assured his brother.

"Please, not too soon. It's nice not having to look at your ugly mug every day."

The two brothers exchanged one last smile, and Christian stepped out of the car. He waved his brother good-bye and looked for a secluded area to speak with Shyra. He ducked behind a vacant truck and contacted her once more. "Shyra, I'm ready. Please bring me back."

For the fourth time in one day, Chris was dematerialized. Christian arrived at the ship's doorstep where Shyra and the others seemed to be having an important meeting about what was to come. He didn't want to tell the team what was going on with him, because the last thing he needed or wanted was pity.

"Welcome back, Irascible Flame," Shyra said. "You are just in time to hear this."

"Why? What's going on? Chris asked.

"It seems we're gonna get our chance to fight the Zenakuu earlier than expected," Alex said.

CHAPTER 13

Memento Mori

"WHAT ARE YOU TALKING about?" Christian said.

"Voltaic Cloud is right, I am afraid," Shyra confirmed. "Everyone join me in the control room." The alliance proceeded to follow their mentor to the control room where they were forbidden to enter unless instructed. The doors sprang open, and before them sat the most advanced technology their eyes had ever seen. The team walked in farther, trying not to let their curiosity get the best of them by touching anything or pressing buttons.

Shyra once again spoke. "If I could have your attention at the main monitor."

Everyone looked up and saw what appeared to be a map of deep space.

Cassie finally asked, "What are we supposed to be seeing here?"

Shyra hit a few buttons on the keyboard, and the image magnified. "Right there," she pointed.

"That meteorite?" Dimitri asked.

"Not quite, Seismic Earth. That is no meteorite. That is a Zenakuu scouting ship that will be here shortly. That is the reason you all were given the chance to see your families again. Soon you will be heading into battle."

"What! No, that's not enough time. We need to train more," Christian said in a panic.

"Calm down, Chris," Cassie said.

"Thank you, Effervescent Rain," Shyra said. "She is right, Irascible Flame. You already have all the training you will need, but do not despair. There are still a couple of months left before they arrive, so we shall concentrate on teamwork. When you are out there, you need to fight as a unit, so we will focus on creating powerful combinations to use in battle. They will not use restraint because you are young. The first chance they get, they will kill you."

Alex stood there, silently weighing out the heaviness of what Shyra had just said. The moment they had been preparing for was finally at hand. This would be the true test of his merit.

"If I didn't know better, I would say it sounds like you're scared, Chris," Dimitri said mockingly.

Still angry over everything that had happened at home Christian lashed out. "You wanna say that to my face, D?"

"That's Earth to the likes of you, punk."

"Knock it off the both of you. This is serious," Alex intervened. "Shyra, exactly how much time do we have?"

"By my calculations, we have approximately fifty-eight Earth days before they arrive."

"That's not much time," he said.

"In these remaining weeks, I want all of you to work together and work in groups that will complement each other's powers. Think carefully about the nature of your abilities. Wind will spread fire, water is an excellent conductor of electricity, earth and water will create landslides, while wind and water create ice—the possibilities are truly limitless."

The next day the five of them woke up at the crack of dawn to practice fighting in unison. Wind, who was still visibly tired, was the first to speak.

"I can't believe you really had us wake up this early, Alex."

"Yeah, well when you survive the alien race that's coming in the next few weeks to wipe out our planet, you can thank me then."

"Whatever," she replied and cuddled up next to Rain for warmth, as the morning sun had not fully risen.

Shyra was already waiting for the group outside. "Good morning, class," she began. "Today we are going to work in teams and master combinations, it is also important you get used to fighting with the protective gear of your uniforms. Voltaic Cloud, partner up with Irascible Flame, and Whisking Wind, you partner with Effervescent Rain. Seismic Earth, there are some techniques I want to show you."

The duos paired off and got some space between them so they could really let loose. Cloud and Flame worked on their aim with some target practice, and after some rounds, they soon came to realize that Cloud had terrible aim.

"Damn, I suck at this," Cloud said, frustrated. "How are you so good?"

"I used to play with a lot of BB guns. You just have to concentrate, take a deep breath, and then aim."

"That's what I'm doing, and it's not working."

"Well, it comes with practice, bro. It's not like you're gonna become a sniper in one afternoon."

"I guess," Cloud conceded. "Let's try the combinations Shyra was talking about. Try to match the electric current I shoot with your fire."

"Okay," Flame agreed. "Hold the blast as long as you can."

For the next few hours, Cloud and Flame did their best to combine energy beams until they mastered the fundamentals of it. The combined blast had incredible destructive force and would prove to be very useful in actual combat.

On the other side, Rain and Wind came up with more creative ways to utilize their powers.

"Okay, you can control water in the clouds, right?" Wind asked.

"Well, it takes me a bit, but yeah, I can gather water in clouds in large amounts, but I can't control its temperature," Rain said.

"Alright, let's do that thing Shyra said where we create ice or something."

"You mean a snowstorm?" Rain asked.

"Yeah, that."

"It's worth a shot. Here goes." Rain closed her eyes, raised her hands in the air, and began to concentrate. At first, it was nothing but a light drizzle, Wind felt a tiny, cold raindrop splash on her cheek. After a minute or so, the rain really started to come down. On signal, Wind controlled the freezing air, and flurries of snow descended upon them.

"Rain, I'm ready. Give me everything you got!" Wind shouted.

Effervescent Rain nodded and got serious. She let out one powerful shout and didn't hold anything back. The rain from the clouds came down in an ireful downpour. At first, it was more than Whisking Wind could handle, but she learned to match the intensity of her friend and let out subzero winds that turned the area into a tempest blizzard. The girls stood their ground but were almost blown away by their own tremendous power. Everything within a thirty-five-yard radius was immediately frozen over. Satisfied with the results, the two girls stopped their display of strength to rest.

"That's really tiring," confessed Wind.

A little out of breath, Rain agreed. "We should use that only if we have to."

"True, I'm beat. Wanna go inside for a minute?" Wind asked. "It's freezing out here."

"Definitely." Rain complied with her friend's request, and the two headed to the ship to get warm.

Elsewhere, Shyra was having a sparring match with Seismic Earth. She rushed in with a few sidesteps to throw Earth off, bouncing from side to side, so he could hardly keep up with her. Shyra got within inches of Earth, but as he threw a quick left hook, his punches connected with nothing but air. Shyra jumped in the air to flip over Earth, and in the confusion that followed, she performed a leg sweep before he could get his bearings back. Earth fell to the ground hard. Shyra was getting ready to finish the match off with an axe kick, but Earth slammed his fist on the ground, creating a tremor powerful enough to send Shyra flying back. The esper got up and started to charge at Shyra. He sent formidable-sized clots of dirt hurtling in her direction, but she deflected each one with ease.

"Seismic Earth, you are stronger than this," Shyra said. "Show me." Shyra reached out to Earth telekinetically and pulled him closer to her. She cocked back her fist, but seeing the impending doom, Earth raised a wall of stone between the two of them that Shyra punched through easily enough. Rocks exploded outward, and a plume of dust covered the battlefield. He inhaled the cloud of dirt and almost coughed his lungs out. Even so, the wall gave Earth enough time to recover his footing. He summoned two adjacent walls of stone to smash into Shyra, but instinctively, she brought up her arms to simultaneously push them away with her telekinetic powers. That was the moment Earth had waited for. He sped in and sucker punched Shyra with a force so strong she slammed into the tree behind her causing the leaves to gently sway to the ground. As the navy blue blood trickled down her lip, she smiled. "Good," she said. "The warm-up is over."

Shyra sprang up, dusted off her pants, and walked over toward Seismic Earth. She got into her fighting stance and motioned for Earth to attack her. He bawled out a roar as he dashed in, but Shyra showed no sign of fear. Earth raised his hands, and stones came flying at them, encasing his hands like literal rock-hard punching gloves. He furiously swung at Shyra, putting all the martial arts training he'd received to use. Jabs, hooks, crosses, elbows, kicks, and knees all came speeding toward Shyra's face and abdomen, but she dodged, blocked, and parried every last one. The difference in fighting experience couldn't have been more apparent, which only led to greater frustration on Earth's part. Shyra's kinetic energy welled up inside of her, and she sought to put an end to the melee attacks by telekinetically lifting Earth up and slamming him into the cold, hard ground.

"You need to be able to block telekinetic attacks, Earth," Shyra reminded him. "The ability is very common, and you must know how to repel it. Concentrate and surround yourself with your own kinetic energy—use it as a barrier. Now get up; we will try again."

Earth struggled to get up. That last slam to the ground knocked the wind out of him, but he was far too prideful so stay down for long. He made his way to his feet and got into a horse stance with his arms crossed against his chest before telling Shyra he was ready. Same as before, she lifted him with her kinetic powers, but this time, she pushed him six feet back to the dirt as if he were some discarded puppet. This process went on for the next forty minutes until Earth got the basics of surrounding himself with his own kinetic power to repel telekinetic attacks.

The team trained for the rest of the afternoon before they called it a day and went back in to rest.

"We will pick up tomorrow where we left off. Good work today, everyone," Shyra said before she returned to her quarters.

Tori and Cassie went to ease their sore muscles in the sauna. They reminded Chris that if he tried to peek inside again, they would literally drown him in a pool of his own tears. He cringed at the thought of the torture that might ensue. As the two girls walked off, the guys decided to have a group discussion of their own.

"In a few weeks, we're actually gonna have to fight aliens," said Alex.

"You think it's going to be to the death?" Chris asked.

"Well, Chris, I don't think they've come all that way just to talk," Dimitri replied in a snarky tone.

"Okay, but that doesn't mean we have to kill each other. Right?"

"Wake up, man," Dimitri continued. "We're not kids anymore. These guys are coming to kill us and everyone we love, and I, for one, have no intention of letting them do it."

"Unfortunately, Dimitri is right," Alex chimed in. "These guys aren't gonna show any restraint if they fight us. We have to be prepared for anything."

"Yeah, so try not to slow me down, *Voltaic Cloud*," Dimitri jabbed.

"That should be my line to you, *Seismic Earth*." Alex said to keep up with the bravado, but deep down he was horrified. He didn't want to die yet, and he didn't want anyone else to die either—but he saw what kind of brutality the Zenakuu were capable of from Shyra's memories and doubted if he'd ever feel truly confident enough to take them on.

"Let's be serious, guys," Christian said. "If anyone is going to shine in combat, it's going to be me. Then maybe Tori will finally recognize me."

"Get your head out of your ass, Christian," Dimitri said. "Both you and she could possibly die in a couple weeks."

"I won't allow that to happen. No one dies under my watch!" Alex snapped back.

"Relax, oh fearless leader," Dimitri responded. "I'm just trying to scare the kid straight."

"Well it didn't work. I've been training my ass off for months now. I'm stronger than I've ever been and so ready for this," Christian added.

"No matter what, we stick together. We'll be fine as long as we stick together," Alex reminded them.

The three friends gave each other concerned looks and wondered if these really might be their last couple of weeks alive. Each pondered the limit of his own mortality, but the one thought that could not be silenced was why they were all fighting and whom they were fighting for. Whether it be for family, pride, love, or revenge, Alex, Christian, and Dimitri had a resolve to see it through that could not be shaken. The three of them went over battle strategies, while elsewhere in the sauna Cassie and Tori discussed the boys.

"So how is it going with you and Alex?" asked Tori.

"You mean lack thereof," Cassie responded. "As much as I don't want to admit it, he's really starting to invade my thoughts. He's strong, confident, and such a sweet guy, but being the team leader, I don't think he sees me like that."

"Yeah, Alex could definitely lay off the leader role and try to relax, but don't blame him too much. I'm sure he just worries about all of us."

"I know," Cassie said. "That's kinda why I don't want to push it any further. We've had some romantically awkward moments where we lock eyes for an instant, and I could swear he's about to say something. But then it's like he gets nervous and looks away. Honestly, it's kind of cute how bad he is at this."

"It's a shame conventional methods of seduction won't work on him, but don't worry. He'll come around," Tori said, grinned at Cassie, which instantly made her blush.

"Anyway … what about you and Dimitri?"

"Oh my God, that boy is hot. Mmm, nothing like my last lame-ass boyfriend," Tori revealed. They both laughed.

"Tori, you really are a mess sometimes."

"What? I can't help it. He has muscles in places I didn't know you could have muscles," she continued.

"Definitely," Cassie agreed. "All the guys have really been working out."

"Still, though, I can't get him to notice me either. Why is it that we're up here in the mountains with the only cute boys on Earth who are more concerned with fighting aliens than cozying up with girls?" Tori asked.

"Well, that's not the case with all the boys. I see the way Christian looks at you."

"Eww, no thanks. He's not my type."

"You mean he's not the bad boy like Dimitri," Cassie added.

"What can I say? He's got edge—besides, you always want what you can't have, and there's nothing like the thrill of the chase."

Cassie laughed at her answer. "I suppose you're right. You know, Tori, I'm really glad we became friends."

"Me too, Cass. I'll watch your back out there if you watch mine."

"Deal," Cassie complied and stood up, "I'm going to bed. I'll see you in the morning."

"Yeah, me too. Besides you just gave me a great idea," Tori said in a stroke of ill-gotten genius. *D will definitely notice me more if I seduce him.*

The two girls didn't stay up for too much longer before hitting the hay. They knew they had a big day ahead of them and wanted to get some rest.

Chapter 14

The More Things Change, the More They Stay the Same

The team had been training and working hard to prepare themselves for the inevitable fight. In the midst of everything they were learning, the group nearly forgot it was almost Christmastime. Cassie strolled by Chris's room and saw him lying down on his bed staring at the ceiling.

She faintly knocked on the door frame twice. "Can I come in?" she asked.

"Yeah," he sniffled. "Sure, what's up, Cass?"

"Nothing. You seemed pretty upset when you came back from seeing your family."

"Nah, I'm fine," Chris said. "I just miss them."

"You have been locked up in your room for a couple days. You can talk to me," Cassie assured him.

Christian's eyes strained, and a teardrop fell and splashed on the metallic floor of his room. He didn't want anyone to see him cry. Cassie closed the door and moved closer to him to comfort him.

"What's wrong?" Cassie asked again.

The knot in Christian's stomach grew larger and larger the more he thought about it. His throat swelled up, signifying to him that he was going to burst into tears. When he couldn't hold back anymore, Christian opened up. "It's my dad," he finally said. His eyes were soaked, and his cheeks turned red. "He died, and I wasn't there for him. I couldn't even say good-bye. I bet he thought the worst of me. He's about to die, and his son couldn't even be there for him. My whole family looked at me with disgust." The tears never stopped.

"Oh, Christian, I had no idea," Cassie said. "They're not disgusted, though. You told me how proud your dad was when he heard you signed up for the military."

"The last thing I ever said to my dad was a lie. How can I live with that?"

"You didn't lie to him. This is the closest thing to—if not more important than—the military. It's the army of Shyra."

That brought a smile to Christian's face.

"That's better," Cassie said. "Your family loves you, your father loved you, and we love you too. You should honor your father's memory by defending this planet with the people who you love and who love you."

"You're right, Cassie," he agreed. "It's just so hard. I can never see him again. I missed my last chance."

"Then you should make it your goal to save the rest of the world, so you can keep seeing the rest of your family."

"That's true. I have to get stronger. I want to get to a point where I can take on the whole Zenakuu planet by myself."

"Hold on there, cowboy," Cassie said. "You don't have to. You have four close friends to share the burden."

The two exchanged a big, elongated hug. Cassie got up to walk out of the room but not before she looked over her shoulder and added, "If you need someone to talk to, don't hesitate to come to me. I'm here for you, ya know?"

"Thanks, Cass. Don't tell the others though okay?"

"Mum's the word." She gave a wink and proceeded to exit his room.

Alex was headed toward Shyra's room when he was cut off by Cassie.

"Hey, Alex," she called out. "We really need to convince Shyra to let us go home for Christmas. I just talked with Chris, and he is really upset. We all need this. And besides, it's the middle of winter. What else can we do?"

"I was just headed there now to talk with her. I'll run it past her," Alex said. "And what's wrong with Chris?"

"I can't say. It's not my place," Cassie answered.

"I understand. I will try and talk with him after I see Shyra." Alex continued on his path. For some reason, he was nervous. He hadn't had many personal discussions with Shyra. It had all been talk of the war. The walk felt like a mile long with everything that was racing through his mind. He thought about when they first met Tori and how Shyra let them enjoy the Californian coast, even though it was rather brief. What would Alex say to the rest of them if Shyra said no to something as important as Christmas? No one had left the base since they'd all gone home in that one-week period. Alex approached the door and had no clue what to expect. He knocked three clear times.

"Come in, Alexander," Shyra called. Alex put on a fake smile and opened the door. "I know you have something on your mind you want to ask," Shyra said.

"Well, we have been working hard with training and have had little time for any kind of normality."

"Go on," she said.

"Okay, the thing is its mid-December now, and we wanted to know if we could go home for Christmas."

"Christmas?" Shyra took a minute to scan Alex's memories of Christmas. "Oh, Christmas. Alexander, I am sorry but I cannot let everyone leave for this 'Christmas' you speak of. You are all are significantly stronger now, and the Zenakuu draw closer. If they were to somehow get here early they will undoubtedly be able to track you down. Divided, you will fall, and I do not think you want to endanger your loved ones like that. Am I correct?" She asked. Alex was upset, but what she said made sense. Getting presents wasn't worth risking their families' lives. "I understand the need of maintaining traditions Alexander, so we can celebrate your 'Christmas' here. I could change the holographic design of the ship into a Christmas décor, but I see that half the fun is decorating. Why do we not go out and acquire some decorations?"

He never thought she would go for it. It wasn't what the team would want but it was better than nothing. Still, Alex thought about how it would be the first Christmas he didn't spend with his granddad, Henry would be all alone. That was the first time Alex seriously considered running away from it all. He believed he could make it back to Houston somehow with his super speed. Alex clenched his fist contemplating what leaving would mean. He didn't care about the consequences inflicted by Shyra, but he could never live with himself if he somehow caused his grandfather's death. Alexander buried his feelings of regret deep inside, and tried to find some solace that he would at least spend Christmas with his newfound friends. Shyra put on a scarf that covered the tendrils on her head and most of her face. Some regular human clothes, face paint to hide her skin, and a jacket completed Shyra's disguise.

"You're coming with us?" Alex asked.

"Yes, I believe this will be good for all of us." Shyra reached out to the others in the ship, telepathically summoning them to her quarters. When they all came in, she announced that they were all going Christmas shopping, decorating the ship, and exchanging gifts. It seemed like a lifetime ago since they had all been so happy. They rushed to their rooms about put on some warm clothes, ready to hit the mall.

The Cherry Creek shopping mall was packed with people rushing to get their Christmas shopping done in time for the holidays.

"I had no idea this was such a big thing on Earth," Shyra noted.

"It's more than just Christmas ya know? There's Chanukah too," Tori butted in.

"You're Jewish?" Cassie asked.

"As a matter of fact, I am," Tori revealed. The group was shocked, she never mentioned it before, "Don't look at me like that, everyone always gets so wrapped up in Christmas, but there are other beliefs too. Like what about Kwanza? Right D? Tori proudly asked.

"What the hell are you talking about? I must celebrate Kwanza because I'm black? I celebrate Christmas like everyone else," he said, outraged by the insinuation.

"Enough you two, we will celebrate all cultural beliefs. This in a way reminds me of the celebration of Kynthos back on Kalryn."

"That's what we're fighting for, right? To save both our worlds so we can go back to living normal lives," Cassie added.

"This is great. Everyone is too busy shopping to even notice we're walking around with an alien," Chris pointed out.

"What's a Kalryn holiday like, Shyra?" Tori asked.

"I could not merely tell you. There is so much detail and history that I can only show you. But we will worry about that later. Everyone split up and get gifts for each other. Alex and I will get the decorations for the ship."

They all went their separate ways, thinking about what each other would want. Chris wanted to get some video games for Alex and used his powers to set off the sprinklers at the Cheat Code gaming store to clear out the crowd. Before the staff could flee, he quickly grabbed the game he was looking for and approached the checkout counter with a devious smile on his face. Tori seemed to be more concerned with getting stuff for herself than anyone else, but still found the time to exhale deeply; blowing over a girl who was standing a little too close to Dimitri for her liking. Alex also used his ability unfairly and super sped between mall patrons picking up his gifts while leaving Shyra to more or less fend for herself. She found Cassie by the front of the mall where the fountain was located. She hid around a corner while the shoppers marveled in disbelief as the fountain water took on an assortment of shapes before their eyes. Shyra smiled at her pupil's master of her power, but pulled her away by the arm, reminding her not to show her powers off in public like that. Once the group was done adding small time property damage to their rap sheets, they met back in the middle of the mall, and with hands full of bags, they exited out the front entrance in unison.

They arrived back at the ship, which had become like a second home to them. Smiles were plastered on everyone's face as they helped each other decorate the ship. They meticulously streamed lights across the front of the ship and around back. They turned a small evergreen that was growing in front of the ship into their Christmas tree by decorating it with various ornaments, tinsel, and lights. Tori grabbed Dimitri under his arms and flew to the top of the tree to put on the star. The tree was complete, and the ship looked beautiful enough to make herald angels sing. Then it was time for the presents. They all rushed back into their respective rooms and wrapped their gifts—some more successfully than others—and awaited the time to put them under the tree on Christmas Eve.

A week passed, and the freezing cold weather, and heavy snow on the ground limited their training, but the group didn't care because it was Christmas Eve. Anxious from waiting, they decided as a group to put the gifts under the tree a day early and a have Christmas dinner on Christmas Eve. Shyra brought back a monstrous turkey that she started preparing early that day. The others were dressed like Eskimos and headed outside to play in the snow and relieve some stress that had been building continuously since the start of this journey.

"Snowball fight!" Christian initiated with a shot to Alex's chest.

Alex retaliated using his super speed to throw a dozen snowballs at Christian, but Christian turned on his heat and melted all the snow before impact. Dimitri caused the ground to shake, which knocked the snow out of the tree Chris was under, essentially putting him out. Dimitri followed with a loud, obnoxious laugh, and Cassie felt it was her turn. She was able to move the snow around her, because it was simply frozen, crystallized raindrops.

She gathered several feet of snow and plowed Dimitri right over, burying him in the mound. His head popped out, and he gave Cassie a smirk. The group shared a laugh and then returned inside to warm up with some hot cocoa.

"That was really fun," Tori said.

They all shared another laugh. The day went by so fast that it was time for dinner before they knew it. Shyra brought out a smorgasbord of turkey, corn, mashed potatoes, mixed vegetables, and three different kinds of pie for dessert. They sat down and marveled at the feast that had been set in front of them.

"Shyra, you have out done yourself," Alex said.

"It was simple, Alexander. I merely followed the instructions. Everyone, we have been working so hard that I wanted to thank you for trusting me and letting me guide you. I know a lot of you have been through some rough times, but know that we are all here for each other. That is what Christmas means to me."

"Couldn't have said it better myself. Good people, good meat, good God, let's eat," Chris jokingly stated. They all grabbed a fork and knife, passed out the food, and feasted.

After the dinner was done, they cleaned up and gathered in the resting area of the ship. Chris looked around the room and said, "You know, in my family it is tradition to open one of our gifts on Christmas Eve."

Just like that, they all got up, sprinted outside, and grabbed one present that had their name on it. They ran back inside and sat in a circle on the floor and looked around.

"Cassie, why don't you go first. Who is it from?" Alex said.

"Let's see. It's from Tori."

"Oh, you're gonna love it," Tori said. Cassie ripped off the wrapping paper and revealed a supply of name-brand makeup.

"Thanks, Tor. I can add it to the rest of my makeup collection," she sarcastically laughed.

"I knew you would love it."

"Okay, Tori, you open yours." Cassie recommended.

"Okay, mine is from Christian. Aw," Tori giggled. It wasn't a big box, but it made a lot of noise. "What the heck is it, Christian?"

His face turned bright red as he looked at the ground in embarrassment. Tori opened the box and found a custom-made wind chime. It had Los Angeles colors: green, yellow, and red. It chimed the softest, most elegant sound, and Tori absolutely loved it.

"Happy Chanukah Tori," he said.

"Oh my God, Chris, this is awesome. I love it." She leaned in and kissed him on the cheek, causing Dimitri to give the two a puzzled look. Try as he might, he couldn't shake his momentary jealousy.

Fighting the urge to pass out, Chris told her, "Thanks. It wasn't easy to get."

They couldn't wait for Christmas any longer.

"It's close enough to midnight. Let's bring the rest in and open them all up." Alex said. In the rush of all the presents opening, Alex pulled Cassie aside to hand her present.

"I got this for you." Alex gave her a wrapped rectangular object. She slowly opened it and recognized the picture instantly. It was a framed picture of the lake where Cassie used to get away from her troubles and practice her hydrokinesis. Tears filled her eyes.

"That's where we first met," Alex explained. "I was also able to get this." He gave her a vile filled with water. "I took some of the water out of the lake and filtered it, so you can have a piece of home with you at all times."

Cassie fell into Alex's arms. She felt safe when she was with him, like nothing else in the world mattered.

After all the commotion, the group wore themselves out and fell asleep. Christmas finally came for the isolated mountainside alliance. The group walked up to Shyra and wished her a merry Christmas and gave her a gift from all of them.

"Oh, I had no idea you guys were getting me something," she said.

"Of course, Shyra, you have given us so much already," Alex reassured her.

Shyra opened it up to find a family portrait of the five young espers posing in front of the spaceship. Alex was in the middle with Cassie and Chris to his right and Tori and Dimitri to his left. Chris had rabbit ears behind Alex's head, and Cassie had her hand on Alex's chest and her head on his shoulder. Dimitri was standing with his arms crossed and a tough look on his face, while Tori was making a kissing face. The frame of the picture read "From your kinetic children with love!" It couldn't have been a more perfect gift for Shyra.

"Thank you all from the bottom of my heart," Shyra said. "Christmas has brought us closer together. You all have used teamwork while decorating and had each other's happiness and wellbeing at heart when you gave presents. I will remember this experience for the rest of my life." Tori left the others to clean up while she covertly snuck away; but Christian noticed, and saw his opportunity to strike.

"Hey Tor, I just wanted to say I'm really glad you liked your present."

She flipped around after being caught. "Oh, Chris… Yeah it was awesome, thanks again," she said with a smile.

"Oh it's no problem, but if you want to thank me, you can do me the honor of not breaking tradition." He said in a devilishly sly manner.

"What are you talking about?" Tori asked. Chris's smile stretched from ear to ear as he pointed up. She looked up and gasped; she couldn't even comprehend when he would have had time to do it. Chris pinned mistletoe above the doorway, and strategically positioned Tori there so that they would be caught underneath it together. She stared at the plant for a moment, and then looked back down at Christian with a glare.

"This was your big plan? It doesn't even make sense, I'm Jewish. Why do you have to be weird all the time?" She took a deep breath and exhaled, blowing Chris clear into the next room. He tumble-rolled, and smacked into the far wall with an echoing thud. He wasn't moving at all but Tori still walked away without remorse.

How could she worry about stolen kisses, when in a few short weeks she would probably be dead?

Chapter 15

Through the Fire and Rain, Through the Joy and Pain

The day after the Christmas festivities came to an end, training intensified even more. They only had nine days left until the fight of their lives, and tension had noticeably risen.

"No, Irascible Flame, that is all wrong," Shyra instructed. "You have to release from your diaphragm. Do it again."

"I'm trying my best, Shyra, but it is freezing out here, and it's not that easy," Flame complained.

"At the moment, your best is not good enough. Try it again."

Flame inhaled deeply and blew out all the air in his lungs, but all that came out was smoke.

"Fire breathing is a common ability with your power. Keep at it until you get it. I must check on the others."

"Yes, Shyra," Flame said.

Twenty yards away Voltaic Cloud was sparring with Earth, and it didn't seem like they were pulling any punches. Snow-covered rocks the size of volleyballs flew past Cloud's head, but he was too fast to be hit by Earth's projectile attacks. He back flipped over one only to jump up and do a no-handed cartwheel over another. Earth created an earthquake to force Cloud to lose his footing, and it tactfully worked. Two more stones came for Cloud's face, but with both hands out in front, Cloud released a beam of electricity that vaporized the first rock and used a lighting-charged back kick to turn the second one into dust.

"Good, you two," Shyra said, "but I know you are holding back. Show me your progression so far."

The two boys looked at Shyra and then at each other. Nothing was exchanged but a simple nod, but they both knew it was time to get serious. Cloud stood up straight, shook any snow off his clothes, and began to power up. Electricity surged over his entire body, and his eyes began to glow. On the other side, Seismic Earth bawled his hands up into fist, and as he raised them, thirteen boulders of various sizes rose from the ground with them. They levitated to the height of his chest and revolved around his body as if he were the sun of his own galaxy. Faster and faster they spun until it was impossible to tell how many he held in his arsenal.

"Get ready, Earth," Cloud announced. "I'm coming at you with all I've got."

Earth threw out one arm, and several rocks went speeding toward Cloud, but he was all too used to this attack. He switched on his super speed, and as the kicked up snow flew through the air, he dodged the assault from left to right as if they were nothing.

"I've seen that trick before!"

Earth grinned as the very same rocks came from behind and smashed into Cloud's left shoulder blade. They hit him at such an angle that he spun around a full three hundred sixty degrees before slamming into the ground, if not for the snow his head would have cracked wide open. He gripped his arm, which ached. An injury like that wouldn't slow him down for long, though. The hero got up, anxious to continue the fight. Once again, he found himself flipping over rocks, but Earth learned to not only throw his element but manipulate its trajectory; they turned into homing missiles that wouldn't stop until they hit his target.

Cloud leapt up, landed on one of the stones, and used it to propel himself toward Earth. In midair, another rock zeroed in on his location. With his left hand, he pushed it away, while he used his right to send a lightning bolt flying toward Earth's head. Earth did his best to jump out of the way, but the explosion left behind from the blast stunned him and created a plume of dirt and snow. Cloud sped in and charged up his fists. Before Earth realized what was going on, Cloud connected with a straight-cross-straight punch combination to his gut. Earth wheezed for air, but all he found was a connecting uppercut to the chin complements of Voltaic Cloud. Earth landed squarely on his ass. Cloud looked to finish the fight, so he threw his hands high in the air and began to gather energy; within seconds, a glowing orb of electric energy grew in his hands and hummed like a bug zapper as it increased in size.

On the floor, Earth struggled to get his bearings back, but his vision kept spinning out of control. He turned over on his stomach and desperately lifted his right fist in the air. The ground in front of him trembled before it unearthed itself and threw Cloud forward, making him lose his ball of electricity. Earth got up and ran in to personally beat Cloud to a pulp. Their breath was clearly visible in the chilling air, and even though they were exhausted, the two boys stood ready for the martial arts display of technique. Earth launched a right snap kick, but Cloud blocked it with his left forearm, which was exactly what Earth was hoping for. Seismic Earth dropped quickly and performed a successful leg sweep, which knocked Cloud in midair. Earth instinctively followed through with a double-fisted axe handle and sent Cloud crashing into the ground, leaving a small crater in its wake.

Sweat ran down the side of his face, but Earth saw his chance to finish the fight, so he wiped his brow and climbed on top of Cloud throwing elbow after elbow to his face. Cloud did his best to block, but each strike felt heavier than the one before it. He knew he was in trouble if the onslaught continued, so he tried the only thing he could think of. He let out a deep roar accompanied by an outward electrical pulse bomb, which succeeded in electrocuting Earth and knocking him unconscious. That ended the fight. The blast radius was only a few yards, but it did the trick.

"Enough! The fight is over," Shyra shouted. She ran over to make sure the shock didn't stop Dimitri's heart. He had a pulse, but it was faint. "Good, Voltaic Cloud. Take a moment to rest, and I will tend to Seismic Earth's wounds."

"Is he okay?" Alex asked.

"Yes, he is fine, but he needs to lie down for a while."

"Alright." Cloud knew Earth was going to be pissed when he regained consciousness. He sat down underneath a nearby tree and let the chilling breeze graze against his skin. His electrical charge was severely diminished as a result of the fight, so he couldn't help but fall asleep and recharge.

Elsewhere, Shrya saw Wind was flying around and attempting to hit targets with her blades of wind as she zoomed past. Sadly, her hit percentage wasn't that high, but she steadily made progress. Effervescent Rain was sitting on the floor thirty yards away meditating. A foot away from her face was a sphere of water that had smaller streams of water circling around it like an oversized molecule. It was easy to see she was deep in thought, honing her skills with water manipulation. She was able to make the most intricate designs, as if anything she could imagine she could re-create with water. This training went on for several more hours until Shyra called the three remaining teammates over and gave them new assignments.

"Irascible Flame, I want you to spar with Effervescent Rain for a while," Shyra directed. "It is good practice to go up against your elemental weakness, because it keeps you on your toes. Wind, I have some exercises for you to do in the meantime. Begin!"

Flame and Rain ran off to a secluded spot.

"Flame, I don't want you to take it easy on me because I'm a girl," Rain instructed Flame. "Give me your best shot, or I won't get any better." Irascible Flame reluctantly agreed.

Some distance away, Shyra spoke with Wind privately. "Whisking Wind, I believe I can show you the most in the shortest amount of time, because you are the most advance out of everyone in the group in terms of control over your kinetic power. What I want you to practice right now is wind manipulation. Your control over air and wind is only limited by your imagination. For the next couple days, practice creating whirlwinds and cyclones that are under your complete control. Do not let them run rampant. Rather, guide their course with your mind."

"Gotcha. I'll try my best." Wind created a pocket of air beneath her and clumsily flew off into the sky. She headed to a spot where she could practice creating hurricane-level winds without causing too much destruction.

Back on the ground, Flame and Rain faced off. Ironically, Rain was nervous about which technique Flame would start with, and Flame was nervous about hitting a girl. The fight started off with a slow pace, but the sound of a distant twister finally set the two in motion.

"Forgive me, Rain," Flame said as he engulfed his own hands in flames and conjured glowing balls of fire that he lobbed over in Rain's direction and blew up on contact. She narrowly evaded the explosions, but it startled her enough to get serious. With her powers, she popped the top of the water filtration tank that was attached to the back of Shyra's ship. Whips of ice-cold water came flying at Flame, two of which cuffed his hands and doused out his fire. They pulled him in close enough for Rain to connect with a spinning high kick to his chest plate. Flame immediately got the wind knocked out of him and fell to the floor on his hands and knees as his lungs begged for air.

"I warned you not to take me lightly, Flame."

"A mistake I won't make twice. Now I'm pissed."

Rain felt the temperature in the air getting warmer. She knew that would be bad, because it would undoubtedly evaporate the fallen snow and her water. It was not a fight she wanted to drag out. She leapt back a few feet and quickly started formulating a strategy in her mind. A frontal attack wouldn't work against Flame; his powers were too versatile. Instead, she bet the victory of the fight on diversion.

"I've made up my mind, Flame. I refuse to be the weak link anymore." With fluid movements, Rain threw her hands in the air, and on cue, the hard work of her training shined through. The sky grew darker, and rain clouds rushed in over the horizon. Flame didn't like where the fight was heading at all, so he sprang into action. He clasped his fists together, and a stream of fire hot enough to melt stone gushed out of his fingers and rushed toward Rain. Effervescent Rain only just dodged that blaze, which landed less than a foot away from her toes. The danger wasn't over, though; Flame wasn't going to turn off the gas until he hit his mark. Rain continued to run, desperately trying to keep a distance between her and the fire nipping at her heels, but the gap was closing hastily.

It's now or never, she thought to herself. She reached out to the tank where the water sat before. Through her training, she had a much better understanding of the feel of her element. She was now able to sense water's general location, and she felt a significant amount sitting in the pipes of the tank. She clenched her hand closed, and the pipeline that once lay underneath the tank exploded outward from the water pressure and was replaced by a geyser of water.

"Crap," Flame said to himself.

Rain wasted no time. She pulled the water toward her and leapt up on it until she was riding the wave. It was a display neither Flame nor Shyra knew she was capable of; perhaps not even Rain knew, but that did not stop her from keeping the momentum going. As she moved along, she couldn't help but think to herself that she wished Cloud could see her. She had more mobility on the wave than her own feet.

Rain was amazed how easily she could maneuver its path with her thoughts and simple arm gestures, but it was no time to marvel at her own mastery of water. It would only be moments before Flame stopped staring and tried to put an end to the battle. She shot a current of water that landed square on Flame's chest, knocking him back once again.

Flame slid on his back until a mound of snow stopped his movement. Angrily, he slammed his fist on the frozen ground, resulting in an eruption of fire from his clenched hands. The blaze grew higher and higher as he got back up. Flame's jaw grinded and smoke snuck out between his teeth. He was searing with anger since Rain was making him look like a fool in front of their mentor, and he could no longer suffer the indignities.

He arched his back and shouted out to the heavens, but his voice was replaced by a sea of fire. He had finally executed the technique Shyra was trying to teach him. It seemed he only needed the right motivation. When he cocked his head forward again, smoke poured from his mouth and flames visibly emanated from his shoulders. His rage now blinded him, and he charged forward lobbing over fireball after fireball that exploded at the base of Rain's wave and sprayed searing water and mist in every direction.

That gave Rain the perfect idea on how to win. She needed to provoke him more. She antagonized Flame until he could no longer take it.

"Flame, you're never going to hit me like that. No wonder no one takes you seriously. If you'd like, I can stand still for you." As if her taunts weren't bad enough, it was the devilish grin she shot at him that sent him over the edge.

Irascible Flame stopped dead in his tracks and powered up his heat. By hell or high water, the fight was nearing its end. The ground began to crack at his feet, and the air around him combusted. There was no doubt he was truly pissed now. Flame brought his hands parallel from each other in front of his chest, and they immediately burst into flames. The space between his hands ignited and glowed with the white-hot intensity of the sun.

Maybe I overdid it, Rain thought to herself, but there was no backing down at that point. She collected all the water she could and dashed forward on a comparably tsunami-sized wave of destruction.

Not even flinching, Flame felt the inferno pulsating between his palms was finally ready. He threw out his hands and released a sea of fire so hot it incinerated the grass as it cascaded over it. Both waves were on a collision course that no one could stop. Fearing her safety, Rain jumped off her wave a few seconds before the hit, which in hindsight was the smartest thing to do. As the two forces smashed into each other, there was a detonation that could have melted the skin of any living being caught in the direct blast.

It did, however, have the effect Rain was hoping for. The entire field was covered in a thick blanket of mist, which made it impossible to see their hands in front of their own face. The only thing bright enough to be spotted in the endless mantle of steam was the intense flames flaring brilliantly from Flame's body. Rain made her move. She ran in for a hand-to-hand fight, knowing Flame would not be able to see where the strikes originated from.

Flame blindly shot blasts in all directions, hoping one would hit, but his efforts were to no avail. Rain was in range for her ambush. The first hit was a high flick kick to the sternum followed by a karate chop to the back of Flame's neck. The force of the impact sent him crashing to the ground. He just barely caught himself and landed on his palms. Before he could react, Rain punted his midsection like she was a professional kicker in the NFL. Flame skidded across the slushy ground before he eventually stopped four feet away. In the distance, Rain could see the once bright light of his flames diminish into nothing. He was incapacitated, and the fight was over. She used her power to clear the mist away and saw Flame lying there.

"Good work, Effervescent Rain," Shyra said. "I knew you had it in you. Your reaction time and battle strategies are worthy of Kalrynian praise."

"Thank you, Shyra."

"You did it all yourself. If you trust in your power, it will never betray you," Shyra added. "Voltaic Cloud is resting by a tree not far from here. Take a break with him while I finish up things out here."

"Okay," Rain agreed. It was the only word she could formulate as she tried her best not to get over excited. She quickly turned around and walked off. Shyra looked toward an unconscious Irascible Flame.

"You did well, Irascible Flame." She picked him up and carried him inside to check his injuries. On her way, she passed Wind, and every target she'd set forth for her had been destroyed. Hope once again showered over Shyra. She believed they really had a fighting chance.

Rain found her way to Cloud, who was still sleeping under a tree. He looked so tranquil with his head rested against the trunk of the ponderosa pine that she didn't want to disturb him. But in all the mayhem that was soon to follow, she didn't know if they would have another chance for a peaceful conversation. She perched herself next to him and gazed up at the vast blue sky. Things were so simple in that brief moment that she wished it could last forever. The thought of everyone risking their lives in a few days was more than Rain could bear. She had grown so close to everyone, yet it all might come to an end soon. Cloud slowly opened his eyes, and Rain sat up at attention. She hated how he had that effect on her. The harder she tried not to think of him, the more her psyche gave in.

As he woke, he looked over to her. "Cassie … hi."

"Hey."

"What time is it? How long have I been out?" he pondered.

"I'm not sure but, it's almost five o'clock," she responded.

"Damn, I must have really been out of it. Where is everyone?"

"Wind is still training, and Flame is inside recovering from our fight."

"What do you mean fight? He attacked you?" Cloud asked with a concerned look on his face.

"Not exactly," Rain explained. "Shyra had us spar."

"Is she crazy? That's too dangerous. You could've really been hurt."

Rain was very annoyed Cloud thought she would be so easily beat. His cavalier attitude sometimes rubbed her the wrong way. "Didn't you hear me? He's inside recovering—not me."

Cloud finally allowed her words to penetrate his male bravado long enough for what she said to register. "How did you beat him" he asked. "The kid is strong."

"So am I," Rain pointed out. "You really shouldn't underestimate me. I'm tougher than I look."

"Cass, that's not what I meant. I'm just saying I've sparred with him dozens of times, and he's a callous opponent."

"I out smarted him—simple as that."

Cloud placed his hand on top of Rain's. "I'm just glad you're okay," he said.

That warm sensation passed through Rain's hand and traveled to her stomach where it felt like a troop of Boy Scouts were practicing their knots. She smiled and looked down at the ground. "Alex, can I ask you something?"

"Of course. What's up?"

"Do you really think we'll all be all right when they come?" Rain asked.

Cloud paused for a moment. He had some heavy doubts himself with the Zenakuu on the way, but his team looked at him as the leader. He'd rather die than fail them.

"I'll be honest with you," he finally said. "This fight scares the hell out of me, but losing all of you scares me even more. I promise I'll do everything I can to keep everyone alive."

"Me too," Rain added. She slid down until she lied peacefully on her back and let the gelid mountain breeze caress her skin. She closed her eyes and listened to birds singing their songs as they passed by overhead. That moment was so serene that she wanted to bask in it for as long as possible next to the guy she grew to care for so very much.

That evening Shyra brought everyone to the main living quarters to speak with them.

"Listen, everyone, we are going to take the next four days to heal up. There is no sense in fighting an enemy when we are battle worn ourselves. I want each of you to spend some time in the healing tanks and let the bruises wash away. Besides, Dimitri is still in no condition to fight. We will spend the last day preparing a battle plan and then get a good night's rest for the fight to come. Is that understood?"

In unison, the group responded, "Yes, Shyra."

Tori was especially concerned with the condition of Dimitri and shot Alex a dirty look before going to check on him. Chris couldn't help but notice how she swooned over Dimitri, and his resentment for him somewhat deepened. Tori reached the medical wing of the grounds before everyone else. There was Dimitri lying on his right side on an angled bed. She knocked on the doorway of the room before entering but was answered with a frigid response.

"What do you want?" Dimitri asked.

"D, it's me—Tori."

"I know who it is, Wind. We can sense each other's kinetic signature, remember?"

"Right, I forgot … I just wanted to check on you and see how you were feeling," Tori said.

"Why?" Dimitri asked. "I didn't ask you to. Besides, I'm fine. Alex just got lucky, and when I get out of this bed, we *will* settle it."

"Why? What do you have to prove? Everyone knows you're tough—probably even the strongest one out of us."

"You really don't get it. I know life must have been awesome growing up rich and privileged, but not all of us had that, so please don't act like you know me," Dimitri snapped back defensively.

"Well how the hell could I?" Tori shouted. "You shut everyone out and exclude yourself from everything. You walk around all tough, but it's not me who thinks they're better than everyone else; it's you."

"Tori," Dimitri said flatly.

"Yes?"

"Close the door on your way out."

She glared at him with enraged eyes. "Fine! Have it your way, but don't you dare act like growing up was so wonderful for me. You don't know a thing about me, and maybe if you ever got over yourself and actually tried joining the group, you'd discover we might have more things in common than you think." Tori grabbed the door handle and slammed it shut behind her. She let out an exacerbated scream right before she passed the others in the hallway.

"How's he doing?" Cassie asked Tori as she passed.

"Who cares?" Tori yelled out and stormed off.

The rest of the group gave each other confused looks and proceeded off to the rejuvenation tanks. Advanced alien technology certainly had its perks, because the team always felt like a million bucks after they spent some time in the refreshing waters and healing properties of Kalrynian medical advancements.

Tori took a moment to get her thoughts together in her room. "God, he can be such an idiot sometimes," she vented aloud. "Why does he have to push me away like that? What did I ever do to him? I know he would like me if he ever gave me a chance. I'm really not that bad, but no … he'd rather fight the world." She continued to pace her room in frustration. "I just can't understand him, no matter how hard I try. If he doesn't want me around, no problem. I'm tired of putting myself out there just to be shot down. He can get himself killed if he wants. I don't care!" Tori paused for a moment before finishing her rant. "God, I wish I meant that."

Chapter 16

Today is a Good Day to Die, and the Day is Not Yet Over

THE NEXT FEW DAYS went by faster than anyone anticipated, but the tension steadily increased as well. Dimitri and Alex passed each other a few times like a couple of gun slingers in an old western movie. The only time the two spoke was when Dimitri told Alex that they'd continue their bout after the Zenakuu scouts. "Anytime," Alex replied.

Nine days had come and gone. The team learned everything they could with the time they had, but the day of reckoning was finally at hand. Tomorrow the scouts would be there.

Early that night the alliance went over battle strategies. The meeting was led by Shyra and Rain, who tried to calculate every possible outcome of the fight. They went over known Zenakuu strengths and weaknesses along with their own. They were pretty confident they had formulated a successful battle plan, but it would all be decided the next day.

"The element of surprise should be in our favor," Shyra pointed out. "They know nothing of your powers, but we know theirs. We Kalrynians use lygokinesis as a means to produce weapons out of ambient light, but they use a power called karyokinesis, which is the ability to control one's own body on a cellular level. We must be careful, because masters of that ability can quicken healing and maximize adrenaline for extra speed and strength.

The Kinetic Alliance had an unshakable resolve. They got used to fighting in their new uniforms with a little bit of training as they mentally prepared for the most important moment in their lives. Night fell on the sleepy Colorado mountaintop as the butterflies in their stomachs grew larger. The scouts could show up any time. The anticipation was metaphorically killing everyone, but it felt odd that they could be so anxious for a situation they'd all so collectively grown to dread.

The sun rose on that fateful day, removing the chill from the morning air. Shyra hadn't slept at all the night before. Even the usually levelheaded Kalrynian had thoughts that raced back and forth in her mind. She could feel the Karyokinetic pressure that uncontrollably filled her senses steadily approaching. The moment of truth was finally upon them. Shyra stepped out of her room to find the alliance gearing up.

"What are you all doing?" Shyra asked when she saw them.

"It's okay, Shyra. We already felt it. When they get here, we will be ready." Flame smiled and winked at her.

Shyra's doubts melted away just then. She believed in her group and knew her team was ready. The five members of the Kinetic Alliance turned back to their lockers and finished gearing up. They put their fighting armor on one piece at a time. Shyra came out of her room with a battle outfit of her own, which surprised everyone.

"Whoa, are you fighting with us? These Zenakuu have no chance!" Flame joked.

Shyra sported a sleek-looking, skin-tight battle suit. The suit itself was the modified Chrentex armor that belonged to Tribus. It was blue, and the armor was silver with white trim. It wrapped around her entire body and went up the back of her neck. The suit had a chest plate, shin and thigh guards, and light armor around her arms and shoulders. The part that ran up the back of her neck had kinetic probes that attached to her cerebral cortex to exorcise the lygokinetic energy that her mind naturally produced. It also made chemical synapses fire off at an accelerated rate, allowing her to think and react faster. Using her mind, she was able cover the armor that protected her with a thin lygokinetic force field that encased her entire body in a coat of arms. With the suit on, using her lygokinesis took a lot more energy, but it was also significantly stronger.

"This is my prototype battle armor that I have been working on for quite some time now," Shyra explained. "It is a lygokinetic-augmented power suit, or LAPS for short. It allows me to use a portion of my energy and enhance it tenfold. Though I am still working out the bugs, today will be my first test run."

"You sure today is the day you want to test out new battle armor, Shyra?" Rain asked.

"On my world, this altered suit belonged to one of the most powerful beings on the planet, so I cannot think of a better opportunity," she replied.

The alliance stepped outside for a stretch. They started warming up for the fight but really had no idea what to expect. Just as the alliance was done warming up, the unfamiliar karyokinetic energy was getting stronger and closer.

"They're here," Cloud said. The knot in his stomach was crippling. He wanted to run away but stood his ground.

The alliance could feel the scouts closing in on them as they ran through the treetops and climbed the mountainside with incredible speed and precision. It was as if they knew the terrain. They flipped through the trees with the agility and endurance of spider monkeys indigenes to the tropical rainforests. The alliance formed a circle.

"Don't let them get behind us. Get back-to-back," Cloud ordered.

At that moment, each of the scouts dropped from the treetops and circled around the alliance.

"There are only five. We can take them." Flame blurted out. As Flame's words left his lips, five more scouts dropped down from the sky almost simultaneously and filed in between the original five. "Whoa," Flame said dumbfounded.

Wind whispered to Rain, "They just fell from the sky."

"I know. Just stay focused."

"I'm just saying that was kinda cool," Wind avouched.

For two minutes, not a word was spoken.

Shyra opened the door to the camouflaged spaceship to find her team surrounded by the Zenakuu. "Ten on five? That does not seem very fair, does it?" Shyra jumped through the air and landed next to her team. "Let us level the playing field. Shall we?"

The Zenakuu scouts stood roughly six feet tall with lean, long legs. They were perfect for running and being kept hidden. Their fur covered just about everything but their faces, palms, pectoral muscles, and abdomen areas. Although their eyes bore strong resemblance to Kalrynian eyes, to Alex, they seemed to have a certain goat-like quality. The Zenakuu's armor was fearsome. Visible claw marks, bullet holes and dents each triggered depictions in Alex's imagination of their past battles without him having to be there. Cloud swallowed his fear, but even in thirty degree weather, he was visibly sweating. Their armor was painted death-black, but shined with golden trims, and royal purple accents. For reasons unknown, this Zenakuu party was careless and took a more upfront approach.

These scouts are different, Shyra thought. *Zenakuu scouts are not meant to be seen, but they are right here in front of us. What is going on?*

"Don't tell me this group of cubs is this planet's weak attempt for a resistance Kalrynian." The scout leader said with a grunt.

"I'll show you who's weak!" Earth yelled. The ground started shaking and soon the entire mountain was trembling.

"Hold on, Earth. We're already out numbered," Cloud attested.

"How did you find us?" Cloud asked the scouts. He wasn't ready to start the fight. He knew they were outnumbered, and this was the first real fight that they, as a team, had encountered. A Zenakuu scout stepped forward, and sniffed the air around him.

"We simply followed the stench of that Kalrynian," the scout growled and began to snort in between laughter. An obvious lie, Shyra knew they must have tracked her lygokinesis. "We are here to see if Earth had any usable resources. This planet is flourishing with everything we need and may even be Zenakuu's new home world, Vizner willing." The captain scout laughed at the thought of taking over the big blue marble.

"Over my dead body, you ugly ass alien!" Flame shouted. "No offense, Shyra."

"That's the idea, sapiens," the scout said and snarled.

Avoiding the attention of the scouts, Earth picked up a boulder from behind one scout to ensure he was ready for the fight. Flame's eyes began to glow a fiery red, and the snow beneath his feet melted. Cloud clenched his hand and surged electricity through it. Earth sent the boulder flying and blindsided the one scout, knocking him to the ground. With that, the actual fight began. The exchange of words was over, and the scouts were determined to deliver hell in a hand basket.

The teamwork that the Zenakuu showed was incredible. "Split up into teams—formation Cammer," the captain Directed as he growled with anticipation. Only one of the scouts ever talked. They split themselves up into two teams of three and one team of four. It felt like they all shared one mind; they all stood the same way, ran the same way, and fought the same way.

Earth and Flame stayed together and fought the second scout team. The flurry of slashes that came from the scouts' blades were blinding, and the boys knew they were in trouble.

"They're too fast. We won't last long like this—we have to put them down." Flame observantly said.

Flame and Earth jumped back to try to change the fight's flow in their favor; meanwhile, Shyra and Wind were fending off the four members of the third team. Wind inhaled deeply and blew two of the four back with a gust of air, while Shyra held off the captain and another scout with a lygokinetic shield.

"We are being overwhelmed, Shyra. What should we do?" Wind questioned.

Just then, a scout broke through Wind's defenses and grabbed her from behind, stopping the gust of wind. The free scout seized the opportunity to attack and came at Wind with a jump kick that hit her in the chest and sent her flying twelve feet back. She held her chest and gasped for air. Shyra saw her fallen student and sprang into action. She pushed back the scout captain and the other Zenakuu with telekinetic force and ran over to Wind's side. Shyra projected her shield up again to protect Wind and herself, while another trigger-happy scout opened fire on the two. At the same time, Cloud and Rain were dealing with the first scout team.

"I can't shake this guy," Rain said while blocking one out of three members of the Zenakuu scouting team.

"At least you don't have to deal with two of them," Cloud said. That was all he was able to convey before taking a shot to the jaw. Every time Cloud was able to block one attack, another scout got a hit in. Even his energy blasts were missing their targets.

"Cloud, we have to switch up the game plan here!" Rain said. Being the tactical member of the team, Rain realized that being separated was not working.

"Quick, Rain, use the clouds above the mountains to get some water and soak these—" Cloud's words were cut off by a leading leg kick to the stomach. Cloud gasped for air and angrily looked up with glowing yellow eyes. He put his hands together and threw an electrical grenade that landed at the feet of his would-be assassin and exploded. The center point of the grenade sprouted vines of electricity that fried the second scout upon contact. Cloud turned and shouted out, "Rain, now!"

"I'm working on it, but this guy is giving me problems," Rain responded.

Cloud ran up, dove, and tackled the last member of the team, allowing Rain to gather water from the clouds above. Rain collected the water from the sky and flooded the area around the scout's team. They stumbled around from the slippery slush, while Cloud gathered electricity from within.

"Do it, Cloud," Rain shouted.

Cloud thrust out his hands and sent several bolts toward the three Zenakuu scouts, frying them with ten thousand volts of raw electricity. Out of breath, he turned to Rain. "Now let's go help the others."

"I agree," she said. "These guys are tougher than I thought."

Cloud and Rain joined Earth and Flame in their fight with the scouts. Earth was holding his own with his two scouts, while Flame was fighting one-on-one with the third. Earth was able to hold the two scouts off because of his extensive boxing training. He may have not been faster, but he was able to meticulously read his attackers' moves. It was tough, but he didn't get cut even once. He dodged endless attacks and waited for an opening.

Earth concentrated all his attention into his kinetic power. He was able to split the ground from under one scout. The miniquake was felt throughout the entire area but still caught the scout off guard. The scout lost his footing and fell off the edge of the cracked ground. As he attempted to climb up from the chasm, Seismic Earth closed the gap, squeezing the scout until he popped like a grape. Now he could focus on one.

"Okay, it's just you and me," Earth stated.

The scout started the fight with a roundhouse, but in one motion, Earth blocked the kick, grabbed the scout's leg and threw him to the ground disarming him. The scout sprang back up as if hitting the snow-cushioned ground didn't hurt. A left straight was thrown but caught nothing but the frigid air. He was not so nimble on the second swing, as the right hook connected hitting Earth's chin. Another punch hit Earth's body, and he heard his ribs crack. He clenched his sides in wreathing pain.

"Jesus these guys are strong," Earth said to himself as he was hunched over, still short on breath due to the blow. He'd already coughed up a small amount of blood. The copper taste in his mouth was confirmed by the blood stained snow under his chin. Earth quickly picked himself back up and went on the attack. He stomped forward, causing snow covered clods of dirt to hurl into the air at shoulder level. When he punched the air in front of it, the dirt was sent jettisoning on a crash course with the scout's face. The scout dodged the lump of ground easily enough, but in the confusion, Dimitri grabbed the scout's head and utilized his Muay Thai. He began thrusting his knees into the scout's face, however, the scout broke free of Earth's clutches, pushed him away, and backed up to regain his composure. The Zenakuu's eye was swollen and his nose bled, but he wasn't backing down at all.

"Earth, Flame, are you guys alright?" Cloud screamed.

"We're hanging in there, Cloud, but we can use your help," Flame answered. "These guys are quick."

The only thing Flame could do was try his best to block and duck all the punches that were coming his way. He took a step back and conjured a stream of flames toward the scout, but he easily flipped over the attack and landed on top of Flame. Before the scout could do anything, Cloud blasted the scout off of him. He flew back from the bolt of electricity and whacked into a nearby tree.

"Thanks, bro," Flame said.

The scout's armor was visibly singed, and smoke lifted off of it, the smell of burnt fur filled Flame's nostrils. He took his time getting up and recovered from the attack. The two battered scouts walked toward each other and glanced at the other four scouts who were fighting Shyra and Wind. They realized they were in trouble, so they stopped their attack and dashed over to regroup. The alliance regrouped as well, and an even six-on-six fight was in the making.

"Formation Exeter," the captain commanded.

The Zenakuu team snapped into a V formation with the captain in the front. The team was puzzled by their unusual formation, and then the scouts rushed after the alliance. They dashed off, kicking up the snow on the ground and continually crossing and flipping in front of each other, never letting Shyra's forces lock on to anyone in particular. They leapt high in the air and came down on Earth, Rain, Wind, Cloud, and Flame, taking them by surprise.

The captain jumped forward and shot at Shyra's lygokinetic shield with his once holstered handgun, which could more accurately be described as miniature cannon. The recoil of the gun pushed the captain two feet back. It didn't take long before he shattered her shield. The force of the shot pushed her back but not down. She mentally turned on her battle suit and got into a fighting stance. The captain scout growled, and bore his fangs before speaking.

"You Kalrynians think you're so high and mighty—better than the rest of us. Do you really think we didn't study your battle tactics before starting this assault? You're no match for us anymore."

"Make no mistake, Zenakuu. I will not let you defile this planet like you did mine. We will fight you to the last breath." Shyra smirked at the captain scout.

"Insolent wretch, what you call defilement we call ethnic cleansing." The Captain spat on the ground and gave the order to his second-in-command to fire away at Shyra and Wind with their artillery. Round after round of ammunition was shot at the alliance, but Shyra did her best to keep up the lygokinetic shield that protected them all. She cocked back her arm and released it with a sphere of lygokinetic energy into the captain's midsection. Not knowing where such immense power came from, the captain of the scouts was thrown back and wasn't able to land soundly.

Cloud didn't have much of a problem with his scout. The scout seemed more hell-bent on slaughter than the others, his icy stare emotionless and militant. The blade of his sword was like nothing Cloud had ever seen. He swung recklessly at Cloud but made careless mistakes and acted more like a berserk beast than a soldier. The Zenakuu paused to press a purple button on the grip of the sword, and it began to make an unfamiliar sound. Cloud couldn't quite put his finger on it, but it sounded like whistling. Sure enough, the scout let the blade hit the ground, and the snow beneath instantly melted and evaporated.

Cloud couldn't believe his eyes. "What the hell kind of technology is that?" he asked, but the scout only smirked revealing his yellowed fangs.

His once black blade glowed with a visibly steamy red hue, and Cloud could feel the heat that emanated off of it even from three feet away. He slowly lifted his steaming sword and pointed at Cloud. The hero's eyes were diverted to the once unnoticeable shine of a golden pendant that dangled from the sword's hilt. He wondered what it was but received little time to think about it as the scout charged in.

Cloud was able to match the scout's speed, but he knew that one hit from that sword would mean certain death. He waited for the perfect moment, and when Cloud saw it he sprang forward. He charged up his hand with electricity, he needed to strike fast before the opening closed. The thrust started at his hips with an explosion of energy and released the blast right into the scout's face. The electricity left his face smoldering as he stumbled backward. Cloud wasn't going to let this one get away. He followed up with another right cross, then a left elbow, and ended with an electrically charged spin kick to the scout's chin. The energy from the kick exploded on the scout's face upon impact and the Zenakuu had an uncontrollable seizure as the currents coursed through his body, forcing him to drop his sword shortly after.

"Give up, Zenakuu," Cloud said. "This doesn't have to end in death." Cloud stood over the bloody and burnt scout. He said nothing at first but then spit up at Cloud. It angered him but luckily didn't push him over the edge. Cloud grabbed the Zenakuu's chest armor and shocked the scout with just enough to render him unconscious.

Wind was not as prepared for the fight as she thought. All the physical training was there, but mentally, she was crippled. The thought of death kept her frozen in her tracks, unable to do anything but block. She threw gusts of wind in an attempt to push the scout back, but he was too strong. He sprinted back to her fast and jammed a dagger deep into her thigh. She screamed in agony as the warm blood flowed down her leg dying her white costume red. At that moment, something snapped in her, and she felt nothing but rage. She levitated in the air and whipped her arms around circularly. She conjured up gusts of wind and fashioned them into surgically sharp blades. The scout ran after her, but it was too late. Wind sent several of the blades at her adversary. At first they just scratched him, but with her accuracy improving, she soon sent one right at his neck. Like a guillotine, the mighty wind cleaved the scout's head clean off.

"Now there are only four," Wind shouted.

Flame was handling his scout well but wasn't making progress in the fight. After disarming him from the hatchet he came with for the fight, Flame pressed on, but both fighters were running out of energy. Flame tried sending grenades of fire toward the scout, but the scout used his karyokinesis to dodge the attacks and leave pockets of evaporated snow in their wake. Both used a lot of their energy and decided to get up close and personal. The scout didn't know that Flame loved to fight with his fists.

"Enough of this shit," Flame said. "Are you ready to get your ass kicked?"

"Do you think you, an earthling, can last in a fight with a master of karyokinesis?" the scout mocked.

The two ran after each other, met in the middle, and collided. The soldier threw a forward punch that Flame ducked underneath. From that, Flame grabbed the fur on his arm and performed a judo flip that tossed the scout over his right shoulder. The scout hit the ground with a loud thud, but Flame wasn't done yet. Flame climbed over and held him down with one hand while he pounded his enflamed fist down on the scout's head. The scout wriggled with throbbing second-degree burns and push kicked Irascible Flame off from on top of him. He crawled over to a pile of shoveled snow and buried his face inside before getting back up.

The cooling sensation was pure ecstasy, but as soon as the relief came, he wanted nothing more than to slowly dismember Flame. The Zenakuu inspected the black gashes that ran up his heavily seared, heat-withered face. Regenerating skin and bone was simple enough, but the humiliation he endured would last forever. He roared, put his hands up, and ran toward Flame. The scout tricked Flame with a sweep kick and took out his legs from underneath him. Before Flame could fall to the ground, the scout grabbed him by the trench coat and pulled him in closer. The imminent collision of fist and face sent Flame flying seven feet away.

The twist punch turned Flame's nose into a faucet of blood, but he wasn't going to stop before he put his enemy down. Still woozy, Flame ignited his fists, cracked his neck, and started hopping around like a boxer ready for round two. Flame went on the offense, darting in and striking the scout with multiple shots to the body, which severely slowed his movements and burned off the scout's gear. The smell of burnt fur filled Flame's nostrils, and he knew what to do next. The battered scout foolishly tried to throw just one punch. Flame sidestepped and kicked out his knee.

From down on one knee, the scout looked up unfocusedly at Flame's palm as though he was gazing at something miles away. The Zenakuu saw the glowing blaze slowly gathering around Flame's hand, begging to be released. Heat surged from Flame's heart to his hand, as though magma were rushing through him. Chunks of Flame's armor charred and flaked away in the wind. Flame smiled, very eager to know what a well-done Zenakuu would look like. His demonic stare suggested that in some twisted way he was enjoying himself. He finally fired the blast at point blank range leaving the scout looking like a piece of newly ignited charcoal.

“Three left,” Flame said.

Chapter 17

Killing Under the Cloak of War is No Different Than Murder

Earth grew tired of the scouts and wished to end his fight as soon as he could. Irascible Flame looked over to see how everyone else was doing and saw his teammates bloodied and beaten. He shouted at Earth, praying he would hear him. "Earth, let's do that meteor shower move."

Earth looked over and acknowledged. Earth's whole body started shaking as boulder after boulder lifted from the ground and ascended into the air. He was too tired to lift them to the appropriate altitude, but understanding his exhaustion, Wind gave her assistance. She summoned all her strength and got those boulders high into the air for launch. On cue, Flame took aim and set each one of the rocks ablaze. Smoldering in the sky, they created quite a spectacle for all those who were around, but it didn't take long for the scouts to realize what was next. The boulders came flying down just as quick as they went up, crashing into the ground and exploding on impact like they were detonated bombs. The collaboration was a bit shaky and didn't kill any Zenakuu directly, but it left them in a far worse state than they were in before.

The fight wasn't over, however. Earth stood in a firm stance, lifted the ground, and formed two slabs of stone one on each side of the scout. The Zenakuu warrior was able to break one of the slates of rock but was hit by the parallel wall on the other side. The slab brought him within striking distance of Voltaic Cloud, who jumped into the air and came down on the arm of the scout with his knee, breaking it into pieces.

The scout screamed in pain but used his karyokinesis to work through the torment. He knew if he could get away long enough, he could use his power to speed up the healing process. Cloud, however, had no intention of giving him the chance. The scout leapt back with his limp arm dangling from its socket.

"Everyone back; I got this," Cloud ordered.

"No way, he's mine. Fall back son," Earth attested. Earth blindly ran, inching closer to the awaiting trap the scout had ready. He jumped up a few feet in front of the scout and came down with a crash. The resulting impact caused the ground to ripple like when a pebble is dropped in a lake. The scout stumbled back, but Earth charged in. He cocked back his arm and connected with a devastating haymaker. The Zenakuu lay there on the cold ground twitching in the snow with a caved in face. Earth waited to see if the scout would get back up, but once convinced he was no longer a threat, he turned to face Cloud.

"See, Cloud? That's how it's done," Earth boasted.

Cloud's heart skipped a beat as he watched the scout sit up in the corner of his eye. "Earth, watch out!" he shouted.

Earth quickly turned around, but it was too late. He saw the glint of a concealed weapon in the scout's hand. The invader lodged a serrated blade deep into Earth's gut. He screamed out in excruciating pain and immediately fell to the ground. In only a moment, the pure, white snow beneath him saturated turning blood red.

"Earth!" Cloud shouted out. "You son of a bitch!" he screamed at the scout.

The Zenakuu soldier grinned, drew the dagger from Earth's stomach, and sadistically licked the blade clean of any blood. He gripped the handle with his teeth before removing his short sword from its sheath and standing up. He had his sights back on Cloud when Earth reached out and grabbed the heel of his boot.

"I thought I told you that I was your opponent," he strained to say.

The scout growled and made a goal kick, with Earth's face being the ball, in order to relinquish his grip. Cloud started to panic. He had to get to Earth fast before he bled out.

"I got him, Cloud. Just finish this guy," Flame said as he jumped in. He launched a couple of fireballs to put distance between the scout and his fallen comrade.

Cloud was relieved Earth had someone helping. He seemed to still be conscious, and Cloud just prayed he would survive long enough for medical treatment. He gazed upon the scout with contempt, eager to resume their fight.

Both combatants stood there breathing heavy into the freezing winter air. Neither one of them had expected such a fight. It was eerily quiet, but the scout charged and Cloud took a moment to power up. The electrical charge visibly surged around his entire body. He attempted to keep the scout at a distance by shooting him down with bolts but was too worn out for a decent shot. The scout easily evaded all of them.

Cloud could feel the presence of his energy getting weaker. *This fight has to end now*, he thought to himself.

The scout was in slashing range, but Cloud had enough power to dip each hack with incredible speeds. The scout came at him with a downward slice, but Cloud caught the blade with both hands. Impressed with his own reflexes, Cloud smiled only to have his victory prematurely ended as the scout elongated his own neck, leaving a huge gash on Cloud's chest with the dagger that was still firmly secured in his mouth. The teen had never been so badly injured and wanted a moment to consider the gravity of his wound, but the Zenakuu was relentless in his attack. Voltaic Cloud couldn't hold out much longer. He tightened his grip around the short sword the Zenakuu scout was wielding and sent the remainder of his electrical power through the blade, effectively electrocuting the scout until his heart stopped from the shock.

The scout fell to knees and slumped over. Cloud wasn't sure if he was actually dead or not, but it was a chance he wasn't willing to take. He ran up behind the Zenakuu warrior sliding across the ground and quickly scooped him up. Cloud tested the waters by placing him in a chokehold. Just as Cloud thought the scout was alive and violently squirmed around to get free. Cloud tightened his grip until the scout was no longer flailing his arms around, rendered to a state that would barely be considered conscious.

The scout desperately grabbed and clawed at Cloud's armguard, but he no longer had the strength to fight him off. Once the wheezing and grunts stopped, Cloud firmly placed his left hand on the back of the Zenakuu's head while his right squeezed his chin. Cloud exhaled letting his breath visibly dissipate in the freezing air. In one quick motion, Voltaic Cloud yanked his hands in opposite directions snapping his enemy's neck. Cloud stumbled backwards as the body dropped to the ground leaving its imprint in the snow. The finishing blow was so vicious and cold that Cloud hated himself for it. The sensation of each vertebrae snapping, and the crackling sound that followed sent chills through Cloud's body, rattling him to the bone. It felt like murder, an act he never wanted to get used to. For him, the ends hardly justified the means.

"Only two now. Rain, do you need any help?" Cloud asked.

No, I have to do this on my own, she thought to herself. Rain spent most of her time dodging and weaving. She was the least aggressive member of the group, but she knew what she had to do. Her shoulders tightened, and an almost paralyzing chill ran down her spine. There was a lake at the bottom of the mountain that she had been trying to reach since the beginning but hadn't had time to concentrate enough.

"Wind, can you distract this guy for a bit?"

"No problem," Wind answered. "You can count on me."

Rain walked back to the edge of the mountain and started moving her hands upward, while Wind acted as bait. Rain gathered the water and brought a huge tidal wave flying up the mountainside that encompassed itself around the battlefield. As Wind looked up, she couldn't help but laugh. "When it rains, it pours," she said.

This was it for Rain. All the training she had undergone would show in her moment of glory. She carefully used the limited amount of water to her best advantage, and a sinuous wave came crashing down around the scouts. The captain had enough sense to dodge the aquatic upsurge, but the other scout did not have such keen reflexes. He was washed away and left to drown in the current as Rain bent its movement to her will. The wave reached twenty feet tall until she finally made it crash down with the scout still inside. That blunt trauma was enough to leave the scout discombobulated for a few moments, and even though he rushed to regain his composure, he realized the fight would not go in his favor unless he played dirty. He struggled to get up, but angered over the embarrassment, he lashed out.

"Human filth, I'll kill you!" he yelled.

Rain couldn't believe he was even able to move after all that let alone rush after her. After being harangued, she took a step back but refused to retreat. She had something to prove to herself that day. With the remaining chilling water, she formed a whip that furiously bombarded the scout with hits to the head and abdomen fast enough to leave a cracking sound in their wake, but there was no slowing him down. He pressed on, despite his armor being in shambles. Cloud moved forward to step in, but Wind held him back.

"This is something she has to do by herself," Wind said. "If she doesn't believe in herself now, she'll never make it. Don't worry, though; we won't let anything happen to her."

Cloud reluctantly nodded and continued to watch the bout. The Zenakuu scout drew closer and closer. He increased his mobility using his karyokinesis and flipped around and over the water whips Rain formed. With the last of the water circling in the sky brought down in front of her, Rain relinquished the idea of ending the fight with a whip and switched to projectile weaponry.

She condensed the liquid into tightly packed bullets and hit the scout with the pressurized water blast that once again brought the Zenakuu to his knees. Regardless of pain, he rose and continued to close the already small distance between them.

"What the freak are these guys made of?" Rain shouted.

The scout was now in striking distance. He pulled out his surprise weapon, which happened to be a fragment grenade, and pulled the pin with his teeth. He had a devilish grin on his face; his plan was to kill the both of them the entire time. "I'll see you on the other side, human."

Rain's eyes gaped open, and in an instant, her life flashed before her eyes. All the pain and suffering, all the disappointment and letdowns—for an instant, she was okay with the end that surely was to follow, but then she saw it in her mind. The reason she fought so hard, the reason she signed up for this crazy intergalactic war—a vision of her sister Katelyn. Rain knew she couldn't let it end there.

"Rain!" Cloud shouted. He ran over using all the speed he could muster, but he knew he would not make it in time.

Effervescent Rain took a deep breath and screamed. Those next few seconds felt like an eternity to her, but surprisingly, she felt no pain. *So this is what death feels like?* she thought to herself, but she once again heard Cloud's voice.

"Rain!" he yelled.

She opened her eyes and turned her head toward his voice. She saw him there, running quick as lightning toward her. Behind him she saw Irascible Flame with his mouth wide open.

What the hell just happened? She thought. Rain turned back toward the Zenakuu scout, who she assumed had killed her. There he was, as if some kind of picturesque statue captured in time forever in a sheet of ice. She couldn't comprehend what had happened. She wondered where the ice had come from. Was it her that literally chilled him to the bone? Her thoughts were cut short, however, when Cloud grabbed her in his arms and ran with her for dear life. It was only a few seconds later when the grenade went off. Earth, who was coherent enough to watch the whole thing, did his best to shield them by putting up slab of dirt between them and the blast before blacking out, but the destructive force completely obliterated the feeble barrier. The two were sent flying in an explosion of rock and shrapnel and landed forcefully several yards away.

Cloud and Rain looked into each other's eyes. "Cassie, are you okay?" he asked. Cloud was bleeding from the forehead but only concerned himself with her safety.

"I think so," Rain said. "Are you?"

"Somehow."

"Did we get him? Is he dead?"

"You did it Rain," Cloud told her. "I don't think he'll be getting up this time."

"Good—and then there was one," she affirmed.

Once they made sure Earth was in stable condition, Cloud ordered Wind to bring him inside, and come back out once he was safe. There wasn't anything else he could do for the battle in his condition. The others ran to Shyra who was fighting the last scout—the captain. Bloodied and bruised the able-bodied team stood back but really wanted to see what Shyra could do. The captain scout was out of breath by now, and despite having the suit on, Shyra had energy to spare.

"Get him, Shyra! He's the last one!" Flame cheered on.

The scout did not accept defeat and proceeded to attack her. He shot at her until he was out of ammo, but no bullet pierced her shield. With the battle suit on, the captain was no match for Shyra. The captain discarded the semi-automatic gun and picked up a discarded hatchet that had been washed close to him from the previous flood.

"We Zenakuu are a proud race, and I swear to you, Kalrynian, you will get what you deserve. Now let's finish this." The scout captain stood tall and began twirling the hatchet between his hands. With his silver-and-green fur and wrinkled red skin, he looked older than the other scouts, but he still leapt into the air with ease and hurled the hatchet at Shyra with amazing speed and accuracy. She was barely able to dodge it as it landed right at her feet. The captain came down with a stomp kick and leg sweep in progression that caused Shyra to stumble back. She had not anticipated he would be so skilled in martial arts combat. She focused her energy and preformed a devastating telekinetic push, but the captain jumped over it with a 540-degree back flip and slid back on the snow from the momentum.

"He is fast," Shyra said to herself.

The fight wasn't over yet, though. The captain rushed in again and picked up the hatchet he'd thrown earlier. Shyra did her best to evade him, but the Zenakuu mercilessly hacked away at her, and she knew that she would soon be overwhelmed if she didn't turn the tide. Shyra grabbed the captain's forearm and used much of her remaining grip strength to break the bones in his wrist. He immediately dropped the weapon and writhed in unspeakable pain. It was her chance to start her own onslaught, and she wasn't going to let it slip by. Shyra threw a feign right hook but connected to his face with a whirlwind kick that sent the captain's head smashing into the icy ground. She got on top of him and secured a grappling arm bar that she was sure would end the fight less he sustain further injury.

"Give up!" she demanded.

The warrior only laughed. "You should have done your homework, Kalrynian." The captain, who had mastered karyokinesis, dislocated his own arm and slipped out of her hold. He kicked Shyra off of him and stood up. "Mastering one's body is child's play to a true Zenakuu warrior." He popped his arm back in its socket and growled.

"I can't believe how tough these bastards are," Cloud blurted out.

Flame chimed in as well. "I know. It's unreal."

"Should we help her? Rain asked

"Yes, let's end this fight. Everyone get ready," Cloud, who didn't want to see anyone else get hurt, said. The three of them started to run over to their mentor and guide.

"No! Stay back" she shouted.

"This is a one-on-one fight. My people are not without their pride either. I will finish off this scout."

The three stopped dead in their tracks and obeyed their teacher's command. She turned back to the scout. "Ready?" she asked.

"More than you'll ever know, coward. By the time I'm done with you, you'll be begging me for death's sweet release."

It was Shyra's turn to charge in. She closed the gap with blinding speed and sent a barrage of punches whizzing past the Zenakuu's head. She connected with one good palm to the chest plate that knocked the wind out of him, but he did his best to quickly recover. It was an all-out brawl at this point with neither combatant showing any sign of stopping. The captain blocked the next two swings from Shyra and connected with a two-handed hammer fist on the top of Shyra's head.

Her vision blurred immediately, and everything became distorted. The scout continued the beat down with low kicks to her stomach, and a stomp to her ribs. Shyra seemed to be at the end of her rope but rolled away on the ground as she tried to get her bearings back. She felt internal bleeding and feared the end may be near. The scout closed in for the kill while the teens watched in terror. They couldn't believe they came this far only to watch their mentor die before their very eyes.

The Zenakuu scout saw the tool he needed lodged into the ground. He walked over to it and picked up a sword. On his way back to Shyra, he cocked back and thrust the blade forward, but Shyra put up her shield to absorb the blow. The tip of the weapon cracked the shield and was lodged inside of it four inches in. Any farther, and the blow may have proved fatal.

Try as she might, Shyra couldn't hold the barrier any longer, and the shield exploded under the force of the sword. She just barely turned her head in time to avoid impalement but not fast enough to avoid the tip of her tendril getting cut off and a gash on her left cheek, which now poured her blue blood onto the snow.

Infuriated, Shyra screamed out and telekinetically grabbed the captain, flung him high in the air, and launched him into a neighboring tree, which splintered and cracked from the destructive force and caused a family of perched birds to fly away in fright. He kick-flipped himself up and flew at Shyra. She got back in her stance but could not anticipate how dirty of a fighter the captain was. He threw a feign punch to her face that she foolishly tried to dodge, but the real attack was the concealed dirt in his other hand that landed in Shyra's eyes. She was momentarily blinded, and he grabbed her by the face and dragged the back of her head against the frozen, rocky ground. Punch after punch landed square on Shyra's face until she was no longer moving. Not even a broken wrist slowed the storm of punches. He merely worked through the agony. The scout stood up, breathing heavily, but he was still satisfied with his victory. He walked over to the three and roared, "See? See what you fools put your faith in? Now lay down before me and await your destruction. There is nothing that can save you now."

A voice came out from Shyra's position—faint but recognizable. She struggled to stand up. "Where do you think you are going?" she asked. "This fight is not yet over." She spit out the blood that accumulated in her mouth.

The scout let out a bellowing howl and then ran toward her. He once again leapt in the air to cock back his jump punch. Shyra anticipated it and stepped out of the way but not before she was able to grab his arm and flip him around. She grabbed the scout by the hair and drove her knee deep into his face. His nose acted as a hydrant for the blood that gushed out.

The captain could no longer move; he'd taken far too much damage.

With his skull fractured, it was difficult to understand him, but he spit the blood from his mouth and gurgled out his final words. "You're still too stupid to understand, aren't you? It doesn't matter what you do to me. The extinction of this planet and all the others in our way is nothing short of inevitable." He chuckled, "The Zenakuu army will go on a full frontal assault when I don't return, so hurry up and kill me."

"I have had enough of your mouth." Shyra generated a lygokinetic dagger with her remaining strength, and with a flick of her finger, it traveled right through the captain's heart. With the fight finally over, she limped over to her battered team.

"Shyra, what did he say about a full frontal assault on Earth?" Cloud asked, obviously worried. "We're not ready for that."

"Do not worry, Voltaic Cloud. It will take years before they get here. The Zenakuu have been a long-lasting thorn in our sides, but by the time they get here, you five will be ready for anything. You showed great promise today, and I am very proud of you all."

"Thanks, Shyra," Cloud said. "We captured one of the scouts. I was able to knock him out by overloading his body with electricity."

"Good work, everyone. We will interrogate him when he awakes. We have a lot of work ahead of us."

There was nothing that could ruin the sweet taste of triumph from Shyra's palate.

CHAPTER 18

I Used to Wish for Better Days, Now I Pray for Nevermore

SHYRA AND CLOUD CARRIED the imprisoned Zenakuu scout back inside the base. They took him down deep into the ship to the holding cells. Cloud opened the cell, while Shyra threw him in. The scout bounced on the hard floor twice before stopping, and Cloud locked him in. The impact jolted him awake, and he struggled to remember what happened. The captured scout held his head while his grunts broke the silence that blanketed the room.

"Now that we are all here, what were you looking to gain from your trip to earth?" Shyra questioned the captive scout.

He frantically looked around, ignoring her question. "My sword. Where is my sword?" he demanded to know.

"Irrelevant. Answer my question," Shyra said.

"Do you really think I would tell you anything, you ugly glabrous?"

"I see," Shyra continued. "Voltaic Cloud, Irascible Flame, Effervescent Rain, can you leave me alone in here? I want to get to know our guest a little better."

"Okay, Shyra, let us know if you need us," Cloud expressed. The three went back up and checked on Earth and Wind.

"Now that it is just you and me, let me share something with you. I would love nothing more than to string you up somewhere and beat you with a blunt object until my arms become sore, but you have information I need. So are you going to tell me what I want to know?"

"You'll have to kill me," the scout growled.

"We will get to that. Tell me, what is the Zenakuu plan for Earth? Will they use it for resources, land, or slaves?"

"How about all of the above," the scout snickered as he bore his fangs.

Shyra almost lost her patience but held on. "What is your name, scout?"

"What does it matter?"

Shyra shot him a look of disgust before telekinetically lifting him up and slamming him to the back wall. "Refrain from testing my patience any further, Zenakuu," Shyra demanded.

It was noticeably hard for her prisoner to breathe as he struggled to growl. "I go by Donikan," he said. The Zenakuu had the same skin color as Shyra but was covered in ocean blue hair.

"Glad you joined the conversation. Now tell me what I want to know," Shyra demanded.

"You tell me something, Kalrynian," the scout said. "What happens when I do tell you what you want to know? Will you let me go, or will you just kill me?"

"What would you do, Donikan?"

"I wouldn't have taken you prisoner. I would have just executed you."

"That is the difference between you and us. We are not barbarians like your primitive race."

"Is that the philosophy you practiced when you left our world to die from the Myriad?"

Shyra agreed that her planet should have helped, but she knew her disapproval of the Savants' decision would offer little to no solace for the captive Zenakuu. "The Myriad massacre was an unfortunate mistake," she said, "but there was not much we could have done."

"Unfortunate? I lost everything! Everyone I ever loved was decimated. All that was left behind were their bones licked clean of any meat by those bugs, though I suppose to you that's just unfortunate. You make me sick," Donikan snapped.

Shyra looked down at the floor in embarrassment. He was right. They should have helped, but the Savants' word is law on Kalryn. "Donikan, listen to me. There is another way to end this. We do not have to kill each other."

"Wrong, Kalrynian. The only way this ends is with an entire ocean of spilt Kalrynian blood." Donikan laughed, "Foolish girl, our cause is avowed, righteous vengeance. We will see who will win this war."

Shyra's patience was wearing thin after the harangues. "What you propose is not vengeance; it is genocide."

"Spoken like a self-diluted pacifist. You really don't know what happened to us, do you? We will never forget that you didn't help us with the attack. You were supposed to be the mightiest force in the solar system. So what stopped you?"

"Show me," Shyra said.

"What?" he asked.

"Show me what happened. Let me see into your mind, so I can see for myself."

"Keep your filthy hands off me," Donikan demanded. "I wouldn't give you the honor of seeing how bravely my people fought."

"It was not a request," Shyra informed him. She telekinetically pulled him to the door of the cage. His chest banged against the bars and made a loud clanging sound.

"Don't touch me!" Donikan roared.

Shyra's eyes glowed white, and she began a mental link with the Zenakuu.

Shyra found herself in an unfamiliar place, but from the knickknacks on the wall and the display cases, she guessed it to be a gift shop or a pawn shop of sorts. She watched everything unfold from the eyes of Donikan who was standing in front of the counter. Festive music in the background and a foreign yet beautiful Zenakuu woman was behind the counter off to the left. Shyra paid close attention her flawless lavender skin and blonde fur; her nametag read "Lusie." She was talking to a tall, lanky male Zenakuu on the other side of the counter. Shyra heard the name Trisque in the conversation. It seemed like they were flirting as she ran her fingers gently down his forearm. Shyra guessed that they must have been dating based on their body language. Then from behind a draped off area in the back of the shop, a brutish, blood-red-furred and mantis-green-skinned Zenakuu came out carrying a broad sword and a shield. He stood right in front of Shyra and placed the equipment down on the counter.

"There you go, Donni. The usual: level-eight Zurekium sword sharpened and refinished and your level-ten Zurekium shield repaired and polished good as new."

The weapons were graceful yet obviously deadly at the same time, a true sight to behold. It was a task only Serafin could handle, so his assistant Lusie was manning the checkout counter. Lusie was a bit of an airhead, but with her good looks, she was stunning enough to draw in customers. The sword was all black and extremely broad but had a serrated edge on one side while the other had a slicing edge. The design on the face of the blade and hilt had such intricate design it could put Kalrynian art to shame. The shield must have weighed half of what its user was and had the royal family's crest painted on it.

"You outdid yourself this time, Serafin," Donikan said.

"Well I had a hunch you needed to look your best tonight. Are you guarding the palace during the Summer Solstice celebration?"

"Yeah, and judging from the music outside, it sounds like the festivities are underway," he noted. "How much do I owe ya, Serafin?"

"You get charged the same every time—soldier's discount and a discount for loyalty. Sometimes I think I do this work for free, but you keep me busy, old friend."

Donikan handed the currency over before picking up his gear and slinging it over his shoulder with ease, despite its tremendous weight. "Thanks, Serafin. You're the best weapons specialist around."

"I should be thanking you. That damn gun law banned most of my customers from carrying firearms and cut my business in half," Serafin said.

"It's for good reason, old friend. Only the royal guard should be allowed to use guns. We need to recycle those precious metals for better use. Do not forget our world is in dire straits," Donikan said.

"Yeah, and we the people have to suffer because the kingdom has led us to this dried up economy." Serafin slammed his fist on the counter, startling Lusie.

"Easy, brother," Donikan said. "We'll get to a better place soon enough. It's always darkest before the dawn, right?"

"Perhaps. I still can't believe we are running out of resources this quickly. I see more and more people on the streets. The amount of beggars has truly gotten out of control," Serafin grunted as he pointed his finger in Donikan's face. "And another thing, Donikan, I don't agree with Emperor Zelix's decision to trade Zurekium to other worlds for resources. We should just keep mining uninhabited planets. He besmirches the honor of his pelage by begging for help."

"Serafin, you worry too much. Who cares if we trade Zurekium? It's our number one export, and we have such an abundance of it I can't see the harm," Donikan said.

"The same can be said about mining planets without sentient life. Where's the harm in sticking to what we do best? I'll give the emperor a piece of my mind if I ever get the chance."

Donikan laughed at the thought of his old friend storming the castle walls and demanding to see the emperor.

"Serafin, you'll never change. Alright, man, I'm gonna head out. Thanks again." Donikan opened the door but was greeted by a loud crash and shockwave that knocked him on his behind.

The blast reverberated through his chest and almost blew out his ears.

"What the Cezial's inferno was that?" Donikan growled. His ears were in severe pain. He placed his hand on them and saw the green blood seep through his fingers. Donikan looked over at Serafin; the windows had shattered, and the lights went out from the crash. Donikan was disoriented, and the dust didn't help his vision. He saw Serafin's lips moving but couldn't hear a thing.

"... look outside. Lusie, Trisque, stay back." As his hearing returned, Serafin motioned Donikan near the front door of the shop. Donikan equipped his sword and shield.

"Be ready for anything," Serafin grunted as he got closer to the door. All he heard were screams and shrieks. He cracked the door just enough to see outside.

"What in the world is that?" Donikan asked. It was some kind of large insect-looking creature. Even though Donikan couldn't see much, he did notice they were about two to three feet tall and had six limbs.

"It's heading right toward us!" Serafin screamed as he slammed the door and backed up right away. The monster repeatedly rammed the door, desperately trying to get in. "Trisque, Donikan and I will hold the door while you find something to barricade it with. Go!" Serafin directed.

The two firmly pressed their backs to the front door, bouncing off a little bit each time the beast slammed into it. After a half dozen attempts, the door pounding stopped, and for a while they believed the insect had moved on—until, that is, the creature's two-foot claw pierced right through the Zurekium door and Serafin's right shoulder with ease. Blood spurted out, and he bellowed in incomprehensible pain. The insect quickly pulled his claw out, and Serafin fell forward.

Lusie rushed to his aid. "Serafin! Are you okay?" she screamed.

"I can heal. I'll be fine," he explained.

They knew boxes and crates would not be enough to stop the insect's advances. It continued stabbing the door. Not wanting to share his friend's fate, Donikan dashed away from it.

"Close the gates," Donikan roared. Serafin and Trisque ran over and reached up over head and pulled the security gates down. "What level is that door, Serafin?" Donikan demanded.

"Level five—same for the rest of the building," Lusie cried.

"And they cut right through it just like that?" Trisque added.

The creature's claw was still stuck in the door behind the gate. Its shriek pierced the ears of anyone near enough to hear it.

"Serafin, is there a back door to this place?" Donkin asked.

"Yes, it's through here," Serafin said, "but before we go, we should get weapons. I've been working on a few things. It's time to put them to the test." Serafin opened up a chest just beyond the draped backroom. He revealed three separate ballistic weapons.

"I call these scatter guns," he said. "They shoot out a casing that explodes in midair and releases smaller pellets. It works best at close range, but it covers large areas." He handed Trisque and Lusie the two scatter guns. "I'll take this," he added, grabbing a third weapon.

"What is it?" Donikan asked.

"I call it a tactical assault rifle. It is equipped with a grenade launcher, an inferred and night-vision scope, and a laser sight."

"I'm impressed. I knew you were the best weapons engineer around outside the palace walls, but I had no idea you had blueprints for guns," Donikan grinned

"I didn't have blueprints. I engineered these myself," Serafin boasted

"Whatever your reason for having guns, I couldn't care less at this point. Now how about that back door? The front door won't be holding that thing for much longer."

Serafin guided the others out the back door of the shop. Lusie was behind him followed by Trisque and then Donikan, the only one without a ballistic weapon. They exited the alleyway behind the shop that led to a main road. There wasn't much left of the city of Xenon. There was no one in sight—only the sound of pitter-patter and shrieks generated by the creatures. During this time of year, you were almost guaranteed to be elbow to elbow with people as they flooded the streets to celebrate. Mothers took their children to the city for various games and rides. Locals gathered for shopping or simply to marvel at the festive decorations. It was a celebration all around with so much energy and life buzzing through the air.

Zenakuu didn't celebrate many holidays, so when they finally came around, it was a party that could almost be felt throughout the entire planet. Natives dressed up in ceremonial robes and costumes, while others danced in the streets until the ground itself rumbled beneath their toes. Xenon had everything; being the biggest city on the planet, it always held these events. Donikan took a look around at the once prospering city. Its large buildings that were built for shelter gave no such thing, because these hideous invaders had the tools to cut right through them. He remembered the claw that pierced the door; it sent a shiver down his spine, and caused his fur to stand on end.

"C'mon. Let's press on, Donni," Serafin alerted.

"We should stay off of main roads and keep to the alleyways," Donikan pointed out.

"Agreed," Serafin said. "Now let's get to the next one without being seen."

The four-person team quietly pressed through the city in a single-file line, alert and cautious. They trolled trough a couple more alleyways and in the distance saw the tremendous crater with what they estimated to be a mile-long smoldering meteorite still inside. The bugs were still shooting up in the air like an exploding geyser and came raining down on victims who were close enough.

"Well, now we know what they came here on," Serafin observed.

"That's not good. Just how many are there?" Trisque asked.

"Judging by the size of this, there have to be thousands—a whole city's worth," Donikan retorted. "We have to keep moving. We're sitting targets out here in the open."

The group continued down the street. While Serafin, Donikan, and the others were moving through the city, they heard a scream from inside one of the buildings to the right side of the street.

"Did you hear that? We have to check it out," Donikan said.

"From the sounds of it, Donni, it would be too late." Serafin pointed out.

"Are you serious? We have to try." Donikan ran off toward where the scream originated.

"C'mon we got to back him up," Serafin exclaimed. Lusie and Trisque followed Serafin. After all, what choice did they have? With no combat training or even survival training, their lives depended on Serafin and Donikan.

Donikan got to the front door. He heard a woman inside screaming "Get back!" He kicked down the door and distracted the attacker by bashing his sword on his shield.

"Hey, over here!" Donikan crouched down and brought his shield to the bridge of his nose. Now he was close enough to the enemy to see it in all of its terrifying detail.

It turned its body to face Donikan. It stood only on its hind legs and had four arms, which were almost three feet long with razor-sharp, scythe-like claws that were another two feet long on the end. Its legs were a lot smaller than its arms and were bent backward. On its head were bulging eyes, protruding fangs, and long feeler antennae. Donikan noticed its legs were much shorter, so he knew right away that it wasn't very mobile when only on its hind legs.

The creature shrieked and stretched out its claws; it then dropped down and raced for Donikan. Utilizing all six limbs, the creature was fast, but its height was cut in half. Donikan stood his ground and backed his shield up with both arms. The creature was close enough now for Donikan to attack. He lunged forward and planted his shield in the creature's face. The contact was so incredible that Donikan did an involuntary front flip over the charging creature. Donikan landed on his back. His sword came loose from his sheathe and slid toward the woman in the room.

"Ma'am, I need my sword. A little hand please," Donikan grunted.

The woman was frozen with fear. Donikan never took his eyes off his opponent, because he knew it was going to charge again. It did. He kept his shield close for the best possible control. This time, before collision the creature sprang up and drove its claw down on Donikan's shield. It was a grazing blow, but it gave Donikan a chance to get behind it and open up some room. The creature, however, jumped on the wall, turned around, and sprang right at Donikan. He barely had time to bring up his shield. The force of the blow caused Donikan to go flying backward through the Zurekium door, breaking it off the hinges.

"Need a hand, old friend?" Serafin arrived on the scene and helped Donikan up on his feet. Donikan looked in the house and saw the woman he sought out to rescue being cut down and feasted upon by the beast. Something snapped inside Donikan. He ran inside the house full of rage, and while the creature was eating, Donikan picked up his sword, enhanced his strength with his karyokinesis, and forcefully slashed down on the creature's back.

The sword bounced off its back, and Donikan finally saw the strength of his enemy. Strong and unbelievably fortified, its exoskeleton seemed impregnable. Donikan wondered if there was a way to stop the creature. He took a couple steps back; the creature turned around, went on its hind legs, and screeched. Donikan blindly slashed. The sword found a joint by the creature's claw, and a gooey, light brown filling plopped onto the floor—the exoskeleton was weak at the joints. No one could have predicted what happened next.

The screech turned into whines, and before everyone's eyes, the creature curled up a bit, similar to a dead bug. Steadily, the severed arm produced a stub covered in the thick, gooey blood.

The stub grew bigger, gurgled more of the slimy blood out, and soon generated a claw. The creature had completely regenerated its severed limb.

"Watch out, Donni." Serafin pushed Donikan out of the way and opened fire. Bullets showered the creature, but nothing really hurt it. Serafin took a couple steps back, shoving Donikan back with his left hand.

"Out the door; stay behind me," ordered Serafin as the creature regained its composure. Serafin loaded his grenade launcher and took aim at the creature, but before he fired, he saw the severed claw rumbling around on the floor. It seemed to have gotten bigger.

Serafin quickly thought to himself, *Could they regenerate new bodies from severed limbs?* He didn't wait around to find out. When the group was behind him and out of harm's way, Serafin fired his weapon and blew the back of the room up into nothingness.

"That will surely attract more monsters," Donikan growled while sliding his sword back into his sheathe. The group heard the creature's noises getting louder and louder, "We need to get back in the alleyways, so we can move hidden from plain sight."

Back in the cramped capital city's alley system, the group kept moving as they looked for sanctuary. The stench of death was choking, Lusie and Trisque were tired and scared, and Donikan was suffering from a couple cracked ribs from their last encounter with the creatures and focused his karyokinesis on healing. Serafin, however, was still going strong. He was metaphorically holding his followers up on his shoulders. The group came to another wide intersection.

"We have to cross this main road here and then more alleys and then we will be out of the city." Trisque informed.

"Great, but what if they have moved past the city?" Lusie asked.

"Well, no matter what, the palace will be the safest spot on the planet at this point. The giant Zurekium walls are impenetrable, they have stationary gunners on all four corners of the palace on two separate levels, and plus they have snipers posted on the walls, guns, and an army. I think it's best if we go there." Donikan made a good argument.

"Okay, Lusie. You go first. Trisque and I will cover you from the alley." Lusie scurried across the intersection without making a sound. "You go on next, Serafin." Donikan suggested.

"Okay, watch my back, Donni." Serafin ran about halfway before the ground began to rumble. Serafin tightly grabbed his rifle close to him as he tried his best to stay balanced.

The ground erupted in front of Serafin, creating a dust cloud in the streets. Rocks and dirt flew in every direction; Serafin guarded his face with his left forearm. When the dust settled, a giant creature was revealed. It had to be three to four times bigger than any other one they had seen yet. It towered over Serafin.

He backpedaled while looking down his scope and gave himself some breathing room. Serafin opened fire, and under a cannonade of bullets, the single insect screeched and drooled at the thought of eating the succulent Zenakuu. Serafin unloaded an entire clip into his enemy but then remembered that even the smaller ones were resistant to his bullets, so they would be no more than a minor nuisance to the monstrosity in front of him. It lunged forward, and in the last second, Serafin dove out of its way.

"Lusie, run. Get outta here and find a place to hide!" Serafin bellowed across the street. Trisque and Donikan stood back and watched in the darkness of the alley, knowing that they couldn't help him. She ran for dear life into dark alleyways and out of sight from the others.

The giant insect's deadly claw swept through the air. The claw was so big it actually generated a breeze that carried with it the creature's putrid smell. Although the creature was powerful enough to take on anything, it was way too slow to get anywhere close to Serafin. He jumped, dodged, dived, and slid out of harm's way as he waited for an opening. One of the claws slashed downward and ended up getting stuck in the ground. That was the opportunity Serafin was waiting for. He ran up the creature's arm and reloaded his grenade launcher. He took aim, jumped backward, and squinted his eyes. He fired, sending the grenade right into the creature's mouth. Its head exploded into a downpour of blood and fragmented exoskeleton; however, all the commotion led the bulk of the invaders to Serafin's location. Serafin knew he was out in the open, so he got the attention of all that showed up.

"Run!" Serafin pleaded. He meant to sacrifice himself and ran out of sight around the corner. With half their group disbanded, Trisque was now stuck with Donikan. Donikan now had to lead Trisque out of the city. Lusie was gone, and so was Serafin; Donikan wasn't sure what to do next. In an attempt to find Lusie, they went into a ransacked store.

"Looks like no one is here. Let's take a break and continue in a bit," Donikan said as he proceeded to sit on an old looking crate.

"A break? Are you out of your starking mind? I can't take a break in a place like this, with everyone dying around us," Trisque snarled. "Lusie and Serafin are alone fighting for their lives. You can take a break, Donikan. I'm going to find Lusie."

"I'm glad you still have some fight left in you. Okay, let's do this." Donikan used his sword as a cane and helped himself stand back up.

"Now we have to keep moving, and fast. I noticed due to their body construct and the speed they travel that they're going to have a hard time taking sharp turns. So if we get into a pinch out there, just stay close to me, and we will be able to outrun them." Donikan walked to the back of the store and found a back door. The two exited and traveled through some more alleys. They traveled to a place Trisque believed Lusie would go to if she ever got into trouble in the big city.

"Are we getting close, Trisque?" Donikan asked.

"Yeah, we're almost there. I'm surprised we haven't seen those things in a couple hours," he said.

"Wait. Did you hear that?" A faint screech reached the survivors. Donikan climbed a fire escape to see where the noise had come from. He saw a flood of claws and fangs; the streets were painted in their greenish-black spotted exoskeletons.

"How many are there?" Trisque asked.

"There are a myriad of them. No wonder they took over the city in just a few hours." Donikan gazed out into the distance for a bit before snapping out of his trance. He jumped down from the rooftop and pushed Trisque forward.

"We need to find a safe haven." Donikan barked.

Try as they may to run away, the beasts grew closer, but Trisque and Donikan never looked back. They heard the claws scrapping the ground behind them and the all too familiar screech that filled their ears time and time again. Donikan grabbed Trisque by his shirt and guided him around a ninety-degree turn. Just as Donikan suspected, the creatures couldn't make the turn. They stumbled and fell over each other. Just then, Trisque pitched a plan to Donikan. "We can't keep running," he said, pointing to a manhole cover. "There … let's head for the sewers. We can hide underground."

"It's worth a shot," Donikan agreed.

The two scrambled to remove the lid and one at a time jumped down in the sewer hole. The floods of creatures were too disoriented from the sharp turn to see where their prey had gone and continued on their hunt for life to consume.

Donikan and Trisque trudged through the thick sewage under the city for a while until Trisque broke the silence. "Maybe this wasn't a good idea," he grumbled while examining the sewage on the lower half of his pant leg.

"You can't think of cleanliness in the middle of an alien apocalypse," Donikan jokingly stated.

"This isn't funny, Donikan."

"I know. I just deal with stress by joking a lot—don't mind me," Donikan confessed.

The sewer plan seemed to work out well. They didn't confront any more threats, and they cut through the city quickly in the direction Serafin and Lusie had run.

"Trisque, I think it's time to go topside again."

"I think you're right," he agreed.

They proceeded to climb up the next manhole and emerged back on the streets. They smelled horrid, but more importantly, they were alive. They noticed a nearby convenience store and sought shelter in it. They quietly entered the store, and Trisque fell on the floor from exhaustion.

"Who's there?" a voice from the darkness shouted, followed by the sound of a gun being cocked.

"Don't shoot. We're just trying to get out of the city alive," Donikan pleaded.

"No way. Donni, is that you, man?" the voice said as a man walked out from the darkness. He was holding a sizable rife with a sniper scope attachment. His fur was grey, and his skin was a caramel brown; he blended perfectly in the dark. He was tall and tone without being too bulky with muscle. Shyra was reminded of herself. He had the body of an Olympic swimmer.

"Greece? No way, man. Is that you?" Donikan answered back. He was a sniper in the Zenakuu army—one of the best.

"Of all the pelage to run into … Ha, I knew you would survive this pandemonium," Donikan joked.

"Well, you know me and my trusty 'problem solver' here get the job done," Greece said, holding up his sniper rifle. "I've been on the roof of this building since the beginning. With camouflage on, these things can't see me in the dark. Seems like they can't smell me either, and you know me, Donni, no one hears me coming till it's too late," he gloated.

"I suppose you're right. Well, let me introduce you to Trisque. He's been watching my back out there."

"Glad to meet ya, son. I hope you're keeping this soldier safe with that gun of yours. Say, what kind of gun is that anyway?"

"It's a scatter gun, sir," Trisque said with respect.

"That's right. Serafin the weaponsmith designed it," Donikan added.

"Serafin—you mean the guy with the shop on the corner of Haian and Putch?" Greece continued, "He was just through here. I told him to stay, but he said he had to find some girl. He was carrying a pretty impressive gun too. I didn't even think to ask—"

"He was here? Greece, which way did he go?" Trisque asked.

"No way, son. You guys aren't going out there without cover," Greece said. "I didn't want to go with him, but Donikan is a fellow soldier. Let me get my things, and I'll show you."

"That would be great. Told you we would find them, Trisque," Donikan said as he beat one hand against his chest.

"Yeah, all we have to do is follow his trail of blood," Greece casually said as he gathered his things.

Chapter 19

Tough Times Don't Last, Tough People Do

THE ONCE TWO-MAN TEAM had grown to three. They ventured off once more into the streets of Xenon, searching for their disbanded team. The screams for help they heard at the start of the infestation were no more. Donikan hoped it was because people had been able to find refuge, but in his heart he knew the real reason. No one had made it out alive. Most would have thought that the two they were searching for would be long gone, but that didn't stop them. Serafin saved Donikan's and Trisque's lives. Lusie was held dear to Trisque, moving on without them was not an option.

Greece led them to a broken-down, condemned municipal building that looked like it had housed no one but strays and rodents. It had broken pillars and crumbled statues littering the ground. In the building they found broken floor tiles and bullet holes everywhere. They got close to the court entrance where they discovered bullet casings all around the area.

"This has to be from Serafin's gun," Donikan grunted.

"Hold on, Donni," Greece said then growled. "We don't want to rush in to anything. You two press on. I am going to go up on that building across the street and will cover you from there."

"Okay, good idea," Donikan agreed. "Be safe out there, brother."

"No need to worry about me. I've got your backs." Greece ran off into the building that offered him the best vantage point. Donikan and Trisque continued to follow the trail of bullet holes and empty casings until they came to a dead stop. A countless amount of creatures lay motionless on the ground. Donikan couldn't believe it was possible to kill them, but there they all were. He did, however, notice that not one of them had a head. Then it clicked—they couldn't regenerate if their brains didn't activate the ability. Serafin had discovered the trick—destroy the head.

They followed the carcasses through the broken-down city hall. They spotted Serafin sitting under the outer wall lights. The lights flickered on and off, and Serafin was sitting on top of a monster he'd killed, which was hunched over in a bloody mess. Donikan and Trisque slowly walked around to get a better look. A half-eaten body rested before Serafin, and the blood-soaked blonde fur hinted that it could have been Lusie. Trisque spotted the pendant around the neck of the body; there wasn't a doubt about it—the mutilated remains were Lusie's. Trisque slowly stepped back and gasped for air. He bent over and began dry heaving. Donikan crouched down and closed her eyelids with his hands.

"Ahhh!" Trisque roared at the top of his lungs. He dropped to his knees and let his emotions overtake him. "I swear to Vizner I'll kill them all!" Trisque shot his scatter gun into the air purposely to attract the ones who had taken his love away from him.

"Are you out of your mind, Trisque?" Donikan yelled.

"I want them to come." Trisque stood still with tears soaking into the fur on his face. Donikan gave the signal to Greece to abort position and regroup. The screeches were louder than ever.

Donikan turned back to Serafin who was still sitting in a trance and staring at Lusie's dead body.

"Serafin, we gotta move—" A gunshot cut off Donikan's words. He felt a splatter cover his back. He turned around and saw a headless creature standing right behind him with its claw lifted up. He looked up and saw Greece was still in position and nonchalantly waved while looking down his scope.

"Thanks, brother. We aren't too far from the palace," Donikan pointed out. "It's through the field about a couple city blocks away."

The gunshot had woken everyone from their trances; Serafin sprang up and reloaded his rife. Trisque realized that taking on thousands of the creatures wasn't such a good idea. The three turned and ran for the field; the sound of gunshots rang in their ears. Donikan knew he was safe as long as Greece was sniping.

They got about halfway to the palace when the gunfire ceased. Donikan looked back, and the creatures were barreling down on them. He started to worry about Greece. Serafin and Trisque began firing their guns to slow down their attackers. One was right on the heels of Trisque when another sniper shot took off the head of the creature, but the bullet traveled through and hit Trisque in the calf. He immediately fell; Donikan and Serafin both stopped. Serafin was able to stop a couple creatures that were close to Trisque, but when he ran out of bullets in his clip, the abominations were all over Trisque.

"Get to the palace!" roared Trisque as he shot a couple from his back. "Save your—" A claw went right through Trisque's chest, and the horde of creatures gathered and eviscerated his remains.

"We have to keep moving, Serafin," Donikan said. They both turned and dashed for the palace.

It was almost in reach when they heard a voice shout from atop the palace wall. "Hit the dirt!" Serafin and Donikan both dove down on the ground. The giant mini-gun tore the creatures tailing them to pieces.

The heavy, twenty-foot, twelve-inch, solid, level-ten Zurekium doors slowly opened. The palace was well fortified; it had impregnable outer walls, and sixteen mini-guns surround the compound, four on each corner. The palace gates opened up, and they stumbled in, exhausted and battered. The two were met at the entrance by soldiers and civilians alike. For the first time all night, they felt safe, but Donikan needed to go back for Greece.

"Serafin, we have to go back for Greece. He saved our lives; I will not take that for granted."

A Zenakuu general interjected. "There is a search party out there looking for survivors. When they come back to resupply, you can go back out there with them."

Donikan nodded, "Serafin, you should come with me. You know how to take them out, and we could use your talents."

"Wait a minute. You know how to kill these things?" the general asked.

"Yeah, you have to obliterate the brain. Without it, they won't be able to regenerate," Serafin explained.

"Brilliant! You must speak with Emperor Zelix this minute and share the news with the troops," the general responded.

"Gladly," Serafin agreed, "right after I help my friend back out there."

The palace doors swung open again, and two bloodied soldiers dragged themselves in. "Medic!" one soldier shouted, and a team of trained personnel rushed to their side.

"What happened out there?" the medic asked while trying desperately to stop the bleeding from the wide-open gash in the soldier's left side. Blood cascaded from the wound and quickly soaked up the gauze.

"We heard survivors in a bank, so we decided to check it out. I'm not sure what happened to the bank, but it looked like a bomb hit it. We got close enough and those ... monsters ambushed us. There was an endless number of them. Not only are they invincible, but they're smart, calculated."

The one soldier who dragged his injured comrade in continued to tell the story. "I am not going back out there. No one should."

After a few moments, the injured soldier gurgled blood and passed away. His wounds were too deep, and there was nothing the medic could do.

"Donni, maybe we shouldn't go out there," Serafin said with a grunt. "Greece is a soldier; he would understand."

"I don't care, Serafin. I will go out there by myself if I have to. I would rather die with honor than live as a coward."

"He gave his life to save us. Going back out there and risking your life will only throw that sacrifice away," Serafin pointed out. "Donni, don't let his death be in vain. I'm going to speak with the emperor."

"Do what you must," Donikan answered. "I'm leaving."

"Donikan, don't be a fool!" Serafin shouted.

Donikan walked out into the baron wasteland that was once Xenon armed with only a broad sword. The ghost town had the smell of fresh blood and gunpowder in the air, and anything heard could be expected to be an enemy. It was amazing how quiet such large, primitive beasts could be. As Donikan crossed the streets of the once prospering town, he showed no fear. With his sword in one hand and his shield in the other, he was ready for anything, including death. Surprisingly enough, he made it to the building where they'd last seen Greece unscathed.

"Greece, where are you, Buddy?" Donikan whispered to himself. He noticed blood on the floor. "This has to be his."

Donikan continued to follow the trail of blood, dead bugs, and bullet casings up the marble stairs and onto the roof. "This must be where he was covering us." Donikan saw the hole where Greece fell and fought with the soulless savages. Donikan jumped down the two stories and found the small room destroyed from the fight that had ensued. He stumbled through the hole in the wall, following his friend's footsteps. Donikan spotted an empty clip by a doorway that led out to an alleyway and into the next building over. He crept to the adjacent building, which used to be a thrift store, and immediately headed to the top where he found none other than Serafin.

"Serafin! What are you doing here?" Donikan asked, obviously surprised.

"Well I couldn't just let you go off on your own," he growled. "I knew where Greece was last, so I figured I could help you out. Oh, and by the way, you're too slow." Serafin smiled as he turned and headed down to ground level.

As the two quietly exited the store, Serafin cautiously peaked around the corner to ensure there were no threats. They continued down the street, and Serafin equipped his infrared scope to scan the buildings for hot spots and living organisms. Unbeknownst to them, the alien bugs were underground tunneling.

"There isn't a single one in sight. What's going on?" Serafin wondered. Just then, he caught a glimpse of thermal energy on the infrared scope. Serafin and Donikan rushed into the building and found Greece bleeding on the floor, gun in hand. He was no longer conscious, but his military instincts made him continuously pull the trigger on his empty firearm as he barely held on to life. As they scanned the room, they saw he was surrounded by headless carcasses.

"Greece, you're going to make it, Buddy. Hang in there," Donikan cried out. There was no doubt that this place was going to be the final resting spot for the brave sniper. Almost as if he waited for confirmation of their safety, Greece stopped breathing as soon as Donikan's voice filled the air. Determined to give his fellow comrade a rightful burial, he picked him up and slung the limp body over his shoulder.

"I've got you," Donikan told his friend. "We'll patch you up good as new." By the time Donikan had left the building, Greece was already dead.

"Donikan, we won't make it all the way back with him on your shoulders. It will slow us down," Serafin pleaded.

"I don't care! I don't want to fight anymore. I just want to bury him," Donikan cried out with tears trickling from his eyes.

"I respect that, Donikan, but is it worth your life?"

Donikan stood there for a moment. He gently placed Greece's lifeless body down and asked Serafin for a few rifle shells. He cracked them open and poured the gunpowder over Greece then pulled out a book of matches. Donikan placed Greece's trusty sniper rifle on his chest with his hands folded across it.

"Rest in peace, Soldier, and thank you." Donikan then flicked the flint of the match as it spontaneously combusted. The smell of sulfur mixed with blood was in the air as Donikan tossed the match on his comrade. His head hung low, Donikan and Serafin slowly walked out of the building.

"Donikan, I'm sorry." Serafin felt his friend's pain—the entire planet felt that pain. The roaring fire behind them quickly brought the creature's attention straight for them.

"Listen, Donikan, we need to hurry back. These things will overrun this place in minutes, and we want to be as far away as possible," Serafin said.

"You can bet your pelage on that, Serafin. Let's get out of here."

With that, the two sprinted back for the palace. Serafin and Donikan made it pretty far unnoticed, but all good things must come to an end. Soon, the ground began to rumble. Serafin turned around and witnessed a building being torn down by the rattling of the planet.

"They're underground!" Serafin shouted. Remembering the freakishly large alien menace they'd encountered in the beginning, Serafin feared the worst. The ground burst open, sending Serafin and Donikan flying in opposite directions and landing hard on the dismembered ground.

"Not again," Serafin groaned.

Donikan picked himself up as thoughts raced through his mind. "This is all my fault. If I hadn't gone after Greece, we wouldn't be in this situation. I couldn't save Lusie, Trisque, or Greece, but I will save Serafin no matter what," Donikan said to himself. "Serafin, run! Get outta here now!" he snarled at his friend. Donikan jumped as high as his legs allowed. His trained eye located a soft spot in the enemy's head, and with surgical precision, he thrust his sword through its eye. The impact sent a shiver of pain up his arm, but he pressed until the blade cracked through the creature's carapace. He twisted the blade and then yanked it out. The beast staggered back for a moment, blood oozing from the wound. Then the carapace began to knit back together. In a moment, the hole completely closed up. The creature shook its head and then let out a roar.

Donikan backed up. *No way this is happening. It just isn't possible. Is it?* Donikan thought to himself. He knew next to nothing about these creatures. He was certain of only one thing: the knife wound had done little more than piss it off.

Donikan gripped his sword by the handle and continued hacking away at the insect. The creature's blood gushed out, splattering all over Donikan as he cleaved the blade through its head. Its lungs screamed for relief as it fell to the ground. Due to his anger, Donikan's body shuddered violently as he stood over his victim.

Serafin had never seen Donikan so angry. He grabbed him by the arm, and they headed toward the palace once more. They ran for their lives, doing their best to not run into anymore beasts. They reached the palace with discouraged looks painted on their faces.

"Are you the only ones left?" the gatekeeper asked.

Donikan and Serafin nodded. "Now where is the king? I must speak with him," Serafin snarled and bore his teeth.

"Follow the emergency tunnels to the safe haven," the gatekeeper instructed. "He waits there with the royal family."

Donikan threw his weapon over his shoulder, and they walked into the dark depths of the palace.

Chapter 20

Heavy is the Head That Wears the Crown

Serafin and Donikan traveled deep into the palace and then underground to get to the Royal Panic Room. The guards stopped them at the start of a long hallway.

"What is your business with the emperor?" one guard asked.

"*Well our planet is being torn to shreds, but I just thought I'd stop by and say hello.* What do you think we're here for!? We must see the emperor," Donikan demanded.

"Enough, Donikan. Calm down." Serafin was a known legend for being a weapons engineer. Many of the artillery and turrets the palace used in their defense were designed by Serafin himself. "I have knowledge of our enemy, and I was told to share it with him," Serafin added.

"Stand down," one sentry said to the other. "Don't you know who that is? It's Serafin."

Embarrassed, the guard quickly stood aside. "Please, Serafin, your forgiveness. I did not know," the guard apologized.

"Just get out of our way," Donikan grunted.

Serafin and Donikan had to give up their weapons to the guards in order to continue. The hallway had paintings aligned perfectly on both sides. The paintings depicted each emperor throughout the years.

When they arrived at the door, Serafin knocked three times. The door was unlocked from inside and was opened by the empress. Serafin viewed Emperor Zelix sitting on his throne, while his family huddled together behind him. With him in the room were all the treasures of Zenakuu—historical books, jewels, armories, rare art, and knowledge passed down by many generations. It almost seemed as though they had no intention of fighting back. Serafin stood there puzzled. *Was he planning on letting everyone die while he stayed safe?* Serafin wondered to himself. The emperor sat on his deep purple throne fit for a king. Clearly, the craftsmanship of the chair was not from Zenakuu, but the emperor always had an unusual taste for art.

"Your majesty, I bring news from the front lines," Serafin said.

The two walked up and kneeled down in front of the emperor. He was large in stature and had fur only the royal family could grow—shiny gold fur and a deep purple skin.

"My lord, my name is Serafin. With me is a member of your great army, a Berserker by the name of Donikan. I have insight on how to kill these attackers."

"Stand before your emperor, Serafin, Donikan. These are rough times, and frankly, I don't have time for pleasantries. However, this is great news. I will get a communication specialist out there and tell the world of your discoveries. We could be the last ones on planet Zenakuu. Hours ago I sent out a distress signal to the planet Kalryn. My words fell on deaf ears, and we are left for dead. If my people get out of this alive, we will make Kalryn pay for ignoring us in our most desperate hour."

"My lord," Donikan broke in. "My wife and daughter were your royal servants. I have not seen them yet. Have you any news?"

"I regret to inform you, but your wife showed sacrifice above what was asked from her. She gave her life to guard your child. From what I heard, she fended off three of those beasts to protect your daughter, but they were overwhelmed by the insect's relentlessness. She did not make it, and your girl was severely wounded. We did what we could to keep her alive for as long as possible, but the rest is up to her now. She is in the back if you wish to see her." The emperor turned to his wife. "Henriella, my queen, take Donikan to see his daughter."

Donikan slowly walked in the back room and saw his daughter held together with medical equipment and strung up to life support. Donikan broke inside and stared at his little girl dying. Her soft blue skin and light orange fur had been dyed brown from their green blood.

"My child, I am so sorry I wasn't there for you and your mother."

The girl was fading, but she recognized her father's voice and struggled to smile. "I love you, Dad," was the only thing she could say before ultimately meeting death.

"I love you too." Donikan roared with agony. He'd lost everything worth living for in one day. He removed the gold necklace he'd bought her for her tenth birthday from her blood-soaked neck and gripped it tightly. He pulled the sheet up to cover his daughter and kissed her on the forehead. Donikan wrapped the chain around his sword's hilt. By doing so, he signified that every enemy his sword hacked down would be in honor of his daughter, who would live on through his actions.

Donikan left the room and entered the adjoining panic room, but as the doors sprang open he was met by a scene of total disarray.

"My lord, they are here. They have breached our defenses," a royal guard informed.

"You have to get out of here, my lord. I'll stay here and destroy their brains. It's the only way to stop them," Serafin cried out.

"I am afraid not, Serafin. I want you to watch over my family. You have survived these horrors for this long, and it's obvious that my guards are no match for them. There is an even stronger panic room thirty yards below this one meant for nuclear fallout. Please take my family down there and come back for any survivors."

Serafin nodded, and the emperor turned to speak his final words to his beloved family. First his wife Henriella, a beautiful Zenakuu woman who stood strong and silent, but in her eyes you could also sense fear from all that had transpired. She possessed black hair, bleach white skin, and a smile that was warm enough to melt polar ice caps.

"My love," the emperor said, "I need you look after the children and world from now on. Follow Serafin. He will lead you to safety."

Despite her unquestionable strength, tears flowed down her cheek because she knew this was the last time she would talk to the man she loved so unconditionally. "I don't know if I can do this without you," she whimpered. "The cubs need their father, especially Xarnoricc. He's so young."

He smiled at her sincerely. "You're more than he'll ever need. Above all else, make sure they survive."

"Of course, my love."

The two kissed and held each other for the last time. Emperor Zelix kneeled down and placed both hands on his son's shoulders to give him one final lesson. With the average life expectancy of 189 years, he was still but a child at the age of twenty-four.

"Son, someday you'll understand all this when you're emperor, but for now, know your father loves you, your brother, and your mother very much. All I do is for the three of you. I'll meet death before I'd let any of you meet harm."

Zuresh was in tears, because he knew it would be the last time he looked upon his father's face. He sniffled and hugged his father as tight as he could.

Emperor Zelix smiled and said, "It's going to be up to you now, so remember the beliefs of our people—integrity, dignity, and honor."

Saddened, Zuresh nodded at the emperor's wishes and did his best to be strong. "Yes, Father."

Lastly, Zelix turned to his youngest son Xarnoricc, who was only six. He knew the young boy would be too young to remember his face. The Emperor lamented over not being around to watch him grow up, but in his heart, he knew it was the only way to ensure their survival.

"Xarnoricc, I love you more than life itself, so please forgive your old man for not being there for you in the future. I'm leaving you my will and resolve so be strong, my son."

"Daddy, don't go," he cried.

"It's okay, Xarnoricc. Everything will be all right soon," the emperor assured his son. "Be good and listen to your mother. Okay?"

The bloodthirsty monsters were clawing at the door of the first panic room.

"Emperor!" Serafin shouted.

Zelix whipped his head back to see the creatures trying to burst through the doors. "Get everyone out of here now!" Zelix barked back. Serafin rushed back, grabbed Xarnoricc, and led the royal family down the passageway that led to the next safe room.

Donikan stampeded toward the door and barricaded it shut. The emperor needed some time to get battle ready, so Donikan tried his best to barricade the door while he readied his armor. First, the emperor put on his knee-high Zurekium boots that came to a point at the knee. He hooked on his leg armor, which fastened over his thigh. Next his chest armor went over his head and covered the vital organs in his chest and sported spiked shoulder pads. He attached his two pieces of armor that went over his forearms. The last piece of armor was the emperor's helmet, which was a sturdy Zurekium piece of armor that had three fins that came up and traveled from the front to the back of the helmet and came to a point. The armor as a set was called the Emperor's Rampart. It was all black with red trim, and the chest plate was painted a vibrant gold.

The creatures had been thrashing at the door for several minutes.

"I don't know how we will survive this, they're a myriad," Donikan said. The emperor sat back in his throne ready to pounce, like a mighty lion waiting for the inevitable kill.

"Then we will hack down these myriad into pieces," the emperor replied. The Myriad's hard work finally paid off. They burst through the doors, knocking Donikan to the floor and rushing for the emperor.

"Come! Show me what you're made of!" The emperor roared. First he tried his necrokinesis, a bloodline ability only inherited by the royal family that zaps the life force out of one's opponent. He attempted to lessen the Myriad's kinetic energy, but the monsters did not use any kind of kinesis. It was all brute strength and incredible regenerative abilities.

The room was small, but the emperor was resourceful. He jumped over the first Myriad, grabbed the chandelier, and then landed right on the head of another, crushing its head beneath his boots as if they were grapes. The familiar clatter of sharp claws filled the hallway; he knew exactly what was next. Three more Myriad found their way to the panic room.

Like a savage animal, Donikan cleft the insects' heads by swinging his sword around and cutting off the heads of anything in his destructive path. He cleared a path for his lord as best he could so they could reach outside and have more room to fight.

The two emerged from the hallway into the wide-open palace where everyone inside the palace waited in suspense.

"Is everyone here? Is everyone alright?" Emperor Zelix asked.

"Yes, my lord, we haven't seen those things for hours," one civilian said.

"Are you okay, Sire? Is that your blood?" a soldier asked.

"I'm okay. How did those insects get past here? There is only one entrance to the panic room."

"My lord, the only ones who came through here were Serafin, the guard you're with, and the royal family, sir."

The emperor was puzzled. He went back down the hallway where he was cut off by a Myriad who had tunneled under the floor. "They can dig under the palace," the emperor said in disbelief. Another Myriad emerged behind him and grabbed him. The first Myriad started digging up, while the other followed and dragged the emperor underground. Donikan shouted for the emperor, but it was too late. Donikan was terrified of going in there. He had no idea if it was an ambush or if the emperor was even still alive, but he had nothing left to lose. He crawled through the tunnel and found himself outside the palace on the ground level where Emperor Zelix fought for his life with a mob of Myriad surrounding him. He charged in but was ordered to stay back by his bloodthirsty emperor.

One by one, the vicious aliens began hacking and clawing at the exploited emperor. He was able to dodge most of the attacks, but the few swipes that were able to breech his defenses did a lot of damage. His armor was durable and withstood several cuts and stabs from the ferocious beasts but would not last forever. The emperor's karyokinesis was the best on the planet. He was faster, stronger, and more stubborn than any other Zenakuu. The Myriad had never faced such a formidable foe, but fear wasn't something the Myriad experienced—ever.

Utilizing his karyokinesis, the emperor was able to make short work of the smaller Myriad. He ripped the heads off one by one with lightning speed. Covered in blood and sweat, the emperor had a moment to catch his breath before the Myriad began their next onslaught. He felt confident and was ready for some more.

"I can't believe my people died from these pathetic bugs," he grunted. Painfully exhausted, he tried to gain his composure from the multiple bites and gashes that he suffered. The sun started to rise, and it seemed like a new day for the Zenakuu people,

"There has to be more survivors. There is no way the whole planet has perished," the emperor said. "I'm sure there are more like Donikan and I to fight back."

As if on cue, a helicarrier flew over the palace, and a voice filled the skies. "Attention all citizens, we are picking up any survivors at the emperor's palace."

"Finally, a way out. These things can't fly—it's genius." The emperor's hopes were raised again

The emperor was ready to put an end to this war but witnessed the army of Myriad trailing the Helicarrier. They stacked over each other, reaching higher and higher until they were almost in range.

No, this can't be, is there no end to this nightmare? Will I ever wake up? He thought to himself.

The Myriad insects saw the emperor standing wearily in the field and quickly turned their attention toward him. He jumped back and tightly gripped his weapon. He was faced with an unbelievable number of Myriad all bearing their razor-sharp gnashing teeth that dripped with drool anxious for their next meal. The only thing he could think was *How could there be so many of them? The rock that landed was not that big.*

The brave emperor was the last defense in between the emotionless Myriad and his family. They quickly surrounded him, but he didn't even flinch. Zelix was ready for the end, which was upon him. The first Myriad lunged at him, but with a quick sidestep and a downward slice, the bug fell to his blade. Another Myriad slashed his back and sliced him open like a ripe piece of fruit, bringing him down to one knee. Shocked at the damage caused to his body, the emperor realized that he'd severely underestimated his enemy. There was no doubt in the courageous emperor's mind that he was going to die that chilling morning.

Quickly getting up, the emperor cut off the head of another unlucky Myriad but fell right back down to his knee. He stuck the sword into the ground and used it like a crutch until he was able to stand on his own two feet. He raised his weapon and taunted the Myriad. They all screeched, which was followed by lunging, clawing, and slashing. The emperor was batted around awhile, but his sword was still able to find its targets and decapitate another two Myriad before he was tossed to the ground. Zenakuu's Emperor was down, helpless, and bleeding profusely, but he miraculously picked himself up again.

Karyokinesis can only get me so far … I can't take any more, he thought to himself.

"Sire!" Donikan yelled.

"I said stay back," the emperor ordered. "No more Zenakuu will die on my watch."

Out of breath and losing energy fast, the emperor knew the fight would soon come to an end one way or another. Desperately, he picked up a spear. "I can take out twice as many now," he said. He spat out a mouthful of blood and charged toward the biggest one he could find with reckless abandonment. He plunged the spear into its shoulder, knocking it to the ground.

The emperor lifted his spear and came down on the throat of the Myriad, cutting its head off completely. The other Myriad took advantage of the situation and simultaneously jumped on the emperor's back and began gouging and stabbing. Blood and chunks of flesh were flying from the claws of the monsters. Donikan could take no more; he ignored his orders and rushed in, successfully taking down two Myriad before receiving a near-fatal laceration to his chest. He fell to the ground helpless to do anything but watch as he and the emperor became breakfast. Serafin came back up from the panic room wielding his custom-made tactical assault rifle and shot the heads off the remaining Myriad like popping water balloons.

Serafin stood over the Emperor and Donikan who successfully killed a baker's dozen of Myriad.

"I don't think I've ever been so happy to see your face, Serafin," Donikan struggled to whisper.

"Easy, Donni. We'll get you two patched up all right," he said and then turned to his lord. "Emperor Zelix, your family is safe. Forgive me for not making it up here sooner."

The dying leader smiled and looked at him. "Don't be foolish. They are all that matter. As long as they're safe, I have no regrets."

"Can you stand, sir?" Serafin asked.

The emperor looked at him and coughed up blood. "No, I'm afraid this is as far as I go. It's up to the next generation now." He held up the family crest and told Serafin to give it to his eldest son.

"It's been an honor, sir." Serafin took the royal insignia from around his neck and laid his king to finally rest. Serafin supported Donikan by the arm, and the two ventured back down to the depths of the panic room and gave the crest to a crying, yet angry Zuresh, who would be the new emperor.

"Do not cry, young king. Your father fought and died with honor. I will stay by your side until you're ready to take on your new responsibilities as ruler of this world," Serafin swore.

Shyra released her telepathic link and snapped back into reality like a rubber band. Almost as if they shared emotions, the aliens looked at one another with tears rolling down their faces.

"I'll never forgive you, Kalrynian," Donikan snapped at Shyra. "You had no right to see that."

"Donikan … I had no idea it was that horrible, but we would have never got there in time," she said.

"Am I supposed to find comfort in knowing that you thought about it? The facts are you were remiss to our pleas for help. We would have thrived if we just had aid. For Vizner's sake, we are your sister planet, and you abandoned us! When I lost my entire family to those monsters, I promised myself that I would kill as many Kalrynians as I could."

"I am truly sorry that this happened, Donikan," Shyra said. "I know you are angry at us, which you have every right to be, but to start a war and involve all of these planets and people goes too far. We could have settled it with words and not transgressed treaties."

"You disgust me with your lies," Donikan snarled back. "Kill me or leave me alone." The scout tried his hardest to hold back his tears.

Shyra tried even harder to get through to the scout. "When is Zenakuu coming to cultivate Earth?"

"They will be here sooner than you think, Kalrynian, and I cannot wait till they rip this boring planet asunder and finally subvert your world from their self-proclaimed sovereignty."

That was the last straw for Shyra. "Do not count on subjugating this world like you did Purix. By the time your backup arrives here, my team will be able to destroy the entire army."

"We knew about the earthlings, and we already accommodated for it. They will be no match for our armada. Then we shall run right through your home planet and kill your father—slowly."

Shyra struck the scout across the face. "That is enough from you, hypocrite! You are no better than the Myriad. You murdered my betrothed as recompense for your imagined slight. Listen well, Donikan. If you want a war, we shall give you one." Shyra turned and stormed out of the holding chambers, leaving the scout with a bloody smirk on his face.

Chapter 21

What's So Super About Being Heroes

"What did he say, Shyra?" Cloud asked as Shyra exited the room. Are they coming?"

"He would not tell me anything, but I have a strong feeling the real battle is yet to come," Shyra said. "Alexander, I need you to rally your team together. There is still a lot we must do."

"That's gonna be easier said than done," he said.

"Being a leader always is," Shyra told him and went to check on Tori and Dimitri, who were tending to each other's wounds. She found Dimitri hanging over the edge of the healing tank as he helped Tori put on bandages and wrap up her cuts. She didn't want to disturb them, so she just peered around the corner and listened.

"You really scared me out there," Dimitri confessed.

"Well I was just trying to carry my own weight," She said sarcastically. "Besides I didn't even know you cared like that," Tori continued.

"Despite what everyone thinks, I care about all of you."

"Well, that comes through loud and clear," she said sarcastically said.

Dimitri gave her a glare and tightened her bandages.

"Ow!" she yelped and winced backward.

"Quit being such a baby. They're only a couple cuts and bruises. You should be used to it by now."

Tori looked down at the cold floor. "I don't know if I'll ever be used to this, D."

It was in that moment that Shyra felt guilty about the way she had been pushing everyone. She forgot that her team was still just kids thrown into a war they originally had nothing to do with. She pushed them to their limits to make them strong, but without even realizing it, they had crept into her heart. She had grown to care for them deeply. It broke her heart seeing them so injured. It was no life for children. They should have been out with friends, going to dances, and growing up normally. Instead, they were preparing for an invasion that could very likely cost them their lives.

"We'll be fine," Dimitri assured Tori. "I'll watch over you out there."

"Really? You mean that?"

"Of course. If I don't, who knows what will happen to you." He smiled at her, but she responded by placing her hand on top of his and looked deeply into his eyes.

"I don't know what I would do if I lost you either," Tori said, Dimitri was startled by the gesture. She had never made such a blunt advance before, and though he wouldn't admit it, he couldn't believe how good the warmth of her hand felt. He was caught by her balmy scent. Despite being in a potentially fatal battle, she still found the time to put on perfume.

"Tori … you know I have a girl—" Dimitri tried to get his words out, but she cut him off and removed her hand.

"When you're feeling better, let's get back to the others. Okay?" Tori said. "I'll meet you out there."

Dimitri watched her as she walked out of the med bay and wondered when things got so complicated. He stared at the tiled floor before letting his head fall back. Dimitri looked at the ceiling and let out a sigh of confusion, while on the other side of the ship Alex, Cassie, and Christian started their group meeting.

"What do you think he said to her?" Chris began. "It had to be something shocking. She hasn't talked to us all night, and I thought I saw a teardrop when she went back to her room. I didn't even know Kalrynians could cry."

"I'm not sure, but whatever it was spooked Shyra," Cassie added. "If he said that they were coming with an army, she would have to tell us. What do you think?" she asked as she turned to Alex.

"I don't know, Cass, but I'm going to find out. I'll talk to her later and make sure she's okay."

Cassie pulled Alex to the side to speak with him privately on the way to see Shyra. "Alex, can I ask you something?"

"Sure, anything," he responded.

"Do you think it will ever get easier?"

"I'm not sure I follow. What do you mean?" he asked

"Killing. I killed someone today, Alex," Cassie explained. "The images of him dying—and, more importantly, me killing him—have been running through my head. It has been plaguing me since it happened."

"I can't say for sure, Cass." Alex always tried to comfort her in times of doubt. "But remember that this is self-defense. In the heat of the battle, you'll get used to doing what you must to survive. Just think—if you didn't defend yourself today, you wouldn't even be here to worry about it."

"Maybe you're right. Thanks, Alex. I think I'm gonna try to get some sleep, I'll see you in the morning."

"Good night, Cassie." Alex wished that with all his heart.

Alex finally made it into Shyra's quarters. "Are you all right, Shyra?" he asked.

"Oh, Alexander, you startled me. Yes, I am just fine."

"How are Dimitri and Tori?" Alex asked.

"Good, none of their vital organs were hit. They should recover soon," she answered.

"Well, that's good," he said as he paused for a moment. "Shyra, what did that scout really say to you?"

Shyra was reluctant to tell him, but she felt it was only right they know what they were in store for. "His name is Donikan, and they have a blood feud with Kalryn," she explained.

"Well obviously, or they wouldn't have attacked you," Alex responded, "but did he say anything about them sending an army?"

"Alexander, even if they do send the full force of Zenakuu, you and the rest of the alliance will be ready for anything."

"So they are coming?" Alex asked again.

"When they find out that their scouts did not return, they will want to find out what happened."

"I understand," Alex said. "I'll leave you alone now. You have a good night, Shyra."

"Goodnight, Alexander."

Alex stepped out and left the room. After his conversation with Shyra, Alex joined his friend at the front of the ship.

"What did she say, Alex?" Chris questioned.

"She said that it's obvious that they will come."

"We need to get stronger," Christian mentioned. "I don't think we're ready for an army. We hardly took care of the ten scouts."

"You may be right, bro. We need to keep training. Tomorrow morning we need to expand our powers, so let's gets some rest," Cloud instructed.

"Agreed, I think we're all pretty beat," Christian said.

The next day, the morning sun flooded the temple and brought with it hopes that the alliance could actually survive the war to come. After a full night in the healing tank, Dimitri was healing steadily. The team started training for the next step with their powers. They were worse for wear but kept moving forward. Shyra stepped outside only to find the team further perfecting their trade and couldn't have been more proud of them.

"Gather around me, everyone," Shyra instructed. "I feel like you all are ready for real-world combat. First things first—you need to go public and show the world that you are here to help.

Last thing we want is to have people afraid of you because of your abilities. For that reason we need to hide your identities."

"Shyra, why do we need to hide our identities?" Tori asked.

"So the bad guys don't find our families," Chris interjected.

"More or less, Christian. It is more so they cannot intervene with training. Your government would want nothing more than to figure you out and dissect an alien, so I think it is best to keep it a secret. I have made these masks. Each of them is unique and will compliment your uniforms."

The masks were more like helmets that covered their entire heads. Earth took his mask first. The mask was all black with a green symbol for earthquakes, which were sharp zigzags going horizontally and led into a ripple sound wave effect. The ripples surrounded his left eye, and the zigzags went over his right eye. There was also a solid green earthquake crack that started wide at the bottom and thinned out at the top. The mask was tight and covered his entire head.

Rain wasn't too keen on the idea of covering up her whole face, so she came up with her own method of concealment, which was a lot more subtle. She passed on Shyra's design and sported a look that could cover her face but still look tough. She found some blue wrapping bandage and fashioned it together so it acted as one mask to cover her nose and lower face. She tied it together in the back.

Flame's mask was given to him and was meant to strike fear into the hearts of his opponents. It was made of a highly dense polycarbonate material that matched the protectiveness of his armor. It was symmetrically black and red, excluding the mask's inexplicable slots for four eyes, and it faintly contoured to the outline of his face. Christian believed his mask was the coolest of them all, because it looked badass and easily attached to his uniform.

Wind followed in Rain's footsteps and asked for a simple white cloth that would cover her face from the nose down. She also requested a metallic forehead protector that looked very ninja-like in design and had intricate markings engraved on it.

Cloud stepped forward next. His mask was hard plastic, and the design was black and sharply angled with defining lines around his cheekbones. There was a yellow circle on the forehead with a lightning bolt within it. There was a yellow tinted visor that was connected to latches that were conveniently placed on the sides of his mask so he could detach if need be.

"Now the five of you can get some real-world experience and still protect your identities," Shyra said.

"That's great and all, but shouldn't we be preparing for the armada? I mean, we don't even know how much time we have," announced Tori.

"This *is* training, Tori," Shyra explained. What I learned from this past battle is that the enemy is tougher than we originally thought, but there is no greater training than experience. That is why I want all of you to go out there and prepare yourselves for what is to come while still remembering what you are fighting for."

Chris raised his hand.

"Yes, Christian?" Shyra asked.

"What about the media and news reporters? Won't they talk about us?" he asked.

Tori, who was initially against the idea, suddenly lit up. "Wait. You mean we're finally going to be famous?"

"More like infamous," Cassie interjected.

"She's right," Dimtri jumped in. "I've seen enough movies to know people don't like what they don't understand."

"Everyone, relax," Shyra said. "That is why I have given you all masks, so people will not discover who you are. You will be fine."

"Don't worry, Shyra," Tori reassured. "I know all about public relations. I will make sure we get the right coverage."

Shyra looked at her and raised her eyebrow. "I am leaving Alexander in charge."

"What!" Dimitri and Tori said simultaneously.

"I was the better fighter out there with the scouts!" Dimitri shouted.

"And what does he know about dealing with the press?" Tori protested.

Shyra, who was visibly annoyed, let out a sigh. "Listen, the both of you, Alexander protected the team while chaos broke loose. He displayed the leadership qualities that kept you alive and had the sapience to keep one of them alive so we could interrogate him. Furthermore, I am not sending you out there to be celebrities. This is all part of your training, so Alex not knowing how to conduct proper interviews suits me just fine. This discussion is closed."

"Sorry, Shyra," Tori said, ashamed by her outburst.

"A house divided cannot stand. You all really need to learn to work better as a team," Their mentor reminded them.

It was the end of January in the year 2015, and eleven months had passed since their normal lives were transformed into a bloody death match of alien force. It was time to embark on a new adventure. The team was more nervous about the world seeing them than the dangers they potentially faced, but Alex was always good at rallying his friends together. They had just acquired their new faces, but after they discovered what they could do with their powers, some of the team was not sure whether they want to fight regular humans.

Shyra left them with a reminder: "I will not lie to you. Nothing will ever prepare you for war short of war itself. However, I will do all that I can to get you to that point. I was so proud to fight alongside of you, and you all did so well. I have no problem declaring you saviors of your planet."

"Where do we begin?" Alex asked. "I mean, the whole planet? The United States? Or just this town?"

"You mean we're gonna be bona fide superheroes?" Chris interjected.

"Don't be stupid, Chris. We're just gonna show our faces—er, masks—and let the public know that we are on their side, so when the Zenakuu do come, they won't be scared of us and think that we are the invaders," Dimitri explained.

"That's what I said—superheroes," Chris retorted.

"Shut up, Christian, and take this seriously," Dimitri snapped back.

"Well you guys can do the whole PR thing. I am going to make a difference," Cassie said.

"Yes, but never forget your task at hand, which is preventing Zenakuu from taking over this planet," Shyra reminded them. Shyra went off to her quarters, while the rest of the team sat in the conference room.

"So are there any suggestions on how we are going to stop local or tristate area crime?" Alex asked, opening up the floor for any ideas. He proved to be more than just a leader but a teammate as well.

"I'm getting the hang of flying down, so Tori and I can always fly around and spot things that are happening," Chris suggested.

"Really, Chris? Do we have eagle eyes or something that we can spot danger from afar and swoop in to save the day?" Tori noted. "Besides, that doesn't make sense. Don't you think people would notice if they saw two kids flying around?"

"Sorry, Tori. It was just an idea."

"Why don't we just get one of those scanners—you know, like the police and firefighters have," Cassie suggested.

"That's actually not a bad idea," Alex agreed. "I mean, we can't be everywhere at once, but we would hear about close things that are in our power to stop,"

Dimitri soon joined in. "I think we can get one at an electronics store. We should go on our first patrol and pick one up."

"Okay, it's settled. We will pick up a police scanner tonight while on patrol," said the proclaimed leader.

"I can't believe this is happening. I'm having a total nerdgasm. We're gonna be real-life superheroes." Chris had an everlasting smile on his face ever since he'd received his mask.

"I know," Cassie agreed. "It's like something out of your comic books."

Chapter 22

May the Bridges I Burn Light the Way

Night fell on the first day that the team went from being trainees to heroes. They couldn't walk into a store decked out with superhero garb, so they changed into their normal clothes and found the nearest electronics store. The door chimed as they walked in and were greeted by the clerk. "Welcome to Tinker Trade. My name is Carl. How can I help you?"

"Hi, uh, we are looking for a police scanner?" Alex asked.

"Sure, we have a number of scanners," the clerk said. "Do you want short-range or long-range?"

"Well, how far does the long-range go out to?" Alex said.

"I've heard police chatter on the edge of the next state over, so I guess about two states, depending on how big it is—not getting much in Alaska," Carl chuckled.

"Right, then we will take the long-range. Thank you," Alex concluded.

"Alright, that will be three hundred and thirty dollars."

"Um," Alex whispered, "Cassie, do you have, um, about two hundred dollars?"

"For God's sake," Tori interrupted. "I've got the money, just charge it on my card."

"Okay, Miss," Carl said. After a long pause, he added, "So are you guys volunteer firefighters something?"

The group shrugged the comment off with some nervous chuckles. They got the scanner and went back to the ship. The team arrived back home just before nine o'clock that night.

"Hey, Shyra, we got the scanner," Tori announced. "Cassie is going to hook it up if you want to join us." Silence answered. "Oh well, she must be sleeping."

An hour later, Cassie marveled at her own brilliance. "Okay, I think I got it," she said. "Gather 'round, everyone." Cassie knew the most about electronics. She spent most of her time in her room avoiding her mom and had nothing but an old computer to tinker with.

"How did you get so good at this stuff, Cass?" Christian pondered.

"It's simple, Chris. I read the instruction manual—something that is quite overlooked by most men."

The voice on the radio came through loud and clear. At first, they heard nothing but a few domestic violence calls and some disorderly characters exiting a bar and being too loud. They weren't aware that on the police scanner they only use codes, but thanks to the Internet, the team understood every disturbance. When 2:00 a.m. struck, they decided to head to bed. They left the scanner on all night just in case something big went down over night.

The sun rose the next day, and the alliance rushed back to the scanner. Chris was the first one there. "There hasn't been anything all morning," he told the others.

Dimitri came stumbling in last. "You guys are still hovering over that stupid radio? We are in the middle of nowhere; of course we won't see any action."

Suddenly, the scanner went off. "Calling all available squad cars, there is a high-speed chase in pursuit south bound on I-25," it announced.

"Now is our chance to show the world what we can do." Alex led the team with confidence and vigor.

Just then, as Shyra walked into the room, the police scanner picked up another emergency. "The Summer Shade apartment complex is on fire and spreading. Fire department is en route."

The team all looked at each other. "Okay, then," Alex began. "Guys, we're going to need to split up. Rain and Flame, get to that fire and put it out as soon as possible. The rest of us will handle the car chase."

"I will teleport each team to their destination. Voltaic Cloud, Seismic Earth, and Whisking Wind, you go first, then the others," Shyra said. "Is everyone ready?"

"Wait, you're not coming with us, Shyra?" Flame asked.

"No, I am afraid. The risk of me being spotted is too great, and your species would not take to an alien walking their streets favorably. I will stay here and be ready to transport you back. Good luck." Shyra stayed behind to watch over the ship.

Wind, Cloud, and Earth were teleported about two miles away from the chase, which was heading their way. It gave them enough time to think of a plan to stop them. Cloud started giving orders. "Earth, bring up a wall of rock to stop the car."

"Are you crazy? If I do that, they will smash into it and die," Earth pointed out.

"Just listen, Earth, okay? Now is not the time to argue," Cloud insisted. "Wind, I need you to direct strong winds against the car to slow it down. I will shoot the car with electricity to short out the battery and shut it down."

The plan was foolproof, but it was easier said than done.

Soon, the car came zooming down the road. There was a determined look on Cloud's face; he was certain that it was going to work. Hovering high above in the sky was a helicopter that was following the chase as the police department's "eyes in the sky."

Cloud looked at his team. "On my mark, after I hit it, Wind, you slow it down. Earth, you work on that wall."

A wall of rock and gravel was erected in the middle of the highway. Luckily for the team, the police shut down the highway, so there were no bystanders. The wind started to pick up as Wind's hands moved, guiding nature's powerful force. When the car came into sight, Cloud lined up his shot.

A jolt of electricity shot out from Cloud's palm. It veered slightly to the right and missed. He switched hands and immediately shot another bolt which hit the car, shutting it down immediately. The wind picked up more, slowing the car down exponentially. By the time the car arrived at the rock wall, it gently tapped into it and ultimately stopped. Earth covered his arm in gravel and ripped off the car door. He reached into the car and pulled the driver out.

When the police caught up, they discovered three young adults with strange costumes had stopped the car and put an end to the chase. Before the police could ask the young heroes what happened, they disappeared before their eyes. The group was teleported back home in front of the main steps, but the three had no idea everything had been caught on video by the circling chopper. Wind pulled Cloud to the side by the arm before the three could enter to have a private word with him.

"You're wrong about Dimitri, ya know," she said. "He would make a great leader if you ever gave him a chance." She let go of his arm and darted up the steps. He wasn't expecting the hit-and-run comment to have such an effect on him. He questioned himself as to whether he was being too hard on Dimitri and went to make amends.

In the next county, Flame and Rain found themselves beside the burning apartment complex just outside of the perimeter the firefighters had set up. The firefighters tapped in to a nearby fire hydrant and began putting out the raging inferno that had the onlookers frozen at the horrific sight. Rain knew what she had to do.

"Flame, go inside and see if anyone is trapped," she instructed. "I will work on putting this fire out."

Flame started walking toward the building when he was stopped by one of the firefighters. "What do you think you're doing, kid?"

"Don't worry about me, sir. I've got this." Flame looked at the building and kicked on his afterburners. He flew up and surveyed the burning building to see what would be the best approach. After getting a decent layout of the scorched apartment complex, he landed. Flame kicked open the main doors and was immediately greeted by a wave of heat so scorching hot that the convection was too much, even for him to bear. He cleared up a pathway so that he and the firefighters could enter the building safely. Windows popped and exploded from the walls causing embers and raging fires to shoot out. Flame cleared another path, and they continued to venture further into the building.

"Just follow me," Flame instructed. "We can save whoever is in there." The fire chief stood there dumbfounded.

"What kind of freak are you?!" He said as he began to step back. It made flame angry that the chief could so easily discriminate against someone who only wanted to help.

"I don't have time for this, you wanna stand there and call me a freak all day, or do you want to save lives?" Flame retorted. The chief paused for a moment before continuing.

"I don't want to believe it, but if that kid can move fire, then we need to use him to save the people in there. Men, get ready. We're going in," the fire chief uttered.

Flame led a small group of firefighters through the building to look for any survivors. Inside, black smoke spewed from every opening, making it impossible to see.

"Help me! Please, someone, anyone—I can't breathe in here!" a voice cried out in the distance.

"It came from over there," a firefighter said. "This way."

"Hey, kid, get rid of these fires down the hallway."

"Leave it to me," Flame said as he pushed the fires out of the way and extinguished them. "How is that, sir?"

"Good, but don't get cocky. We still gotta find those people. Now let's move!" the firefighter replied.

The group ran down the hallway, but the floor gave out. Flame fell down into the basement and landed poorly on his ankle, lucky not to get impaled by the crashing floor above him. "Argh!" the hero screamed out in pain.

"Dear God! Kid, you okay?" a firefighter screamed from above.

"Fine," Flame answered. "Just go on without me and save the woman. I will catch up."

The group of firefighters grudgingly pressed on without Flame. Rescuing the survivors was the most important task at hand. Flame attempted to use his Pyrokinesis to propel himself, but the pressure from the thrust proved to be too much for his twisted ankle that screamed in pain with each step taken.

Now how to I get back up? he wondered. Flame thought for a moment, aimed his hands down, and blasted himself like a rocket ship back up in to the first floor through the same hole he'd fallen through.

"What the heck is Rain doing?" Flame said aloud. "This fire should be out by now."

Rain could feel the water's current beneath the street. She gathered the strength to control the water that dwelled within the fire hydrant. The fire department was doing what they could to manage the devouring inferno that turned the complex into nothing more than an oversized pyre, but it was a battle they were quickly losing. The hoses suddenly lost pressure, and water ceased to flow.

"What in God's name is going on?" the fire chief snapped. "Manny, I thought I told you to keep the water flowing. It just stopped."

"Um, Chief," the rookie firefighter responded back.

They looked back and saw Effervescent Rain standing next to the fire hydrant with her hands lying upon it.

"What are you doing here, Kid? You're going to get hurt," the chief directed. "Get back."

Rain disregarded the man's instructions. The ground started rumbling, and Rain slowly walked back away from the hydrant. With her hands wide open, she reached out to it as it violently shook and with one quick movement clenched her right hand into a fist, causing the water to burst out of the top of the hydrant and peel the metal like a banana. The firefighters were pushed back by the force of the water. Rain brought the water high in the air and then moved it over the building. "Where should I put the water, Chief?" she asked.

The chief of the fire department looked in disbelief. "First a kid who can walk through fire and now a kid who controls water. What the heck is this world coming to? We have to wait for the guys who went in to get back to us. Just hang in there, Kid," the chief instructed.

The wait felt like hours. Rain patiently held the water over the building. Sweat dripped down the tip of her nose from the struggle. Her arms began convulsing and, as a result, large pools of water fell and doused small fires on the building's surface. She was growing increasingly tired, and desperately wanted to release the water on the points of the building where the flames roared the loudest.

"Hey, Chief, turns out the fire was caused by a faulty electrical outlet near the rear of the building. We just have to wash out the flames and call it a day," a firefighter announced.

The chief acted quickly and relayed the message back to Rain. "Listen, girl, the fire started in the rear of the building. Usually, we would have to fight through, but with you here, we can wash from the back to front."

"Okay, I will try my best," Rain said with doubt subtlety mixed in her voice. Suddenly, loud explosions of fire crashed through all the windows on the south side of the building. Rain wasn't so sure in her abilities and found herself to be a more intellectual element to the team rather than hands-on.

"Okay, here goes nothing!" she screamed.

The water came rushing down like a waterfall, flushing out the flames. The amount of water that crashed down on the building soaked any material that could burn. There was nowhere for the fire to go, hissing gray and black smoke poured out from every orifice. Soon after, all was quiet, and then the firefighters cheered and yelled in victory. There had never been a fire put out so quickly; it was definitely something to celebrate. Steam and smoke came bellowing out of the complex, and the team of firefighters walked out of the building with a middle-aged woman. They found the lady screaming from before, but the kid who made it all possible was nowhere to be found.

The chief yelled out, "Where's the kid?"

One of the firefighters shook his head, signifying that he didn't make it out with them.

Rain's eyes began to welt up with tears. "Flame, no."

Suddenly, there was a coughing figure among the smoke. "Hey, Rain, you couldn't warn me that you were gonna flood the place? I was still in there," Flame joked around a lot but always got the job done.

Rain gave a sigh of relief that her teammate—dare she say, friend—was okay.

"Luckily, we got everyone out." Flame said, he survived by the skin of his teeth, wrung out his coat and tapped the side of his helmet to force out the water he thought was in his ears.

Both Flame and Rain saw the news reporters out of the corner of their eyes and knew it was time to go. Rain telepathically told Shyra that the fire was out, and they were ready to go home. The reporters came running up to the two pint-size heroes, but before they could line up a proper shot, they were gone. The only thing they caught was an overzealous Irascible Flame giving the thumbs up.

CHAPTER 23

Pandora's Box

CASSIE AND CHRISTIAN MATERIALIZED in front of the steps of the ship. Cassie helped him up on account of his ankle was swollen to the size of a grapefruit. Shyra met them at the top.

"Today was a step in the right direction for the world to welcome us. I am extremely proud of the both of you. Cassandra, head inside with the others while I look at Christian's injury," Shyra told her.

"Yes, Shyra." Cassie handed Christian off to her and went in to regroup with her team.

"So how did it go?" asked Tori.

"As well as can be expected, I suppose. Christian twisted his ankle, but he'll be fine," Cassie said.

"Did you guys put out the fire?" Tori asked.

"Yeah, it felt great actually using our power for stuff other than fighting. I kinda get why Chris is into comic books so much now," Cassie said.

"Dear God, not you too." The two friends shared a much-needed laugh.

"C'mon, they're not that bad," Cassie finally said. "Where are the boys?"

"Last I saw them they were playing ping-pong in the rec room."

Cassie looked a bit puzzled. "You're telling me Voltaic Cloud and Seismic Earth are getting along and playing a game?"

"Weird, I know," Tori agreed, "but I think they had a breakthrough or something."

Cassie's curiosity only grew. "Did something happen on your mission I should know about?" she asked.

"Ha, *sarcastic pause* ha," she said. "Okay, I'm serious—go check it out for yourself."

"I think I'll do just that." And with that, Cassie walked off to let Tori finish her television program. She met up with the guys who indeed were in the recreational room that hosted games like darts, pool, foosball, ping-pong, and a multitude of playing cards. The room itself wasn't that large, but the gang found themselves spending more and more time there as they became better friends. For some reason, the allure of television faded in the distance as they felt less attached to current events.

Alex and Dimitri were playing a ferociously intense game of ping-pong. Cassie knocked on the doorway to alert them of her presence, but neither one of them even looked up to acknowledge her existence. Annoyed, she purposely coughed in a loud tone, "Ahem."

"Oh hey, Cass," Alex said. They still didn't look up, but at least one of them responded this time. The white ball was sent hurtling back and forth between the two; it was like their very honor depended on the outcome of the match.

"Yeah, hi," Cassie said. "So I heard the car chase went well."

"Of course it did. I was there," Dimitri butted in as he smashed the ball with his paddle back at Alex.

"You were? I couldn't even tell," Alex snapped back at him not only verbally but physically and sent the ball right back in its original trajectory.

"Whatever, bro," said Dimitri.

Cassie was beside herself in shock. *Bro? Are they actually friends now? What did I miss?* she rhetorically asked herself.

The mission itself had been pretty lackluster, but what she had missed was Alex asserting himself as a capable leader and Dimitri actually responding to it. Dimitri gained a little bit of respect for Alex that day, and that game was his way of saying "good job." Cassie left them to their own devices and took the opportunity to get some needed quiet time.

With everything being as hectic as they were during that fire, Cassie wanted time to reflect on everything. She smiled as wide as her cheeks would let her and had a very simple thought, *I'm a hero.* She couldn't believe it.

Those abilities of hers weren't a curse at all. This whole time she'd searched for meaning behind her powers and existence. For so long, she'd rejected them, but now she was overwhelmed with bliss. She wondered to herself what other great feats she would be able to accomplish with her powers, but one thing she was sure of was soon the world as they knew it would change forever.

Just as they predicted, it wasn't long before the stunts of the team were all over the news. The videos of their heroics quickly went viral over the net, and overnight, it seemed as if their popularity spread like wildfire. Everyone wanted to know who the five were, how they were able to do the things they did, and where they had come from, but fame wasn't the only thing their semantics segued to. They would soon find out that for every action, there is an equal and opposite reaction.

It had been less than a week since their exploits hit the web, but they had already been viewed millions of times. The young adults gathered around the living room after an intense workout, but Tori had other interests. She grabbed her laptop and eagerly checked the status of her own celebrity.

"This is awesome! Guys, check it out. I look great in that clip," she proclaimed. "I'm glad they caught me flying." The other four peered over her shoulder to watch the clip.

"That's not why we do it," Alex said.

"Ugh. Whatever, Alex," Tori said as she rolled her eyes.

"I knew this would be big news—people with superpowers, of course—but I never thought it would spread this quick. What if they find out who we are?" Cassie asked.

"They won't. As long we're quick about it and keep our faces covered, we'll be fine," Alex said.

"I don't know, man. This is how a lot of movies start," added Christian.

"What are you even talking about?" asked Dimitri.

"Think about it, man … A couple super-powered teens or, better yet, an advanced alien race gets caught on tape doing some miraculous feat, and next thing you know the government catches wind of it, and they get abducted then experimented on."

"Shut up, Christian," Dimitri responded.

"You shut up," Christian murmured under his breath not loud enough for anyone to hear.

"Guys, seriously," Alex cut in. "We'll be okay. Let's just stick to the format we've been doing."

And so it went for the next few weeks. Their routine was train and stop petty crimes. The team's hard efforts paid off. In no time at all they mastered new abilities. Cassie was able to draw moisture out of the air so she did not have to rely on nearby sources of water, and Christian mastered his rocket-powered flight and heat absorption. Cloud and Earth amped up their repertoire by learning the advantages of static cling and creating stone weapons. Even Wind concentrated her efforts by learning to create gale-level winds.

The alliance powered up with no time to spare. In the upcoming months, there was a live broadcast on television of a bank robbery taking place. Normally that wouldn't be a big deal, but it was taking place in Washington, DC and the team was located in Colorado.

"Guys, check this out," Chris called out.

The four others walked over to the big-screen TV and glued their eyes to the events that were unfolding. The news anchor in front of the camera seemed frantic.

"This is Elizabeth Liao coming to you live from the Channel Five news van with this breaking news. Titan National Bank is being robbed by two assailants with what can only be described as superpowers. They have the police pinned down behind their squad cars with possible hostages inside. Nobody appears to be hurt, but the criminals have yet to make their demands. More as this horrifying story develops."

The team stared in disbelief. Their mind had just been blown.

"What did she just say?" Tori asked.

"She said we're in trouble," responded Dimitri.

"Everyone stay calm," Alex said. "Shyra will know what's up." He turned his head toward her room down the hall and shouted out for her. She came out of her bedroom and asked the nature of all of the squalling.

"Is there something you want to tell us, Shyra?" Dimitri asked.

"What are you referring to exactly, Dimitri?"

He pointed to the television set as it flashed images of cop cars being hurled into the air and police officers ducking for cover. "I'm referring to that."

Even Shyra had a hard time believing what she was seeing. As far as she knew, only the five had kinetic abilities.

"What's going on, Shyra?" Alex stepped in.

"I do not know, Alexander."

"Well, in case you were wondering, there are other people with powers out there wreaking havoc," Tori butted in.

"It has to be because of the first Kalrynian guide who crashed here. When he let out his kinetic force to trigger the latent powers in your species, he must have affected more humans than I calculated."

"Great … How many people may have been affected?" Alex asked.

"There is no way of knowing, unfortunately," she replied.

Flame interjected, "I thought you had equipment that could pinpoint us or something."

"I have esper-tracking technology, but the kinetic signal you all put out was so strong I could sense it internally. I never predicted so many earthlings would be affected by such a low-level guide."

"So what do we do now?" Cassie asked, finally joining the fray.

"We will overcome this like every obstacle thrown in our path, Cassandra. Worry not."

"I just don't understand why now, Shyra. Why are they all of a sudden coming out of the woodwork?" Cassie responded.

"Well, as your people say, it would appear we have opened Pandora's Box with our media-covered heroics." With a troubled look on her face, Shyra attempted to rally her team together. "I will consult the Kalrynian Savants regarding this development. In the meantime, everyone suit up. I am sending you in. Subdue the espers and await further instructions."

The gang's morale took a bit of a dip. Fighting Zenakuu with powers was one thing, but to take down humans was another. The team looked to Alex for reassurance, but even he was at ends with the turn of events. Ever the leader, he spoke to snap everyone out of it.

"You heard her, guys," he said. "We can't do anything from here. Let's just get there and see what can be done. Suit up."

And so they did. Chris jumped off the couch, and they simultaneously darted to their rooms to put on their uniforms. Minutes later, they were ready for transport.

"Is everyone ready?" Shyra asked.

"Ready as we'll ever be," replied Flame.

"Good. Good luck, everyone."

"Shyra, wait ..." Cloud cut in.

"What is it, Voltaic Cloud?"

"What if they don't surrender?"

"You will do what you feel is right, and that is all that can be asked of you."

The five teens looked at each other, not really knowing what to expect, and were instantly teleported. It wasn't the reassuring answer Cloud was hoping for. She couldn't have expected him to take a human life. It just wasn't something he was capable of doing.

Shyra teleported the alliance two blocks away from the actual robbery. They slipped on their respective masks and headed toward the crime scene where more than thirty police officers had their weapons drawn, ready for a shootout. Captain Sanders met Cloud at the edge of the scene. Yellow "do not cross" tape was the only thing in between the two.

Up on the ship Shyra ran to the communication room and incautiously attempted to patch into her home world. In less than a minute, she was connected to a Kalryn Advisor. "Guide 5142-K, what is the nature of your hail?" The man on the screen asked her.

She spoke out, "I implore you, Advisor. It is my whim to bear call upon the Savants."

"Child, surely you jest. We are in the middle of an intergalactic war, and you saw it fit to call away the one force capable of saving the universe? Under what merit, or do I need not guess? Is it your desire to speak with your precious father? You think a fool of me child?"

"Advisor, it is not that at all," Shyra insisted. "I have questions that I need answered."

"Indeed, well it seems Lady Luck still keeps you in her favor. Savant Hartell just became available."

He was not at all the Savant member she would prefer to speak to. In fact, Hartell made her father look like a cuddly teddy bear in comparison, but she supposed he was better than nothing—or at least she hoped.

Soon, his image appeared on screen, and he spoke. "Ah, the prodigal child of Rayvaar the mighty, whose wit is only matched by his mastery of lygokinesis and charm with the ladies." He sarcastically laughed before finishing his thought. "What is it that we can do for you, Child?"

Oh how she wished everyone would stop calling her that. She bit her lip to subdue her raising frustration over the condescending tone. "Please, Councilman, I need to hear the final transmission of the first guide who was sent here to planet Earth."

"What difference does it make? He is dead and of no consequence at this point."

"His self-sacrifice has given way to an unforeseen crisis here on Earth," Shyra explained.

Hartell arched his right eyebrow. "Of what crisis do you speak?"

"There are an unascertainable number of earthlings who have had their kinetic powers awoken. His actions opened the flood gates, and I know not how to find all of them."

"That does prove to be quite the dilemma, young guide, but alas, you biting off more than you can chew does not warrant being granted an audience with the entirety of Savants. I shall convey this news to the other members, and we shall get back to you at our earliest convenience. Hartell out."

"But—" Shyra began; however, before she could finish her the sentence, the line was cut. She was left staring at a blank screen.

"That son of a sulca!" She cursed. The Savant members were notorious for being pretentious and having poor manners, but back on the ground, the group was about to face a threat that would make the scout fight seem like a stroll through the park. Not to mention that Alexander Carter may just have to kill another human being…

CHAPTER 24

No Good Deed Goes Unpunished

"WHAT THE HELL ARE you supposed to be?" Captain Sanders asked. "Get back behind that line."

Cloud had a simple response. "We're here to help."

"Help? What can you do?"

Cloud took a step back, letting Flame step forward and ignite his hands.

"Holy Jesus, you're on fire," Captain Sanders exclaimed.

Flame quickly put it out before anyone else saw.

"Well, I don't know what to say. I didn't think you freaks were real, but after what I've seen today …"

Cloud gave the officer an unappreciative look. "What do you mean?"

"Those two who are in there—they're not normal … I saw one of them tear the vault door right off the wall."

Alex turned back to his team. "They sound powerful, so be on your guard. Officer, do they have any guns?"

"Do you think they even need them, kid? I didn't see any."

"Okay, then call your men back. We will take it from here."

"Under whose authority? This is my jurisdiction."

"How about the we're-trying-to-save-your-sorry-asses authority?" Wind lashed out at him.

Earth stepped in. "Look, we're the good guys, so you either move your men back, or we'll move them for you."

"What did you say, punk?" the captain snapped.

"Enough!" Cloud yelled. "It's your choice, Officer, but I promise you we're going in there one way or another."

"Disrespectful brats. Whatever, it's your funeral." He ordered his men to move back another twenty yards with his police bullhorn and told the team that "the stage was theirs."

The five espers made their way to the front of the bank. Cloud took a deep breath. There was no turning back now with all those TV cameras on them. The entire nation was watching his every move. *How did things get like this? I just wanted to be a hero, not kill people,* he thought to himself. "Wind, do me a favor clear out all this dust," Cloud said.

"Piece of cake, boss." The whistling winds started gathering, and a strong gust blew all the smoke away until not a particle remained.

Two silhouettes were all they could see. It seemed to be a man and woman. They stepped into the street and were greeted by the Kinetic Alliance. The man looked almost six foot tall and was dressed in tattered blue-and-black flannel shirt with black denim jeans, and army boots covered his feet. A simple ashen ski masked pulled over his face with only the eye area revealed was all that kept his identity secret. The woman was wearing a very tight, contouring T-shirt that was mostly comprised of purple and pink. She had on fitted denim blue jeans, sneakers, and the same gray mask the man was wearing.

"What's this? Kids playing dress up?" the man mocked. "I had no idea we were invited to a pajama party." Prolonged laughter followed the comment.

"And I guess this is the right way to use your powers, you irresponsible jerk!" Wind yelled out.

The man looked at his partner and laughed uncontrollably. "What else could I do with these powers? Money makes the world go round, and I'm tired of being the poor, disrespected 99 percent."

"Why don't you join us and do some good?" Rain questioned, but only more unstoppable laughter broke out from the masked man. An agitated Cloud furrowed his eyebrow, wondering why she would even offer that to a criminal.

"Join you, some rag tag, do-good vigilantes? Sorry, but no thanks. I appreciate the police department rolling out the red carpet but run along to your mommies before you get hurt."

"What about you? Do you have anything to say, Miss?" Flame asked as he turned his attention the woman beside the criminal.

"She has nothing to say to you," the man bellowed. "Now outta my way!"

A giant steel girder came out of the darkness of the crumbled building headed in the direction of the alliance. The team scattered, narrowly escaping the incoming projectile.

"What was that, Cloud?" Flame questioned. His heart was pounding from not knowing what they were dealing with.

"Looked like a support beam," Cloud noted. "What the hell is his power?"

"Look out! Here comes another one!" Rain warned. Another beam whizzed by, crashing into a police truck across the street and demolishing it. The reverberating sound of metal banging and crashing scared all the civilians in the area, and they ray away petrified. The team could hardly hear each other over all the screaming.

"Can you imagine if that hit one of us? There's no way we would survive," Wind shouted. The team had to be cautious with him. They hadn't encountered someone with such powers besides sparring with one another.

"We need to put him down—and quick," Earth said.

"Agreed. Everyone get ready. We're going on the offense," Voltaic Cloud said.

"But how?" Rain desperately questioned.

The two steel girders were coming back around, and the alliance had to hit the dirt as they zoomed overhead. With both hands controlling the metal, the man was open for an attack, and Cloud seized the opportunity. With his lighting speed, Cloud was able to close the gap between him and his masked foe. With a running start, Cloud leapt and came down with a flying lariat, leveling his opponent and forcing him farther into the bank. The man sprung back up and slowly wiped the blood off of his lip as he sized up Cloud. Cloud ran in after him, followed closely by Earth. They assumed their fighting positions, ready for what would be a very special duel.

"Looks like Cloud has his hands full, but where is the girl?" Wind asked.

Just then, Rain felt herself getting heavier. "What's going on?" she asked. "I feel like something is pushing me down." Rain found herself collapsing under her own weight. She slammed into pavement below as she struggled to even breathe. "Ugh. I can't take this. What's going on?" Any longer, and her internal organs would have gone into apoplexy from being crushed. Rain looked all around and spotted the purple shirt high in the sky.

"Wind, she's … up … there." Rain pointed skyward as best she could.

Wind picked up on it and wondered how she was up there flying. "Are you kidding me? I'm the master of wind, and I don't even have flying down perfectly. She is up there just chillin'." Wind used the air to lift herself up and pushed toward the masked girl.

The girl caught a glimpse of Wind in the corner of her eye and aimed one hand in her direction, which slowed Wind down substantially. Wind plummeted back to the ground but then gathered more airflow and was able to break through whatever was slowing her down. She grabbed the mystery girl's leg. Wind judo flipped the girl over her shoulder, followed by a violent gust of wind to speed up her plummet back down to the ground.

"That's right! You picked the wrong chick to mess with," she yelled.

The masked girl didn't know what was up and what was down as she flipped through the air, but she was able to sort it out and stop herself from falling. Rain felt a debilitating weight lifted from her shoulders but was weakened from struggling with the strange force. Wind glided back down to the ground slowly and landed safely.

"If you want to fly, then so be it," the mysterious woman said.

"So she *can* speak," Wind said mockingly.

The girl turned her hands right side up and began raising them. At first, Wind felt better than before, but when she took a step forward, she looked like Neil Armstrong walking across the surface of the moon. The girl quickly stepped forward bending her left leg and extended her right leg backward, getting low to the ground. She raised her hand and stood straight up in one fluid, yet almost meticulous motion. In an instant, Wind was thrown above to incredible heights.

Speeding through the clouds, Wind entered the planet's troposphere and struggled just to get a breath of air. Flame came running up from behind the girl and put her in a full nelson, cutting off her control over Wind. Unconscious and coming down fast, Wind slowly woke up as the ground was coming into view at an alarming rate. She knew she would be dead if she hit the ground at her current velocity. Thinking surprisingly fast, Wind had enough time to send a gust of powerful wind toward the ground to act as a cushion. Her quick thinking slowed her decent, although the impact still left her disoriented.

Flame held the girl still, but he started feeling heavy himself. However, Flame was not going to let go. Their feet went through the ground, because of the outrageous force that was on Flame. When he couldn't take it anymore, he gave out a painful yell and spontaneously combusted, blowing the girl several feet away and tearing her clothing almost clean off. Rain and Wind helped Flame up and placed him down on a nearby bench, beaten up Wind sat down next to him.

Effervescent Rain ran next to Earth and watched as Cloud and the unknown man battled it out in the bank. Cloud rushed in one more time, but the unknown esper was all to used to the speedy attack. He anticipated where Cloud was going to be and hit him in the chest with an incredibly strong trailing leg kick. Cloud flipped backward and landed on his chest, unable to get back up. Earth and Rain jumped into the fight. Earth headed at the man with a flurry of beach ball-sized stones that were thrown up from the destruction of the bank, but the shady criminal had footwork that was good enough to avoid Earth's attack.

With a flick of his wrist, the enemy whipped a large chunk of rebar toward Earth and wrapped it around him. Rain decided to jump in with a sidekick, but the unidentified man took Rain's other leg out with a sweep kick followed by a stern casting punch to her midsection that snatched the air from her body. She fell to her knees, curling up in the fetal position. The nameless man walked up to Earth, who was still wrapped up. He summoned a thick sheet of metal to his hand that he fashioned to look like brass knuckles. He cocked back his fist and with all his might slung his arm forward. The swing connected with the left side of Earth's face and shattered his jaw. Earth was knocked unconscious, his body went limp, and he bled profusely from his mouth where a gash had been ripped open. His mandible was fractured.

"Bastard!" Cloud yelled as he found his second wind. He couldn't believe how fast his team was dropping. The esper they faced was merciless.

Cloud approached his assailant in a more defensive stance. He saw Rain in the corner of his eye, and the rage built more and more within him. Electrical charges zapped from his body and crackled through the air. Cloud's hair stood up, and his eyes were glowing yellow and matched his surging hands. The unknown man hid his devilish grin as he rushed Cloud with two straight right punches that Cloud easily blocked. He followed by grabbing the back of Cloud's head and driving uppercuts toward his face, but Cloud put both hands out and stopped his barrage. Cloud turned the tables and went on the attack, starting with a picture-perfect left sidekick to the man's side followed by a jump kick to the side of his head. After connecting with two sequential kicks, Cloud backed up into another defensive stance.

Shaking off the two air kicks, the nefarious man came at Cloud for another assault. This time he started with a left-right-left combination that Cloud narrowly blocked but was clipped by the fourth overhand punch. The seemingly master of metal looked as if he was actually enjoying the fight. He summoned a steel channel bar that was sitting tight in a piece of broken-off wall. He usurped it from its position and held it tight. It was clear to Cloud that the man's intention was to bash his skull in. As the man charged in, Cloud had to think fast. He threw both hands on the ground and sent his electrical charge coursing through the floor's surface. The electricity surged in all directions, including the general directions of his teammates. It was in that very moment Voltaic Cloud displayed mastery over his element. He telekinetically willed the electric current away from his team and sent it racing toward his enemy.

The current connected with such a force that it exploded on impact and knocked the steel bar, which was a great conductor of electricity, out of his hand and instantly brought him to his knees. As he convulsed out of control, Cloud thought the fight might be over. He looked around and saw the building in ruins. Small fires were left strewn about, while in other places electrical wires dangled from the ceiling and violently sparked. Once again, his team looked worse for wear. Alex walked over to the others and looked for a way to set Earth free. Not paying attention, he didn't see that the man had gotten back up. The villainous miscreant got to his knees and looked left. He spotted a metal desk that he easily picked up and brought over Cloud's body.

Cloud leapt out of the way as it came down on top of him. He zapped it with so much electricity that it actually exploded, sending shrapnel all over the bank. No one was hit by the pieces, but they became a suitable weapon for the malicious magnetized man. He lifted several pieces of sharp metal and held one at Rain's throat.

"I didn't want to have to do this, but you've left me no choice," the man growled. Blood trickled down Rain's neck, and Cloud stopped in his tracks.

"If you hurt her ..." Cloud warned. Wind and Flame stumbled in and saw the situation.

"I won't if you all just back up."

Thrown into a classical Mexican standoff, everyone just stood their ground. Next, that same unfamiliar force came over the team for the second time and brought them all to their knees.

"Looks like my ride just got here," the man said. "Come after us again, and I promise you I'll make you regret it." The two bank robbers were unable to grab what they came for, so the girl lifted them off the ground to escape.

The police were tired of waiting and decided to go in, but the entire bank dropped under the force of the mystery woman. The building collapsed on top the defeated alliance and pushed back the police. Shyra, no longer able to hold back her worry, was able to pinpoint where they were under the ruble and teleported them out, along with some debris from them building.

"Rush Seismic Earth into the healing chamber right away, fully submerged!" Shyra ordered. "Irascible Flame and Whisking Wind can go into the regular healing tanks."

Though also beaten up, Cloud and Rain were the only two who were still conscious. They quickly but gently helped Shyra move the three to the medical bay of the ship. After removing their uniforms down to their undergarments, they got everyone ready for the tanks. Shyra attached a breathing apparatus to Earth's face and placed him in a cylindrical tube where the healing process would be accelerated for more severe injuries.

Flame was coming to, so Cloud assisted getting his groggy friend into the healing tub. Flame slowly entered, but once inside, he immediately tilted his head back to the edge of tank and went back out. It was becoming more and more evident he was suffering from a concussion.

"Alexander, just make sure his head stays above water."

"Yes, Shyra."

While he did that, Shyra and Cassie brought Tori to the tub next to him. Her injuries weren't that bad, so she would be able to walk again shortly.

"Everyone's condition is stabilizing, Shyra," Cassie reported.

"Thank you, Cassandra. Now I need to talk to you and Alexander in the communication room. I want to hear exactly what happened."

Alex and Cassie followed their mentor to the room and sat down beside her.

"Okay, what happened down there?" Shyra asked.

Cassie turned to look at Alex, who had his head down in shame. Cassie knew he felt responsible for the defeat and wanted to come to his aid. "Well, Shyra, they were just really strong and—"

Alex looked up. "It's okay, Cass. You don't have to cover for me. Shyra, the truth is we lost because of me. I didn't have control of the situation. The enemy was more powerful than I anticipated, and by the time we finally figured out their powers, it was too late."

"Too late? What does that mean?" Shyra asked.

"We became separated after the girl esper neutralized Rain and Wind, and from there, the male esper started attacking us. He was just too fast for us."

"That is no excuse," Shyra said. "The five of you have taken down five times as many Zenakuu combatants, but you got beat by two earthlings?"

"I take full responsibility, Shyra. I'll step down as leader."

Cassie was shocked by his sudden decision. "Alex, no."

"If I can't keep the team safe, what good am I, Cassie?"

"That decision is mine alone to make, Alexander," Shyra interjected. "The fact of the matter is that the five of you have suffered your first real defeat. Learn from it."

"But, Shyra—" Alex began before being cut off.

"But nothing, Voltaic Cloud. Everyone is still alive, and we will persevere from this like we always do. Ask yourself, Alexander Carter, does the rest of your team stand a better chance of surviving with or without your leadership?" Somehow, Alex knew she was right.

"Alex kept us alive, Shyra," Cassie added.

"That I have no doubt of. Do not doubt your ability, Alexander. I have placed my faith in you for a reason. The two of you get some rest. We shall discuss this more in the morning."

Alex and Cassie slumped off down the hall to their individual bedrooms. Cassie noticed how quiet Alex was being and could tell he still blamed himself for all the injuries.

"You okay, Alex?" she asked.

"Why does it always end up like this?"

"What are you talking about?"

"You really haven't noticed yet? After every mission we come back beat the hell up," Alex pointed out.

"Well, yeah, but doesn't that just come with the territory?" Cassie said.

Alex tried to make sense out of it all. "It shouldn't have to be that way. I mean, is this really what we signed up for? At this rate, how long will it be until one of us is dead?"

Cassie stopped him in his tracks and placed her hand on his left shoulder. "You won't let that happen, Alex."

"If only it were that easy … I need to get stronger—a lot stronger."

"We all will," Cassie assured him. "We'll just train harder."

"No, it's not just that. I don't think you'd understand," Alex said.

"Help me understand then," she pleaded with him.

"I can't. This is something I have to do alone." With that, Alex walked off by himself down the hall but passed his room. He walked all the way to the rear of the ship where he pressed his forehead up against a large plate glass window and slammed his fist down on the windowsill. He struggled to calm his nerves, but as he looked up and gazed into the starry night, his resolve to be the best intensified. The next time he came across that criminal he swore to himself he would win for sure.

As darkness retreated to the west and morning light bled from the east Chris, Alex, and Cassie met at the breakfast table where they knew a talk over the events that transpired was inevitable.

"How's your head, Chris?" Cassandra asked.

"Pounding headache," he said, "but if not for my helmet, I'd be dead."

"Yeah, I saw it when we got back. There's a long crack in it," she added.

"How the hell did the roof fall on us anyway?" Chris wondered.

"It was that girl with the short hair," Tori said as she limped into the room.

"Tori, you're up." Alex was relieved to see another teammate on their feet. "Are you okay?" he asked.

"I'll live. More importantly, that girl … she has the power to control gravity. I just know it. No one has ever been able to prevent me from flying before, but around her, I felt like I weighed a ton. Next thing I know, the whole place comes down around us, and I wake up in a tank."

"That makes sense. How else could she pin us down like that?" confirmed Cassie.

"Alex, what about the guy? What power did he have when you fought him?" Chris asked.

"It all happened so fast, but he unmistakably had the power to control metal."

"Damn. That's a good power to have," Chris said within his usual inappropriate timing.

Shyra was the last to join the others in the dining area, but before she could even speak, Tori, who was on pins and needles, shouted out, "How's Dimitri?"

"He is fine, Tori," Shyra answered. "He should be ready to train again in less than a week. Something all of us will be doing soon enough."

"Shyra, what did your elders say about the espers here on Earth?" Cloud impatiently asked.

"They have their hands tied with the Zenakuu over there and will get back to me shortly, but worry for not. We will be prepared for any and all challenges next time."

"That's not exactly comforting," a worried Cassie protested.

"We will be removing ourselves from the spotlight until I can gather more information on this matter, so rest up for the next couple of days while Dimitri heals. When the five of you are together again, we shall resume training."

"Okay, Shyra," Chris responded. He was thankful for any kind of break,

"Oh, and one more thing," Shyra said. "You guys better never worry me like that again." Shyra smiled at her team and walked off toward the communications room. There was a world of questions she needed answered. What really happened to the first guide intended for planet Earth, and just how many people had kinetic powers?

Chapter 25

From the Top Will Be the Very Same Place You Hang From

For the next few days, the group took it easy. They only kept up with their meditation as they waited for the last member of their alliance to join back into the ranks. Tori spent a lot of time by his tube, hoping he would wake up, but he just floated, subtly going up and down. She would talk to him, not knowing if he could hear her, but she wanted to believe he could. Almost a week passed before it finally happened, and Dimitri opened his eyes. Tori ran to get Shyra and tell her the great news. It took her mere seconds, and before the end of the hour, they had removed him from the tube and placed him in a rejuvenation bath where he finally spoke.

"Why do I feel like a raisin?" he asked.

"You were in that tank for the better half of a week, my young hero," Shyra reminded him.

"What happened to me?" he wondered.

"We got into a fight with other espers, D, and let's just say we didn't exactly win," proclaimed Tori.

"Yeah, I remember that part. Some guy and a girl were robbing a bank I think. I remember chasing after the guy with Alex, but it starts to get blurry after that," he recited.

"Well your jaw was broken in two places, Dimitri," Shyra added.

"That would explain why it's so stiff and why it hurts a little to talk," he said.

"Indeed, we surmise the two have the ability over magnetism and gravity," Shyra told him. "Are you ready to get back to training?"

"Hell yeah, I owe that guy a world of hurt."

Tori looked upon Dimitri with concern. He'd just gotten out of the tank a few minutes ago, and he already wanted to fight again. "Don't you think you should eat something first, D?" she suggested.

"Later," he said. "Let's get to work. Call everyone else and tell them to get ready."

"In this instance, Tori is right, Dimitri. You just woke up. Regain your strength today, and training will start first thing tomorrow."

"Fine," Earth muttered. He wasn't happy about this decision, and most importantly, he didn't want to be seen as weak. The fact that someone bested him so easily would never sit well with him. He had a score to settle with the stranger who'd broken his jaw. He slowly stood up spilling the healing liquids of the bath all over the floor and went to regroup with the others. Still a little shaky, he put on some decent clothes and stumbled through the ship. Tori offered to help, but he quickly pushed her assistance away. He found his three other teammates eating lunch and sat down beside them.

"Dimitri! You're up," Alex blurted out.

"No shit. You thought that weak ass punch would keep me down?"

"Weak ass punch? He put your lights out, man," Chris added in.

Dimitri shot him a death glare and punched him in the arm.

"Ow! What was that for?" he asked.

"Tell me something, Chris. Do you have to practice having such horrible timing, or does it just come naturally?" Cassie questioned.

"It's natural, I think."

She rolled her eyes at him and turned back to Dimitri. "How are you feeling?"

"I'm fine," Dimitri insisted. "I wish everyone would just drop it already. Alex, when can we start training again?"

"As soon as possible," he said. "Next time we go up against those two, we will be ready."

Dimitri nodded and got up to make himself a sandwich. Christian got up with the intention of finding Tori, who he discovered lying on her bed. She was by herself and was playing with a miniature air ball she created in her hand. Christian knocked on her doorframe to announce himself. "Hey, Tori," he said.

Startled by the noise, the air ball dissipated into nothingness. "Christian. What is it?" Tori asked him.

"Well, I saw Dimitri in the kitchen. You must be really happy that he's okay."

She sat up, tucked some hair behind ears, and gave him an intense look. "*What* are you trying to say?"

Christian's heart began to pound. He didn't understand what he could have said that was so wrong or why she always had such an effect on him.

"Well nothing," he said. "I just thought you were worried about him, ya know? From the way you spent so much time by his tank."

"So? I would have done the same for anyone. That doesn't mean anything."

Oh how he desperately wanted to believe that, but he knew if it were him floating up and down in that giant tube, she'd barely notice. "Right. Of course. I knew that, Tori. Don't mind me.

How is everything else?" Christian said, trying to change the subject. It was his awkward attempt to make small talk.

"I'm a little busy, Christian. I was meditating or whatever." It was obvious she wasn't, but he wasn't going to argue.

"Sorry, I'll leave you alone," Christian said.

"Appreciate it," she said snidely. And with that, he walked away.

It was like she didn't even like him as a friend. She only had eyes for Dimitri, but Chris thought that there must be a way to win her affection. The day passed quickly on the ship. For the most part, everyone was happy to see Dimitri back in action, and his spirit couldn't have been more up. They all anxiously waited for the night to pass so they could start more training. The next morning came just in time.

In the morning, Alex walked down the hall to see Cassie in her room already suiting up.

"Hey, Cassie, when you're done, could you grab everyone?" Alex asked. "I want to have a meeting in the war room."

Cassie, who was putting on her boots, happily complied. "Sure thing, Alex." Cassie met up with Tori a couple of minutes later. "Hey, Tor, Alex wants to see everyone in the war room."

"Okay, I'll be right there," Tori said but went right back to fixing her hair.

Not shocked by her nonchalant demeanor, Cassie continued on to round up the others. The boys weren't in their room, but she did hear a lot of commotion coming from the recreational room. Sure enough, there they were, engaged in battle.

"D, Chris, we're meeting in the war room."

"Okay, right after I beat D in this ping-pong match," Christian said.

"Never gonna happen, kid," Dimitri attested.

"Just be there in five minutes." Cassie was always punctual.

When the rest of the team showed up, Alex was ready for his speech. The war room was the place where all of the meetings took place and where they observed the threats of the United States, gathered information, and observed any channel and live video feed through any satellite the ship was able to hack into. The team wasn't allowed in there a lot, but it always made Cloud feel like he was in some kind of secret army base with all the high-tech equipment. His first time there he was left utterly speechless.

The room was a deep metallic blue. The words on the giant screen centered in the room appeared in white, but everything else was in sharp ultramarine blue and very easily visible. There was a huge holographic screen that wrapped around the whole room and was able to bring any piece of the screen to the transparent round table, which seated ten people. The entire room was interactive by means of your hands or voice. The super computer that Shyra set up in the room was able to scan the entire country, acquire geographical maps, and pull any information from any resource that was available through the World Wide Web. This was where Shyra spent most of her time when the team was training.

"Alright, guys," Cloud began, "I just have a few things to say. First of all, I can't help feeling guilty about what happened last week. I should have been there for you, D, and I should have helped Tori and Chris with the other criminal."

"Don't be so hard on yourself. You can't be everywhere at once," Flame interrupted.

"I know, Flame, but if Shyra put me in charge, then it is my responsibility to bring everyone home unharmed. We have a lot of work ahead of us, but there was one thing that those two didn't do that we can capitalize on."

"What's that?" Earth asked. He desperately wanted to get even with the man who'd put him out of commission for a week.

"Teamwork, D. There wasn't one time that those two worked together."

"But they were strong enough on their own to put all of us down," Wind joined in.

"Yes, but did we work together? Did we attack as one? What about combining our powers like Shyra taught us? I want Earth and Rain to work on their powers together, and as for Wind and Flame, I want the two of you to come up with some kind of powerful combination."

There were mixed feelings about splitting up the group in the fashion that he had. For example, Earth wasn't exactly thrilled about being teamed up with Rain. It wasn't as though he had anything against her, but he viewed her as the weakest member of the group. Although they have been friends, even Rain felt a little weird about spending alone time with Earth. On the other side, though, there was one person who was ecstatic about the team up. Flame believed he would finally be able to show Wind what he was capable of, and she would be impressed by his valor and male bravado.

"Alright, everyone, you heard him. Let's do this," Flame enthusiastically said.

"Kiss ass," Earth added in before about-facing and walking off.

"Cloud, what are you going to do?" Rain questioned.

"I have some intense training that I want to work on with Shyra."

"That's a good point. Where is Shyra? I haven't seen her all morning," Wind finally noticed.

"She's waiting for me outside," Cloud answered. "That's enough questions for now. We all have our assignments. Good luck, everyone." Voltaic Cloud got up from his seat and headed for the front door entrance of the ship where Shyra was indeed waiting for him in full battle gear.

"Are you ready Voltaic Cloud?" she asked him.

"Yes, I'm ready. Let's go." Master and student started walking off away from the sight of the others to start the most dangerous training of his life.

Chapter 26

A Match Made in Heaven Said the Fires of Hell

Outside, Rain met up with Earth, who was sitting down on the stump of a fallen tree. He heard Rain approach and stood up.

"So," he stiffly said.

"Yeah, so," Rain responded with the same ineptness.

"This is dumb. Why did he match us up, nothing happens if you combine rocks and water," Earth noted.

"True, but what happens when you combine dirt with water?" Rain asked, trying to nudge him in the right direction.

Earth thought about it for a second before letting out a not so impressed answer. "Um, mud?"

Rain was baffled by how slow he was grasping what she was trying to suggest. "Yes, but what happens if you have mud and raging waters?"

It finally clicked in his head. "Oh, a mudslide!" he exclaimed.

"Exactly."

The immediate terrain surrounding the ship was fairly lapse from all the fighting, but Seismic Earth did his best and brought up the softest soil he could kinetically unearth. He swung his arms back and forth, mixing the ground below their feet until it was a quagmire and malleable.

"Okay, ready when you are," he shouted out.

Rain was still concentrating. "Almost done," she answered

There was a decent amount of water gathered in the air but nowhere near enough to achieve the desired effect.

"Rain, we're gonna need a lot more water than that," Earth pointed out.

As much as it pained her, he was right. It wasn't enough water, and the process was taking too long. She put her pride aside and threw her arms in the air.

What the heck is she doing? Earth thought to himself, but within seconds, his question was answered. Almost instantaneously, dark clouds hovered above the two and it began to downpour.

Earth smiled. "Let's do this," he uttered as he became drenched in the storm.

The two slowly got their arm movements in unison, and within fifteen minutes, they were completely in sync. They roughly guided the path of the mudslide as it increased in strength, unaware of the fact that it was still raining and collecting more and more dirt as it moved.

"Rain, I think we have enough water," Earth noted.

"You're right," she agreed. "Take the reins of the mudslide. I'll just need a second to turn it off." She cut the telekinetic link she had with the water in the landslide, and Earth immediately felt the added pressure. He hadn't taken in consideration how much of it she was controlling. Despite all that, he told her he would try his best. With attention turned toward the sky, Rain hurried to end the rainfall, but just before she was done, she was startled by Earth shouting at her. "Rain, look out!"

Rain dropped her head to see why his voice sounded so terrorized, but in a split second's time, it was far too late to get out of the way. Earth lost control of the landslide around a sharp corner, and it was speeding toward a crash course with Effervescent Rain. She thrust her hands out in front of her as some form of a feeble defense, but the current swept her away and tossed her around like a ragdoll.

"Crap!" Earth used his powers to lift a clot of dirt four feet by five feet long that was mostly composed of sedimentary rocks. He leapt on top and used it fly over and survey the area. There was no sign of Rain, and she had been under for at least thirty seconds. He began to panic. How was he going to explain to Shyra that he'd drowned one of the teammates? All he could see was a river of brown, murky water falling down the mountainside.

Please be okay, he thought to himself. As he thought his prayers would go unanswered, he spotted it—an arm flailing around and then quickly going back under. With a flick of his wrist, he was off. He flew down to where he saw her arm and jumped in. He too underestimated the force of the mudslide as he bounced around like he was the little silver ball in a pinball machine. Determined, he felt around until he grabbed on to what felt to be a foot. Earth pulled Rain in close and forced her head above water.

"Breathe!" he shouted. Relieved to see his face, Rain took in a deep breath. "I'm gonna get us out of this, okay?" Earth reassured her.

She wanted to believe him, but she was riddled with fear and doubt. "How?" she yelled out over the crashing waves.

Earth looked around as they gained momentum and spotted they were heading for a few trees. "I have an idea. Just hold on to me tight."

Willing to try anything, Rain grabbed on to his hoodie for dear life. They were seconds away from a patch of evergreens, and Earth threw out his hands, which were able to grab on to the trunk of a tree. The immediate danger was over, but they weren't out of the woods yet. He turned to Rain, who was holding on but being pelted by dirt clots and broken off branches.

"Listen, hold on to this tree," Earth directed her. "I'm going to end this."

She nodded and moved her arms into position to grasp the tree as best she could. Once secured, Earth knew it was his time to move. *God, I hope this works,* he thought to himself. He let go of the trunk and was instantly swept away again in the slide.

"Earth!" Rain screamed out, but it was far too late. He was gone, and she could only trust in her teammate's words and pray for the best. Underneath the mayhem, Earth fought to gain control, but all of it was too much for him. In a last-ditch effort, he curled himself into a ball and concentrated. He was already exhausted from creating the mudslide in the first place, but nonetheless, he gathered his remaining strength and condensed it deep within his being.

This is it! he thought to himself. He threw out his arms and legs and let his geokinetic power explode outward. The destructive shockwave blew the landslide out until the river was no more, and the forest was covered in mud. The technique worked but left him severely weakened. Rain trudged through the mud to reach him.

"Are you okay?" she asked.

He just barely opened his eyes and spoke. "As right as rain."

A little less than a mile away, Irascible Flame and Whisking Wind sat in awkward silence. "Any ideas?" Flame asked to break the silence.

"Nope," she quickly answered back.

"Yeah, me neither." He picked up a stick from the ground and started drawing in the dirt, allowing another five minutes of silence to go on before Wind let out her displeasure over the team up.

"What was Alex thinking? Everyone knows wind blows out fire."

Flame dropped the stick. "That's actually not entirely accurate," he pointed out. "In many scenarios, wind can actually spread fire, making it considerably stronger."

Annoyed that he'd corrected her, she answered in a solitary, "Whatever."

How could he fail so miserably with her with such minimal effort he wondered to himself. He finally got up the nerve and asked her. "Did I ever do something to you, Tori?"

"Um, what do you mean?" she asked.

"It's just that you always give me such a hard time, like you don't like me, and I'm not sure if it's because I did something to make you mad."

A little confused by the unexpected question, she replied as best she could. "It's not like that. I just … I don't know … You're kinda like an annoying little brother to me."

"But I'm older than you," he reminded her.

"Yeah, but you know what I mean."

Flame was really hurt by her comment. He'd never done anything to warrant such a verbal lashing. "Yeah. No, I get it. I'm just some annoying brother to you. I'm a joke," he threw back.

"Only because that's how you act, Christian," Wind continued. "I mean, I just don't get it. With your power, you could probably be the strongest one among us, but all you do is joke around and not take things seriously. It's frustrating."

He'd had just about had enough at this point. *Since when am I on trial*, he thought. "Well maybe if you ever took the time to get to know me, you'd see we have more in common than you think!"

The words cut Wind deep. It had been the same thing she shouted at Earth just a few months ago. She wondered if she could really be treating Christian the same way Dimitri treated her, and she was immediately ashamed. "You're right, I'm sorry."

Taken a little aback by her response, Flame arched his eyebrow and repeated it for confirmation. "I am?" he asked.

"Yes. I haven't been very fair to you, but I'd like to change that from now on. Friends?"

"Yeah, definitely." He didn't know what brought about this change of heart, but he honestly didn't care. He didn't want to lose that momentum, so he threw out an idea. "Listen, Wind,

I've been thinking about how you and I could have the sickest combination of them all, and I think I've finally got it."

"What did you have in mind?" she asked.

"Okay, check this out—a flaming tornado. What do you think? Badass right?"

Wind was actually impressed. If it worked, it would have incredibly destructive power.

"Actually, yeah, that's surprisingly a great idea," Wind admitted. "But how do we do it?"

Flame hadn't thought that far ahead. Truth be told, he expected her to shoot down the idea, so he tossed out his most basic strategy.

"Well, um, you make a tornado, and I'll set it on fire."

"Yeah, but what's fueling the fire?"

He knew the answer but didn't want to seem too much like a nerd. This kind of science was his forte. "Well, technically, you are. It's like this: In a fire, there is a substantial updraft due to the fact that flames are, of course, hot and naturally want to rise. Now, should there be any kind of rotational affect, it will actually amplify the flames and stretch them out. As they stretch, they will then become a column and grow much more intense. By this time, the tornado is actually feeding itself, so we don't need any fuel, but it will still need us to direct its course."

"Scary, but that actually made sense," Wind said. "You're pretty smart, Flame."

He blushed at the compliment. "Let's get to it, shall we?" he said.

"Yeah, here goes nothing." Wind took only a second to concentrate, and suddenly, the skies turned dark green from all the leaves, grass and tree limbs that were violently ripped from their roots and swirled around. It horrified Flame because he had never such a sight. The winds picked up dramatically, and there was a loud racket almost like an old freight train barreling through. The strength of the raging wind was more than Flame could have ever imagined. He had never seen a real tornado up close before. If not for Whisking Wind's control he would have been ripped to shreds in seconds. In that instant, he learned to respect her destructive power—almost as much as he feared it.

The swirling vortex of fierce winds made its final decent from the heavens and kissed the ground. Flame couldn't believe how precisely Wind was able to direct her energy. The control she demonstrated seemed to have come so easily to her. Flame knew from then on he would have to step up his game.

Under her guidance, she stabilized the twister, which was picking up incredible speed. Even the landscape around them was feeling the effects as small shrubbery and blades of tall grass were sucked up.

"Okay, Flame, gimme your best shot," she said. She still wasn't sure if it would work, but she placed her faith in him.

Flame rubbed his hands together as if he were back home in New Jersey standing outside in the middle of winter trying to get warm. In seconds, they caught on fire, and he shouted out to his teammate. "Okay, hold her steady," he chuckled.

"Will you just do it already?" she yelled back.

As commanded, he put his hands out and shot a continuous stream of fire at the base of the tornado. His theory was spot on, and the tornado instantly burst into flames. It was actually quite the sight to see, and the two of them marveled at their creation. Wind flew up to get a better look and could really feel the difference in temperature. Eruptions sporadically spurted from the sides of the twister, looking like fiery claws reaching out for victims. It was much hotter as she got to the top—almost unbearable, in fact, so she kept her distance. The two did their best to keep it under control, but they knew they would soon have to extinguish it, as anything close enough to the immense radiation that emanated off of it was immediately incinerated. Before that, though, Wind called out to Flame, who was keeping the fire lit from below.

"Flame!" she yelled, but she was too far for him to hear. She flew down a bit closer in hopes he would catch it. "Flame!"

"Yeah?" he shouted back. It had worked.

"Come up here! You have to see this thing from the top!" She smiled at him. There was no way he'd ever turn down an invitation from the stunningly beautiful Whisking Wind, so he kicked on his afterburners, flew to her altitude, and greeted her with a hello.

She grabbed his hand. "Follow me," she said, leading him to the top.

All he could focus on was the feeling he got from such a subtle gesture. His heart began to beat out of control, and he could only wonder what the act meant. Did she like him now? Was there a possibility that she loved him? It was a stretch to say the least, but maybe she finally forgot about Dimitri? Of course, it was none of those things, but he held on tightly to not only her hand but also hope. When they reached the top, Wind released her grip, but in the heat of the moment, Flame held on a little longer. Flame felt flustered, he couldn't understand how a simple graze of her skin could send tingles throughout his body. She had a touch so gentle yet, so overwhelming, it made even his scorching body temperature sky rocket to new heights. It took everything he had not to burn her.

"Um, Chris," Wind said.

"Yeah, Tori?" he asked as his voice cracked.

"Can I have my hand back?"

Very embarrassed, he let go of her hand. "Right, of course. Sorry." Flame lowered his head and tried not to make eye contact.

"Ready to get rid of this thing?" Wind inquired.

"Yeah, ready when you are," he replied.

"Okay, on three," Wind directed. "One … two … three!"

Flame summoned up his energy and put out the fire. It was strong, but with Wind's help, it eventually died down into nothing. While up in the air, they noticed pitch-black clouds forming in the distant sky.

"What do you suppose that is?" Wind asked.

"I don't know, but isn't that where Shyra and Cloud are?"

"I think so. Let's head back to the ship. I wanna tell Cassie how awesome our flaming tornado was." Wind paused for a moment and looked into Flame's eyes. "This was fun. Thanks, Christian."

He was on cloud nine. Not only had they held hands, but now she was admitting to enjoying time with him. The young hero couldn't be happier. "Yeah, I'll catch up with you," he said as he needed a minute to compose himself.

"Suit yourself," she responded and flew down toward the ship.

CHAPTER 27

The Pretentious Company of Dreams

A FEW MILES AWAY, Shyra and Alex trailed through the woods until the ship was no longer in sight. They set off to a remote area where the vegetation was green and thick, but it was an ideal spot to be alone.

"Why are we so far away from the others?" Cloud wanted to know.

"What I am about to teach you is too dangerous to be around everyone else. Do you remember the first night we met, Voltaic Cloud?"

"My first encounter with an advanced alien species? Yeah, it's pretty fresh in my mind," he joked.

"Good, then you recall me telling you about all the incredible things you are capable of, correct?"

"Well, I remember you telling me I could fly, but that didn't turn out so great."

"I am sure you will get the hang of it eventually. More importantly, there is another power you have inside of you that I will attempt to bring out this day. It should allow you to protect your friends."

Alex grew tremendously excited. "Are you serious, Shyra?"

"I hardly joke around, Voltaic Cloud," she replied back.

"Well, what is it? What else can I do?"

With a grin on her face, she told him. "Today I will show you how to summon lightning from the very heavens to strike down your enemies."

His young heart skipped a beat, and he stepped back in total shock. "I can actually do that?"

"By the time I am done with you, yes," Shyra confirmed.

"Great! What do I have to do first?" he asked with gleaming eyes.

"Voltaic Cloud, I should warn you. This technique is extremely dangerous. It draws power from your raw emotions and, if done incorrectly, could cause serious injury to you and your teammates. Do you wish to continue?"

Cloud paused for a moment. The thought of accidently electrocuting the people he swore to protect was more than he wanted to imagine, especially after all the pain they had already endured. However, the alternative of staying at his current level was unacceptable. He stood tall and looked at her. "I do, Shyra," he finally answered.

She smiled back. "I knew you would. Let us get started."

He nodded and immediately got into a fighting stance.

"It is too early for that. Sit down, Voltaic Cloud. You must realize one thing about yourself and your power," she attested as she walked back and forth in front of him.

"Which is?"

"That you are the quintessential form of electricity—a matchless conduit for the unrefined power of lightning."

"Awesome," he boasted in self-admiration.

"Your spark is the same that ravages the skies during every thunderstorm; you must concentrate and reach out to the source. The lightning that strikes down is the bridge that connects you to nature. Call out to it, Voltaic Cloud, and demand recognition!"

"Right," he shouted back.

"Then show me, Voltaic Cloud. Show me the full extent of your power."

"Here goes!" Cloud closed his eyes and let out a thunderous roar, but alas, nothing happened.

"I was afraid that was going to be the case," Shyra proclaimed.

"What am I doing wrong?" Cloud asked.

"Well, to be honest, you do not believe it in your heart. I am afraid you do not have the need for it, and you are not resolved enough."

Cloud grew ill-tempered by the critique. "That's crap! I do have a need for it."

"Apparently not, Alexander Carter!"

Cloud gritted his teeth with resentment. That was the first time he was ever truly enraged by Shyra.

"Since you must think this a game, we shall try a visualization technique," Shyra suggested. "I am going to enter your mind and draw out that power. Are you ready?"

"I'm ready for whatever it takes," Cloud agreed.

"Good. I sincerely hope you mean that."

Cloud closed his eyes and let his mind go blank. It was as if he could feel the telekinetic hands of Shyra pierce his consciousness. In an instant, he was off in another world. He questioned his own sanity. How could he have been in the woods one second and in the next walking down some long corridor? Dark blue carpet stretched over the entire length of the hallway, and long flowing silver tapestries with alien markings written across them draped down each wall.

A thick smoke pooled out from the distance, so it was impossible to see what waited for him at the end. Cloud was scared, but he pressed on, only able to see far enough in front of him to ascertain his own hands. Step by step, he crept through the mysterious hall, letting his fingers trace the walls until he tripped over a figure. He fell hard to his knees but quickly scurried away to a safe distance. It was fear that was preventing him from unleashing his power in the first place, and he knew it needed to be cast away.

Cloud inched over to the figure to see what he'd tripped over and was so shocked and disgusted at what he saw that he felt as if he just lost a year from his life. There in front of him was Tori Hannon with the same kind of saber that the Zenakuu scouts had with them lunged deep into her sternum.

"Tori! Oh my God, what happened? Who did this to you?" Cloud screamed, but there was no response. Despite obviously seeing that she'd bled out a long time ago, he cried out, "God, no! Please not this."

Cloud was interrupted by a shaky yet familiar voice. "Cloud? Is that you?"

He turned his glance in the direction the sound was coming from and ran over. Victim number two, his best friend, lay before him wallowing in a pool of his own blood. Cloud propped Christian up against the wall, grabbed him by the shoulders, and desperately tried to figure out what happened. "Flame, what the hell happened here? Where are we?"

Flame coughed up blood that landed on Cloud's cheek. "We're on Kalryn, man."

"How did we get here? Where is everyone?"

Irascible Flame struggled to breathe. "The Savants summoned us here to help with the war, but there was a surprise attack. They came out of nowhere, bro. I tried to take out as many as I could, but there were too many. Where were you, Alex?"

"I … I … I didn't know, Chris. I would have been here sooner, but I just didn't know."

Flame's eyes began to dim, and as his eyelids closed for the last time, he spoke his final words. "Save the others." With that, he was dead.

"No … no!" Cloud violently shook his best friend, praying he would open his eyes, but there was no such luck. Tears started streaming down his cheeks. This all felt too real to be a dream. The smell of blood was fresh in the air, and all around him he saw only corrosion and death. He stood up and clenched his fists, which were freshly painted with his best friend's blood, tightly. He felt utterly defeated but trudged on down the hall. He thought he could still save the others. Then it hit him—Cassie!

He needed to believe she was okay, still safe until he could reach her. He ran in a hysterical frenzy until he heard action in the distance. That's when he realized that Earth was fighting up ahead.

Yes, there's still hope, he thought to himself. He couldn't make out all the figures, but it definitely wasn't a fair fight.

"I'm coming, Dimitri!" Cloud yelled. Despite how fast he ran, the gap between him and his teammate never closed. Cloud remained at a distance close enough to vividly see what was happening but not close enough to intervene.

His electric bolts and bombs faded off into nothingness, making him seem only more remiss to the situation. It was a three-on-one fight that Earth was steadily losing. With each enemy he put down, another one took his place. Yet, he still fought on, hurling jagged stone after jagged stone through the monstrous Zenakuu warriors. It was a valiant effort, but an adversary struck him over the head from his blind spot, causing Earth to fall to the ground. Two other soldiers picked him up, each grabbing one arm tightly, and stood him in front of the tallest solider. They said something to him, but Cloud was too far back to make out the words. Earth grinned and spat in the face of the Zenakuu. Enraged by such insolence, the solider removed his gun from its holster and emptied a full clip into Earth's gut at point-blank range. Smoke arose from the barrel of the gun, and Earth dropped to the ground dead.

"No!" Cloud screamed out. This time, his voice penetrated the void, and the soldiers were onto him. They charged, firing their automatic rifles, but matched to Cloud's reflexes and speed, they might as well have been throwing one hundred-pound barbells. Cloud easily evaded the ballistic rounds and in a flash was face-to-face with his friends' executioners. He charged up his right leg and spun kicked one of the soldiers so hard that he sliced through his midsection. He flipped over to the second Zenakuu, and before the alien warrior could react, Cloud unleashed a storm of berserker punches faster than the human eye could follow. He had never accelerated the upper half of his body before, and even though the feeling was strange to him, he reveled in it. It was like time slowed down almost to a standstill, but left Cloud to move freely. In seconds, he'd already landed hundreds of punches, but it only took a dozen or so to crack all the ribs in the soldier's torso. The others were for Dimitri's sake.

It was down to Cloud and Dimitri's gunman, the one who pulled the trigger. Cloud slowly walked over, blocking out all emotions other than murderous intent. Electricity sparked all around him, and the hallway lights exploded with excess power.

"You'll pay … I'll make sure you pay for what you did in full." His threat was no empty rhetoric, and there would be no subterfuge today.

The alien backed away in fear. He stumbled to reload his gun, dropping several bullets as he did. He scurried to pick them up, but by the time he'd reloaded enough, Cloud was only a few feet in front of him. He aimlessly fired away at the hero at point-blank range but caught only air. Cloud moved so fast it was impossible to tell if he'd moved at all. The bullets appeared to just phase right through him. Cloud gritted his teeth, lunged forward, and grabbed hold of the Zenakuu's face. He bellowed out deeply from within his soul, discharged a little less than half of his electrical power directly into the body of the alien, and did not let go until his heart exploded and his body stopped convulsing.

The Zenakuu's body hit the ground smoldering, but Cloud felt no kind of remorse and stood over the corpse while breathing heavily. Drops of blood ran from Cloud's nose. He had exerted too much power, but he could care less about the consequences. He wiped his nose and continued to advance. He concentrated his power into his speed, and within seconds, he was at the end of the corridor that led into a decorated chamber room. It was heavily damaged with sporadic fires scattered about the floor. What was left of the roof sustained the most damage. It looked as if it had suffered from an aerial bombardment. The sky above was dark and rising smoke blotted out the sun. The only hesitation for Cloud was the horrific sight of Cassie suspended by her neck, dangling a full two feet above the floor at the mercy of a Zenakuu general. Cloud stopped dead in his tracks and then cautiously approached them.

"Ah, little earthling, so nice of you to join us. I was just about to show your friend here the broader side of my sword," he mockingly said.

"Please, no. Don't do this," Cloud pleaded.

"What's the matter? I'm giving you the same satisfaction that we received as we watched our loved ones slaughtered right before our eyes, powerless to do anything."

"No! We didn't do this to your planet."

"Maybe not, but your self-proclaimed saviors did, so you're just as guilty," the general informed him.

Cassie struggled to breathe. She didn't have much time.

"Wait! Allow me to trade places with her," Cloud offered. "Take my life instead and let her go."

"You would give up your life for this measly human girl?" the general snickered.

"Yes, I'll do anything you want. Just please don't hurt her."

"Good, then today I will teach you the same lesson the Kalrynians taught my people when they ignored our desperate pleas. Endless torment."

Cassie knew she didn't have long left in this world. With her final words, she wanted to let Cloud know it was going to be okay and how she really felt about him. Finally, she mustered the strength to speak. "Alex, I lo—"

Her words were cut short as the general unsheathed his sword and drove it deep into her heart. With one motion, he threw her to the ground like yesterday's trash. The sight of it was more than Cloud could handle. His eyes widened and allowed for electricity to surge out of his overly dilated pupils. Like a threatened feline, every hair on his body stood on end, and everything slowed down in that instant. He momentarily lost his ability to hear anything besides the erratic pounding of his own heart.

That next second something snapped inside of him, and he finally let it all go. The doubt, restraint, tameness, and limitations—he finally let it go. The skies above turned midnight black, and the remnants of thunder echoed all around. Alex struggled to hold onto his humanity, and let out a shout that stirred his very soul. A loud crack strong enough to shatter eardrums filled the room accompanied by a powerful lightning bolt that fell down from the heavens, striking down the general as if he'd just been smote by the gods for sacrilege. It was all over very fast, but there was no trace or residual of him. All that was left was the smoking singed floor where he once stood. Alex crawled over to Cassie's lifeless body and embraced her in his arms,

"This is my fault, Cassie, I'm so sorry. I wasn't strong enough to save you and the others. Please forgive me."

The body he gripped so tightly in his arms turned into a milky, white-colored vapor and dissipated into the air. The chamber room where he so bravely fought began to vanish right before his eyes. The floor cracked from under his feet, and he fell into an endless sea of darkness until he was completely swallowed up. A moment later he awoke from the illusion and opened his eyes. The ground around him was soot black, and the plant life near him had been scorched dead. Shyra stood there at a comfortable distance away. The only thing he was sure was real at that point were the tears rolling down his face.

"None of it was real?" he asked her.

"It was as real as it needed to be," Shyra answered. "You did it, Voltaic Cloud. You summoned a ferocious lightning storm. Use that rage and draw from its strength."

"Shyra?"

"Yes, Voltaic Cloud?" she replied.

Cloud shot an electric bolt at the Kalrynian faster than she could react, launching her into to air and slamming her into ground several feet away. "Never do that again." He walked off back in the direction of the ship, anxious to see his friends alive and well. He never realized how much they meant to him, but with that new power, he refused to let that illusion ever come to pass.

Back at base, Cloud met everyone at the entrance of the ship. They were all exchanging stories. A sense of calm poured over him as he saw his team safe. Even better, they were laughing and having a good time.

Christian was first to spot him as he approached. "Alex, how did it go, man? Did you learn something cool?"

"Yeah, I think we're ready to get back out there now. How did it go with you guys?" Alex asked.

"Great. We all learned some pretty powerful combinations," Chris answered.

Alex looked at the rest of the team, who all nodded in agreement with what Chris said.

"Good. Let us put them to the test," Shyra said as she hovered down next to the group. You have caught me in a benevolent mood, Voltaic Cloud, so I will overlook that recent outburst. Let us go inside and eat. It is important we keep our bodies nourished."

The team started to walk up the steps to the main doors, but Dimitri grabbed Alex by the arm. "What did she mean by that?"

"It's nothing," Alex said. "Don't worry about it."

With that, the five went inside and prepped themselves for whatever was to come next.

CHAPTER 28

You Never Seeing It Coming, You Just Get to See It Go

IT HAD BEEN ABOUT a month since the alliance met the two tight-fisted combatants. Although they had gone through extensive training and come out victorious in skirmishes against other espers who were abusing their powers, the rest of the team was still unsure if they would be able to beat the two next time around.

"We just have to shake it off," Alex told the team. "At least now we know we're not invincible."

"Yeah, whatever Cloud. We knew all that already. You don't always have to be Captain Obvious," Dimitri snapped at him.

"Yeah, well maybe if you followed orders, we wouldn't have been beaten so easily."

"What did you just say to me?" Dimitri balled up his fist.

"You heard me," Alex snapped back.

Shyra finally interjected. "Stop it the both of you. If you spent half the time you do fighting among yourselves on training, you would not have been defeated. Next time you encounter those two, you will win as long as you stick together."

Dimitri lowered his head and stared at the floor for a minute, knowing that his rash actions may very well have cost them the fight. "Shyra is right," he admitted. "We do need to work more like a team. I'm sorry."

Alex's jaw dropped. A sincere apology was something he never expected from the stone-cold Dimitri Williams.

"Well, I guess I can cut back on the leader role I play so well," Alex conceded.

"What about those other two espers we fought? They're still out there," Chris said.

"We have them join us," said Rain.

Earth whipped his head around in her direction. "What! Damn that! They're just as crazy as the Zenakuu. Are you guys forgetting we almost died fighting them?"

"No one forgot, D," Alex said.

At that moment, Shyra stepped in. "The decision is not yours to make, Seismic Earth. There is strength in numbers, and we will need all the help we can get when the Zenakuu army comes to destroy your world."

"I think we're overlooking the fact that they hate us. We'll be lucky if they wait ten seconds to talk before they try to kill us again," Chris said.

"Luck favors the prepared, Christian, and so all of you will be ready the next time you face them," Shyra affirmed.

The gang looked very concerned, but they had all been training so hard.

"Shyra, that reminds me," Alex interrupted. "There's something we need you to teach us before things get crazy again."

"And what might that be, Alexander?"

"Telepathy. Last time we fought them we got separated, and I think that's part of the reason why we lost, so can you teach us how to talk with our minds?"

Shyra stared at him for a few moments. Telepathy was no easy feat, so she gave them the blunt truth. "Technically, I can. With the limitations you all have broken through mentally, telepathy is within the realm of possibilities, but make no mistake—it will not come easy. You have to clear your thoughts of distractions and allow yourself to be susceptible to having someone probe into the depths of your mind."

Everyone was a little hesitant about letting each other see their most private thoughts.

"Sounds intrusive," Cassie complained.

"Maybe, but we're fighting for peace," Chris said.

"How do you *fight for peace*? That's an oxymoron," Cassie retorted.

"You're face is an oxymoron," Christian murmured underneath his breath. Alex tried his best not to crack a smile.

"In any case, it is indeed intense, Cassandra, but that is the risk you run when you let someone peer into your head. It is a two-way street that links the minds together," Shyra explained.

"Let's just get this over with," Dimitri said. He was clearly annoyed at this decision.

"All of you have had a long day, so we will start first thing tomorrow. Take some time to reflect and meditate on today's events," Shyra suggested.

The group did their best to focus on their new telepathy training.

The ship became a little quieter as they honed the skill, and so it went on for two weeks. It was just sounds and noises at first, but they focused on clearing out their minds of unnecessary distractions until they had all mastered speaking with each other without audible words. The team was ready to get back out there, there had been reports in the news of the two criminals they ran into from Washington, D.C., who the media has dubbed "Full Metal" and "G-Force," causing trouble, so everyone got together to come up with a plan.

"Why don't we just make a video challenging them to a fight and send it to a news station to air?" Dimitri suggested.

"Call them out on national television? You can't be serious," Cassie said.

"Dead serious," he responded.

Alex, however, was not too keen on the idea and shot it down. "That's not really the publicity we're looking for; besides, there has to be a better way to get their attention."

"Why don't we catch them in a trap or something?" suggested Tori. Everyone gave her a surprised look.

"That's actually a great idea," Alex replied.

"Of course it is. I'm tired of everyone thinking I'm dumb," Tori said.

"No one thinks you're dumb," Christian reassured her. "Now what was your plan?"

"Oh, I don't know. I thought you guys would kinda take it from there."

Everyone's eyebrows dropped and quickly got over her moment of genius.

"Well, let's think about it. They're bank robbers, right? We just have to stage a large enough fake shipment of money that not even they can pass up," Cassie suggested.

Shyra, who was listening to the conversation, agreed it could work.

"Could you do it, Shyra? Can you really hack into the Federal Reserve and authorize that transfer?" Cassie asked.

"Kalrynian technology is light years ahead of your own. I can crack it within minutes," she bragged.

"Good," Alex said. "Set it up then. We're going after these guys."

And so she did. Shyra set up a shipment of money to be transferred to the Potomac Trust Bank. The stage was set for their fateful reunion, except now the team was ready for them. The delivery was scheduled for a week later, and the team was already in place waiting for the two to arrive. They stationed themselves at different vantage points around the bank and communicated telepathically. If anyone saw anything, they were to immediately alert the others before engaging.

"What if they don't show?" Flame asked from his lookout spot on the rooftop of an adjacent building.

"They'll show. There's no way they can resist such a huge haul," Earth said, but he was two blocks away in hopes he could spot them coming from a distance.

The team looked on in concealment as the armored truck with the money pulled up.

"This is it, guys. Everyone stay sharp," ordered Voltaic Cloud, who was strategically hidden in the bank's bushes.

Wind kept an aerial view of the bank from above, and Rain peaked around the corner of an alleyway to the west. The transfer was almost completed, and there was no sign of the two.

"Damn. This is looking like a bust, guys," Wind said. "I don't think they're coming."

"Just keep your eyes open, Wind. They'll come; I know they will," Cloud ordered.

"The transfer is done, and there's no sign of them. Call it, Cloud," Rain said.

"No, there's still money in that truck, so it's still a target. We're not pulling out yet." Cloud was determined to catch the two espers, but as the truck pulled away, it wasn't looking good. Morale was dropping, but right as the truck stopped at the intersection in front of the bank, it began to hover a few inches off the ground before it quickly shot up in the air and was tossed on its side on the other side of the road. Flame, who heard the crash, was the first to call in what the others had already saw with their eyes.

"They're here!" he mentally shouted.

"Everyone, wait. We know they're here, but we don't know where they are. Don't make a move until we know their location," Cloud broadcasted to the others. He was being extremely cautious this time around.

The armored truck sparked as it skidded across the street until it came to a complete stop. The espers whom everyone wanted a piece of hovered over a distant bridge while getting closer to the truck by the second. It looked like the girl who could control gravity was carrying them over with her power. The three guards who were in the truck were shaken but crawled out the back doors and opened fire on the two. However, the male with ferrokinesis put up his hand, and the two were protected in a magnetic force field.

The girl placed them down near the truck, and the bullets continued to bounce off the barrier like they were rubber balls being thrown at a wall. With his other hand, the man ripped the doors off the truck and launched them at the guards, who were instantly knocked unconscious. The man and woman walked into the toppled truck with the intention to loot the money inside, while the group watched at a distance.

Cloud was hesitant to approach the duo. They had never suffered a defeat like the one they had been dealt by the mysterious man and woman. Even though there was a sense of fear, Cloud couldn't help but feel excited over the chance to square up with such a powerful adversary. The long-awaited rematch was finally at hand—nay, a bout demanded by the fates.

"Everyone move out," Cloud ordered. "Circle around them. Don't let them escape."

In a flash, they were out. Within moments, all routes were blocked off as Flame and Wind circled from above, Rain covered the area encompassing the sea, and lastly Earth and Cloud barricaded the ground exits. They all swarmed the two and prevented any form of escape.

The man stepped out of the truck only to realize that he had been set up. He was visibly angry, as he did not appreciate being made a fool of. He looked all around, realizing there would be no easy escape, and vocalized his annoyance. "Are you serious? You guys again? How many times are we going to do this? I thought you learned from the last time."

"Yeah, well I guess we're slow learners," Wind shouted back.

Flame looked at her with an arched eyebrow. It was not at all the best comeback, but it was all she could come up with.

"Anyway … Full Metal, right? Put down the money and come with us. This doesn't have end in a fight," Cloud added.

"That depends entirely on you, kid. Walk away now, and the only thing hurt will be your dignity," he said. By that time, his female counterpart had also stepped out into the open.

"I'm afraid we can't do that," answered Cloud.

"Have it your way, kid." With that, Full Metal raised his hands, but before he could get his attack off, the local police and highway patrol was on the scene.

They formed a perimeter around the seven and called out on the loud speaker. "This is the Metropolitan Police Department. Put your hands in the air and step away from the armored car."

Full Metal laughed at the idea of surrendering. "What now, hero? They see you as terrorists just like us."

"Only because of what *you've* been doing. You and G-Force have been ruining our names."

"Oh, I suppose we should turn ourselves in, right?"

Cloud wasn't sure what to do. There was no way of telling how many could be hurt if they fought in a crowded area, and he couldn't risk endangering his team by allowing them to be arrested. He reluctantly decided to move the fight to a less-populated area.

"There's a highway not far from here," Alex suggested. "We can fight there—unless you're scared."

Full Metal gave him a stern look. "That's it. Keep on digging your own grave." He turned his head to face his partner. "G-Force, we're following these kids to the highway, and then we kill them. Understand?" She nodded in hesitant agreement.

The officer once again spoke. "Final warning. Hands in the air!"

Even Cloud was getting annoyed at their persistence. It was now or never, so he telepathically hailed his team. "Guys, listen we're moving this fight. As soon as I'm done explaining the plan, move out. Wind and Flame, you're our fliers, so grab Rain and Earth and follow me by air to that highway over there. We'll set up a blockade so no one can interfere."

"Cloud, what about you?" Flame asked.

"I'll be fine. I'll stall them and give you guys some time to escape," he said.

"Okay, but don't do anything reckless."

"Don't worry. I won't," he assured his friends. "Everyone go."

Cloud held an electrical spark in his hands, and when he clapped his hands together, it exploded in a blinding light. With that, the rest of the team simultaneously took off. Even Full Metal and G-Force followed suit. The police department didn't see the diversion coming and were instantly blinded by the bright light. The whole plan only took a second, but in one fell swoop, everyone was gone, and Cloud dashed away with super speed to regroup with the others. They all arrived on the interstate near the river. Drivers immediately slammed their feet on their brakes. The smell of burnt rubber and sound of crashing waves were fresh in the air.

The images of those seven people were plastered in almost all forms of media known to man at that point. They were infamous whether they liked it or not. Upon seeing the group, every last person grabbed their families and ran for dear life. They abandoned their precious cars as if they meant nothing. Once the alliance was sure the area was clear, they battened down the hatches for an all-out brawl.

"Let's do this before the authorities ruin our fun, shall we?" Full Metal said, cocky as ever.

"Fine by us," Earth shouted back. He was still angry over their last encounter.

"Earth, don't lose your cool. We're not fixin' to give in to this guy's pace," Rain said.

"We're taking the fight to them. Got it?" Cloud asked.

"Whatever, man. Just show me the target, so I can lunge and attack it." Earth responded, anxious for the fight.

"Guys, remember the plan," Cloud directed. "These two are dangerous, so split them up. Flame and Wind, you two attack the girl and bring the fight to the air. The rest of us will overpower this guy on the ground. Remember your training, and don't do anything reckless. Fight in pairs—always."

The group nodded, and the plan was immediately implemented. The alliance just got deathly serious.

Chapter 29

Ask My Shoulders How Much the World Weighs

Wind took off to the sky, and Full Metal signaled for G-Force to pursue her. In seconds, the two of them were high in the open air and faced off. Wind knew that G-Force was more powerful than her, so she had to play it safe. Wind and G-force were face-to-face in midair approximately seventy feet off the ground. Flame noticed that Wind was facing off with G-Force alone, and he could not have that. Like a rocket ship blasting off, Flame shot fire from his feet and boosted up toward Wind. He flew next to her and cut back some of the firepower to hover there with her. Flame knew this fight wasn't going to be easy, but when G-Force spoke, it changed his mind.

"I don't want to fight you again," G-Force said. "We only need the money. If we get it, then you won't have to deal with us again."

Flame boosted forward. "We can't let you harm people and steal money for your own personal gain."

"It's not for me. It's to fulfill his dreams."

"I still can't let you do it," Flame repeated.

"Hey, Flame, ease up on the comic talk," Wind said, embarrassing Flame, before turning to G-Force. "Listen, hun, why are you involved with this guy if he is into all this stuff?"

"He isn't bad," she answered. "He just ran into some bad luck. I can see past all that, though. Deep down, he's good."

"You can end this now," Wind told her. "If you wanted to come with us, we could help you and your friend."

"I can't do that. I am with Full Metal, and he needs the money."

"Fine. Let's do things the hard way." Wind surrounded herself with gusts that reached a hundred miles per hour, and the smell of the ocean vanished. Displaying her power, Wind's sphere of bursting winds grew larger and larger, and even Flame had to give her space.

"I am not impressed," G-Force said. She pulsed a gravitational incorporeal blast with her right hand that connected with Wind's defense but wasn't able to push her back. She then realized that they had gotten much stronger and she had underestimated them. G-Force brought her left hand forward to increase the intensity of her attack. It pushed Wind back a bit, but she put all of what she had into the defense in order to drive forward and fight the force of gravity.

G-Force closed her eyes to concentrate and increase her efforts. She released a gravitational shockwave that pushed back both Flame and Wind. The two tumbled back for about twenty seconds before Wind regained herself. She saw Flame tumbling toward her and threw out her hand, which Flame grabbed.

"I got you," Wind frantically called out.

Flame boosted back up and got ready for a fight. "How are we going to get close to her?" he asked.

"One of us will have to distract her," she suggested.

"Okay, leave it to me. I'll cook her in that force field of hers."

The two leaned forward and burst onward. Flame was still getting used to using fire to project himself, but this gave him good practice. Wind was a pro at flying at this point.

"How far did she push us away?" Wind asked.

"Not sure, I don't see her anymore, but we have to be getting close." Soon, they saw G-Force in the distance. Wind slowed down and let Flame take her head-on. He came in fast, swung both arms forward, and unleashed an astonishing amount of fire, though nothing could penetrate her gravity shield. G-Force was well aware of both Flame and Wind. Even though all of her attention was on Flame, she knew what Wind was up to. Wind attempted to flank her from the back. G-Force turned to the side, one hand still shielding herself from Flame, and brought her other hand facing Wind. Wind stopped in her tracks when she saw G-Force's hand aimed at her. Instead of sending her flying endlessly into the sky, she applied gravity's unrelenting force upon her tenfold.

Wind fell out of the sky like a meteor plummeting down to the ground at terminal velocity. Flame saw her falling and knew he had to save her. Wind was about ten feet away and about fifty feet from the ground, so Flame kicked on the jets and zoomed toward her. He caught her but couldn't lift her, because the gravity was too strong. Flame got the idea that if he got under her, he would be able to use his rocket-like flight to stop her or, at the very least, slow her down.

He positioned himself back-to-back with her, so he was facing down. Flame gave it all he had as he tried his hardest to shoot up and break the gravity, but he couldn't do it. Although he did slow down the descent, he was getting too close to the ground. The flames from his feet charred the dirt and burned a hole right into the ground. Wind turned her head and looked at Flame. He looked back up at her; his face was strained from struggling to lift her. Flame saw a worried look on Wind's face and did not want to let her down. He let out a holler at the top of his lungs and executed a boost as big as a space shuttle lifting off into space. Suddenly, Wind felt herself being lifted off the ground. They were fighting gravity that was ten times Earth's normal level. G-Force couldn't hold them down any longer, and any more gravity could seriously injure them, which wasn't an option to her. The last thing she wanted to do was hurt people. She released her hold on Wind.

"I don't want to hurt anyone," G-Force stated while Flame caught his breath.

"Hurt anyone? What about the people in D.C.? The building collapsed, millions of dollars lost in the rubble, hundreds of thousands of dollars to rebuild that building, not to mention all of the people who had money in that bank and lost it. Also, they will be without jobs for months. You and your little boyfriend have hurt a lot of people already," said Wind.

"No, we just needed the money. If you hadn't come in, everything would have been fine."

"I don't have to listen to this," Flame cut in, obviously annoyed.

"Flame, take it easy. Listen, we can help, give you a place to live and a reason to fight, more of a reason to help than your boyfriend's financial problems," Wind reasoned.

"Can Full Metal join as well?"

"I'm not sure. He doesn't seem to feel the same way you do," Wind noted.

"If he can't come, then neither can I." G-force used her gravitokinesis to create a shield of gravity not around herself but around the area, entrapping Wind and Flame. Next she used gyrokinesis to send three separate waves of gravitational power that pounded Flame and Wind against the inner wall of the gravity dome. Lastly, G-Force held a continuous wave that pressed the two heroes against the incorporeal gravitational barrier.

Wind strained to even breathe but was able to verbalize, "We have to do something to stop her!"

Wind and Flame couldn't move a muscle. The centrifugal force was squeezing the air from their lungs. Flame couldn't take it anymore. Instinct kicked in, and he ignited his body into a burst of flames. Wind exhaled and covered her body with a flowing armored suit of wind to protect herself from the fire but was still in danger of being broiled alive by her teammate. Flame screamed and filled the entire gravitational field with fire and flames. G-Force was once again overwhelmed by Flame's unyielding resolve to live and had to take down the field to escape the riotous fires. The clothes on G-Force were singed and smoking. It reminded her of the last time they met.

He was severely fatigued, but Flame shot forward using his pyrokinesis, and his fist found G-Force's face. She was pushed back from the force of the shovel punch. Flame grabbed her foot, and she struggled to break his hold. They tussled and spun around in the sky for a minute, neither of them knowing which way was up, which only testified how aerial fights were not as elegant as they were portrayed in the movies. Wind wanted to attack, but she withheld in fear of accidently hitting Flame. He finally spun her around and released, sending her right toward Wind. She created a minitornado that caught G-Force and spun her with enough RPMs to send her thrashing around like a ragdoll at one hundred miles per hour. She cushioned her fall with antigravity, but G-Force grew tired of being thrown around.

G-Force had her eyes locked on Flame at this point. She raised her right hand and aimed at the troubled hero. Another gravity pulse traveled to Flame, and even though he was able to dodge the girth of the beam, it still caught his left arm. The pulse that she put out wasn't just to push out. She magnified the gravity around Flame's arm to five times Earth's gravity. Flame had a hard time keeping his arm from ripping out of its socket, but he managed to keep his altitude, even though his arm was useless. She increased the gravity again, and he screamed out in pain.

"Wind, help!" Flame lost his balance but was able to regain it by holding his left arm up with his right.

"I'm working on it, buddy." Wind was finally able to redirect the wind that shielded her to force it into a vortex to attack G-Force.

Flame witnessed the twister aimed at G-Force and saw the opportunity for their scorching tornado. He let go of his left arm with agony painted on his face, He shot out a flamethrower attack at the base of Wind's vortex, but being so off balanced, he missed entirely. Nevertheless, the tornado touched down on the shore's surface, but without the additional destructive power, it wasn't enough to take G-Force down. Without holding on to his arm, Flame quickly plummeted out of the sky due to the overly stressed gravity. He plunged deep into the Potomac River that was directly beneath him and created a gigantic splash. Flame's left arm grew heavier as it dragged him under into the soon to-be-abyss. Fearing that he might drown, he screamed out for help but only succeeded in squandering what little air he had left in his lungs. As the air bubbles left his mouth, he knew it was over for him. He disappeared into a watery grave.

"Christian!" Wind shouted out, although it was too late. In the blink of an eye, he was gone. She looked at G-Force but only saw red. "You bitch!" she screamed and threw wind blade after wind blade toward her enemy.

Each of them easily bounced off G-Force's protective force field, which worried Wind a lot. She was running out of time if she was going to save Flame. She knew she had to switch tactics, so she hunched over and put her hands five inches away from one another. She focused all her aerokinetic energy to her palms and created an extremely concentrated ball of air that shot out like a jet stream from her hands and barreled toward G-Force, punching a hole through her barrier after spiraling hard against its surface. Wind was not done there, though, she clenched her right fist, and the ball exploded outward, causing G-Force's gravitational shield to implode. G-Force was thrown from the force of the blast and found that Wind was able to anticipate her trajectory, as she was hovering a few feet above her.

With all of her might, Wind shot a gale into G-Force's abdomen. Before she was able to block it, she dropped out of the sky and smacked the water's surface hard. Wind was determined to show her the same brutality she showed Flame. Out of blinding rage, she screamed and shot multiple gale-level winds to the pinpoint location of where her combatant had nosedived. The water surged up after each blast, and after awhile G-Force could no longer be seen, but it was different this time—this time she couldn't control the winds. She created a hurricane that took on a life of its own Wind understood her own power, but not the science behind tropical storms and things were getting worse fast. Not knowing her recklessness might have caused more harm than good Whisking Wind began to panic, the barometric pressure plummeted and she didn't know how to fix the situation. The deep, warm water, cold prevailing winds, dense moisture, and a source of power were all the necessary ingredients for a rampaging storm that she became the eye of.

The torrential rain was astonishingly blowing sideways. She could hardly speak let alone hear herself think over the roaring winds. She circled in the air, struggling to catch her breath. She had never used so much of her power at once and could already feel an excruciating headache coming on. Wind knew that last attack would not be enough to finish the fight, so she formed an air bubble around her to protect from the hurricane and waited. She looked for any kind of movement, but there was none—just people from the port fleeing in terror.

From above, Wind saw the water shake, and she knew round three had begun. G-Force exploded with gravitational power, sending water, boats, fish, debris, and even an unearthed Irascible Flame outward. She rose out of the river like the lady of the lake holding Excalibur for King Arthur in the same gravitational field she had sported before.

Wind swooped down at incredible speeds and caught her sunken treasure of a teammate by his ankle. She carried him to the ground and placed him down gently, but he wasn't breathing. She was careful to land in a spot out of sight, but she didn't know how long it would be until G-Force discovered their location. Wind dissipated her air sphere, and tried to awaken her teammate.

"Flame, are you okay?" Wind asked, but there was no response. "God damn it, Christian, you are not allowed to die!"

From her time on the Californian beaches, Wind had seen CPR preformed enough times that she felt she could wing it. She didn't have much choice at the moment. She pinched his nose shut and lifted his chin. She only hesitated a second before she firmly pressed her lips to his and blew air into his lungs. With her ability over air, she was careful not to overinflate him, but she could still visibly see his chest cavity rise and drop. Yet, nothing happened. She placed one palm over another and continued with a series of chest compressions. She listened for a heartbeat, but she feared the worst. Once again, she blew air into her friend until he finally coughed up a large amount of water. He was alive, and she couldn't be more relieved.

He slowly opened his and gazed upon his savior.

"Chris, thank God you're okay," Wind exclaimed. "Don't ever do that to me again."

He struggled to sit up, but he was still disoriented. "What … happened to me?" he stammered.

"You went under for a long time, but she must have dropped her gravitational hold on you when I—" but her sentence was cut short by a water-logged and very angry G-Force.

"Watashi wa anata o korosu darou!" A death threat in her native language that she had every intention of fulfilling. She had found their location and picked up Wind with her ability. She suspended Wind high in the air and slammed her to the ground, guiding her every movement with her hand.

"Wind!" Flame yelled out, but he couldn't get to his feet yet. He reached out for her, but she was beyond his help. Their enemy wasn't done with the onslaught; she threw Wind from side to side, slamming her into any object blunt enough to endure the bash. She once again lifted Wind, but after seeing that her body had completely gone limp, she dropped her to the ground causing the hurricane to clear out. That was all Flame needed to see. With reckless abandon, he stood up. His mask covered his tears, but he was overwhelmed with emotion over the thought of losing Tori. With eyes void of any shred of humanity he looked up at her, and responded to her actions.

"¡Quiero que te mueras, puta!" A mutual threat he shouted back. His face twisted in fury and hands lit up with a blue flame that he had never seen before, but he felt the increased heat and intensity. He could do it with this power, so he aimed both hands at her and let forth the strongest flame he'd ever produced.

The blue fire blazed from his fist and was so hot it melted his hand armaments before fully engulfing G-Force's protective force field. Even she doubted if she could withstand such a force as it showered over her. She exuded all of her power to strengthen her shield, lest she be incinerated. No one had ever pushed her so far, and she was clearly at her limit.

Flame wanted to end the fight, so he flew up to her eye level. He was worried about Wind. "She better be okay, G-force, for your sake," he growled.

If looks could kill was the first thing that went through her mind. G-Force looked down at Wind with sadness. She knew herself to be a good person, not a deliverer of death. When G-Force looked back up, she saw Flame leaping toward her with a flaming fist. She immediately focused power to her shield, and Flame hit it with such force that it made a loud clap, but looked similar to a balloon popping. G-Force saw her shield ripple where Flame connected, but all she could do was defend. Flame continued with a blazing left, then a right, followed by another left. Every punch was fueled with fire and made the same loud clap.

G-Force knew she couldn't keep it up, but her mind was distracted by the thought of Wind being seriously injured. She let her anger get the best of her, and she knew she was better than that. Flame lifted both hands, held them together, and came down with a heavy ax handle, which finally broke through G-Force's shield. She didn't know that breaking the shield also meant breaking her psyche. It rendered her unconscious, and she dropped out of the sky. Flame realized it was far too high of a fall to survive, so he swallowed his pride and caught her, gently put her on the ground, and stood over her. Wind came limping over not long after that. Her sleeve was ripped and her arm was scratched, but all around, she was fine.

Flame smiled at her. "I'm glad you're okay, Wind." But he was still unsure what had caused G-Force to pass out, so he telepathically called Shyra. "Shyra, I broke through the female esper's forced field and she passed out. What happened to her?" he asked.

"Well when you broke through her kinetic shield you technically broke through her mental defenses. She more than likely could not handle the stress, so she fainted. She will be fine with due time," Shyra explained.

"Okay, good," he said with a confused sense of accomplishment.

"That was impressive, Flame," Wind said. "Didn't know you had the strength to get through. I certainly didn't. I'm glad you did."

"Thanks, Tor." Flame's cheeks turned red under his mask. "You did really well too."

"Yeah, yeah, you find something to tie her up. I'll go see if the others need me and meet you over there." Wind winked at Flame and flew off.

Flame felt on top of the world at that point, and he blissfully followed her orders. *Good job, Chris. You took down the bad guy, and you may finally get the girl—not a bad day's work*, he thought to himself. Flame's ego sometimes got the best of him. He took out a zip tie and closed it around G-Force's wrists. He hoisted her over his shoulder and went to join his team.

CHAPTER 30

Death Before Dishonor

WHILE FLAME AND WIND fought G-Force, it was up to Earth, Cloud, and Rain to take out Full Metal. The three of them stood twenty feet away from their enemy. The fight had already gotten out of control. Cloud worried for his two friends who were waged in an aerial battle, but he knew distraction could mean death. He gathered his nerves and formulated a plan in his head. He spoke to his teammates telepathically so not to be found out by the enemy.

"Rain, listen. Earth and I will keep him distracted, while you gather all the water from the air you can. I need you battle-ready when we break through his defenses. Odds are we're only gonna get one shot at this, so we better make it count."

"Understood. Good luck," Rain responded.

Cloud turned to Earth, "Okay, I'm fista rush him. You come in right behind me and follow through."

"Okay, but this better work," Earth said.

"It will; trust me," he replied. Cloud turned to Full Metal, who was growing impatient.

"You princesses finally ready?" he asked mockingly.

"Last chance to surrender," Cloud shouted out.

"Yeah, thanks but no thanks, kid. You can take your offer and shove it," Full Metal said.

"Have it your way." Cloud ran as fast as humanly possible without kicking into super speed so that Earth was able to keep up. When he was finally in striking distance, he cocked his fist back for what would be a devastating knockout punch. Full Metal threw his arms up to block, but the punch was a feint. Cloud super sped forward, leaving only his after image to phase through Full Metal, a technique he learned training with Shyra.

When Full Metal dropped his arms to try and comprehend what had happened, Earth leapt forward and on cue drove his fist deep in their enemy's solar plexus, which caused him to drop to his knees and gasp for air. Cloud came in from the left and slammed his knee hard into the side of Full Metal's head. The assault launched him outward, forcing him to skid along the pavement. He was laid out and not moving. The two thought the fight may have actually been over.

"Let's finish him," Earth demanded.

"No, we keep our distance for now." The words were spoken none too soon, as the two heard a blood-curdling yell come from the motionless body.

"Guys, be careful," Rain stressed from behind.

Full Metal used his magnetic pull to bring himself to his feet. "You thought that would stop me? All you've done is succeeded in pissing me off!" He drove out his hands and started ripping guard rails off their hinges.

"Rain, get ready. We're all going to attack him," ordered Alex.

She was finally done gathering water. "I'm ready," she replied.

The loose guard rails flew toward the three in an attempt to impale them, but they took evasive maneuvers and narrowly dodged the rails. Rain shot a jet stream of water that forced Full Metal back but not off his feet. Cloud instinctively knew to electrocute the ground that was now covered in water, but Full

Metal jumped on a silver midsized sedan where the rubber tires acted as an insulator for the electrical charge.

Earth stomped his foot down on the road, which created a deep fissure that stretched to the car Full Metal was using for safety. The vehicle tipped over, and Rain lunged forward with a spinning back-handed hammer fist that hit his right cheek. She continued her melee attack with continuous right- and left-handed jabs and hooks to the ribs. Rain started low in a southpaw stance, her balance came from her core center of gravity. She jumped forward and raised her left leg at a forty-five degree angle, and snapped back with the right leg. Her left foot connected with the ground and her right foot connected with Full Metal's throat and face. With precision she was able to find the right timing. She performed a perfectly executed crane kick that left him shaken up and barely able to know up from down.

She leapt up again to end the fight with a jump ax kick, but Full Metal parried her foot and shot a magnetic pulse into her abdomen that changed her polarity. Unbeknownst to her, she had become magnetized and crashed into the hood of a nearby abandoned car from the magnetic pull.

"Rain!" Cloud yelled out.

"I'm fine," she responded. "I just can't get off of this car. I think he magnetized me."

"I'll get you free." He connected to Earth's mind with an important task.

"Earth, can you hear me?" Cloud asked telepathically.

"Yeah, what's up?" he responded.

"I'm going to create a diversion. When I give the signal, everyone shut their eyes, and then I want you to rush him while I help Rain."

"Got it," Earth confidently said. He had been waiting for payback the entire fight. Cloud put out a surgically charged hand and released a slowly pulsating orb of electrical energy that crackled as it traveled through the air. Even Full Metal was curious as to what strange technique it was, but when the ball was close enough to him, Cloud telepathically shouted, "Now!"

Rain and Earth closed their eyes, and Cloud clenched his fist. The orb exploded with a blinding bright light. He had made a flash bomb that took away Full Metal's sight. Blinded, Full Metal magnetically lifted cars and guard rails and arbitrarily launched them in all directions, hoping one would hit one of the heroes.

Luckily, none did, and Cloud raced over to Rain, while Earth charged Full Metal. Cloud tried his best to pry her free, but she was stuck tight.

"What in God's name did he do to you? I can't get you free," he said rhetorically.

"Don't worry about me, Cloud. Just finish him."

"I'm not leaving you here. I'm not fista lose you again."

Rain looked confused. "Again?" she asked.

"Never mind. I'll explain it later. Right now I just have to get you out of this."

Rain had an idea on how to liberate herself from her situation, but it was not something she was looking forward to. "Cloud, listen. I know how to get rid of the magnetic pull."

"How?" he asked.

"Electrocute me," she replied.

"What! No way."

"Cloud, we don't have time for this. You have to shock me," she insisted.

"What are you talking about, Rain?"

"Ugh. I don't have time to go into detail, but it works like this: using Ampere's Law, one can determine the magnetic field associated with any given current or current associated with any given magnetic field, providing there is no time changing electric field present."

Cloud had no idea what she was talking about. He knew she was smart, but this was on a different level. "Layman's terms please," he said.

"Alex, you can take over his magnetic force with your electrical charge through electromagnetism. Now hurry!"

Cloud didn't like the idea at all, but it was the best chance they had, and desperate times called for desperate measures. He broke through the driver's side window of the car and grabbed what seemed to be a baby's rubber toy.

"Bite down on this," he instructed. "It will help with the pain." Rain nodded and took the toy into her mouth.

A few yards away, Earth was having a heated, super-powered battle with Full Metal. He attempted to spear Full Metal with pointed mounds of raised rock, but he stepped back and rolled out of the way of each spike. The combatant ripped down a billboard with his control of magnetism and telekinetically folded it into the shape of an oversized spiked mace.

The ball chased Earth around the road as he flipped from side to side and ducked out of its way, just missing his head by a few inches. That last dodge was too close for comfort for Earth, so on the next come around by the mace, he stood tall and lifted a solid wall of concrete and stone no less than a foot thick. The mace smashed into it, embedding itself deep within, and even though it caused quite an explosion, the wall had succeeded in halting the mace.

Enraged by the scene, Full Metal charged in and threw punch after punch to Earth's head, but Earth instinctively ducked. A cool breeze fanned his face as Full Metal's fist rushed by. His days trained as a boxer were too much for his opponent to handle.

Full Metal threw his right knee to Dimitri's abdomen but was blocked by him lowering his left elbow. The criminal's left low kick was blocked by Earth's raised right calf muscle. The entire fight was happening at near superhuman speeds, and with their instincts running the show time might as well have halted all together. Full Metal's blood was boiling at being toyed with by what he perceived to be some young punk. He threw an uppercut that Earth sidestepped and a right hook that he ducked underneath. Earth countered by throwing a feint right jab that Full Metal foolishly tried to block, and then drove his right knee forward into Full Metal's stomach, which made his whole body concave and sent it crashing through the highway median. Seismic Earth stood confidently and assertively said, "My turn."

Voltaic Cloud concentrated on spreading his power out evenly from his hands. He looked into Rain's eyes and let the electricity pour from his fingertips until it looked like a miniature lightning storm egressed from his hands. Cassie convulsed and contorted as her body was writhed with amps of electrical discharge. She screamed, but before it appeared like her life was in serious danger, he ceased the flow. Even though Cassie fell to the ground in pain with smoke rising off of her body, the technique luckily worked. Cloud canceled Full Metal's polarization with his powers. He kneeled down to check on his teammate.

"Rain, are you okay?" Cloud asked.

She was a little woozy, but other than that, she'd live. "I'm fine. Go help Earth, and I'll be right behind you."

Cloud nodded and was off. It was a bad way to discover it, but Cloud was overjoyed that he knew he could cancel out their enemy's affect with his own kinesis. He approached where the two were fighting, but it didn't seem like Earth needed help at all. He was too busy pummeling Full Metal with elbows and knees. Earth tried to continue his barrage with a spinning sidekick, but Full Metal stopped it midair with a cushion of magnetic force. In that instant, Cloud super sped over. Before he could get there, Full Metal spun around, caught Earth with the backside of his fist, grabbed the very same foot he was almost struck by, and javelined Earth to the other side of the road. However, before Full Metal could even put his arms down, Cloud landed a flying jump kick to his spinal cord.

Taking all three of them on was proving to be more of a challenge than Full Metal anticipated. Full Metal stumbled forward, while Cloud charged up his electrical current. Full Metal reached out his hand and tore a highway sign that read, "I-

66 Theodore Roosevelt Memorial Bridge ¼ mile," from above. As Cloud shot a concentrated ball of electricity toward him, Full Metal shielded himself with the sign. The blast left the sign a jagged heap up of metal, but Full Metal still saw it fit enough to mold into the shape of a lance and hurled it at Cloud in hopes it would skewer him like a shish kebab. Earth stepped in and raised a pillar of dirt from the cracked ground that deflected the attack.

The miscreant knew he was getting nowhere fast, so he made the conscious decision to take off the kiddie gloves and end the fight. Full Metal threw out his hands and focused; a vein pulsated on his forehead, and he tightly gritted his teeth. He never thought those brats could improve as much as they had, but it was obvious that victory would not come easily.

The space around him became wavy and distorted. The massive magnetic energy pouring out of his vessel could be seen with the naked eye. Rain and Earth converged back on Cloud's location.

"What's he doing?" Earth asked.

"I don't know," Cloud said, "but we're not fixin' to just stand here and find out. Hit him with everything you've got."

Cloud whirled his hands outward and powered up. The charge visibly originated from his feet and manifested itself through his body before gathering between his palms. The energy glowed and blustered violently as it gathered. In one motion, he released his raw power that met face-to-face with Full Metal's magnetic field head on. The blast sparked and surged around it, but Full Metal appeared to be safe in the epicenter of his impenetrable force field.

"Pathetic," Full Metal shouted out over the storm.

With that, Rain and Earth stepped forward. Rain twirled her arms around in a series of martial art movements designed to gather water from the air, while Earth pounded his fist into the ground and caused a miniature earthquake. Full Metal stumbled back but kept his magnetic field firm. Earth's real intention was to split the ground enough to supply himself with an artillery of metamorphic rocks. When the two were ready, they followed suit and joined their captain in a barrage of projectile force. The firing went on for what felt like an eternity to the three, but Full Metal held strong.

Cloud reached out to Earth and Rain telepathically. "Listen, I want you two to fall back."

"Are you nuts? It's gonna take all three of us to put him down," Earth protested.

"I have a plan," Cloud explained. "I'm going to try and take over his magnetic field."

"Alex, no. That works both ways. He could take over your electrical field," Rain pointed out.

"Don't worry," he said. "I won't let that happen. Trust me."

"That's the second time you've asked me to trust you, bro. This time it better work," said Earth.

"It will. When his powers are down, I need the two of you to quickly subdue him."

"We'll take care of things on our end. Just be careful, Cloud," demanded Rain.

The two stopped the hail of their elemental power and left things to their leader. Full Metal didn't know if it was some kind of trick, but he wanted to seize the opportunity he was presented with, so the villain forced his field to recede inward. He absorbed the energy like a sponge.

Just like Voltaic Cloud, he channeled it through his hands and released it forward. The two were locked in an intense power struggle of opposing forces. The beam fluctuated back and forth as Cloud and Full Metal fought to take over the other's power. Full Metal, who had been pushing so hard that his nose began to bleed, tensed his muscles and slowly pushed forward, which caused Cloud to momentarily lose his footing and step back.

"Cloud!" Rain shouted out.

"I'm okay. Just be ready." The hero knew he couldn't let down his team. He remembered what it felt like losing them and immediately became enraged.

The image of his team slain at the hands of those who threatened his very life haunted his consciousness. Once again, dark clouds formed from up above as a ferocious thunderstorm poured in. Cloud's eyes surged with electrical power.

"I won't let you hurt them," he roared out, and from the sky, an astoundingly luminous lightning bolt cuts through the sky and crashes down on top of him, magnifying his power tenfold. Everything brightened for a split second, and the power raced up through his body looking for the path of least resistance. It found its escape in the already terrifying current of electrical power his hands created. The lightning broke through Full Metal's field and sent him careening through the air until he came to a stop when he slammed into a truck. Smoke rose from Cloud's body as he dropped to his knees.

"Now!" Earth yelled, and the two were off. Earth jetted for Full Metal, while Rain rushed to Cloud. Before Full Metal realized what was happening, Earth formed two slabs of rock that entombed tightly around him so he could no longer use his magnetic powers.

Across the street, Rain propped Cloud up on her lap. "Cloud, are you okay?" she asked.

"I think so," he responded. "Did we get him?"

The selfless question reminded her of the time they bravely fought the Zenakuu scouts, and he was so worried about her. With a smile, she gave him the same response he gave her. "You did it, Cloud. I don't think he'll be getting up this time."

He smiled back, and Effervescent Rain helped Cloud to his feet. Earth stood in front of the fallen criminal with a disturbing look in his eye. He raised his arm up and held out his hand. He slowly closed its grip, and the two slabs began to tighten. Full Metal screamed in agony as his body was being slowly flattened.

"What the hell is he doing?" Cloud asked.

Earth continued to clench his fist, and the slabs grew closer and closer, inch by inch.

"Earth, no!" Cloud shouted.

"Shut up, Alex. I'm doing this for all of us."

"We don't kill people. You know that," Rain pleaded.

"He's not a human," Earth exclaimed. "He's an emotionless monster." Earth held his position; any tighter, and the criminal would die.

"Dimitri, I said no! Don't do it," Cloud shouted.

Earth looked at Cloud. Cloud's right hand was pointed at him and surged with electricity. He had a very serious look on his face, as if he would really do it—shoot his own teammate.

"It's like that, huh?" Earth asked.

"Only if you make it," Cloud responded.

Earth looked back at the barely conscious enemy for a second before finally releasing his grip. "Whatever, man. When shit hits the fan, it'll be on you," he said.

Rain walked Cloud over to the defeated Full Metal. He was still unconscious, despite the torture, which was a relief to the three as they were all physically and mentally drained. Wind touched down two minutes later, a little disappointed she had missed all the action.

Cloud called out telepathically to Flame. "Hey, how you holding up?"

"I'm good, man," he responded. "I'm bringing the girl over to you guys now. See you in a few."

The four of them wanted to relax, but now that the sparks were done flying, it would only be a matter of time before the cops tried to apprehend them once again. Flame landed with the tied up G-Force on his back.

"Yo," he said. He looked down and saw the state Full Metal was in. "What happened to him?"

"I'll explain later," Cloud said. "Shyra, we won. What do we do with them now?"

"They are too important to let your government get a hold of them," she responded. "I am preparing all seven of you for transport. Stand by."

With sirens blaring in the background, the team knew they had officially overstayed their welcome and could only imagine what the news was going to say about their exploits this time.

As always, they dematerialized and were gone in a flash.

CHAPTER 31

Keep Your Friends Close, and Your Enemies Closer

THE TEAM HAD FOUGHT tooth and nail and arrived in front of the ship doors where Shyra was waiting for them with proper restraints for their new guests. The two awoke in a cell adjacent from Donikan, the captured Zenakuu scout, who was running his mouth as usual.

"More prisoners of fortune Kalrynian? And this time you've taken to enslaving this world's native species, I see." Donikan said as he turned to the Kinetic Alliance. "Tell me, earthling children, how is she any different from me? At least we would've killed you quickly."

"Silence, Donikan. I am not in the mood for it today," Shyra snapped back.

"What the hell is this? Let me out!" Full Metal started shouting,

"In due time, Full Metal," Shyra said. "Right now it is important we treat your injuries, but we cannot do that if you do not calm down."

The room was dimmed, but Full Metal knew something was amiss. His captor didn't look human at all.

"What are you?" Full Metal asked as he stepped back from the cell doors and faced G-Force, who was curled up in the fetal position in the corner. He demanded that G-Force get them out of there, but even if she hadn't been frozen in fear over their predicament, their powers were being blocked inside the cell.

"Useless!" he yelled at her.

"I need you to calm down. We are not your enemies," Shyra said.

"I am," Dimitri voiced out as he raised his hand.

"Seismic Earth, enough," she sighed, as she knew this was going to be a long night. "I am known as Shyra, and as you have surmised, I am not of your world. I am from a planet called Kalryn, but trust me when I say I have come a long way to find you."

"What do you mean me?" he asked.

"You and others like you. Your powers are not coincidental. Light years away there is an intergalactic war being waged between many planets. The war was initiated by the home world of the individual you see before you."

"Lies! We didn't start this war, but I swear we'll finish it," Donikan objected.

Shyra beat her hand on the wall, leaving a small crater on the face of it. "I said shut up. You besmirch my people's honor with your slanderous remarks for the last time!"

Donikan backed away from the cell door.

"As I was saying," Shyra continued, "you received your powers to save your world from invasion to put it simply. There is an army coming to eradicate this entire planet, and you are its only defense. If you will let me, I will show the two of you."

Full Metal paused and looked at G-Force, who nodded with compliance. "Show me," he said.

Shyra entered their minds and, like the others, showed them the Kalryn massacre at the hands of the Zenakuu. She showed them the carnage the war had brought down on the galaxy. The two were in disbelief; it was a lot to take in, and with no way to know if she was telling the truth, they were skeptical.

"Will you join us?" she asked.

"I don't like the idea of risking our necks to clean up your mess. I'll have to think about it." Full Metal replied.

"Fair enough," Shyra said. "I am going to let you out of this cell now and show you to your quarters for the night, providing you can control yourself and not cause trouble."

The tension in the air was almost palpable, but Full Metal knew that his captors had the upper hand. "We'll behave," he replied.

Shyra looked back at the five others who were watching the whole thing from the other side of the room. Their expressions were a mixture of concern and distaste, but as their mentor, she had to consider all possibilities. The two new captives' powers could not be denied. They very well could tip the scale in her favor when the Zenakuu came.

"I pray that you do," she said as she opened the cell door.

Full Metal stretched his arms out wide as he exited. G-Force was still reluctant to make a move.

"That went for the both of you," Shyra reminded her.

G-Force slowly got to her feet and inched over to her freedom.

"You have my word that though my appearance may be startling, I am not here to hurt you," Shyra reassured her.

Dimitri, who had enough of the display of hospitality, got off the wall he was leaning on and walked upstairs to the main floor. Tori followed behind him, and soon the others went up behind her.

"The kids you're babysitting don't seem too happy about this," Full Metal avouched to Shyra.

"And for good reason, as you have tried to kill them twice. Worry not about them. I will speak to them. Follow me to your room."

They followed Shyra up and out of the brig but not before Full Metal gave Donikan a menacing stare. A stare that was reciprocated as they passed the alliance whom formed a circle in the shared living quarters.

"Shyra has lost her damn mind inviting those two back," Dimitri declared.

"He's right. They can't be trusted," Christian agreed.

"Guys, I'm skeptical about it too, but Shyra has to have a reason for this. What do you think, Alex?" asked Cassie.

Even though they looked for clarity from their appointed leader, he was just as much riddled with doubt as they were. "I don't know yet," Alex admitted. "Let's just see what happens. They're strong and could help us, but they may not even want to join."

In the meantime, Shyra lead the two their room. "Will you be needing separate rooms?" she questioned.

"No, that won't be necessary. We'll be fine here," G-Force said, speaking for the first time. Full Metal glared at her but didn't try to object.

"Very well," Shyra said. "I will leave you to talk it over, but know this: your world is in danger of being wiped out, and the two of you could really make a difference. There is a lot about your powers I can teach you. I can give you the strength to beat them. You would forever be known as heroes."

Full Metal and G-Force looked at Shyra with sincere eyes and nodded, signifying they understood what was at stake. With that final thought, she closed the door and walked back to the others who were still in a heated debate.

"I see everyone started without me," Shyra said.

"Yeah, well we normally don't question your decisions, but this affects all of us. That woman almost killed me," Tori said.

"As have the Zenakuu, except they will not show mercy to members of your species who cannot defend themselves like she did. They will decimate your entire planet without hesitation. There is a saying here on Earth that I have recently heard and become fond of: 'The enemy of my enemy is my friend.'"

Shyra made a good point, but no one wanted to admit it.

"This is bullshit," Dimitri said. "We should have finished them off when we had the chance."

"That is not our way, Dimitri. We do not kill needlessly," Shyra reminded him.

The rest of the team was a little shocked that Dimitri could offer such a dark and morbid resolution, but he was the only one who grew up with death being a constant reminder on the streets.

"I understand everyone's concern, but I have grown very fond of the five of you in the time we have spent together. I would give up my life before I ever let something bad happen to you. These two can be an incredible addition to our team. Please give them a chance for me," Shyra requested.

It was the first time she was ever so humble as to ask for the team's permission. It took great humility, and the five appreciated that. They unanimously agreed to give the two a trial run.

Before heading to bed, Dimitri pulled Tori off to the side. "I heard you held your own out there today," he said. "Good job."

Tori blushed and responded. "Really? I mean, thanks. I just never thought I'd be getting praise from you."

Dimitri rolled his eyes. He didn't like it when people weren't able to just accept a compliment. "Well, you really did ya thing today. I'm proud of you."

Her face lit up, and she wrapped her arms around his neck. "Thanks, D!" she said.

Dimitri stumbled back a bit from being jumped on but reciprocated the hug and cautiously placed his arms around her waist. The smell of her hair was intoxicating to him, but he despised that she could cause such a reaction in him. When they finally loosened their arms long enough to actually look at each other, they realized they were in inches away from each other's lips. Tori tried to look as alluring as possible, but Dimitri awkwardly ended the moment.

"You're welcome," he said. "I'll see you in the morning." And then he walked away to be alone.

Back in their room, the two newcomers talked about what they should do. The room had always been vacant, so it was basically bare besides the essentials. They sat down on a king-sized mattress that was lined up against the wall with a dresser and lamp within arm's distance and went over options.

"I think we should join them," G-Force said. "You saw what's about to happen, and we finally have a chance to wipe our slate clean and be part of something big."

"You *would* say something like that. Look, this isn't some camping trip where we sit down by a fire and sing 'Kumbaya.' They aren't our family, okay? The only people we can count on are ourselves."

"Baby, why do you have to always be like this? I don't want to live this life of crime anymore," she pleaded. "We're gonna get ourselves killed doing it. I've only been helping because I love you, not because I enjoy it."

Full Metal placed his hand on her cheek to calm her down. "Hey, I've always looked out for us. I would never let you get hurt."

She looked back deeply into his eyes. She so desperately wanted to believe him, but it didn't matter if he was telling the truth or not. Somewhere along the line she grew to love him unconditionally and would follow him wherever he led her.

"I know," she said ever so softly.

"One thing is for sure—we do need to do something. I just can't believe it, though ... Aliens actually exist and, even more, are coming to kill us." Full Metal laid down on the bed with his fingers intertwined underneath his head and let his knees hang over the edge of the mattress.

G-Force twisted her waist and laid down with her head on his chest. "Let's do it, okay? Let's join them. I don't know how, but I know it's what we're supposed to do," she said.

He sighed out loud and responded. "Alright, but no matter what, we look out for each other."

Overjoyed that he had finally come around, she moved up and kissed him. "Alright."

"I'll give them our answer in the morning," he told her. The two positioned themselves under the sheets and turned out the lights.

Chapter 32

You Never See It Coming, You Only See It Go

DAYLIGHT BROKE THROUGH THE ship's windows, and the usual five were interested to see if the potential new members had restrained themselves enough to not sneak out in the middle of the night. The Kinetic Alliance assembled in the shared living area where Shyra was standing on the side of Full Metal and G-Force.

"Good morning, everyone," she said with a smile. "I would like to introduce you to the newest members of our little family: Lucas Wright and Sora Morikami."

"Pleased to actually meet you," Sora said as she bowed to greet them.

It was the first time the team had really gotten a good look at their bare faces. Lucas looked a few years older than everyone else. His chocolate-brown hair, a shade darker than Tori's, had that perfectly messy just-out-of-bed look, the kind that most people spent hours in the mirror trying to recreate. When he casually brushed the hair back from his face, he revealed his gauge-pierced ears. But, the real lady-killer features were his penetrating gray eyes and his cleft chin which looked like it was perfectly chiseled out of marble. He also had just the right amount of danger in his smile to make the girls swoon. Lo and behold, he was actually quite handsome. He had great bone structure, stood five eleven, and looked to be about 215 pounds. He also had a toned body and let his five o'clock shadow grow in. It was no wonder Sora fell for his devilishly handsome good looks.

Sora was much shorter, standing at only five feet, two inches, and appeared to be no more than 125 pounds. She was very basic looking and didn't wear too much makeup, only enough eye shadow to accentuate her individuality. Her short hair was like a waterfall of black silk that descended to her shoulders. She was very easy on the eyes herself.

Dimitri, who still wasn't thrilled about them joining, stood there with his arms crossed in an attempt to be aloof.

"They don't look like a Lucas and Sora," Tori said under her breath.

"Alright, allow me to introduce you guys to the rest of the group," Shyra said as she walked over to her team. "This is Alexander, Christian, Cassandra, Tori, and Dimitri. Codenamed—"

"I got this, Shyra." Lucas didn't even let her finish her introduction.

"From our battles, I've figured out your monikers."

"Is that right?" Cassie sarcastically asked.

"Yes. That's Spark Plug and Burnout. You're Wash Up, that's Blockhead, and that's Air Bag." Lucas laughed, but of course no one else found him funny at all.

"Call me that again, and I'll personally flip your teeth upside down," Dimitri stepped forward and challenged.

"Oh, you must be the tough guy of the group. Right? The badass," Lucas mocked.

"Would you like to find out, *Lucas*?"

"Sure, why not? I think it's time we settled the score, don't you?"

Shyra stepped out in front of them. "Stop it! The both of you," she reprimanded.

Lucas looked at Shyra and then back at Dimitri and chuckled. "Relax, man. I'm just messing with you. Look, let's put the bad blood behind us. I know I was in the wrong, and that's my bad. I really needed that money, though."

"For what? We'd like to know what your deal is," Alex said.

Lucas looked around, and since no one objected, he complied with their request. "Sure, I suppose I owe you that much," he agreed. "Everyone grab a seat."

Everyone went further in the room and each found a comfortable spot on the couches to listen to his story.

"I don't know about the rest of you guys, but growing up wasn't easy for me. I was born in D.C., and I'm an orphan. I never had what society would deem proper parents. I've had 'caretakers.' People would adopt me, but they kept returning me when I didn't turn out like they expected. After awhile, it didn't even faze me anymore. The revolving doors of that orphanage became second nature to me. I just buried my nose in the books," Lucas leaned back and continued. "I'd read about all kinds of things from the sciences of molecular energy to the history of Sun Tzu's art of war. I had an unquenchable thirst for knowledge. Time flew by, and before I knew, it I was eighteen. I wanted to go to college, but even with an academic scholarship, I didn't have enough money to stay there more than a few semesters, so I dropped out. Out in the real world, no companies were hiring kids with such little work experience. I had to eat, so I did what anyone would do when the threat of starving to death appeared—I stole."

The group had no idea things were so hard for him, but Tori was familiar with the lack of parental attention and argued back. "That didn't give you the right to take what didn't belong to you."

"Maybe it didn't, but what do you know about not knowing where your next meal is coming from? Or having your clothes literally falling apart but not having any money to buy new ones? I was smarter than half the people at that college, but because I didn't have enough money, I ended up being homeless for a year. Where's the fairness in that? I had to sleep with one eye open every night, or I would wake up the next morning to find someone had stolen my dilapidated shoes. Don't preach at me with your holier-than-thou moral compass, because I've seen the darkest side of this nation and survived thanks to my wits and power."

"Ahem." Sora deliberately cleared her throat, and everyone looked in her direction. "That's not the only thing that kept you alive," she interjected. "Lucas and I met when he saved my life. I was going to college in Washington, DC with a scholarship much like his own, but I was still young and naïve. One night I was walking home from a night class when I was mugged. The man held me at knifepoint and demanded everything I had. I was too scared to even speak, let alone use my unrefined power. I was just frozen with fear. I gave him all that I had, but he still wanted more. This guy walked me off campus with that knife tip in my back until we reached this underpass near a freeway away from spectators, even now I can recall the feel of its point against my skin. Then he ordered me to strip, and in my mind, I couldn't believe I was about to be raped. I wanted to scream or at least beg him to stop, but other than shaking and crying, I couldn't pull myself together long enough to make a sound. Turns out I was taking too long for the mugger's taste, so he ripped my shirt. I finally cried out, begging for help. He placed one hand over my mouth and the other held his knife tight against my throat. He told me if I made another peep, he'd slit my neck. I just closed my eyes and prayed for it to be over soon, but it never happened," Sora said as the group hung on her every word.

"The feel of sharp, cold steel pressing against my jugular just disappeared. When I opened my eyes, the knife was lodged in the adjacent wall, and I dropped to my knees. There he was, standing tall like some kind of vigilante superhero. Lucas threw out his hand and pulled in the mugger out of thin air. It was only later that he revealed his magnetic power, so I figured he must have controlled him from all the piercings and metal that mugger must have had on him. I didn't care, though. He gave that guy the beating of his life. Like a knight in shining armor, he walked over to me and asked me if I was okay. I was immediately in love. Once I understood his powers, I knew it was fate that we met. After dating for a bit, he moved in with me. I showed him my abilities, which was a shock for him too, and we've been together ever since. Before all that, though, I was born in Japan. My parents moved to America when I was still a baby, because my dad's job transferred him to run a department store in Savannah, Georgia. I hated it there. I was made fun every day because I looked different, but as soon as I graduated high school, I got out of there as fast as I could. The rest is history."

There was an eerie silence in the room. No one really knew what to say, but the consensus was to bury the hatchet.

"You two have been through a lot," Alex said. "Let me be the first to say welcome to the team." Alex walked over to Lucas and put out his hand. Lucas hesitated but ultimately accepted the heartfelt welcome and the two shook hands for the first time. Sora, who wanted to keep the momentum going, walked over to Tori and Chris and apologized.

"I'm really sorry about what happened between us before. Do you think we can start over and be friends?"

Christian and Tori looked at her hand and then at each other. They had a quick telepathic talk. "What do you think?" Christian asked.

"I don't know. She seemed sincere, but it's tough to forget that she almost killed us yesterday," she rebutted.

"True. Do you wanna give her a chance to redeem herself?" he asked.

"We're all on the same team now. I don't think we have much choice," she answered.

"Okay, let me handle this." Christian shook hands with Sora and told her, "We can't forget that you tried to end our lives, but we're willing to give trying to be your friend a shot. That's the best we can do."

She smiled, gave each of them a huge hug, and said, "I'll take it!"

Cassie was second after Alex to shake Lucas's hand and say, "Welcome aboard."

"With beauty such as yours, it's nice to be aboard," Lucas replied.

The compliment caught Cassie off guard, and she awkwardly blushed. "Um, thanks," she responded.

Only Dimitri was left, but it didn't seem like he was budging. Lucas walked over to him and under his breath told him, "For what it's worth, you have a hell of a right hook. I haven't been hit that hard in a long time."

He tried to fight it, but even the tough guy Dimitri cracked a smile over the compliment.

"I love it when we all bond like this. However, now that the pleasantries are over, we have a lot of work to do," Shyra interjected. "We need to get Lucas and Sora caught up to the rest of you guys. I shall be working individually with them for a while, but I also encourage you all to help out should they need it."

"We've been training for over a year now. How are they supposed to catch up?" Chris asked.

"It is true that there is not much time before the Zenakuu threat will come into fruition," Shyra admitted. "We must all work together to bring Lucas and Sora up to speed. Voltaic Cloud, I am teaming you and Lucas together first. I believe there is plenty you can learn from each other." The two gave each the same look you would give when a teacher partnered you up with the weird kid for the class science project.

"As for the rest of the team, work on your newest techniques. You must perfect them before the Zenakuu arrive. I will be showing Sora the motions that might help her to control her powers more effectively. Her specific kinesis is rare, but I touched on it briefly in my studies."

Sora bowed, and said, "Take care of me, onegai shimasu."

Interesting, Shyra thought, she never encountered someone so well-mannered like that before.

Shyra dismissed her students. They were all too used to the training that took place on the windy Colorado mountaintop.

However, on their way out, Alex stopped Cassie with some concerns.

"Cassie, hold up!"

She turned around quickly and greeted him with a smile. "Hey," she responded.

"What was all that about?" Alex asked her.

Cassie raised her eyebrow, bewildered by his question, and retorted, "What was all *what* about?"

"Well, you just seemed really taken by Lucas, that's all," Alex said.

"What are you talking about? He's strong, he'll be a big help," she answered.

"He can't be trusted, Cass. I don't know why you're so determined to have him fit in. Is it because he called you cute? Big deal."

She was disgusted by his attitude. Cassie stood up straight and crossed her arms, clearly ticked off by this point.

"Why are you getting so jealous?" she asked. "I can talk to, or flirt with whomever I want."

Alex was thrown by her response; he didn't know if he was being jealous but he couldn't let her believe he was, so he scoffed sarcastically to confuse her.

"Ha! Me jealous? I don't think so; you guys can do whatever you want. I'm only looking after the team," Alex said confidently.

"That's it? All you care about is the team collectively?" She demanded to know.

"Of course, what else is there?" Alex said.

Blood rushed to Cassie's face as she turned red with anger. She moved in close and shoved her finger in Alex's face.

"You know, for once, it would be awesome if you dropped the superhero role and acted like a normal guy." Cassie turned around and stormed off the ship.

Alex could tell she was mad at him, but didn't understand her frustration. Everything he ever did was to keep her safe, but he knew his feelings for her made her a liability. He did all he could to bottle them up, but when she was around him, he didn't care about fighting, nor did he care about aliens. He only cared for her.

Rain went on her side of the mountain to collect water from the atmosphere and the clouds and focused on converting it into ice. With that kinesis perfected, Rain would be one of the most deadly espers on the planet.

Wind headed to her side of the mountain and worked on wind blades. She had no problem creating manipulated winds, but she couldn't seem to get the hang of condensing and pressurizing them. She was also obsessed with the idea of breaking the sound barrier by flying at Mach speed.

Earth and Flame decided to spar together and try their hand in combining their abilities. Besides setting rocks on fire and launching them at a crowd of targets, Earth remembered how powerful he and Rain's mudslide was and gave it a try with flame. Earth opened a crack in the earth's crust, and Flame raised the fiery lava that was underneath. The heat was sweltering and each found it to be too challenging without the help of the other. They discovered that neither one of them could harness the destructive power of magma and lava single-handedly. However, together it proved to be something they could use in the upcoming battle.

Being able to control lava wasn't enough for Earth. He wanted to become more powerful and learn more abilities. He had an idea of what was next but needed confirmation from Shyra before he tried and went in over his head. He practiced structuring the technique the rest of the day but couldn't finish without Shyra. Flame perfected his combustion technique but also tossed in flight practice on occasion. He knew being able to rise above the fight played a very important part in the war.

Shyra was far away from the ship due to Sora's powerful kinesis.

"Now from what I gathered in my training of many different kinesis around the galaxy, gyrokinetics mainly rely on their powers rather than hand-to-hand combat. With such a powerful kinesis, one should not need to confront an opponent head-on," Shyra began. "But with a closer look, gyrokinetics are extremely strong and versatile. Most of your training will involve yoga and proper stance and balance. To get the most out of the power of gravity, balance is required. We do not have much time, but we should be able to get your endurance and strength to where they need to be. Your attacks and movement will consist of many thrusts and attacks that hammer down as well as lift up from the ground."

Shyra and Sora worked together to perfect her stances and balance as well review an entire encyclopedia of yoga exercises that she would be busy with during downtime.

Cloud and Lucas practiced right in front of Shyra's ship.

"Hey, Sparky," Lucas said, commencing the conversation.

"It's Cloud. What is it?" Cloud replied with a somber tone.

The two were going through the motions of their respective techniques. Although very similar in scientific means, the two styles were very different. While electrokinesis was fast-paced and accurate, magnokinesis motions were powerful, straight movements that seemed to pan out over a large area. There wasn't much deviating when it came to manipulating metal; however, it was a kinesis that had limitless possibilities.

In theory, a powerful enough magnokinetic could disrupt the geomagnetic field that surrounded a planet and tamper with the magnetosphere, allowing planets to be harmed by solar winds and cosmic rays that travel through space. Also using the natural geomagnetic field that surrounds planets, a powerful enough magnokinetic could condense the field and crush the entire planet to an infinitesimally small singularity point, to about the size of a peanut. There were even stories of a demented magnokinetic who simply ripped the molten iron alloys in a planet's core, causing the world to destabilize and throwing the planet off of its rotation with its sun and its perfectly tilted axis. These, however, were all techniques Shyra would never divulge to Lucas. Instead, she just let him continue training with Alex.

"Have you learned how to fly?" Lucas asked.

"Not exactly," Cloud replied.

"I think I found an easy way, but I'm not sure if you can do it."

"I'm listening," Cloud said.

"I've tried it in my spare time. Get this: I surround myself with an electromagnetic field, and I lift it up." Lucas surrounded himself and Cloud with such a field and easily lifted the two up clear over the mountain.

"Okay, I get it," Alex said. "Put us down!"

"You still have to try it. Start small; create an electromagnetic field. I read up on all sorts of magnetism and things like that. At first, I didn't think I could do it because it needs electricity to charge matter, but after our fight, I read that it can be found in the air as oxygen. It expands into a field, but since I control magnetism itself, I can skip the step on manually electrifying the objects. I just magnetize them and control how large the field expands to."

"If you say so … You're a bookworm, aren't you?" Alex asked.

"You'd be amazed what you can learn from a book," Lucas grinned.

"Alright. What do I have to lose? I'm only thirty feet in the air in a magnetic bubble," he said sarcastically. Cloud concentrated deeply and started with an electric arc; he felt the air being electrified around him.

"Create a positive and a negative charge, so it attracts and forms the field," Lucas explained. "Then, since it is electricity, you should be able to control it."

Cloud had never attempted to produce both a positive and negative charge. He diverted the negative charge to his left hand and the positive to his right. As soon as the charges reached his fingertips, the opposite electrically charged hands attracted to each other and smacked Cloud's hands together. The force caused a thunderous boom and an electromagnetic pulse. It decimated Lucas's magnetic field, and the two fell out of the sky not knowing what happened.

"Lucas, do the field thingy!" Cloud yelled. But due to the electromagnetic pulse, he couldn't produce the necessary combination.

"I'm trying! It's not working!"

They both hit the ground rather hard. Cloud had the wind knocked out of him, but Lucas twisted his knee attempting to land on his feet.

"What the hell was that man?" Lucas asked.

"How should I know? You're the electromagnetic expert here," Cloud said as he gasped for air. He happened to glance to his left when he saw Shyra's naked spaceship. "Hey, Lucas, wasn't Shyra's ship cloaked as a temple?"

"Yeah. Shit, my knee is jacked up. I guess it was. Why?"

"Well why isn't it cloaked now?" Cloud asked.

"Hmm not sure. I'm new here, remember?"

Cloud sent a telepathic message to Shyra. "Shyra, come back to the ship ASAP."

"I am on my way," she responded. Shyra got to the scene, and the first thing she noticed was Lucas was limping but knew it was not serious. More importantly, she saw her bare spaceship. "What happened to the ship?"

"Not sure," Cloud shrugged.

Shyra entered with caution. She rebooted the system and proceeded to diagnose the ship's onboard computer diagnostics. Shyra exited the ship after a few moments. "There was an electromagnetic propulsion occurrence," she said.

"Now it makes sense!" Lucas said. "When Alex created the positive and negative charge, it created a chain reaction the second his hands met and repelled my magnetic field. It flowed through me, acting as the conductor, and that's why I couldn't remake the field right away. It then repulsed, causing an extremely powerful electromagnetic pulse, because our two powers combined." Lucas fell victim to blank stares, except for Shyra.

"That level of comprehension is incredible, Lucas. I see you have done an ample amount of research in the science of your ability. I am impressed."

To hear Shyra give such praise to Lucas was a knife in the gut to Cloud. He was painted green with envy that afternoon. A refutable competition had subconsciously begun to not only prove to Shyra why he should still be the leader but to prove it to himself.

Earth watched as Lucas stole Cloud's metaphorical thunder. Cloud dragged himself inside the ship, while everyone else was fixated on Lucas. Earth came to Cloud's room where he was sitting in a chair charging his portable mp3 player with electricity. Without turning around, Cloud asked, "What do you want, Dimitri?"

"I know we don't always see eye to eye, but I know what you're going through. Now you have something to push yourself to become even stronger." After that, Earth left and continued his own training.

"He's right. Dimitri has been training harder than all of us put together, because he fears that someone else is tougher than him," Alex thought aloud. "Is that what motivates him? Do I motivate him? Is this all a competition of who is strongest? If I want to lead this team to war, I better have what it takes to bring them home. And I'll be damned if some magnetically powered, smart, emo-looking guy will bring me down." Alex marched through the vacant ship to the war room.

"Computer, bring up everything on electricity," Alex commanded. He spent three entire days researching the possibilities he could accomplish with his power. The rest of the team, including Shyra, was left in the dark about Alex's research and his training regiments. As his team began to admire and put more faith in Lucas, Alex began to fear that Lucas would soon be designated to replace him as leader of the alliance.

Chapter 33

I'd Risk the Fall Just to Know How It Feels to Fly

A FEW WEEKS HAD passed since Lucas and Sora were recruited, most of the team was getting accustom to their two new members. Everyone was doubling their efforts in preparation for the attack. Back on the ship, Cassie, who finally mastered being able to draw water from the air quickly and change it to ice, approached Shyra with a concern.

"Shyra, is there anything you can do to help me with this flying problem?" she asked.

Puzzled, Shyra looked at her and asked, "What flying problem?"

"You know … Everyone can fly by some means or another but me."

"I see … But who told you that you could not fly?" she asked.

"I know I can ride waves and stuff, but I want to be able to really fly like the others," Cassie explained.

"Cassandra, you are a hydrokinetic, and the human body is made up roughly about sixty-five percent water. So, once again, I must ask. Who told you that you cannot fly?"

Cassie was mad at herself for not coming up with that by herself. "Of course! Duh, Cassie, so I can control the water in my body and fly, right?"

"Well, yes. Theoretically, it will work," Shyra said. "I have read that human blood has an average density of approximately 1060 kg/m^3. That is very close to pure water's density of 1000 kg/m^3, but you must be careful. You can truly hurt yourself by manipulating the water in your own body. Worst-case scenario, you could die, so you should start off small."

Cassie burst out grinning. "I will, Shyra. I promise." And with that, she ran off to find Alex and tell him the great news. He was in his room with the door open getting some necessities together. "Alex!" she shouted, and he jumped up.

"Dear God, Cass, you scared the crap out of me. What's wrong?" he asked.

"Nothing's wrong. Shyra just told me I'm able to fly. Isn't that fantastic?" The two of them seemed to be civil, but ever since their argument their exchanges felt phony.

"Yeah, that's great news. Hey, about what I said about you and Lucas—" he began with a distraught face. The awkwardness between them had been killing him, and he just wanted to apologize and go back to the way things were.

"Don't worry about it, okay? We're cool. So, where are you going?" Cassie wondered.

"Well, actually, I was heading to this quiet side of the mountain to meditate and practice flying myself. It's too noisy here now to concentrate."

Cassie thought this might be the perfect chance to get some alone time with him. "Yeah, I know what you mean. Lucas is really loud and obnoxious sometimes. Do you think I could come with you and practice?"

In his normal, oblivious manner, he welcomed her along. "Sure. It's a long hike, and I could use someone to talk to."

She tried to hold back her smile but only succeeded in reducing the level of her blushing cheeks. "Cool. Give me five minutes to get ready, and I'll meet you out front."

Alex nodded and passed Christian before going outside to wait for Cassie at the monastery doors.

"Broham, where you heading?" Chris asked.

"Cassie and I are fista practice flying," he replied.

"Oh, you should get a pair of goggles then. That's one thing they never really talk about in the comic books. It's really freaking hard to keep your eyes open with all that air blowing in your face," Christian said.

Alex looked down at the floor, arched his eyebrow, and then looked up at the ceiling as the remark left him deep in thought and said, "Hmm, I never really thought about that, but I guess you're right. Anyway, I gotta head out, so, I'll catch you later."

Alexander threw his hand out for a fist bump. Christian happily reciprocated, and began to walk off. Alexander was just two steps in front of the doors when Christian shouted back, "And be sure to keep your mouth closed, there are a lot of bugs in the air, trust me…"

Alex chuckled, and threw his right hand in the air to wave goodbye, and to verify that he heard the warning. Ten minutes later, Cassie ran down the steps to the front doors with excitement and stood in front of Alex.

She was wearing hiking shorts and a low-cut blue tank top. She had her dark red hair tied back in a French braid and seemed to be glowing as the sunlight bounced off her skin. Even Alex took notice of how beautiful she looked but had trouble articulating his thoughts appropriately. Instead, he just asked if she was ready to head out.

A little bummed out he didn't say anything on how she looked, Cassie walked down the steps in silence, and the two were off. They were walking and chatting for almost an hour when Cassie finally asked, "My legs are starting to hurt. Are we close?"

"Yep, it's right on the other side of that bridge," Alex pointed out.

Cassie looked over and saw the decrepit wooden bridge that spanned across a chasm they needed to cross. "And you're positive that thing is safe?" she asked.

"I've crossed it dozens of times. We'll be fine," he assured her.

She reluctantly agreed and followed her crush over the rickety bridge. Through a thicket of shrubbery, they finally arrived at their intended destination. A breathtaking open field that was heavy with wildlife, beautiful flowers, and a crystal clear pond.

"This place is gorgeous, Alex. How did you find it?"

"By accident, really. Sometimes I like to run, because it helps clear my head. One day I ran farther than I realized and stumbled across this spot. Don't tell the others, though."

"I won't," Cassie agreed. "But why did you share it with me?"

"I don't know. You're different from the others. I feel like I can share things with you that I can't with them."

Cassie turned bright red. "Really? I kinda feel that way too. About you, I mean."

Alex smiled and grabbed her hand. "C'mon, let's sit by the pond and practice," he said.

Is this finally happening? He's actually admitting he likes me? Rain thought to herself.

The two sat peacefully by the water and meditated. Cassie did her best to clear her head, despite the obvious distraction Alex was. Once they were at peace, Alex built up a small static electrical charge around his body, and his hair began to stick up. Cassie peeked at him and giggled but quickly went back to her own meditation. She summoned water from the pond and kept it suspended in the air as she became one with her element.

Alex created the same charges in his hands as he had when training with Lucas—negative in the left and positive in the right. He was nervous, but like before, he clapped his hands together. The resulting sound wave was overwhelming, and the distinct sound of thunder rang in his ears. However, this time, without the trigger of a magnetic field, no electromagnetic pulse exploded. Alex just began to hover slowly off the ground.

Despite the noise of static Cassie remained still and became perfectly zazen, a state of perfect relaxation and meditation. She looked inward until she could feel the pumping blood coursing through her veins. It was faint at first, but she sensed the water inside. In her first several attempts, her body didn't budge an inch, but after twenty minutes of concentrating, she lifted a few centimeters off the grass and then immediately dropped. It was a minor victory, but she was ecstatic.

Alex was already floating twelve inches off the ground, but because he wasn't used to it, the strain proved to be too much, and he dropped. While he rested, he watched Cassie try her hardest to float. In a short time, she learned to hover four inches from the ground. He marveled at her radiant beauty and was blown away at her raw talent and comprehension of her power. The sun was beginning to set on the two, so Alex suggested going back.

"Hey, Cass, we should head on back. The others are probably wondering where we are."

"But I was just getting the hang of it."

"We'll come back soon and pick up where we left off," he reassured her.

"Promise?" Cassie said.

Alex gave a heart-melting smile and replied with a simple, "Yes."

They got up and headed back to the trail with Cassie in front. They came upon the bridge that swayed in the strong breeze. She hesitated and looked back at Alex.

"It's okay," he promised her, and she stepped forward.

After her sixth step, the board underneath her foot snapped in half. As her leg went through the bridge, she screamed. The weight of her body and her momentum broke the plank of wood directly behind her, while her chin cracked the board in front, subsequently knocking her unconscious. Cassie's whole body fell through the bridge instantaneously, and Alex looked on in fright as she surely plummeted to her death.

"Cassie!" he yelled, but it was too late.

Chapter 34

A Second Chance at First Impressions

Alex panicked. He refused to lose her but didn't know what to do—until it finally hit him. He figured out what needed to be done, but didn't know if he had the ability to do it. In an instant, he found his resolve. He created a crudely fashioned positive and negative charge in his hands and loudly clapped them together. It sounded like distant thunder, as he bravely did a front flip into a swan dive over the side of the bridge.

Like an illuminated bullet, he accelerated into the darkness until only a dimmed glow was visible. Seconds stretched into years, as he lit up the abyss in search of Cassie freefalling. She regained consciousness for only for a second to see some sort of light at the end of a tunnel and wondered if she should head toward it before passing back out. Alex spotted her and within a second was close enough to grab her. He clutched her by the waist, but the pit was so dark and deep that the bottom was still nowhere in sight. It was do or die, so Alex focused on the feeling he got from hovering. Their descent slowed down, but they didn't gain any altitude.

"C'mon!" he shouted, begging for his power of flight to work. *I can do this*, he thought to himself. The thought of Cassie dying because of his impetuousness triggered his latent power, and the two stopped midair. Alex's eyes turned yellow and surged with electricity. He finally flew up with her in his arms and landed on the other side of the basin. Alex kneeled over her and gently placed his hand on Cassie's cheek.

"Cass, are you all right?"

She slowly opened her eyes and was relieved by the soothing sound of his voice. "What happened?" she asked.

The hero was truly allayed as he fell backward on his butt. "We had a close call, but it's all right now," he said.

Cassie sat up and looked over at the broken bridge. Her chin was sore, but she quickly pieced together what had taken place. "Did you really jump in and save me?"

Alex nodded.

"And did you fly the both of us back up?"

Once again, he nodded to confirm her suspicions.

She jumped on him and wrapped her arms around him. "Thanks for saving me, Alex."

It was his turn to blush. As they both fell back, he told her, "Anytime." A momentary silence broke loose, but as they stared at each other, the quietness seemed to connect them in a way words never could.

"Alex," she called out.

His heart started beating hard enough to burst out of his chest. She was dangerously close to Alex, he even felt the curvature of her breast press against his body with every exhale. As near as their lips were to each other, he wondered if they were really about to share their first kiss.

"Yes, Cassie?"

She was scared, hesitation kept her from doing what she felt in her heart to be right. "Are you ready to go back?" she asked.

"Oh, um … yeah," Alex responded.

She got off of him, helped him to his feet, and they hiked back to the ship.

The next day during one training session, Sora offered to help Earth with kinetic strength building by adding surplus gravity to the boulders he was lifting. He kept them levitated a few feet over him despite the immense pressure. Everything was going as planned, but Dimitri's ego wouldn't let him admit he was getting tired. However, Sora was concerned by the beads of sweat dripping down his face.

"Do you want to stop?" she asked.

"No. I can handle it; keep going," he answered.

"Okay, I'm going to ten times Earth's normal gravity," she warned him.

"Do it," he told her, and the boulder instantly increased in weight. The force brought Earth to his knees as he buckled under the pressure. Try as he might, he couldn't withstand the heaviness of the load. As it threatened to turn him as flat as a pancake, he let the boulder smash into the ground below after jumping out of the way. The collision shattered the boulder into sharp, rugged pieces that blasted outward. Sora had the good sense to put a protective barrier around herself, but the explosion was too fast for Earth. He was bombarded with rocks and gravel, which pelted various parts of his body. Dimitri fell to the ground while Sora rushed over.

"Earth, are you okay?"

"One of those rocks really got me in the thigh," he told her.

"Can you stand?" she asked.

"I think so." Earth attempted to rise but collapsed back to the ground when his injured leg gave out. Sora kneeled down, placed his arm around her shoulder, and helped him up. As she walked and he limped back to the ship, Earth asked her not to tell the others he'd been hurt.

"Don't worry. I won't," she replied. "Someone's gotta look after you."

Earth looked at her and chuckled.

"What is it?" she asked.

"Nothing. It's just that my older sister used to say the same thing to me. You actually remind me a lot of her."

"Oh yeah? What's she like?"

The smile on Dimitri's face went away as he remembered that she had been viciously gunned down. "She died, but I keep on fighting for her. I don't want to see anyone else I care about die."

"I'm sorry, I didn't know," Sora said. "You don't have to worry, though. We're all strong and not going anywhere."

Earth became very close to Sora from then on, which only made Tori despise her even more, but they were not close for the reason she thought. Sora reminded Dimitri of his murdered older sister, and Sora didn't mind playing the part. She told him he could come to her anytime, and so he did. They formed an unshakable bond. The same held true for Sora and Cassie, who seemed to find the maternal figure she always wanted in her.

The group even warmed up to Lucas, who treated all of them as little brothers and sisters. After getting over his initial jealousy, it was Alex who became closest to him. Their powers synced so well that Alex found a mentor of sorts in Lucas. Shyra was more than pleased with everyone's progress. Everyone was relaxing on the couch watching television when Shyra requested their attention.

"I want all of you to know I am very proud of the progress you have made, and I have no doubt we will stand victorious when the Zenakuu come," she announced. "I just have one final thing to do, and that is to present your new brethren: Vigorous Polarity and Laden Gravity."

The newly named Vigorous Polarity and Laden Gravity entered the room where the other espers were and showed off their new uniforms. Polarity came out with a sleeveless, tattered black-and-gray trench coat. The sleeves of his tight-fitted shirt were covered with clipped-on forearm armor. A matching gray scarf covered his neck and was also used to pull over his face to keep his identity hidden. The black on the trench coat had a gray pattern that symbolized a sort of tribal design. He had a skin-tight undershirt that was a darker shade of gray with the symbol of magnetic waves in the middle of his chest. Polarity's pants were loose fitting and mostly black but had gray trim that matched his shirt. His boots came halfway up his shin and strapped in and connected to his metallic kneepads, which matched the tattered look of the trench coat.

Lucas had never felt so at home in a family before. He was truly happy, and Sora saw the positive change of attitude in her man. Laden Gravity came out with purple lipstick on that matched the purple streak dyed in the front of her hair. She had on a black trimmed, purple leather tank top that was cut short and fitted over her rib cage, exposing her stomach. She wore black gloves that had thin purple padding. The gloves had yellow squared designs that matched her loosened belt. Her black, skin-tight pants had a purple fill-in that covered her pelvis. Gravity's boots were knee-high and colored purple while symbolizing zigzagged gravity waves in yellow near the top on the boots. The top of the boots were trimmed in yellow fur. Gravity was welcomed with open arms in the alliance, but the team felt as though she only joined because Polarity agreed to. Unfortunately, Gravity was a blind follower to wherever Polarity ventured.

"Oh, before I forget, while Lucas and Sora master their kinesis training, I do not want the five of you to think your training is complete. We are adding something new to your fighting repertoire," Shyra announced.

"Like what?" Dimitri asked.

"I am glad you ask, Dimitri. You all shall be going through weapons training."

"Why do we have to learn to fight with weapons?" Cassie asked.

"They are another way of defending yourself. The armada is almost at our doorstep, and we will utilize every chance of winning we have," Shyra explained.

"I don't know … It's not like I'm against it, but a lot more mutilation will happen with weapons training," Christian added.

"Maybe, but I'd rather have it and not need it than need it and not have it," Dimitri pointed out.

"Good point, I guess," Christian said.

"With that matter settled, let us get started," Shyra said.

Their guide laid out each weapon of the eighteen arms of wushu and let the group choose their own specific weapon. Alex walked up first and picked out a dao, a curved saber that was very simple with its design. It was a one-handed weapon capable of duel wielding. He whipped the sword through the air with slashes and stabs. Following in his footsteps, Chris was next to pick his weapon. He decided on hook swords, the sleek metal felt cool to the touch. They were very versatile, the hook swords were often duel wielded and hit the enemy fast and hard. With the ability to hook the swords together and swing them around, they covered more ground than any other sword.

Tori walked up next, and her eyes widened as she saw her future weapon—a chain whip. The chain whip was one of the most aesthetically pleasing weapons, and most would think that was all it was for. However, made of all metal and wielding various lengths of chain. It rattled as she gripped it, the chain whip was perfect for her wind-related abilities. One end of the whip was a hilt where the user gripped, and the other end was a five-inch dagger.

Cassie was a little apprehensive at first, being the passive one of the group, but then something caught her eye. "Is that a trident, Shyra?" she asked.

"Actually, it is known as a ranseur. It is a combination of a trident and a halberd."

"That sound kinda French," Cassie said. "I thought wushu was supposed to be Chinese."

"I do not make the names, Cassandra, maybe it is."

Cassie lifted the ranseur, and it was about the same size as her, and gleamed when light bounced off of it. Cassie gripped her new weapon, and a smile grew larger on her face. Its intricately welded metal design was actually beautiful, but still deadly. "I think I could do something with this. With my water powers, it only makes sense."

Dimitri was patiently waiting for everyone else to get their weapons together. As he did, he eyed up the one weapon to the left of the mat. He chose the tonfas, two thick wooden clubs with the handle connected to the side. It was used over the forearms and ascended two inches past his knuckles, which made for close combat. He ran his fingers over their smooth surface before spinning by the handles. They were brutal when on the offense and durable on defense. It catered to his fighting style, which was a mix of wushu, muay thai, and shuai jiao.

With the exception of Lucas and Sora who still needed to master kinetic training, each member of the alliance received a new means to tear down the enemy, but calling their moves clumsy would be an understatement. They did their best not to lob off an appendage as they practiced and Shyra worried deep down they would not have enough time to become proficient before the Zenakuu came to earth.

CHAPTER 35

Ask No Questions and Be Told No Lies

THE WEAPONS TRAINING FELT like it went on longer than the actual combat training, and the gang received their fair share of cuts, bruises, and close shaves. While the five were busy with that, Lucas was up late at night and often wandered around the facility. He made his way down to the holding cells where Donikan was still a prisoner.

"What are you doing down here, earthling? They let you out. Why would you return?" Donikan asked, snarling at his visitor.

"I'm actually not sure myself," Lucas admitted. "Shyra showed me what you did, but she didn't show me your side of the story. My curiosity has bested me, and I suppose I'm here to discover why your race is on this crusade." Lucas offered his ear if the scout was willing to share.

"Ha! You're barking up the wrong tree, earthling. What makes you think I would give you the time of day?"

"When I was locked up in here, you said that you two weren't that different—you and Shyra. Explain what you mean by that," Lucas inquired.

Donikan posed a misleading question. "Why are we the bad guys in this war?

"Is that a rhetorical question? It's because you enslaved planets, invaded Kalryn, and got your asses kicked," Lucas laughed.

"Is that what she told you? We hardly enslaved planets. I do not have telepathy, so grab a seat. It's a long story."

Lucas summoned a cold steel chair that was leaning up against the barren gray wall. The chair slowly dragged two of its legs across the floor, causing long scratches to appear. Lucas turned the chair around and sat backward.

"My name is Lucas Wright," he said.

"The name is Donikan. I was ... *am* the only surviving member of the most successful team of Zenakuu scouts. We never had any real invading missions, but we had a 100 percent mission completion. We never failed—until we came here. Zenakuu is a planet of karyokinesis. We can manipulate our bodies to whatever we wish. From changing the way we look to changing our DNA to make us faster and stronger."

"I'm aware of your abilities and how you do them," Lucas said, becoming impatient. "Get to the story."

"As you wish. It's not like I have anything else better to do. In the Renfari solar system, there was a peace treaty, and we all were involved. We began running out of resources on our planet, so we decided to mine other planets with their permission. This has been a long time ago now, but there was an uncharted and seemingly innocuous planet on the outer rim of the solar system. No one ever stepped foot on that rock until we decided to cultivate it. We awoke a terrible menace. We don't know the details of what happened on that planet, but somehow a chunk of it landed on planet Zenakuu. Those creatures ran through our planet in one day. We fought back, but they were countless, truly earning their name of Myriad."

"We were able to finally push them back, but there is a twist. We sent a distress signal to Kalryn, the biggest and baddest planet in our system. They claimed they couldn't help, but they were the closest planet to us at the time. No, I will not accept it. They stood idly by and witnessed us being slaughtered. Who are the real monsters here?" Donikan's emotions flared as he fought himself, trying not to tear up.

"We told other planets of the situation, and they joined us. We did not force them."

"What about the planets that didn't want to join you?" Lucas questioned.

"Technically, there weren't any. When they heard our story, it was obvious to them who was in the right. They kneeled in submission, but the tough part was building up an army without alarming Kalryn so we could attack. We invaded and tested the waters. We found that they weren't the powerhouse we thought them to be. But with other planets helping their side, this will be the biggest war in anyone's history."

"Hmm, gives me something to think about." Lucas stood up, grabbed the back of his chair, and leaned it up on the same wall where he found it.

Lucas went back to his room, but didn't sleep much that night. When morning rose, he was the first one up and about. He kept quiet most of the day. The only thing on his mind was who was right and who he thought would win the war, as he secretly sought out a second encounter with the Zenakuu scout. The day continued on, and so he discovered another opportunity to meet with Donikan. He secretly strolled down to the holding cells where he found Donikan once again.

"What are you doing here now?" Donikan asked.

"I wanted to ask you—why did they take you prisoner?"

"Because they are cowards. They didn't have the stomach to kill me," he said. "It will be their biggest mistake."

"I want to talk to your commanding officer," Lucas said. "I won't get the answers I need from a lowly scout like you."

"Who the hell do you think you are?"

"I'm the only chance you have of escape," Lucas reminded him.

"Escape? Surely you're not serious."

"How can I come into contact with your higher-up?"

"Simple. Get me a portable communication device, and I will set you up with a conversation," said Donikan.

"I will meet with you tomorrow with the device," Lucas said.

Donikan was elated, because he knew he would soon be as free as a bird once more.

The next day was a slow one for everyone. The rain made it impossible for anyone to train outdoors, except for Cassie, of course. Dimitri and Alex were in the rec room setting up the pool table.

"Do you want to break?" Alex asked.

"Yeah, let me show you how it's done back home."

Alex set up the billiards in the appropriate position on the table. Dimitri chalked up the end of his cue stick. His stance was text book, and his form was perfect. His arm thrust forward, and the triangle of billiards broke apart. Multiple striped and solid balls entered various pockets.

"Stripes or solid?" he offered.

"I'll take striped," Alex accepted.

"So what's on your mind?" Dimitri asked.

"What makes you think I have something on my mind?"

"We've been here for about a year, fought side by side, and encountered aliens. Yet, we have never played a game of pool together. You obviously have something to talk about."

"Touché," Alex conceded. "Well, I have been thinking a lot about Lucas."

"Pause.... What about him?" Dimitri asked as he sunk another ball.

"Well, after he got his uniform, he has been a shadow ever since. I don't like it."

"What do you want to do about it?"

"I'm not sure. I mean, he can be a very good asset to the team and help us grow stronger. Also, I've done so much more with my powers because of him. On the other hand, he is dangerous. That punch that broke your jaw—he didn't have to do that."

"Don't remind me," Dimitri said. "I still owe him for what he did to me." Dimitri didn't want to say anything, but the look on Lucas's face before he threw the punch was psychotic.

"I'll try to talk to him tonight. I just hope he doesn't do anything reckless," Alex said.

"That's the difference between you and me bro. You hope he doesn't act up, but I *wish he would*… I'd love the chance to return the favor for that broken jaw her gave me. Anyway, eight ball, side pocket." Dimitri sunk his game-winning eight ball and put his cue on the rack.

"And you wonder why I never asked you to play." Alex hung his hardly used cue stick next to Dimitri's on the rack.

Chapter 36

Freedom is a Light for Which Many Men Have Died in Darkness

The veil of night bestowed itself upon the temple once again, but this time Lucas procured the communication device found in the Zenakuu scout's personal belongings that had been taken from him when he was captured.

"Do you have the device?" Donikan questioned.

"Does switching polarities in a magnetic field redirect magnetic flow from positive to negative?" Lucas yet again drew a blank stare. "Yes, I got it … Damn alien."

Donikan gave him a cold stare, but freedom was worth taking a few insults from a kid.

"Alright, I'll call the general of my sector, and you can speak with him."

Lucas slipped the device through the bars, and the communications opened. "This is Donikan from scout team E-1337."

The general heard his lost scout team on the radio and interrupted. He appeared on the miniscreen. "Where have you been, you flea bitten mongrel? We thought you were dead." The general had a roaring tone in his voice that shook the walls around him. "I have an eighty thousand-man army heading toward that little blue ball you were sent to."

"I apologize, sir. My team was annihilated, and I have been taken prisoner," Donikan reported.

"Good. Then we don't have to turn around. We will wipe that planet clean for starting war with us."

"They had help, sir—a Kalrynian, and there are powerful warriors here."

"You call yourself Zenakuu?" the general said as he spat on the ground.

"One more thing, sir. An earthling requested to speak with you."

"Oh really? What does he want? To beg for mercy?" the general snickered.

"I'm not sure, sir," Donikan grunted.

"Put him on, you disgrace."

Donikan placed the device in Lucas's hand. Lucas saw the video feed of the Zenakuu general and could tell from his demeanor that he was a strong and ruthless warrior.

"Speak, human."

"There isn't much to say. I just want to be on the winning side. Guarantee me an army like yours, and I'll hand over the Kalrynian," Lucas promised.

"Are you toying with me, vagabond?"

"Why is this such a hard concept for people to understand? To win, you need power, and power isn't given. It's taken. I'll help you take it away from the Kalrynians." Lucas spoke with extra bass in his voice and had never been more serious.

"You think you have what it takes to be a Zenakuu general?" the general growled. A long pause overwhelmed Lucas.

"Of course," Lucas replied.

"We'll soon see, now put me back on with your prisoner," the general demanded. Lucas tossed the device to Lucas with a grin on his face.

"You have disgraced yourself soldier, getting captured by a lowly Kalrynian, then being spared by an even lower earthling.

Once you get out of there, be sure to shear your pelage," the general ordered.

"But sir!" Donikan tried to beg for a lesser punishment.

"Enough!" the general roared. "We shall be there in one week. Do not let me see you with your pelage still intact when we meet again." The transmission cut out, Donikan growled over the thought of losing his fur. It was their point of pride, and would mark him as dishonorable once he was back on his home world.

"Let me out of here human," Donikan said.

"No, I don't think that will be happening," Lucas smiled maniacally. Ice water coursed through his veins. He cracked his neck and rolled his right shoulder to loosen up before turning to Donikan. "You ready?" Lucas asked.

Donikan's face turned ghostly white. He said as he stumbled back to the corner of the cell and pressed himself against the wall. Their eyes met, but all Donikan saw in Lucas's eyes was darkness. "But, you said you would set me free," he said grudgingly.

"Stand still, you coward, and die like a man. I'll give you the death the others were too weak to give you." Lucas picked up the keys and threw them at him.

"The Zenakuu escaped!" Lucas screamed as he kinetically detached one of the metal bars from the cell and impaled Donikan through his chest. Donikan coughed up blood and dropped the keys on the floor. He fell to his knees and lay on his back before he passed on—murdered in cold blood. The ruckus caused everyone to come rushing through the entrance of the brig.

"What happened, Lucas?" Shyra asked.

"Your guess is as good as mine. I don't know how he did it, but he was out of the cell holding the keys. I tried to stop him, but I didn't mean to kill him."

Shyra stood in shock as Donikan's blood pooled around her feet. "It is all right, Lucas. Let us clean this mess up," she said.

"I'm so sorry, Shyra. It was an accident," Lucas said.

Accidently on purpose, Dimitri thought to himself.

"At least he didn't escape," Tori pointed out.

"What's this doing here?" Chris asked as he picked up the communication device. "I could have sworn we locked this up."

"He must have been out for longer than I suspected," Lucas said, trying to make sense of it.

"Oh my God. He could have killed us all in our sleep." Cassie started biting her lip.

"Well, we can sleep easier now," Alex comforted her.

"Yeah, good thing Polarity was here," Dimitri said suspiciously. He couldn't shake the feeling that Lucas was a wolf in sheep's clothing.

"Lucas, can I talk to you?" Alex asked.

"Not now, Sparky. It's late. Catch me tomorrow," Lucas answered.

"Oh … yeah, sure. I'll catch you later."

Lucas walked off anxious for what was to come.

Sora wasn't around much that day and hid in her room all night. Shyra knocked on her door to check on her.

"Come in," Sora answered with a downtrodden tone.

"Are you feeling all right, Sora?" Shyra asked.

"Fine. Just thinking, that's all."

Not convinced, Shyra reminded her of the obvious. "You realize I am telepathic, right?

"Yeah, I know."

Shyra wanted to comfort Sora, who seemed to be deeply troubled. "Well, I do not need powers to see that something is wrong."

"I'm just worried about Lucas," she replied.

"You love him, do you not?"

Sora looked at her briefly and then up at the ceiling but said nothing at first. "I suppose I do," Sora replied.

"Well, what is wrong with that? Love is an invaluable thing," Shyra told her.

"Nothing. I just want to see him happy and help him see his dreams come to life."

Shyra understood what that implied. "Whatever they may be?"

"Oh, Shyra, I just don't know anymore. Ever since we came here, he's been pulling away from me, and it's tearing me apart." Sora started to cry.

Shyra was sympathetic to headstrong lovers, so she left her with some food for thought. "Sora, you have a kind heart and good soul, but when the time comes, will you have what it takes to do what is right? Think about my words and decide what is most important to you."

The next day, Sora came up to Lucas, who was working on lifting a condensed slab of osmium weighing over a metric ton. He was finally able to make it rise and spin in the air when he heard Sora.

"Lucas," she called out. She startled him, and the slab dropped. Lucas turned around to see who had disturbed his training.

"Oh, it's you. What is it? Can't you see I'm busy?" he asked, obviously annoyed.

"Yeah, I just wanted to talk, though."

Lucas let out an exacerbated sigh. "Fine, whatever. Just make it fast, okay? I need to get back to training."

"That's what I wanted to talk to you about … Who are you getting stronger for?"

Lucas was angry at the subtle insinuation. "What's that supposed to mean?" he asked.

"It's just that we're already stronger than the others. They look up to us, and I just don't want to let them down."

Lucas looked at her with contempt. "They mean that much to you?" he asked.

"Yes, they do," she avowed.

"Duly noted. Well, in that case, shouldn't you be training? You wouldn't want to let them down when the decisive battle happens." Lucas turned back around and continued to lift the heavy metal.

Sora did her best to fight the tears and walked back to the ship. She knew she was losing him, and it broke her heart. The group felt uneasy over what had happened among their ranks, but there was a much more dangerous situation unraveling. No one could have predicted the rapine and massacre in the week to follow. The final battle was finally at hand.

Chapter 37

We Were Never Meant to Last

The Zenakuu exited their time-warp drive, which allowed bigger ships to safely bend the fabric of space and venture many light-years in mere days. Planet Earth was in the grasps of the tenacious Zenakuu armada armed to the teeth with soldiers, and lock, stock, and barrel with advanced weaponry that they acquired from the planets they'd already overtaken.

According to calculations on board the Zenakuu ships, they were entering the atmosphere above Arizona. The nearing unidentified object was getting closer, and with Arizona having seven separate military bases, troops were already being deployed. The Zenakuu warship ripped through the atmosphere and broke through a layer of clouds.

It looked as though they were headed toward the Army Camp Navajo. The jet-black warship was in sight, and the Zenakuu soon discovered a small army waiting for them on the ground. They came out with minimal forces to receive their first encounter of the fourth kind.

The first wave of soldiers came in the form of three full-sized M1 Abram tanks, two infantry fighting vehicles, and two H92 transport helicopters. Those men and women brave enough to ride the tanks and light-armored vehicles were some of the most valorous soldiers the American army had to offer. They immediately sent a message to the nearest Air Force base for air support. They scrambled their jets and were on the scene before Zenakuu's intimidating colorless ship dropped any closer.

Suddenly, a glint of light blinked in the cloudy sky of the dry, humid Arizona day, and with little warning, a twenty-five-foot wide amethyst-colored laser beam shot down upon the tanks. The intensity of the laser first melted the metal on the tanks before disintegrating it completely. One soldier attempted to escape before it was destroyed, but the laser had the same effect on her. First her skin and muscles melted away, and then her bones disintegrated into thin air. The aftermath was a mushroom cloud that had an ominous formation often seen in the sky following a nuclear explosion or volcanic eruption, complete with a bulbous top and a centralized stem.

Everyone in the group sat there and watched the armies get decimated. Shyra was especially sick to her stomach, because it reminded her so much of the invasion on her planet, except at least her people stood a chance. What was playing on the TV was nothing short of genocide.

"Everyone suit up. I want us ready to go in ten minutes," she ordered, and with that, everyone sprang into action. The Kinetic Alliance ran to the locker rooms where their uniforms lay ready.

In the room, Chris reached out to Alex. "Alex, are you worried about the battle?"

"Of course, but we're a lot stronger from the time we fought the scouts. We'll get through this somehow."

"I know. It's just that there are so many of them," Christian said.

"I didn't realize with the apocalypse coming we had so much time to talk," Lucas added.

Alex hated to admit it, but Lucas spoke the truth. The more time they wasted, the more soldiers would die.

"He's right," Alex agreed. "Hurry up, Chris. We have to move."

In the other locker room, the heaviness of their situation finally got to Cassie. The last thing she wanted was to die without telling Alex the truth.

"Alex," Cassie telepathically called out.

"Cassie, we're getting ready to head out, what's wrong?" He asked as he frantically made last minute preparations.

"I have to talk to you about something," she said.

"I'm kind busy at the moment, can it wait 'til we get back?" Alex asked.

"No, it really can't, okay? Just listen for a minute." Cassie demanded.

"Okay okay, what's up?" Alex asked, and put on his last shin guard.

"In case we don't make it back, do you know how I really feel about you? Do you know that I love you?" Alex couldn't believe what he mentally just heard. They had spent so much time together throughout the course of everything, but they never came out and said how they truly felt. For so long he had wanted to hear those words come out of her mouth, but not now. They were about to enter what would presumably be the most lethal batter of their lives, and he didn't want his emotions to cloud his judgment. Alex was in such utter shock he didn't realize he'd gone a full minute without responding. "Alex?" Cassie called out again.

"Yeah, I'm here… I'm just shocked. I don't know what to say," he finally answered.

"'I love you, too' would be a nice start," she said, but again, there was silence.

"Cassie, can we talk about this when we get back?" Alex asked.

"Wow, um, okay. That wasn't the answer I was expecting, but that's just it... Why do you think I'm telling you now? What if we don't come back?" She said.

"We will! No one dies today. We've come too far to fail now. Look, there's a lot I've been wanting to tell you, too, but I don't want it rushed. I want to do it on my own terms. So, let's talk about it when we get back, alright?" he requested of her.

"Yeah...sure thing, Alex," she said with a broken heart.

Before long they were done and shot over to the weapons locker to grab their melee weapons—all except for Lucas and Sora, who hadn't had enough time to be trained for it. Eight minutes later, all seven of them stood in front of Shyra suited up and ready to go.

"I do not know how they got past our defenses, but we will not let them take this planet. It will get crazy out there, but I want everyone to look out for each other. Try not to get singled out, and we will all make it home," Shyra instructed.

In unison, the group nodded. They walked behind her toward the front doors, not knowing if they would ever return the ship they called home. Tori grabbed hold of Cassie's hand. She wasn't only a friend but an anchor when things got their craziest. Cassie squeezed her hand back as if to say, "Things will be okay." But not even someone as thorough and analytical as Cassie could be certain.

Christian was dealing with his own problems, as he felt mortified over the impending carnage. Only Lucas seemed to walk out of the temple with overflowing confidence, which didn't sit well with Dimitri at all. Their enemies were so many, and yet they were so few. Once out in the open, Shyra about-faced and looked at her team. They were young but brave at the same time.

"This is it, everyone. All your training has been for this event. Trust in your teammates. You all are more powerful than you will ever realize."

Sora was trembling, but Dimitri put his hand on her shoulder to calm her down.

The eight of them were instantly transported to a plateau of the Granite Narrow, an area in the Grand Canyon where they could overlook the ongoing bloodbath between the United States forces and Zenakuu military. The terrain was ideal for fighting, with a river a half mile away and endless rocks. Yet, it was far enough from civilization to avoid innocent bystanders. The image would forever be burned in their subconscious—waves of American soldiers were sacrificing themselves as they tried to defend their planet. As they peered over the precipice, Shyra was forming an attack strategy in her head to help them out. Two warships had already unloaded their ground troops and returned to the air, while the third ship descended to do the same.

"We need to take out those ships," Shyra finally directed. "Laden Gravity, take down those warships. We are going to destroy as many Zenakuu from afar as we can." Grav stepped forward and aimed her hands at the first hovering ship. She felt the density of the craft, and struggled to compress it. Her arms shook as she gained control, and the very air around the warship rippled as it tilted. Cloud stood in amazement at her raw power, and realized that if she'd truly wanted, she could have killed them in battle at any time.

"What is she doing to the sky?" Wind questioned.

"It cannot be…" Shyra said under her breath.

"Cannot be what!?" Wind demanded to know.

"She's creating a black hole." Polarity casually said, and the rest of the group whipped their heads toward him.

"She can do that?" Flame asked in bewilderment.

The ship's main thrusters glowed with bright blue propulsion and attempted escape, but Laden Gravity would not let them go that easily. Lucas let out an exacerbated sigh as he was tired of explaining the science behind everyone's powers.

"Don't you guys ever pick up a book? Mathematically speaking, technically anything can become a black hole as long as it is compressed enough to a small enough space. Everything in the universe has what is known as a Schwarzschild Radius. A tiny amount of space that were you to collapse the entire mass of the object into, its density would be so infinitesimally heavy that its gravitational pull would be so great you would create a black hole," he explained.

"I don't know if I can hold them," Grav said. "It's too strong."

Her hands shook violently, and the closer they got to each other, the space around the Zenakuu warships became more displaced. Sweat poured from Gravity's forehead, but she continued to press on until she was finally able to clasp her hands. The ship seemed to crack and break as it collapsed in upon itself. A loud explosion boomed in the distance, and she fell to the ground in exhaustion.

"See? She compressed the ship's Schwarzschild Radius to a singularity, its density became infinite therefore its gravitational pull became so strong that nothing could escape—not even light and—," Lucas said before getting cut off.

"Okay shut up, we get it. You're smart, and she made a black hole," Wind attested. The Zenakuu warship vanished leaving a formidable-sized black hole in its wake. The others couldn't believe their eyes, they never saw a real black hole before, and the depths of her power finally hit them. Even Shyra took breath to be sure of the moment.

The second ship drew closer and closer to the hole until it had reached the point of no return. The vessel crumpled under the extreme force, and was seemingly gone forever.

The alliance watched closely to what they thought to be the ship's final moments. In actuality as the ship approached the black hole, the distortion in the sky grew greater and greater, but the alliance didn't actually physically see the ship get sucked into the hole. Instead, they saw what appeared to be the ship decelerating in speed as it reached the event horizon or point of no return. They didn't realize that what they saw was merely an illusion, a collection of photons that were reflected off of the ship in its last moments. Because black holes warp not only space, but time as well the ship seemed to be frozen in place, but then, the light started to shift red as it slowly faded into nothingness.

All was going to plan until the black hole started pulling in everything, Zenakuu and American military alike.

"Grav, you've got to shut it down!" Rain yelled. But creating a miniature black hole was no easy feat, and she was still on the ground in a weakened state. Polarity couldn't help but smirk at the situation. The black hole continued to pull in everything around it while the gravitational pull around the clouds produced smears and smudges in the sky. The resulting image resembled a reflection seen through a fun house mirror.

"Help me up," she pleaded, and Flame and Earth grabbed her arms and lifted her to her feet. She was drained but extended her right arm and reached out to the black hole that was drawing in tanks and jets by the second. She battled to close the rift in the sky, but it would not go down easy. With heavy breath and trembling body, she forced the black hole into submission. It fluctuated, and with the clinch of her fist, it imploded into nothingness. Though she couldn't save the F-22 and F-4 Phantoms fighter jets that were in combat, the ejected pilots owed her their lives.

"We are continuing." Shyra ordered. "We have to take out as many as we can from afar before we get dragged into close-quarters combat."

"There are too many of them," Wind stated.

"Then we shall thin out their numbers," Shyra said. "All of you, long-range attacks." The group got ready for what would be forever known as their defining moment.

"No," Polarity answered.

Everyone whipped their heads and stared at him.

"Excuse me?" Shyra asked.

Lucas stepped closer to the precipice's edge. "I said no. I'm done with this. How do you all not get it? In this universe, power is everything, and you all don't have enough to win."

"So what? You're fista' run away?" Cloud shouted.

"Nothing of the sort. I'm ensuring my own victory." Lucas continued to inch over to the edge of the cliff.

"This isn't funny, Lucas," Cloud said.

"Open your eyes. She is nothing more than a false prophet selling foolish pipe dreams. Now who wants to join me on the other side of sanity?"

Chapter 38

Great Minds Don't Think Alike, They Think for Themselves

The alliance glared at him with contempt, but did not make a move.

"I figured as much. Maybe one day you'll understand." Vigorous Polarity threw his arms out and fell over the edge backward with a smile on his face.

"Lucas!" Cloud shouted as he reached out for him, but it was too late. Halfway to ground, Lucas shrouded himself in a magnetic barrier and flew off toward the last intact Zenakuu ship. The rest of the group looked at Shyra, who was boiling with rage over the betrayal.

"Leave him. We will deal with him later," she ordered.

Grav, who always felt in her heart it might end up like this, couldn't let it go. With her remaining strength, she lifted up and flew after him toward the war grounds.

"Sora!" Earth shouted.

"Dammit! Does anyone else want to defect while we are at it?" Shyra yelled. The original five members of the alliance didn't move. "No? Good! Then let us finish this. Attack!"

The group was disheartened by what had just happened, but followed orders. The ground below rumbled from being covered by Zenakuu and enslaved alien races as far as the eye could see. Going down there would be a suicide mission. Seismic Earth stomped the ground with his left foot, summoning a massive quake that split the ground, swallowing flanks of enemies whole. At the same time, Voltaic Cloud sparked with electricity as the skies grew black. He called forth a lighting storm from the clouds that decimated everything in its path. Irascible Flame and Whisking Wind dispatched a series of flaming tornados that scorched the unsuspecting victims to the bone, while on the left side of a chasm, Effervescent Rain created an ice storm that left behind a subzero, frozen tundra of shimmering crystallized Zenakuu statues. The area had never seen such destruction.

They had successfully reduced enemy numbers by half, but they were far from in the clear. Zenakuu soldiers took aim at their location, and the gunners shot a barrage of cannon rounds that exploded mere yards away from the team's location.

"Shyra, we can't stay here anymore," said Rain.

"I know," she agreed. "It is now or never. Everyone get ready. We are bringing the fight to them. Remember what I said—stick together."

Everyone who was now proficient in flying took the air and headed to battle except for Earth, who was still worried about Grav. He levitated a flattened boulder and surfed his way down, passing the rest of his team. Ten feet from center of the Zenakuu wave, he leapt off the rock, twirled his tonfas in his hands, and brought them crashing down to the ground.

The force of his hit sent a shockwave through the ground, flinging up every soldier in a forty-yard radius. Earth was in rare form as he sent the Zenakuu infantry flying to their deaths. His teammates landed immediately after the blast subsided and began fights of their own. Even though the enemy's numbers seemed endless, they fought on.

Wind took in all the air she could, inflated her lungs to their limit, and let out a super breath that launched everything in its path into orbit. Flame took notice of its effectiveness and inhaled a deep breath of his own. Heat welled in his chest and smoke pooled in his lungs. The sensation it brought him was borderline sadistic; he lived for the rush of it all. Like a dungeon dragon, he roared and passed a fiery sentence of death to the surveying area. The Zenakuu battalion was not prepared for such a force, and hardly seemed like a match for the heroes. From the combination of high heat, cold winds, and thunderstorms, a derecho formed over the battlefield that shrouded the alliance and Zenakuu in darkness.

Shyra, who donned her LAPS gear, blasted away soldiers who got too close with her telekinesis. A few yards away, Rain called forth a raging river that came crashing through the chasm and swept away dozens of enemies. They were the lucky ones; the soldiers foolish enough to hang on to the edges were electrocuted and died a conductive and painful death by Cloud who was providing backup.

Their leader then offered moral support to his team. "Everyone keep it up!" However, they needed no invitation. Zenakuu were dropping like flies, and the alliance's teamwork was impeccable.

Polarity landed a few feet away from the Zenakuu ship when Fleet Admiral Graz spotted him. The doors slowly opened, and Polarity proceeded forward when Gravity landed with a crashing thud a yard behind him. He turned and smiled at her. "Sora … I knew you would do the right thing and follow me."

"I am here to do the right thing, Lucas, but I'm not following you."

"Not you too. I really gave you too much credit, you know that?" Polarity began to rant. "Ever since the day I saved you, you've been like a lost puppy always at my heels, but I really hoped some of my intelligence would have rubbed off on you."

Grav was shocked. This was a new level of cold-heartedness for him. "Is that all I was to you? A lost puppy? You told me you loved me," she said credulously.

"I loved things about you—things you did for me," Polarity went on.

The tears began to roll down Gravity's face. "You bastard!" she shouted out and lunged after him.

Grav shot a gravitational pulse beam that Polarity deflected with his barrier. She raced in and closed the gap between them. With Grav in range, Polarity threw a claw punch that she evaded by somersaulting over him. However, with Polarity's reflexes, he caught her ankle midair and slammed her to the ground. Grav was only momentarily stunned and preformed an axe-wheel trip with her legs that she prayed would connect. However, her prayers were not answered, and Polarity jumped back and grinned at her.

Now frustrated, she pounded her fist on the ground, which expelled all gravity in the area. It caught him off guard, but Polarity stabilized himself by hovering in his force field. It caused just enough momentary distraction for Grav to unearth a nearby tank and hurl it at Polarity. Being ever quick-witted, he caught the tank with his magnokinesis.

"You've got to be kidding me," he laughed. "You use metal to attack me? You can't be that dumb." He shot an energy blast that Grav was not quick enough to dodge. She slammed into a rock pillar before bouncing off and being clothes-lined by her once love. She couldn't believe he was capable of such ruthlessness.

The others were almost a mile away fighting their hearts out against the remaining thousands of Zenakuu warriors. Flame was running through Zenakuu soldiers the size of linebackers with similar purpose to the cause. They swung widely at him with lances and maces, but he dipped and dodged them all.

Once in the clear, he started to snap his fingers in rapid succession, and the soldiers he passed spontaneously combusted bursting into flames. He was overjoyed the technique worked but was blasted away from a nearby explosion. He survived the fall, because Earth, who saw the whole thing, turned the stretch of ground into soft sand. Flame looked up and nodded, thanking his teammate for the assist before taking to the sky and continuing the assault. Rain and Wind were back to back in the center of a ring of Zenakuu armed with rifles, ground-to-air missiles, swords, and axes.

They looked for an escape route, but there was none. There they were in a sea full of sharks that all smelled blood. They tightly pressed their backs to each other as the circle became smaller. Wind closed her eyes and hoped that when they opened, it would all be just a bad dream, but the nightmare she found herself in was reality.

"Rain," Wind called.

"Yeah?"

"If I don't make it back today, will you tell D how I really felt about him?" she asked.

"No. Forget that, Tori. Alex said everyone is coming home today. I'm not gonna let you die." At least that's what Rain told her, but she knew deep down she was making empty promises. Cassie could feel herself becoming emotional. "Now get ready," she directed, "we're going to attack."

"I'm ready," Tori replied.

"Let's go!" Rain shouted, and they propelled themselves forward.

Over on her side, Rain charged at the fighters and used water whips to lash out at the swarm. Wind twirled her arms in a clockwise motion creating whirlwinds that forced soldiers to cling to the ground for dear life right before being blown away. Others who were dumb enough to use their free hands to muffle the sound of the whirlwind's ear-shattering whistles were launched high into the air before smacking into the ground with a devastating crack. No one was safe from its wrath as it left a trail of death in its wake.

Using so much power took its toll on the girls, but they pressed on. Rain summoned all the surrounding water and drowned dozens of enemy soldiers in a maelstrom of vicious waters. At the same time, Wind threw her arms out, letting a current of air carry jagged quarry rocks that shredded everything in their path. Wind and Rain held their own admirably for a long time, but the troops were relentless. They ganged up on the two heroines with various blades as they hacked and slashed. Some connected, which caused torn uniforms to be the least of their worries, as they were now randomly covered in nicks and cuts.

Now separated, the two girls were all alone. A horde of alien races advanced on Rain, bearing their teeth. Rain fluidly motioned her arms and encased herself in a ball of thick ice. The Zenakuu were puzzled but instinctively weighed down on the ball, cleaving away at it. Inside, Rain heard as the blood-drunk Zenakuu worked desperately to rip her limb from limb, causing the hairs on her arms to stand on end. As chucks of ice chipped away, she felt proud that she held lasted alone for so long but did not see a way out of her situation. It was then that the first axe finally penetrated the bubble of ice. She cried out for help, but everyone was already up to their necks in battle. She was on her own.

Not willing to give up without a fight, Rain slapped both hands along the inner walling of her ice ball and sent out hundreds of needlepoint ice quills that speared and killed every alien within four feet of her. As their dead bodies dropped to the ground, there was silence. She thought to herself that she may have won and contemplated exiting the ball, but instead, she peeked out of the crack the axe had made.

That is when she saw it—a Zenakuu soldier with a rocket launcher aimed right at her. She panicked and used iced breath to mend the crack and fortify the ball. She wasn't sure if it was strong enough to survive an explosion of that level, but she had no choice now. Rain braced herself; the missile struck the ball with such force that it exploded on impact. The wall of ice did save her life, but she was flung away from the ear deafening explosion high into the air and smacked down on the unforgiving ground below.

Wind only saw the aftermath of the explosion and found an unconscious Rain on the floor. She screamed out for her friend, but an army of alien soldiers still stood between the two. Wind was seething mad at the sight of her best friend so gravely injured. Her eyes turned opaque, and she began to spin like a top. A ferocious twister formed at the base of her feet, and she lifted to the skies. Twenty feet high, the whistling air current covered everything up to her waist. She was the master of the tornado that twisted and turned to her every whim, but she remained perfectly still inside.

Countless Zenakuu fired at her, but the bullets deflected off her wind shield with minimal effort. She towered over all enemies and sliced them to shreds with razor-sharp blades of wind she'd fashioned. She continued to clear a path to her friend, as approaching infantry spiraled out of control around in her twister. Once close enough, she dissipated her tailwinds and grabbed Rain. She held her friend by the waist and took to the sky with Mach speeds leaving behind a sonic boom that cracked through the air seconds later. They landed on the other side of the Grand Canyon, where the armada could not see them. Wind prayed to God they could just have a moment to rest.

Chapter 39

Heroes Come and Go, but Legends Never Die

On the other side, Shyra was doing her part, sending hordes of soldiers to their graves. The power of the LAPS suit was immeasurable, but it took a heavy toll on her. The death count was in the thousands by her hands, but she was noticeably exhausted. She pulled out all the stops and created a jet stream of lygokinetic swords, daggers, spears, hatchets, bayonets, battle axes, scythes, arrows, chains, halberds, and much more. The weapons made any and everything in their path look like nothing more than heaps of broken armor and chucks of flesh.

Those who dodged the current of weapons charged in and demanded blood for their fallen brethren. Shyra created a psionic shockwave that extended outward and blew away a dozen more soldiers, but their advancement never ceased. The only path to survival relied on staying focused, but her thoughts were on her young team who had been thrown into the midst of chaos.

Three elite soldiers, who did not appear to be from planet Zenakuu, walked up and pushed the others out the way. The sun-deprived pale skin covering their bodies looked dry and cracked like stone. Skinny spiked black bone extruded from their foreheads and gangly arms, elongated necks, glowing blue eyes that illuminated the air around them even in the middle of day. Slim leathery appendages that hung only a foot or two off the ground gave them a unique look, but they stood almost seven feet tall. Shyra quickly realized they were Purytes from the captured planet Purex. Each carried different weapons—a katana, double-barreled pistols, and, lastly, a sickle with an attached chain known in Japanese culture as a kusari-gama. The two carrying melee weapons ran in crossing paths a few feet in front of her, while the gun user stood motionless. He waited for a window of opportunity to strike.

The sickle-using Puryte, who went by the name Aster, launched his weapon at Shyra's chest, aiming for her vital organs. She dodged to the left but was almost decapitated by Heaux, the katana wielding Puryte. Deken, who had the double pistols, still just stood there, guns in hands with his arms crossed. For some reason, he concerned Shyra the most. But if she wasn't careful, she would lose her life far before he posed any immediate threat. After her close call, she rolled on the ground away from the three but was once again nearly impaled by the sickle blade. Luckily, she stopped her roll before she was skewered, but with the constant onslaught, she could barely defend herself, let alone counterattack.

Shyra did a back handspring on to her feet and telekinetically pulled a large boulder from the basin where they were. She threw it at Aster, but Heaux jumped forward and sliced it in half before it got to his team member. Shyra created a lygokinetic bow staff, the perfect midrange to long-range weapon for taking on multiple opponents. She displayed her mastery of the staff by twirling it around and hoping to strike fear into the Purytes' hearts. They showed no sign of backing down as Heaux swung a downward slash that Shyra blocked. The two of them exchanged blows for several minutes with no clear victor.

With sickle in hand, Aster jumped high in the air and came down on Shyra, hoping to cut her in half. Shyra blocked the slash, but it cracked her staff. She side kicked Aster away and swept the legs underneath Heaux. Her staff wouldn't last much longer, so she intended to end the bout. She brought the staff down in a piercing motion on Heaux, but Deken finally made his move and saved his partner. His pistol shot a bright, neon green laser that flew by Shyra's head.

"I was wondering when you would make a move," Shyra said.

Deken smiled and circled around her, blasting off laser beams. Shyra deflected the majority of shots but couldn't keep up with his rapid fire. Aster jumped off Heaux's shoulders and wrapped his chain around Shyra's staff, yanking it from her grip. Heaux sprang forward and started slashing away at the unarmed Kalrynian, who, at best, was able to put up a lygokinetic shield that parried away the swings. Heaux jumped out of the way and immediately following him was a supercharged blast from Deken's pistols. Their timing and synchronization were perfect and proved to be too much for her. The shield shattered into hundreds of tiny fragments, and the force knocked her back.

Very stunned, Shyra flipped back to put some distance between them. She fought admirably, but the suit was draining her of her power at a steady rate. She had one trump car left, but it was kill or be killed. The three Purytes stood in a line in front of her, anxious for Kalrynian blood, while Shyra stood several feet away, exhausted from continuous battle.

In a last-ditch effort, Shyra tapped further into the raw power of her LAPS, knowing it may kill her. Pulsing white energy circled the ground around her, and it began to shake. She glared at the Purytes, who had never seen such power. Shyra had never pushed the suit that far and was fearful of the consequences, but with careless disregard, she brought it to its limit. She was coated in lygokinetic power so prevalent that it shot into the sky like a distress signal beacon high enough for anyone in the Grand Canyon to see.

The Purytes stepped back, but their fate was already set in stone. Shyra moved faster than the soldiers could follow, and with seconds, she was behind Heaux. She placed her left hand on his chin, the right on the back of his head, and followed through by snapping his neck. The remaining Purytes had never seen such speed in their lives. Shyra formed a lygokinetic, serrated dagger and jettisoned forward. Aster jumped back, but Shyra followed his movements to the bitter end and remained in his face. She lodged the dagger deep into his chest, and he coughed up their signature black blood. Aster died before he hit the ground, dousing the floor with his innards, and once again, Shyra took off running. Deken ran backward and relentlessly shot at Shyra, but she deflected the spray of lasers faster than the eye could follow.

She toyed with her pray before savoring the final kill by running around him in circles so fast that she created a series of after images. It looked as if Deken now had to face ten Shyras, but he knew it was just a trick. He shot at her but connected with nothing but air. Shyra's heart began to palpitate, and she knew she had pushed herself too hard. She lunged at Deken, slicing off his left arm in one swipe. Before he could grip the stump where his arm once was, Shyra hit the brakes and dashed at him again, severing off his right arm. Deken fell to his knees. Shyra sprinted right toward Deken but stopped inches away. He jerked his head back due to the shock of being amputated.

Shyra looked down on him and uttered one word, "Pitiful." She sliced his jugular, and the blood sprayed out as if it were shot out of a cleaning bottle on mist mode. Soon, it painted the upper half of Shyra's body. She wiped her face clean and ran toward her team.

Farther down the canyon, Flame and Cloud were contending with their own hordes of Zenakuu. They fought on bravely, combining their powers in a fiery, electrical energy blast that incinerated everything in its path until there was nothing left. Tired from overexerting themselves, they desperately sought refuge.

Flame and Cloud ran through the canyon, avoiding detection until their lungs burned with exhaustion. They stumbled upon an elevated hill, but when they looked down, they saw an ocean of enemies waiting for them below. Alex and Chris were still ragged and bloodied from previous battles. The initial shock vanished. They looked down at sea of soldiers and simultaneously chuckled. It was a laugh as if to say, "There's no way we're going to survive this one."

Depleted of energy, Voltaic Cloud turned toward his partner and asked, "You ready, Buddy?"

Irascible Flame smiled and replied, "Never been more ready in my entire life, bro."

They both let out an epic battle cry and charged the legion below them like Custer's Last Stand. When they reached the enemy front lines, Flame widened his stance and pulled out his hook swords, which were sheathed on his back. Cloud reached back and took out his dao saber. Between the long, high-powered attacks and going around taking out thousands of Zenakuu with their abilities, the team's powers were almost fully drained. As a result, they resorted to brutal weapons combat.

Zenakuu snarled at the earthlings daring them to fight. The boys did their best to defend, but the stampede was unyielding. Flame was able to block and counter a brute by letting him hit his one hook sword, while with the other sword, he stabbed the arm of the Zenakuu. The alien let out a screech, but before it could react, Flame removed the hook from its arm and drove it into its neck, severing the juggular. Blood flow didn't cease until the corpse was drained.

"These guys aren't so tough." Flame had a warranted level of confidence on the battlefield.

"Don't get too cocky, Flame," Cloud warned. He was having trouble with his half of the aliens. All he could do was block. There were too many to charge head-on. *If I attack, I will leave myself open. I have to wait for Christian to help,* Cloud thought.

"All you had to do was ask," Flame responded, having read his mind. He pushed away the Zenakuu he was fighting, performed a back flip and turnaround in midair, and found himself facing Cloud's enemies. One was pushing his sword into Cloud's dao. Flame quickly responded by lopping off the arm of the attacker. Blood soiled the ground as Flame and Cloud were surrounded once more.

Cloud was desperately trying to keep from being sliced open as he dodged, rolled, and blocked his way out of near-death several times. It seemed like every time Cloud got out of the way, another sword was headed for his neck.

"We can't keep this up all day," Cloud yelled at Flame.

"I know!" Flame responded, straining to keep the Zenakuu broad sword back from cleaving him in two. He shifted the weight to his side, and the broad sword hit nothing but dirt. The berserker came around with his shield and bashed it into Flame's chest, lifting him up and then causing him to fall on top of Cloud. The two were on their backs. One look up, and several swords plummeted down after them. Quick reflexes saved the two, as they immediately shielded themselves with their weapons. However, one got by the defense and sliced a gash in Flame's arm. He screamed as the blood spilled out.

"I've had enough!" Flame declared. "Cloud, get outta here!" Flame looked over and glanced at Cloud, who was being pulled away by his leg.

"Alex, no!" Flame went for broke. He ignited his hook swords to super nova temperatures and sliced through sword, shield, and flesh alike and he barreled down to save his friend. The only saving grace for the Zenakuu was that the heated blade immediately cauterized any gash it inflicted. He jumped over a small row of them to land next to Cloud.

"Don't worry, bro. I'll get you out of here," he assured his friend.

Flame hooked his two swords together and swung them around and around like he was pruning hedges until there was a space large enough to help Cloud with his escape.

"What are you doing? If you keep this strain up, you'll get an aneurysm," Cloud warned.

"I don't care! I'm sick of this. Now you need to get out of the basin."

Chris's rage had been building up since the beginning of the fight. Flames were literally jumping off his body and catching anything flammable in the air.

"Flame stop!" Cloud shouted.

"I'm sorry about this Cloud."

"Huh? Sorry about what?!" He demanded to know.

"Please get out of here. I don't think I can hold it back any longer," Flame said. "I'm trying to be the hero here, but I can't promise you won't get hurt." Cloud had never seen him so ballistic before, and wondered if he always had this rage driven monster inside of him.

As if reduced to hardened clay, Flame's heat resilient armor splintered and cracked off his body causing half of it to fall to the dirt. The scorched mass of protective gear in front of Flame looked no better than a lump of used charcoal. Cloud held his hand over the brow of his eyes to shield them from the intense radiation that emanated off his friend. All of the warnings to his best friend fell upon deaf ears, and he knew there was no going back. If Cloud hadn't left in the next few seconds he would have been engulfed by Flame's inferno.

All of Christian's pent up emotions only added fuel to the fire.

"I'd shake your hand, but I like my skin intact." the two shared a shortened chuckle.

Cloud was then serious and nodded his head. With a flash of light, Cloud used his super speed to run up the side of the canyon with his cape undulating on his back. Back at the bottom, Flame was increasingly getting hotter. The Zenakuu reached Flame but were instantly flash cooked and reduced to ashes. Flame was ready for whatever was to happen next, some might say, he even wanted it. A change seemed to be washing over Flame. The more he used his powers to kill, the stronger his taste developed for it.

His powers were slowly corrupting him. In the distance Cloud heard an echoing roar.

"Para ti, padre!" Suddenly, an explosion swallowed Flame and the remaining Zenakuu army that was in the basin in a white-hot fiery demise. The flames were nearing Cloud as he made his ascent up the side of the cliff. He jumped with all his might, but the fire slowly reached him and burned off the majority of his cape. Cloud narrowly escaped and landed on top of the cliff's edge.

"Christian … I didn't know he had such power," he said to himself. Flame was ready for whatever was to happen next, some might say, he even wanted it. A change seemed to be washing over Flame. The more he used his powers to kill, the stronger his taste developed for it. His powers were slowly corrupting him. In the distance Cloud heard an echoing roar.

"It's my turn to be the hero now." Cloud had barely enough strength to walk, let alone carry another person, but he was determined. He thunderously clapped his hands, and the resulting sound wave echoed through the trenches. He slowly flew up the steep hills of the Grand Canyon to reach the top and keep Flame out of the fray. Cloud placed Flame down and then collapsed next to him from exhaustion.

Earth found himself alone—exactly what Shyra instructed them not to do, but there was little he could do to regroup with the others. Swarms of soldiers fired away at him as he ducked for cover. He was scared. Never before had the odds been so against him in a situation that his life depended on, and his heart was in danger of beating out of his chest.

Earth dug his hands into the ground. He struggled only momentarily as he lifted a three-foot thick block of redwall limestone that flew from the canyon's floor. Not even the strongest of Zenakuu warriors would be capable of such a feat, but Earth made it look easy. The block crushed an advancing, platoon leaving no survivors, but there were plenty more where they came from.

Once again, Earth found himself under fire. He jumped forward and tumbled along the ground until his entire body was covered by a rock coat of arms. The bullets chipped away at his armor but not enough to hurt him.

Earth made an uppercut motion in the air, and a wave of rocks sprang from the ground and pummeled another squad. He was pleased by how well he was doing, but his moment of glory was cut short when his rock armor cracked and broke apart from some kind of blunt trauma. Earth was sent careening into a nearby mound of rock and stumbled to figure out what had just happened. He looked in the direction from where he flew, and a beast with drooling fangs grunted at him. He was wearing Zenakuu armor but clearly wasn't from their home world, as it barely fit his brown skin that stretched tightly over slabs of bulging muscle. He was at least nine feet tall with raptor claws capable of cleaving the meat off bone clean, talons that dug into the ground with every step, and a long muscular tail strong enough to show an anaconda how it's really done. Thick veins popped out of his muscular neck, and his skin looked like a scaly reptile. Whatever the monstrosity was, he appeared to be more muscle than man. He wielded a gigantic hammer, but the way he lifted it made it look like it weighed nothing at all.

Earth stomped the canyon floor and a half-sized boulder jumped up. He cocked back and overhand punched the rock as hard as he could. With incredible speed, it flew at the beast. The alien didn't even flinch; instead, he stepped forward and hit the projectile with his hammer like a line drive into left field.

Earth didn't appreciate being toyed with. He stomped the ground once more, and three larger boulders bolted up. He jabbed the first, left hooked the second, and front kicked the third in succession. They flew toward the beast once again, but like before, it seemed like the beast couldn't care less. With a subtle gesture, he leaned his shoulders to the left, and the first boulder skidded past his chest. He used the back end of his hammer to pierce the second rock, and he caught the last one with his right hand.

"One handed?" Earth gasped.

The creature roared at Earth and crushed the rock in his bare hands. He charged Earth, hammer in hand. Seismic Earth raised a stone slab between the two of them, but the alien easily broke through it and the rest of Earth's armor. Earth was sent back and slammed into a wall. He tried to get up but was too disoriented. The unidentified alien walked over and grabbed Earth by the hoodie. He lifted him four feet off the ground and threw him away like a rag doll.

Earth tried to crawl away, but the monster was right behind him. He lifted his hammer above his head, wanting to end Earth's life. The hammer came down almost instantaneously, but Earth barrel rolled out of its way. The hero was out of options. He couldn't see straight, let alone put up a decent fight. Earth got to his knees and, in an act of desperation, slapped both hands on the ground, turning the solid ground underneath the beast to fast-acting quicksand. The monster bellowed and growled, but there was nothing he could do. He sank in a matter of seconds beneath the earth's surface until only his head was visible.

Earth solidified the ground again, and the warrior stopped sinking. He violently threw his head around, twisting and turning his neck, but he was entombed in solid rock. Earth grabbed his side as he tried to breathe normally. He walked over to the canyon wall and gave it a powerful hammer fist. The impact created a rockslide that cascaded from the top. It was more than a little sadistic, but Earth intended to bury the alien alive if the rocks didn't crush his head first. They came down, knocking into the side of his head, and in flash, he was gone.

"The bigger they are," he said under his breath.

The soldiers who watched the fight from afar were furious at the malicious act and charged in. Tired of all the brawling, Earth looked to end the war quickly. He lowered his center of gravity and leg-swept the floor. With his geokinetic power, dozens of stone spikes shot up from the ground and impaled the advancing soldiers. He may not have won the war, but the battle was surely his.

CHAPTER 40

After You I Will Never Be the Same

BACK NEAR THE WARSHIP, things were heating up between Polarity and Gravity, while the Zenakuu sat back and enjoyed the show.

"Babe, stop this right now! I don't want to fight you," Grav pleaded.

"No, you can't fight me," Polarity argued. "There's a difference, and don't call me that anymore. You still don't get it? I've moved on to bigger and better things."

"Are you crazy? By joining the Zenakuu, you're on to better things?" she asked.

"That's your problem, Sora. You're weak, and you've always been weak with no ambition. You'll latch onto whoever is stronger than you, because you're scared."

"Maybe you're right. Maybe I held on to you because you're strong and made me feel safe, but that doesn't make me weak. However, giving in to the allure of temptation does. This isn't you, Lucas. I know it isn't. You were meant to be a hero," she attested.

"You got the wrong guy. I've picked the role of the villain, and so I'm ending the miserable lives of all those pajama-wearing superheroes first chance I get, starting with Dimitri who you've grown so fond of."

"I won't let you!" she screamed out. Grav stomped her right foot on the ground, and everything in the surrounding area fell hard to the floor. She amplified the normal gravity fivefold.

Polarity was brought to his knees as Grav slowly walked up to him. She picked up a nearby sword on her way over. It seemed she finally found her resolve to do what needed to be done. Polarity gritted his teeth and struggled to lift his head as his executioner approached. As she walked closer, she was reminded of the life they shared together and how much different it had been before Shyra and the others entered it. Ever since the day they were recruited, she slowly started to lose him. He was the love of her life, but now they might as well have been strangers—at least that would be better than enemies. The thought of him dying by her hand was more than she wanted to bear; each step toward him was more painful than the last.

"Sora, let me go!" Lucas shouted, but she would not release him. She let the sword drag on the floor until she was right in front of him. Grav dropped to her knees and spoke what would be their last conversation together.

"It's you, Lucas. It's always been you. I have loved you since the moment I saw you and wanted more than anything to spend the rest of my days by your side," she divulged.

"Dear God, Sora. I was using you! I was always using you. It was always me and you 'til it was me *or* you."

"I know, but I didn't care," she confessed. "I was just happy being with you. I guess I just thought one day our love wouldn't be so unrequited, and we could give up being criminals. We could have been happy together, just the two of us."

"You're even more naive than I thought," Polarity laughed.

Grav dropped the sword, lifted Polarity, and suspended him in the air. "Lucas, please … stop this. I don't want to hurt y—" Her sentence was cut short by the sword embedded through her chest plate and the stream of blood running down her chin. The force of the abundant gravity vanished from the battlefield, and

Polarity dropped to the slate rock he was once compressed on. Grav gurgled and coughed up a mouthful of blood, "How?" she barely managed to ask.

"Like I said, Sora, you're weak." Polarity yanked the sword from her small chest, "Don't think your power over gravity is stronger than my control over metal. You were already dead the second you dropped your weapon," Polarity said.

She clenched the deep gash in her chest tightly, desperately trying to apply pressure, and stop the bleeding, but the blood simply cascaded through her fingers painting the ground red.

Mortally wounded, Gravity fell over and laid her head down on the ground. Her vision faded to black, and she slowly closed her eyes as the blood spilled out. Tears streamed across the side of her face as she watched Polarity walk toward the Zenakuu warship.

Laden Gravity fought with all her heart and died heroically on that day. The team felt Sora's kinetic link sever from theirs. Earth whipped his head due east in the direction of Gravity. The rest of the team faced the same way, distracted by what felt like the fall of a teammate. Earth finished bashing a rock into an alien's head and peered out over the horde. Rage filled up his body to a staggering amount.

"If you've hurt her," Earth threatened under his breath. The Zenakuu slowly backed away. They sensed the anger Earth was radiating. "I'll rip off your head if you hurt her!"

Every wisp of air in Earth's lungs exploded in a fit of insanity. He thrashed his arms apart, causing the ground from under the horde to split open wide. The Zenakuu army fell through the abyss created by Earth and landed in lava that was exposed at the bottom. Earth's power increased to a whole new level in that moment. The lava shot out of the ground like a geyser, and then several sprang out following the first.

Earth ran toward the fissure he had created and jumped in. When his right foot reached the blackness of the pit, he instinctively raised a rock big enough to plant his foot on. Never slowing down, every step was supported by a new piece as the one before it fell. He was headed toward the last location of Gravity's kinetic signal.

"I need to get there—now." Earth brought a large rock big enough to surf so he could reach her before it was too late. Surfing through the sky, bullets whizzed by him and crashed into his mode of transportation, but nothing was going to distract or stop him.

Earth arrived at the scene where he witnessed Gravity still on the ground and Polarity with his back toward her wielding a sword. That sword represented the evil that was inside Lucas Wright.

"What have you done?" Earth yelled as he stood in shock.

After seeing what power Sora had, he would have never guessed that she would fall so easily, but she was weakened. Dimitri fell to his knees. His eyes began to tear up as he lifted his friend off the dusty canyon ground. Her hair was soaked with blood from the hole in her sternum. The blood spread to Dimitri's hands as he laid her head down gently. He took off his hoodie and placed it over her face, exposing his black wife-beater undershirt. Dimitri stood up with a homicidal look in his eyes. His teeth grinded into each other and his fist clenched shut, shaking violently.

"Blockhead, what a wonderful facial expression you have there," he tilted his head to the left and grinned as he continued his taunt. "Is there a problem?" Polarity laughed as he told Earth that his emotions would soon get him killed. "I knew you two were growing fond of each other, but to shed tears over her—I thought you were big, bad Dimitri Williams."

"There won't be enough of you to positively ID when I'm done with you, Lucas," Earth swore.

"Ya know, you and I are a lot more similar than you think. We both strive for power to be the best, which is why I respected you the most. I would ask you to come with me if you weren't so tied to this sorry excuse of a world we live on. It sickens me."

"I loved her like my own sister, you piece of shit. Why would you do this to someone you loved?" Earth shouted.

"I never loved her," Vigorous Polarity admitted. "I loved her power, and since she was batting for the other team, I had to exterminate her."

"You're an animal, and I swear I'ma put you down like one," Earth vowed.

"No time like the present, gangsta," baited Polarity.

Earth had heard enough and jumped forward. He punched Polarity with knee-jerk reaction speed, which caught him off guard. The solid right punch rocked Polarity to the core, but it wasn't enough for Earth. He followed his first punch with three more to the body. Earth grabbed a handful of Polarity's hair and pulled him in, bashing his own skull into Polarity's forehead. He grunted loudly and staggered backwards as blood trickled down from his hairline. An honorable fight was the last thing on Earth's mind. The only thing that would sedate his rage now would be to stand over Polarity's lifeless body.

Polarity tried to swing back, but Earth gracefully dodged the poorly executed punch and countered with another solid right hook to Polarity's cheekbone. He slid back on the ground and wiped his bloody lip.

"It looks like you're finally getting serious." Polarity carried a depraved look in his eyes and smiled, exposing his bloodstained teeth. He spat out a chunk of his ripped open inner cheek and opened his arms wide. "Come to Papa."

It was clear that he reveled in the bloodshed and desperately wanted more. Earth rushed at him again, but Polarity pushed him back with a negative magnetic pulse. Earth stopped his momentum by digging his feet into the ground, but there was now distance between the two. Polarity knew he couldn't win in a fistfight, so he turned it into an ability showdown. Lucas reached out to the downed warship for resources. He surrounded himself with Zurekium and formed armor for himself. He also laid all the metal he could reach behind him, effectively setting up an endless supply of ammunition. Earth had his own endless supply—the battlefield itself was his weapon.

Metal began to levitate, mending together to create several solid spheres. Earth glared at Gravity's lifeless body and relapsed into blind fury. He attempted to suppress his anger, so his head was level for the fight, but it overwhelmed him. His powers reflected it as such.

The ground cracked and rumbled under their feet. Polarity lost concentration and dropped his metallic spheres. Chunks of bright angel shale and mauv limestone broke off the ground and floated around Earth as if he was a red giant star in a newborn solar system. Most of them hovered in midair and exploded, but the ones that survived his power-up spun faster and faster around him. The earthquake reached the rest of the team, and they all looked over simultaneously in fear of what Earth might do.

"I can't … believe you can do this to people … to help an evil alien race," Earth spat out. More rocks lifted off the ground, and it became increasingly difficult for him to speak complex sentences as his rage took over. The angrier Earth got, the more power he emanated; nothing could mitigate his rampage.

"I won't let you gather any more power," Polarity shouted and came running up.

When he got close enough, Earth dispersed the crowd of boulders. The rocks fell like a meteor shower. Polarity was able to dodge a few, but thanks to his control over metal, he took cover behind a barricade he'd made for himself. He stretched the metal overhead and formed a metallic igloo. Rocks pummeled the outer layer of his defenses, relentlessly trying to break through. Lucas turned the barricade of Zurekium into a full sphere with him inside. Like a hamster in a wheel, he bowled down in Earth's direction.

Earth saw him coming and raised the ground the metal ball was on. Higher and higher the pillar grew until he crumbled it. Polarity's means of defense fell from high in the sky. Freefalling to the ground in this metal orb surely meant death. Lucas dispatched the metal around him and formed a slide. He slid down about eleven feet before Earth sent a boulder through the slide, bending and twisting the metal into scrap. Polarity jumped off and dropped several feet before he triggered his magnetic field, which slowed him down to a gradual stop.

Polarity kept his shield up and slowly walked forward. "Nothing you can do will penetrate my shield," he taunted.

"That won't stop me from trying," Earth lashed out. Several rocks around Earth broke off, and small pieces soon formed hundreds of javelin-shaped spears. He released them in a stream, and one by one, they shattered upon the magnetic shield Polarity had produced. Earth's patience wore thin. He delivered every last remaining javelin in one last attempt to break the force field. Not one penetrated his defense, but it did provide cover for Earth to close the gap. He was mere feet away before Polarity laid eyes on him.

Polarity reached out and snatched an elongated shard of metal that he fetched to wrap around Earth and stop his assault. He prevailed just in the nick of time. Earth was pinned down by that heavy chunk of Zurekium. Earth struggled to free himself but couldn't bend the metal. He even tried prying it open with his teeth. Polarity confidently walked up to Earth and stood over him. "I am your superior in every way," he said. He followed with a low kick to the kidney.

Earth struggled to sit up only to be kicked over.

"Just like I thought. All bark and no bite," Polarity said mockingly. He lifted Earth by the strap of metal around his midsection, and as it pressed his arms closer to his chest, breathing became a chore.

"Any last words, D?"

"My name… is… Seismic Earth," Earth leered at Polarity and pierced his soul with his eyes.

Polarity became enraged. He leaned in and gave Earth a few light slaps on the cheek. "Your misery and torment would be so much more satisfying than just killing you; but honestly, the thought of your bones shattering and ripping through your flesh is too exciting to pass up. So, you've got two choices: you can die here and now and stop all this futile fighting," Polarity said and let out a wispy sigh. "Think about it, no more fighting, no more suffering, just endless peace and quiet. *Or*, you can live with it, knowing you could have saved her if you weren't so weak, but you didn't did you? You let Sora down, just like your sister. A shame really, but whichever one happens, I swear to God if you get in my way again I'll kill your entire family in front of you, one by one."

"Lucas," Earth called out before continuing. "I'm personally gonna be the one to dig your grave, and bury you one day."

Polarity smiled at the threat. "See you then," he sarcastically replied.

With that, Polarity lifted and hurled Earth into the vast chasm. He flew through the air for a while before his back met a pillar of rock. Earth exploded through the giant stone structure and landed on the other side, of the deep chasm beaten, battered, and broken.

Fleet Admiral Graz ordered his men to lower the hatch doors, and Polarity walked toward the Zenakuu warship the victor. Back on the lower battleground, everyone felt Earth's pulse weaken.

"Dimitri!" Wind shouted.

Shyra didn't want to lose anyone else. She called out to her team telepathically, "Everyone converge on Seismic Earth's location. We are regrouping now!"

The alliance abandoned their current battles, leaving a few hundred or so Zenakuu still alive. In the distance, a thunderous clap was heard, and Cloud carried Flame on his back. They all flew over to the last Zenakuu ship where they felt Earth's presence fading. The alliance arrived to an unconscious Earth less than a minute apart and were glad to see that everyone was more or less still alive.

"Christian, is he?" Rain asked.

Cloud set him down on the floor. "Knocked out, but he'll be okay," Cloud was relieved to say.

"What about D?" Wind asked frantically.

"The same. If we can get him to the ship, he will recover," Shyra said to relieve her worries.

"Is Sora really dead?" Cloud asked. "I thought she went along with Lucas."

"Apparently not," Shyra said. "I caught portions of her final moments telepathically. She died trying to stop him."

"He won't get away with this. If it's the last thing I do, I swear I'll pay him back for this," Cloud vowed.

"Shyra, what are we going to do? We're too outnumbered now, and half our team is down," Rain voiced.

Shyra's hands glowed bright with blinding white lygokinetic power. "We are finishing this fight," she said. "Whisking Wind, Effervescent Rain, I want the two of you to get Seismic Earth and Irascible Flame as far away here as you can. Voltaic Cloud and I are not letting them get away. We will avenge Sora Morikami."

Cloud was in no condition to fight, but he would ignore the crippling pain for just one chance to even the score.

"Let us go, Voltaic Cloud." Shyra flew off with him right behind her. They landed a few yards away from the bow of the ship. Polarity was more than halfway up the ramp when the two landed with a thud.

Chapter 41

Fairy Tales Don't Always Have a Happy Ending

"Lucas!" Shyra shouted.

He turned back to see his former mentor seething with rage. Cloud never in his wildest dreams imagined Shyra could get so mad that she would foam at the mouth, but there she stood, fist tightened, tendrils quivering in the air, and facial markings sporadically and rapidly moving about.

"Where do you think you are going?" Shyra demanded to know.

Polarity took a few steps down the ramp for what he believed to be the last time he would see his former team. He felt no remorse over his betrayal. Instead, he only grew excited over worlds he would soon see.

"To heights you could never reach, Shyra," he answered.

She had never seen evil so singularly personified than on his face at that moment. "You are not leaving this planet alive, Lucas Wright," Shyra threatened, but Polarity only grinned with anticipation.

"You don't know how long I've been waiting to fight you for real, Shyra. Let's finally decide who's stronger."

"No, Polarity," Cloud cut in. "If you want Shyra, you'll have to go through me first."

Up on the main deck of ship, the Zenakuu watched as their cargo was about to be annihilated.

"Sir, the Kalrynian means to kill the magnokinetic," a solider said, but the Fleet Admiral disregarded him completely. He couldn't quell his hatred. The blood feud between the Kalrynians and Zenakuu took over his senses.

"General Zander," he shouted.

"Yes, sir," Zander replied.

"Give that filthy glabrous a lesson in torment. Kill everyone she loves in front of her and then finish her off," he ordered.

"Yes, sir," the general complied.

He had the ship's gunners aim for Rain and Wind, who sluggishly tried to carry Flame and Earth out of the chasm to safety while avoiding any sneak attack from straggling Zenakuu soldiers. A smaller cannon mounted on the nose of the ship had its sights locked on the other members of the planet earth's Kinetic Alliance. The cannon's barrel glowed a vibrant amethyst hue like before, and the ship began to shake, but due to Shyra being fixated on Polarity, Cloud was the first to notice.

"Shyra, the canon isn't pointed at us," he alerted. But by the time she snapped out of her tunnel vision, it was too late. Cloud concentrated every ounce of his remaining power to his super speed. Only a brilliant trail of yellow light was left in his place as Cloud ran faster than he ever had before. He knew if he did not reach the others in time, they would all die. He stopped only a couple feet in front of his team. There wasn't enough time to get them all to safety.

"Alex, what are you doing here, where's Shyra?" Rain asked.

"Get down!" he shouted back. Wind looked around Cloud and stared down her inevitable death. The canon fired, and she threw herself over Rain's body. Cloud stood there face-to-face with the impending beam with unwavering nerve. He believed in himself. He had to succeed, because if he didn't, he would lose everyone.

He powered up his hands and released the most powerful electrical current he could muster. The two forces met head-on. Cloud did his best to overpower the blast, but the canon was too much for him in his weakened state. He knew he would soon lose his footing, and then he and the rest of his friends would be disintegrated by the beam.

Cloud knew there was only one hope. He remembered all the things he learned about taking over energy from his time spent with Polarity, and although he didn't have the strength to negate the blast, he believed he could deflect it. He channeled all his electrokinetic energy to his right arm and attempted to push the blast skyward. He screamed out until he had half a lung left, but he won. He'd saved the rest of his team. It all happened in a matter of seconds. The Zenakuu canon round bounced upward at a ninety-five-degree angle, but not before blasting off Cloud's arm. He fell to the ground screaming in pain, as all that was remaining of his right arm was a vaporized stump.

With his left hand, Alex grabbed the mangled flesh and continued to kick around on the ground until he eventually passed out from shock. Cassie, who was only a few feet away, couldn't believe the once-so-strong Voltaic Cloud was lying on the ground mutilated. "Alex!" she screamed as she crawled over to him, but he was already unconscious. "Oh my God, what do I do?" She was as pale as a ghost but held him tight and deliriously cried out for help. "Shyra!" Rain screamed.

Whisking Wind was still trying to get her bearings back when she noticed the increasing pool of blood. With her hands trembling, Rain frantically ripped her sleeve off at the top, and tied it tightly around Cloud's stump. Using it as a tourniquet was the best she could do to prevent him from bleeding to death.

Back at the Zenakuu ship, Shyra stared off in her team's direction with her eyes gaped open. Another member's energy dropped almost to nothing. Polarity, who had a knack for pointing out the obvious, looked directly at Shyra to deride her. "That looked like it hurt. You might wanna get over there."

It was in that moment Shyra's inexperience in war shined through. She was frozen in fear and unsure of what she should do.

The canon once again took aim and began to glow, but this time, Shyra wouldn't allow it to fire. Like the Chrentex of her world, she activated a feature on her LAPS that granted the user godlike powers for a short time at the cost of some of the user's life force. A white lygokinetic energy ring quickly spun with its face toward the ship. As it grew in strength, the ring filled with power until it was solid. In a flash, the ring shot out a beam four times larger in size than its wielder right down the barrel of the canon, destroying it on impact.

Shyra raced to the others. Her vision was blurred, but she unmistakably saw Cloud bleeding to death. Shyra needed to telekinetically link to her ship. She took a breath and closed her eyes. In the next second, she and everyone else were lying in her ship near the Colorado mountains. She wanted to pass out from the pain the suit had inflicted internally, but Cloud would surely die if she did.

Tori, Cassie, and Shyra found themselves in the war room of the ship.

"How did you teleport us from the battlefield?" Tori asked.

"Never mind that, Tori. You need to get Christian and Dimitri prepared for the intensive healing tanks. Cassandra, I need your help prepping for Alexander's surgery. We have to hurry if we are going to save him."

Tori obeyed, while Shyra and Cassandra hoisted Alex on a stretcher and raced him to the surgery/intensive-care unit of the medical bay. Tori struggled with Christian. She carried him with his arm over her shoulders as she held his torso.

She stripped him down to his underclothes, strapped the breathing apparatus to his nose and mouth, and then dunked him in the tube. She quickly ran back down the hallway to grab

Dimitri. He was even heavier than Christian, and she heard the bones in his body cracking with every step she took.

"Don't worry, baby. I got you," she told him. Tori did the same for Dimitri as she did for Christian, but before she put him in, she gave him a kiss on his lips. "I love you, Dimitri, please come back to me." She released him, and as he sank, bubbles rose to the top. Since teaming up with the Kalrynians on this crusade, she had seen enough blood to last her a lifetime.

Polarity, who watched Shyra's last display of power, stood in amazement. "That was incredible. Such power … she got me all excited. I'm gonna have to kill someone just to calm down." Lucas couldn't restrain his sinister smile as he boarded the ship.

"Damn Kalrynians. Damage report!" Admiral Graz shouted.

"Sir, the canon is completely offline. It will take some time to repair," A diagnostics solider reported.

"I don't care about the canon. Can this starking thing fly?"

"Yes, sir. Our jump capabilities are still operational, but scanners show we do not have enough life support for all of the ground troops to make it back safely." The crew of the ship looked to their leader to see what his decision would be.

"Leave them here. They will have to fend for themselves until reinforcements come," Admiral Graz decided.

"Um, yes, sir."

Polarity eavesdropped outside the doors of the main deck to hear the conversation and to make his own demands. He entered the main doors, "Prepare for departure. We are leaving now," Polarity ordered.

"Who do you think you are? Commanding my troops! Our men are loyal to Admiral Graz and me only," General Zander barked.

"Things are going to be different for a while," Polarity informed the fleet. "I am in command of this ship now."

"Over my dead body!" General Zander said, but Polarity's eyes had grown so cold since killing his love that his stare was enough to send shivers down Zander's spine. Polarity deucedly grinned at General Zander's comment. Polarity put out his hand and slowly squeezed the air. The general's metal body armor dented at first before crumbling under the weight of the magnokinetic's power like a balled up piece of paper.

"Wait, please stop," Zander begged.

"I love it when they beg right before they die," Polarity stated in an emotionless tone. The armor collapsed in on itself, flattening the general's chest. Blood poured out the orifices in his head. The imploding armor severed his arms and legs from the torso.

"I like your style, human. What is your name?" Graz asked.

"Vig— Formidable Polarity, and I am your new Paramount."

"Confident too, but you'll be my subordinate before anything else, human." Admiral Graz grunted, and looked around. "Where is Donikan?"

"Unfortunately, Donikan died in battle heroically. I'm terribly sorry," Lucas said as he channeled his unbeknown acting skills."

"I see. It is of little importance at this point. May Vizner watch over him," he turned to his subordinate, "Prepare for departure," Graz ordered.

Back on the ship, it was a race against time to save Alex's life. Five out of seven members of Shyra's team were unconscious, defected, or dead. They slew thousands of Zenakuu soldiers, but at what cost?

In the operating room, Shyra and Cassie did their best to stop Alex's bleeding, but his skin turned pale. Alex was drifting in and out of consciousness, and with each spasm followed a series of convulsions. The screaming was so intense that it threatened to burst Shyra's sensitive eardrums, but she worked through the pain. Saving him was all that mattered. She knew failure was not an option from the tears that profusely streamed down Cassie's face.

Minutes turned to hours, but they finally stabilized Alex. He was lying peacefully with the life support hooked up to him and a type O blood transfusion steadily pouring into him. His Electrocardiogram showed eighty beats per minute.

Shyra and Cassie closed the wound and were relieved to finally be out of the woods. Alex would live but would never be the same. Shyra blamed herself for not being able to see the writing on the wall, but all they could do was wait. Being covered in his blood made Cassie hysterical. She buried her head into Shyra's chest and cried her eyes out. Each time their lives were threatened, she came to terms more with how much she cared about him. The thought of losing him made her chest tighten, and the fear refused to let her breathe.

"He will be fine, Cassandra; we all will," Shyra said, trying to reassure her. "I will not rest until Lucas atones for what he has done. We will have our retribution."

A fire forged out of hatred burned intensely within Cassie. "I'll kill him myself," she said with a cold stare, but their conversation was interrupted by Alex's violent seizure. His heart rate spiked out of control as he entered cardiac arrest. The two girls ran over to him and tried to hold him down.

"Shyra, what's wrong with him?!"

"I do not know. Alexander, can you hear me? You have got to stay with me!" Shyra shouted.

Alex's heart rate monitor showed that his heart was beating at more than two hundred beats per minute. He was in critical condition.

"Alex, please don't do this!" Cassie screamed, but it was too late. His seizure abruptly stopped. His body lay motionless, and the life support sounded off a long, continuous beep …

End of Book One